THE
BATTLE
IS NOT
YOURS

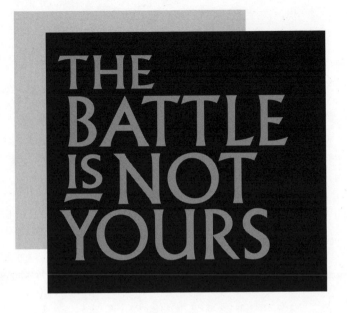

THE
BATTLE
IS NOT
YOURS

Rita J. Bunton

Michigan State University Press
East Lansing

⊛ The paper used in this publication meets the minimum requirements
of ANSI/NISO Z39.48-1992 (R 1997) (Permanence of Paper).

Michigan State University Press
East Lansing, Michigan 48823-5245

Printed and bound in the United States of America.

13 12 11 10 09 08 07   1 2 3 4 5 6 7 8 9 10

LIBRARY OF CONGRESS CATALOGING-IN-PUBLICATION DATA
Bunton, Rita J., 1949–
The battle is not yours / Rita J. Bunton.
p. cm.
ISBN 978-0-87013-799-0 (pbk. : alk. paper) 1. Trust in God—Fiction.
2. Life change events—Fiction. 3. Self-actualization (Psychology)—Fiction.
4. Poor—Fiction. 5. Heroin abuse—Fiction. 6. Abused women—Fiction. I. Title.
PS3602.U564B38 2007
813'.6—dc22
2006100332

Cover and book design by Sharp Des!gns, Inc.

Michigan State University Press is a member of the Green Press Initiative and is
committed to developing and encouraging ecologically responsible publishing
practices. For more information about the Green Press Initiative and the use of
recycled paper in book publishing, please visit *www.greenpressinitiative.org*.

Visit Michigan State University Press on the World Wide Web at *www.msupress.msu.edu*

THE
BATTLE
IS NOT
YOURS

❈ WAY BACK WHEN

Warm thrusts of air from registers at each end of Grandma's glass-enclosed porch made it possible to sit out there year round, even in Michigan's freezing winters. Grandma rocked in her favorite wooden rocking chair. I rocked next to her in mine. She was my very best friend.

One chilly March evening after dinner, we were rocking on the porch, watching the daylight turn to dusk, when I mentioned a rumor going around the school.

"There might be a fight after school tomorrow, Grandma. That's what Albert told me. He said all the kids been talking 'bout it."

Albert was my brother. We hung around each other a lot, even though I was almost two years older.

"Y'all bet not be standing 'round watching no fight. Y'all know better. You and Albert better come straight home from school tomorrow, else I'm gon tear y'all up good," Grandma said, her voice booming from her stomach, her brown eyes piercing mine, over rimless bifocals that sat halfway down her nose.

We watched the fight. Then we tried to avoid Grandma's house by walking a different route home from school. We had almost made it to our front steps when Grandma stuck her head out of her screen door and beckoned us.

"Yoo-hoo! Oh, Jasmine. You and Albert come here," she hollered.

Grandma whipped us with three slick, green, skinny switches twisted together that were so long they bent on the ceiling every time she swung. The whipping was so hard that each time the switches met flesh, they stung like hot grease and bore big red welts. We hopped and skipped around Grandma, ducking and dodging and swearing we'd never do it again—long before she showed any signs of letting up.

Albert cried the loudest and was still crying when we trudged home and told Momma.

"Grandma's whipped us with a *tree*," Albert stuttered, a speech impediment he'd never overcome.

I kept trying to tell him that the switches were just really long, but was never able to convince my brother otherwise.

— ॰ —

THE MATRIARCH of our large, close-knit family, Grandma was my grandfather's mother and actually my great-grandmother. Everyone in our family called her "Grandma."

We lived five doors away from her on Page Avenue in Jackson, Michigan. Located an hour west of Detroit, Jackson was a small, predominately white Midwestern town with a population of about fifty-five thousand. Jackson's claim to fame was having the largest walled prison in the world, Southern Michigan Prison, known as SMP. Jackson was also the home of several large factories that supported the state's auto industry, manufacturing car parts such as tires, mufflers, and brake shoes. Jobs were so plentiful that nearly every home I knew had at least one male earning good money in the shops.

We were one of the few families who didn't. There was no adult male in our house when I was growing up. Momma and my dad divorced so long ago that I never remembered them being married. She raised the six of us alone in a small, two-bedroom apartment that Grandma rented to her for thirty dollars a month. We lived in the rear of the two-family flat from as far back as I could remember. Momma's sister, Aunt Bernice, who was three years younger, lived in the front apartment with her husband. They eventually moved, and we gained the front apartment, where there was a larger living and dining room but still only two small bedrooms. We shared the only bathroom, which connected the two apartments, with other tenants.

I had just turned seven when Momma started sending me to pay Grandma the rent. She'd place a ten- and a twenty-dollar bill in a white envelope and seal it, before writing "Grandma" across the front in big, pretty handwriting.

"That sure is nice of Grandma to charge us only thirty dollars for rent," I said to Momma one day, not having any idea what other people paid landlords, but assumed ours cost less.

"Humph! Grandma knows she couldn't get anybody else to pay thirty cents for one of these dumps," Momma snapped. "This house is so old it's about to fall in. And the wood is so dry, that if somebody struck a match, it'd probably burn to the ground before somebody could throw some water on it."

I wished Momma didn't say things like that. She fussed and complained a lot—especially about Grandma. She said Grandma was too nosey and stayed in her business all the time.

"All she does is sit on that porch all day long—trying to see what everybody else is doing. Then when night comes, she goes inside and sits on the phone talking about church folks," she said.

Usually when Momma got mad at Grandma, she ended up fussing at me, too.

"And Jasmine, you ain't got *no* business sitting up under Grandma all day, running your mouth. I know you be telling her everything going on in this house—and then some."

Momma was right. I told Grandma most things. If we hadn't eaten that day, I'd tell Grandma. If Momma cussed or whipped us, I'd tell Grandma. I told Grandma when Albert didn't wash his face or brush his teeth. I even kept Grandma updated on Momma's longtime boyfriend, Rolland Shavers, who was my three youngest siblings' father.

—— ❧ ——

IF IT HADN'T been for my great-grandmother, I would have been penniless growing up. Grandma paid me a nickel to dust the knickknack shelves in her living room. She gave me a dime whenever I dusted everything, including the big mahogany table with thick, sculptured bowed legs and a matching china cabinet that furnished her brown-carpeted dining room. When Grandma's scalp itched, she paid me a nickel to scratch and grease it with Royal Crown hair dressing. She promised to let me wash her dishes when I turned seven, and kept her word. I felt so grown up and important when that day finally arrived.

Every summer Grandma surprised her great-grandkids with a new toy. One summer she bought us hula hoops. Another year she bought us roller skates. Whatever became the neighborhood kids' craze, Grandma made sure we had it, too. I figured she did it partly because she wanted us to enjoy our childhood, and partly because she felt sorry for us.

Of Momma's nine siblings, our family had the most kids—six. But we also had the least amount of money, and Momma was the only one of the five adult sisters without a husband. She also was also the only person in her family who received welfare.

—— ❧ ——

WE HAD THREE different fathers in my nuclear family, which raised lots of questions among people who didn't know us. I was the sole offspring of Eugene and Malena Armstead and didn't look anything like my sisters and brothers. But it never bothered me.

Albert and Lisa had the same father and looked a lot alike—tall, dark, and slender. Lisa was four years younger than me and the neediest in the family. Extremely shy and soft-spoken, Lisa cried at the drop of a hat.

My youngest siblings, Penny, Terrance, and Keith, were also each two years apart. They favored their daddy, Rolland Shavers. Penny was the fourth born and spoiled rotten. She was Rolland's oldest child and only daughter. Penny had thick, long, nappy hair and cried every time Momma combed it. I felt sorry for her but wished my hair were as long. Penny tended to be selfish and seldom got whippings. And when she did, my baby sister got so terrified I thought she'd have a nervous breakdown. Momma would have to chase her down and even pull her from under beds to get at her.

Terrance was the quietest and most stoic of our bunch. Nothing seemed to bother him. But he liked meddling. One evening he toddled to the kitchen table and pulled a big bowel of hot chocolate over on him. It burned all his skin, from his neck to his waist. All we saw was pink flesh. Momma rushed him to the hospital in a cab, but they returned home that same night. She doctored on Terrance for weeks, and my brother healed without leaving one scar. Momma always wanted to be a nurse.

We all helped raise our youngest brother, Keith. Ten years old when he was born, I quickly learned how to make his formula of clear Karo syrup, evaporated milk, and water. I changed lots of diapers, too. It seemed that every time we went outside to play, we had to take our baby brother with us. Keith kept us in trouble with Momma because he loved sitting in the middle of the street. We'd be in the backyard playing and suddenly hear car horns honking.

"Keith's in the street again!" the five of us would say, almost simultaneously.

We'd rush to the front yard, and sure enough, there would be a line of cars, waiting for someone to get our eighteen-month-old brother out of the street. It was only by the grace of God that he never got hurt because it must have happened at least once a week.

— ⁂ —

ROLLAND SHAVERS ALWAYS wore a scowl on his chestnut brown face. His dark eyes felt as cold as a January freeze and caused my stomach to knot up whenever I saw him staring at me. Rolland came to see Momma nearly every day, usually before he went to work. Penny, Terrance, and Keith always looked forward to seeing their father.

Rolland helped Momma out in his own self-serving way. He bought several bags of groceries a few times a month, but expected Momma to fix his lunch for work every day. I dreaded seeing him coming. He'd pull up in his dark blue 1949 humpback Ford around one o'clock every afternoon and stayed until two forty-five. Working in a small factory, Rolland had to punch in at three o'clock. We didn't see him much on the weekends, and I was glad.

Momma dutifully prepared his lunch each day as if she were his wife, while he strolled around the house with his broad nose stuck up in the air and his mouth poked out. Sometimes he talked to Momma and his kids, but he seldom said anything to Lisa, Albert, and me. And when he did say something to us, it was usually criticism.

"Don't be so messy when you eat. You three are old enough to know better," he'd say with glaring eyes that screamed of contempt. "Jasmine, don't you know how to wash dishes? I saw you drop that fork on the floor. Pick it up and wash it again. I know you were going to try to put it in the drawer without washing and drying it again."

Even Momma seemed more uptight whenever Rolland was around. Although she loved him, she didn't appear happy in their relationship, and neither did he. The tension rose in our house each time he came and died down a little after he left.

One time Rolland and Momma got into a spat. It started in the kitchen, but they took their arguing to her bedroom. I figured they didn't want us listening, but I was scared and listened anyway. When I heard bumping and knocking against the wall, I snuck out and ran up to the front apartment where my Aunt Bernice lived and called Grandma. We never had a telephone while living in the back apartment.

"Grandma, come quick. Rolland's hurting Momma," I whispered into the receiver.

That was all Grandma needed. She despised Rolland anyway, and I knew it. I often told her how mean and nasty he treated us older kids, which made her dislike him even more. It was risky calling Grandma because I knew that Momma probably would be mad at me, but I had to. Never having seen anyone lay a hand on Momma, I was terrified.

Within minutes Grandma had stormed down the sidewalk to our house holding a broomstick in her hand as if it were a club. She didn't have to use it, but she sure bawled Rolland out good, saying, "If you don't get the dickens out of here, I'll warm your jacket!" He left without saying a word, but glared at Momma and me before hurrying out the front door. Then Grandma gave Momma a piece of her mind. Tears streamed down Momma's face, and I felt sorry for her. I'd never seen my mother cry before. Later that afternoon I went to Grandma's house, and she was still fuming.

"Malena outta be shamed of herself, letting that ole no-good niggah put a hand on her, and letting him treat you and Albert and Lisa the way he do. I don't like it. Don't like it one bit. And I ain't gon put up with it no longer. Not in no place of mine. I'll stop Rolland Shavers from coming down there. Now I sho will. He's gon fool around and make me lay my religion down and go upside his head," she fussed, rocking so hard that the plants and ferns lining her porch rustled as if disturbed by the wind.

— ❧ —

ROLLAND BROKE UP with Momma one time, and it really hurt her. I could hear it in her voice one night as she told her oldest sister, Cynthia, over the telephone after we had gone to bed. I had trouble sleeping as a child because of reoccurring nightmares, so I spent lots of nights lying in bed listening to Momma's conversations on the telephone.

The next day Momma wrote Rolland a letter and told me to drop it in the mailbox on the corner when I went outside to play. Afraid they'd make up, I hid it under the mattress of my roll-away bed instead. A month later Rolland started coming back around again. I got scared and took the letter to Grandma and confessed. She chewed me out good.

"If Malena knew you done this, she'd whip the daylight out of you," Grandma scolded, her head shaking so hard that the loose skin under her neck rippled like small waves of water.

I hung my head in shame. Grandma avoided eye contact with me when she promised to destroy the letter. The subject never came up again.

THE BABYSITTER

Mrs. Willa Mae Matthews was in her late fifties and reminded me of Aunt Jemima on the pancake box. She was dark skinned, was overweight, and always wore a red-printed rag tied around her head that hung lopsided just above one eye.

Momma hired her to baby-sit us while she cooked and cleaned for a prominent lawyer and his family in town. It took my siblings and me one day to decide that we didn't like anything about Mrs. Willa Mae.

She dipped snuff, which made an unsightly bulge under her bottom lip, causing her to mumble when she talked. Thick brown saliva dripped from the corners of her mouth, staining her dark lips even darker, and making me sick to my stomach every time I had to look at it. The three-hundred-pound woman who stood less than five feet tall didn't seem the least bit ashamed or embarrassed when she talked about being too big to fit in a bathtub.

"I just do a good wash up every day," she claimed, wiping coffee-colored saliva from her mouth with her bare hand.

I'd turn my head in disgust.

When Mrs. Willa Mae combed our hair, I had to hold my breath while sitting on the floor between her legs because of her body odor. When playing on the floor, we often scrambled to get out of her way when she had to go to the bathroom. Sometimes she didn't make it, and peed on herself. That's when I found out she wore rags, torn from old dresses and shirts, between her legs instead of panties, because she forced me to wash them.

"They don't make drawls big 'nough to fit me," she said, flashing a toothless grin.

I hated washing out her rags, or "diapers" as she called them. I barely touched them, dipping the strips of colored fabric up and down in the water with my fingertips whenever she wasn't around.

"How does she keep these things from falling down?" I often wondered, holding my head stiffly back from the bathroom sink and trying my best not to breathe.

I tried pretending to throw up, hoping she'd feel sorry for me and stop making me wash her "underwear." But that didn't work. She started standing over me and watching more closely—even giving more specific instructions, while appearing amused by my contorted facial expressions.

"Go 'head and put yo hands in that soapy water, girl. Use both those hands God gave you. You act like you scared to get your hands wet or something. Ain't you ever washed rags before?" she said, wiping drippings from her mouth with the tail of the faded blue and white flowered dress that she wore nearly every day, her breath smelling like snuff.

Mrs. Willa Mae and "Tex" Matthews, her husband, lived around the corner on Plymouth Street, a five-minute walk from our home. Their house was a one-story, green, dilapidated structure that sat on cement blocks and appeared to be leaning to one side because the porch sloped downhill.

I dreaded when she took us home with her to baby-sit, which was two or three times a week. Her house was always dark, closed up, and too warm or too cold, and it smelled like stale cigar smoke, musty clothes, and whatever food she had cooking on the stove.

Her husband was the local numbers man. Kids in the neighborhood used to laugh at Tex as he sped up and down the streets in a 1948 car that was beat up and badly in need of a paint job. The fender bottoms were so rusty they looked like jagged teeth. And when he drove fast, which was all the time, the back end of his car bounced off the pavement whenever he hit a bump, causing sparks to fly from the muffler, which needed replacing. We could hear his car coming a block away.

Every now and then Mrs. Willa Mae made me ride to the store with Tex. Embarrassed, I'd crouch low in the backseat, hoping that none of my playmates would see me.

Neighbors whispered about the heavy wool overcoat Tex wore year round. The dark gray coat was so long that it dragged on the ground, and always looked as if he had slept in it all night. They said Tex carried a gun underneath the coat to protect himself because he handled so much money. All I knew is that Tex was almost always by himself, and no one ever tried to rob him.

Mr. Eddie Jones rented a room from the Matthews. A short, golden brown man with a bald head and pot belly, Mr. Jones appeared to be several years older than Tex and Mrs. Willa Mae. He spent most afternoons in their living room, peeking out the front window while sitting in a tattered navy blue chair with busted seams and dirty cotton and rusted springs popping through the tweed upholstery. An old wooden console radio with an arched top sat in a corner, sending scratching sounds of static, rather than music and voices, into the air of the dusty room.

Mr. Jones wore brown suspenders that were so tight they hiked his pants up three inches from his shoes, revealing clean white socks. His shoes never appeared polished or scuffed, and his shirts were well pressed but worn at the elbows.

I was about six years old when Mr. Jones sent my sisters into the kitchen with Mrs. Willa Mae. I'll never forget that look in his eye once we were alone. He motioned for me to come sit on the side of his chair, away from the kitchen, enabling him to put his fingers in my panties. I knew there was something wrong about it, but he was an adult, and I was a child, and kids obeyed grown-ups. That's the way I was raised.

Sometimes I pretended not to see him when he'd beckon me, but that made him mad. His smile would melt, and his face would take on a more serious look. Then he'd make up any excuse to get my sisters out of the room. The boys usually were playing outdoors. Mrs. Willa Mae didn't believe in letting girls play outside. She said, "There's too much that goes on out in the streets."

Once we were alone, Mr. Jones would slowly get up from his chair, grunting with each move, then shuffle across the room without saying a word. He'd pick me up and carry me to his bedroom, located on the other side of the living room. Afraid to say anything, I'd freeze. I never understood what he was doing, but didn't protest. I'd just close my eyes and pretend to be asleep, while Mr. Jones stroked me in places that no one else did.

— ❧ —

ONE HUMID EVENING just before dark, the lightning bugs were floating through the thick summer air while I was playing hopscotch in front of my house with my first cousins Arlene and Robin. They were Aunt Cynthia's daughters and my best friends. They lived two doors up from Grandma on Page Avenue in a three-bedroom bungalow that she owned.

The three of us were laughing and having a good time when we heard a siren in the distance. The screaming siren grew louder until the ambulance passed us, our heads following the red vehicle as it sped by. Neighbors pulled back curtains. Dogs howled. Heads poked out of screen doors, everyone trying to see what was going on. When the ambulance turned down Plymouth Street, adults and kids darted out of their houses, all headed in the same direction. We started running, too.

A crowd had already started gathering in front of Mrs. Willa Mae's house when we got there. Many stood whispering and speculating on who inside needed an ambulance.

Standing on my tiptoes, I watched two white men dressed in dark blue uniforms jump out of the ambulance, hurry to its rear, and pull a stretcher out of the back of the vehicle. They rushed into the house and stayed for about thirty minutes.

By the time they appeared again, Arlene, Robin, and I had drifted apart and lost each other in the crowd. The two stoic-faced men carefully rolled the stretcher out of the house and down the broken steps, with someone lying on it, covered from head to toe with a light brown blanket. Word spread quickly among the crowd that Mr. Jones had died, probably of a massive heart attack, because it took him so quickly.

"I just saw ole Ed Jones yestiday," a neighbor man lamented. "He walked past my house goin to the store. Didn't look like a thang was wrong with him. Umph! Umph! Umph! You never know . . . here one minute and gone the next. Sho gon miss my friend. He was a good man."

I stood flat-footed after hearing the news, unsure how to feel or what to think. After sighing deeply, I turned and squeezed my way back through the whispering crowd and headed home alone.

"Least I don't have to worry 'bout him messin with me no more," I thought, while walking down the sidewalk.

I easily pushed thoughts of Mr. Jones to the back of my mind, where they faded into vague memories within weeks. It would be nearly three decades before the memories resurfaced and I realized the damage he'd done to me.

❀ DO'S <u>AND</u> DON'TS

Grandma sent one of us to the store several times a week to buy her favorite snack—a Cho Cho Pop. Vanilla ice cream on a stick, covered with a thin layer of chocolate, Cho Cho Pops were one of the many treats we bought for a nickel at Bozak's grocery. The Polish family who owned and operated the store referred to most of their customers by their first names, even adults. The entire family knew Grandma and always called her "Mrs. Thomas."

The east side of Jackson consisted primarily of Polish people. Blacks were sandwiched between them, living in the 200 and 300 blocks of Page Avenue, with both ends anchored by small, Polish-owned stores. We lived at 214 Page. Grandma lived five doors away at 302.

Page Avenue stretched about seven miles and was heavily trafficked and dotted with bakeries, gas stations, hardware stores, cleaners, Polish bars, and the only black mortuary in town, which was three doors up from us. I can remember Momma waking us up excitedly on Memorial Day and the Fourth of July so that we could sit on our front steps, still dressed in pajamas, and watch parades pass our house.

A large Catholic church sat two streets over on Pringle Avenue. All of its parishioners were white, as were the students at the Catholic school and the people who filled the bingo hall on Tuesday nights. The Polish National Alliance hall was several blocks east on Page Avenue, and I often wondered what it was for. White people were always standing around, inside and out, whenever I walked by. Sometimes I tried to see inside the large, brick building while en route to my maternal grandparents' house, who lived about a mile and a half away on Tomlinson Street. I never saw anything but people, and never understood why they were there or what a Polish National Alliance hall meant.

Growing up surrounded by Polish people fascinated me. Walking past their houses, sometimes I could hear them speaking in their native tongue. I thought it would be neat to speak in a language that most people didn't know, so I'd jibber jabber to myself, pretending to speak Polish, too.

Our Polish neighbors kept their thick green lawns well manicured and planted flowers every spring. I figured that the insides of their houses were just as spotless, but later discovered differently. While selling Wolverine salve or flower and vegetable seeds door to door, I managed to glimpse inside of a few homes. They were dark, dusty, and cluttered, even though the yards were immaculate. It never made sense to me.

Although our neighborhood was racially and culturally mixed—including two Mexican families living nearby—there was an invisible fence that separated us. Adults spoke to each other in passing, but not much more. And we didn't dare step foot in one another's houses, even though I don't ever remember being told not to. We just knew that black kids didn't go inside white and Mexican homes and vice versa. Every once in a while some of the Polish kids in the neighborhood would wander into our yard, wanting to play with us. We always welcomed them but held our breath because we knew what was coming next. Sure enough, within minutes, a parent or a grandparent called them home, speaking in Polish. We'd laugh because it became so predictable, but deep down inside I felt like something was wrong with us—our skin color.

— ℀ —

GRANDMA HAD SEVERAL close friends who lived in our neighborhood. Most of them were widows or "old maids," a term we whispered among ourselves when no grown-ups were around. Grandma cooked hot meals for her friends who were ailing and had Albert deliver them. The older women always gave Albert some change, which he proudly came back to flaunt in front of us. We eventually started teasing Albert, calling the seventy- and eighty-year-old women his "girlfriends," but it never seemed to bother him. He continued to be at their beck and call.

Grandma and Mr. Thomas owned three houses on our street, including their own. Each had a fenced-in garden in the backyard. Kids and adults alike were forbidden from entering the gardens or picking any fruit off the trees, even though they were in our backyards. Grandma and Mr. Thomas tended to those things.

Mr. Thomas was my step-great-grandfather and Grandma's second husband. Her first husband died of a heart attack when their two children were very young.

Grandma met Israel Thomas through a mutual friend. They wrote each other for several months before he asked her to marry him. She said yes, and he sent her a train ticket to come up north and relocate to Jackson from Ethel, Mississippi. The couple married in 1936, thirteen years before I was born, yet everyone in our family still called him "Mr. Thomas." He called everyone in our family "John," even the females. No one knew exactly why, but I figured it was because our extended family was so big that he couldn't keep everybody's names straight.

— ℮ —

EVERYONE KNEW BETTER than to mess with our great-grandparents' fruit trees and vegetable gardens, but we discovered that small green peaches made great weapons because they stung like rocks when thrown. One midsummer afternoon my siblings and best-friend cousins and I got bold and decided to have a peach fight in our backyard.

We were laughing and pelting each other with the tiny green peaches when Grandma came sneaking around the house and caught us. I spotted her first and froze dead in my tracks. At the same moment, Albert fired a peach at me, smacking me upside the head as I stood there stricken with fear. Grandma whipped all nine of us right there on the spot. It was my second and last whipping from my great-grandmother—not because I never disobeyed her again, but because I made sure she didn't know. I didn't like disappointing her, plus she gave worse whippings than Momma.

Grandma loved growing flowers and plants. Her long, narrow porch faced east and was lined with ferns and ivy that gracefully hung over their large ceramic and clay pots. There were so many that squeezing by without bumping them took some effort. Whenever I accidentally bumped one, I could feel Grandma's uneasiness, even with my back turned.

— ℮ —

OUR GREAT-GRANDMOTHER was a creature of habit—sometimes to our amusement, other times to our dismay. She had a large console, black-and-white television in her living room and refused to let anyone change the channel. It stayed on channel 6 so that she could watch the six o'clock news each evening.

"Changing the channel will break it," she'd fuss, the few times we got up enough nerve to ask her. We snickered about it, but understood that Grandma knew little about televisions and her thinking was a bit old-fashioned.

Every day at sunrise she raised the green shades on her porch, then pulled them down when night fell. Grandma cooked full-course meals every day and baked a pan of cornbread or biscuits to go with them. One of my favorite memories was of her and I eating crumbled-up cornbread in a glass of buttermilk with a spoon, while sitting on the porch in our rockers talking about whatever came to our minds.

If Grandma noticed our toes being cramped in our shoes for too long, she'd take us downtown on the bus and buy us new ones. Grandma always bought our shoes in the basement of Field's department store. She gave us two choices—black and white or brown and white saddle oxfords.

"I wish grandma would let us get a different kind this time," I'd think during our bumpy ten-minute bus ride to town. "I'll ask her when we get downtown."

By the time we arrived at the store, I always chickened out. The salesperson measured our feet, which had always grown at least a size larger, then searched for saddle oxfords that fit. I hoped he couldn't find any in my size, but he always did. I usually chose brown and white saddle oxfords, then smiled all the way back home. I loved wearing something new.

One winter Grandma sent me downtown with Mr. Thomas because he wanted to buy me a wool coat. A tall, lanky man with skin like dark, tough leather, our step-great-grandfather never owned a car and walked most places. I loved walking with him, although he walked faster because of his long legs and strides. Mr. Thomas wasn't much of a talker, so we didn't say very much as he trudged down Michigan Avenue, with me jogging alongside him. And whenever I did ask him a question, his reply was "Uh huh" or "Uh uh," in a voice that boomed like thunder.

Mr. Thomas allowed me to pick out whatever coat I wanted from Peoples department store, one of Grandma's favorite places to buy clothes. I chose a purple and gray plaid wool coat with a navy-style collar made of purple fur that draped over my shoulders. It cost forty-nine dollars, a lot for a young person's coat at that time, but Mr. Thomas didn't bat an eye. I liked going places with him because spending money didn't seem to bother him.

Our step-great-grandfather walked to and from work every day. His job at Goodyear Tire and Rubber Company was located eight blocks away, and I never knew him to miss a day's work. Mr. Thomas was well into his seventies when Goodyear officials discovered his age and forced him to retire. Relatives said he had forgotten his age because he couldn't read or write, something I'd never realized.

Momma used to say that Grandma and Mr. Thomas showed favoritism toward my cousin Arlene and me because our skin was lighter than most others in the family. My skin color was caramel. Arlene could pass for white. I never contradicted Momma's opinion, but didn't believe it either. I figured our great-grandparents did more for us because we got good grades in school and were the oldest in our families.

During the summer, Arlene and I walked up to the A&P supermarket to meet Mr. Thomas after he got off work on Friday afternoons, when he got paid. He'd always give each of us a shiny fifty-cent piece, and caution us not to tell anyone. We didn't.

I often hid mine under our couch cushion until I could spend it without anyone noticing. My stash was spent on Big Mo candy bars, New Era potato chips, and comic books. Albert often teased me about reading so many Richie Rich comic books.

"Jasmine, you must think you're gonna be rich like Richie Rich one day," he'd say, looking at me out of the corner of his eye with a smirk on his deep chocolate–colored face.

"I sure do. One of these days, I'm gonna have a bathtub full of money just like Richie Rich," I'd reply, with a sly look of my own. I daydreamed about being rich a lot.

— ℘ —

AFTER HE HAD to retire, Mr. Thomas became a full-time repair man, coming up with all kinds of unexplainable projects. He built a spare bedroom onto the back of their house, but seldom, if ever, used it. Twice he fell out of a tree while trying to trim its branches. Grandma forbade him from getting on any more ladders. That didn't stop him though. He kept busy by raking and mowing lawns, clipping the hedges around our house, replacing fuses, changing light switches, and even picking Grandma's toenails and sanding her feet when she asked.

I never knew where Mr. Thomas was born, or much about his family. He had a few relatives, including a son, who lived in Jackson. Every once in a while they'd visit him, but most often they saw each other on Sunday mornings at church.

On more than one occasion Grandma made a promise to Albert and me and told us not to tell anybody. "Me and Israel gon buy y'all a car when you get old enough to drive and get a license," she said. "That-a-way, y'all can take us around town to tend to our business, and y'all won't have to ask other folks to take you places."

Albert and I never put much hope in that, even though Grandma delivered on most things she promised. Owning a car seemed too far-fetched to us.

One of Grandma's biggest worries was being forgotten by her family. I sensed that it was a painful subject for her, but every once in a while she'd bring it up to me. "Young folks grow up and get busy with their own families. Then they go to forgetting about old people like me and Israel. They stop coming 'round," she'd say quietly, while rocking slowly in her chair with a padded seat covered with black imitation leather.

Those conversations made me feel very uncomfortable, but I did my best to reassure her that I'd never let that happen.

"Don't say that, Grandma. I'll never get too busy for you. When I grow up I'm gonna still come see you every single day—just like I do now," I'd say.

We'd just sit there in dead silence for several minutes, rocking in our chairs. It hurt me to think that she worried about something like that. I loved my great-grandmother dearly and couldn't imagine abandoning her when she needed me most.

IT TAKES AN ENTIRE VILLAGE

Daddy taught me how to fight the summer I finished first grade. I was the smallest kid in my class, and probably the entire school, and got picked on a lot.

"I don't want your momma telling me 'bout nobody else running your ass home from school crying again. You hear me?" Daddy fussed as he drove me to Flint for summer vacation. "You better be glad you live with your momma and not me. Humph! You'd have two choices—take a whipping from those kids at school or else get one from me when you got home."

My father lived in Flint, Michigan, where he was born and raised. He and Momma weren't married long enough for me to remember us ever living together as a family. But despite their failed relationship, my daddy, Eugene Armstead, the man who loved to dance, drink, party, and womanize, continued to play an important role in my life.

Throughout my summer vacation, Daddy forced me to wrestle with him on his front lawn, giving me lessons on defending myself. Sometimes I thought he took things a little too far, and teaching me to wrestle at six years old was one of them. But I grew up the apple of my daddy's eye and never wanted to disappoint him, so I listened and learned.

By summer's end, my confidence in defending myself soared. I could tell that Daddy was also pleased with my progress, although he would never admit it. He wasn't the mushy type.

My cousins Arlene and Robin hurried to our house to greet me, minutes after we arrived back in Jackson. My siblings and best-friend cousins were always glad to see me return from summer vacations in Flint. I was always glad to see them as well.

Daddy started boasting about my newly acquired skills as soon we had settled into a group conversation. My cousins and siblings loved to be around my daddy. Most people did. He was a good-looking man with a great sense of humor and loud belly laughs that were contagious. Daddy loved to argue and knew enough about most topics to hold his own in any debate.

"I bet none of you can get Jasmine on her back," he said, flashing a big smile on his freckled face with skin so light he was mistaken for white when he was born. "Tell you what. If one of you can get her down, I'll give you a dollar. And Jasmine, you'll get the money if none of them can do it."

Arlene, who was three years older than me, volunteered first. She tussled with me for a minute or two, then quit. My cousin, whose long, thick, golden brown braids were the envy of every girl, including me, said she didn't want to dirty her new red Bermuda shorts. Her sister, Robin, tried next. Eight months younger than me, the most strenuous thing Robin ever had to do was get her hair washed every two weeks. Robin batted her arms blindly, with her head back and her pretty, cocoa-colored face turned to the side, until she got tired. It took all of a minute. Then I grabbed one of her arms and shoulder, put my leg between hers, and flipped her to the ground. She got up mad and threatened to go home.

Albert, who was three inches taller than me and outweighed me by eight to ten pounds, took up the challenge last. We lowered our heads and locked our arms, then twisted and turned. We bent forward and backward. Our legs tangled, causing both of us to nearly trip several times. We scuffled for about three minutes before I remembered what Daddy said about headlocks.

"Once you get their heads trapped in the crook of your arms—you got them cause they can't see shit," he had instructed during one of our self-defense lessons.

I reached up and grabbed Albert around the neck and pulled, tugged, wriggled, and squeezed until I got his head between my bony arm and body. My brother pulled and twisted for half a minute or so, before pleading in a muffled voice.

"Let me go, Jasmine. Let me go. I can't breathe. I can't breathe," he stuttered.

I'd forgotten that Albert's lungs were weak because he drank lighter fluid when he was only eighteen months old. All I remembered about the incident was that most of our relatives came to our house to see Albert the day he got home after a two-month hospital stay. I let go of my brother's head. Daddy must have felt bad, too, because he gave Albert a dollar, and me three.

That school year I got into my first real fight. One snowy afternoon, I was walking back to school after lunch alone, which was unusual for me. I never liked being alone and had plenty of relatives going to the same school, including my aunt Valerie, who was only ten months older than me and one of my best friends. We all usually walked back and forth to school together and had so much fun.

I didn't see the snowball coming, but it smacked my face so hard that it stung with precision accuracy. I wiped the snow and ice from my face with my bare hands, only to see our next-door neighbor, June Bug, whose real name was Delbert Harden, laughing and pointing at me. His younger sister, Rhonda Jean, stood watching and trying to hold back a chuckle. I wanted to throw a snowball back, but I had no gloves or mittens and had forgotten to put a pair of old socks in my coat pocket. I used holey and mismatched socks for gloves when the weather was bitter cold, but only pulled them out when other kids weren't around because I didn't like being teased.

"Don't you do that again," I shouted at June Bug, with frozen puffs of breath spurting from my mouth with each word. "You do that again, and I'm gonna beat your butt!"

He and his sister, dressed in matching coats, hats, and mittens, acted as if I had said the funniest thing they ever heard. By then I was so cold my teeth chattered, and my frail, under clothed body shivered so hard my bones ached.

"Ain't nobody 'fraid of you. Your ole bony butt can't whip a flea," he hollered back.

I knew June Bug well. His family lived across the street from us from as far back as I could remember. With four younger sisters, he was the only boy and was spoiled as all "get out." June Bug kept the neighborhood in an uproar by fighting other kids, his sisters, and sometimes even his parents. I had no intention of tangling with him and hoped he would leave me alone if I talked tough enough.

My approach didn't work. So I stuck my hands in the pockets of my army-green wool coat and started walking toward the school, pressing my arms tightly against my body and hunching my shoulders to shield the cold air from my neck.

I was two blocks from the school when another ice ball whizzed past the side of my face. Within seconds, another one slammed against my back. I turned around and saw June Bug stooping down to pick up more snow. I charged at him and collided into a hail of swinging arms and punching fists. Before I knew what was happening, June Bug grabbed one of my arms and slung me so hard that my feet left the ground. I tried to keep from falling in the snow by grabbing his coat, popping off one of the buttons. That made him so mad, he growled.

Out of sheer fear, I reached for his head, and using every bit of strength that my fifty-four-pound body could muster up, pulled it to the crook of my arm, placing him in a headlock. He grunted with every twist and turn he made, pushing and pulling me so hard I nearly lost my balance several times, but I locked one hand around the wrist of the other and held on with all my might.

Rhonda Jean, who had been watching and cheering her brother on until I got the upper hand, jumped into the fight. She pulled and yanked at my arms until June Bug freed himself. As soon as he got loose, I pulled away from her and took off running and didn't look back. I reached the school building just as the tardy bell rang, panting and my side hurting from running so hard. I hustled up the stairs to my second-floor classroom just as our teacher, Mrs. Fischer, had started to take roll. Stepping quickly around the back of the room, I slid into my seat in the far corner of the front row, feeling the stares of several classmates and struggling to stop trembling and breathing so hard.

I was still trying to settle down several minutes later when Mrs. Fischer instructed the class to line up single file at the door for our weekly visit to the school library. Thoughts of June Bug faded from my mind as I scoured the library's wooden shelves for a book to read. Before long I was sitting at a small, wooden, round table with three other classmates, totally engrossed in my book.

Suddenly my chair flipped backward, causing me to land flat on my back. Before I realized what was happening, June Bug was punching me in the face with his fists and yelling and calling me names. It took Mrs. Fischer, the librarian, and a male teacher who came running from his next-door classroom when he heard the commotion to pry my neighbor off of me. I never saw what happened to June Bug that afternoon, but Mrs. Graham, the principal, soon appeared in the library and escorted me to the office.

A tall, stoic white woman who appeared close to retirement age, Mrs. Graham always dressed as if going to church, in well-pressed suits or dresses, with high-heeled shoes and matching earrings. Her salt-and-pepper hair, pinned back in a bun, always had perfectly formed waves accenting the sides. Dark-rimmed glasses hung from a strap and rested on her chest.

As we passed the school secretary's desk in the main office area and headed toward Mrs. Graham's office in the rear, I noticed the legendary black paddle with holes in it positioned on the wall over her door. Students who had been paddled by Mrs. Graham swore that the holes provided more sting to each swat. I was so scared of getting a paddling in school that the very sight of the office always made me nervous.

"Have a seat and tell me what happened this afternoon," Mrs. Graham said, stern faced with penetrating brown eyes that made me squirm. Stammering at first, it took me a few minutes to loosen up and tell my side of the story, but I did. Mrs. Graham listened intently, occasionally asking a question or nodding her head.

Mrs. Graham knew me as a quiet, straight-A student who had never gotten in a fight before. It was my first trip to the office, and it showed. My eyes were wide and teary, and I twisted the tail of my faded brown and white dress as I recounted what had happened. Half an hour later I was back in class. Several days passed before I saw June Bug again and found out what had happened to him.

"Jasmine, you got those people thinking I'm crazy," he said, grinning from ear to ear. "They're making me see a psychiatrist now."

June Bug's parents had to agree to six months of psychiatric visits for their son before he was allowed back in school. We made up the same day we saw each other after the fight and grew as close as sister and brother.

"That's why I don't believe in getting involved in kids' fights," Momma said after seeing June Bug and me playing together. "Kids fight one minute and make up the next. But full-grown people will fall out about their kids and never speak to each other again."

CHURCH RULES

Momma made a rule in our house. If we didn't go to church on Sundays, we couldn't go anywhere else during the week. And she made us stick to it most of the time. Missing church also meant having to answer to three other people in our extended family—Grandma and our maternal grandparents, whom we called "Mother" and "Daddy."

Grandma would call soon after she got home from church and would fuss at everybody.

"Malena need get up outta that bed on Sunday mornings and see to it that y'all get to church and Sunday school," she would say. "And if she don't do it, Jasmine, you better. Now you're old enough to get yourself ready. You and Albert both. Ya'll can ride with me and Lula Mae and Israel. She picks us up every Sunday morning at twenty minutes to eleven. All ya'll got to do is be up here on my porch by ten thirty."

Mother wasn't nearly as forceful but still made her point. She'd bring the subject up during her Sunday night telephone call to our house.

"Did ya'll go to church today?" was one of the first things she'd ask.

No excuse was good enough.

"You say you didn't have anything to wear?" she'd calmly ask. "Now, Jasmine, I've been knowing how to get myself ready for church since I was a young girl. I'd get my clothes ready on Saturday night. Now, I sho would. I'd shine my shoes, press my dress, and even put hog fat on my hair and roll it up with pieces of paper. And my mother didn't have to tell me to, either."

If Mother had her way, everybody she knew—children, grandchildren, other relatives, friends, and neighbors—would all be churchgoers. She was a church missionary and devoted to bringing others to Christ.

My grandfather, a Baptist minister, didn't apply as much pressure as his wife and mother. He'd wait until we saw each other before giving his thoughts on the matter.

"Now sugar, you outta come go to church with me and Verlie down to Adrian on Sunday mornings. You know I don't mind picking ya'll up," he'd say in his soft, gentle voice.

Daddy was pastor of a small church in Adrian, Michigan, called Second Baptist. I liked going to church with him and Mother, and soaked up all the attention that came with being the pastor's granddaughter. Members of his congregation took turns hosting dinner for Daddy, Mother, and anyone who rode with them every Sunday, enabling him to hold morning and evening worship services without the expense of eating out. Adrian was a forty-minute drive from Jackson, so they seldom returned home before dark. That was too much church for me, so I only accompanied my grandparents three or four times a year.

—— ℰ ——

THE SERVICE AT our place of worship, Trinity Missionary Baptist Church, lasted too long. The wooden pews were hard and uncomfortable, and in the summers the tiny cement block building located on Franklin Street was burning hot inside. Women wearing fancy hats fanned the heat and nodded their heads with angelic smiles on their faces, while hanging on every word of Rev. Amos Whittington's message. Their dutiful husbands sat beside them, wearing starched white shirts and pressed suits. Their kids, hair slicked and feet swinging, sat next to them. I used to sneak peeks at some of them and wonder what it was like to have a father living in the house, and a family who came to church together.

Half of the time we rode with Grandma and Mr. Thomas. Aunt Lula Mae picked up her mother and stepfather every Sunday morning at ten forty five, exactly. The other half of the time we walked. There were groups of us—cousins and neighbors—walking to Sunday school, a two-and-a-half-mile trek.

"And Jasmine, you and Albert better not go over that vidock," Momma would warn us every Sunday morning when we headed out the door. "I'm so glad that somebody finally boarded up that old bridge before somebody got hurt."

She might as well have been talking to the air. I never knew where the name "vidock" came from, but when walking, we seldom missed a Sunday morning crossing the bridge on our way to church. The black wooden structure rose about twenty feet into the air and arched over several sets of parallel train tracks that divided the east side of Jackson from the south. We'd hoist each other up over boards that crisscrossed the entrance, then climbed up the stairway, which was missing steps. We even had to leap across missing planks in the walkway of the old and rickety bridge to get to the other side. I was adventurous but always scared of heights. So while the others stood and looked over the sides, I refused to look down and hurried across the bridge.

—— ℘ ——

GRANDMA ALWAYS MADE all of us sit alongside her in church—sisters, brothers, cousins, young aunts and uncles, everybody. Our family took up an entire pew, sometimes two. And it didn't matter whether it was eleven o'clock or evening worship service at seven, Grandma sat in the same spot in the same pew every single Sunday. People must have known that it was Grandma's seat because I don't remember anyone else ever sitting there.

None of us kids liked sitting right next to Grandma, and we would bicker about it under our breath before we got there, when the adults were distracted or engaged in other conversations. Grandma didn't stand for any fidgeting, feet swinging, or stretching. Yawning was allowed, but limited. If we dozed off, Grandma tapped us lightly on the head with a paper fan, donated to the church by the only black mortuary in town, its advertising on the back. If we squirmed too much and weren't sitting within Grandma's reach, she'd clear her throat first to get our attention, then give us the eye. That look always made even the toughest among us think twice, even my uncle Samuel, Momma's younger brother who was the sixteen-year-old hell raiser of the family.

Three stoic-faced deacons stood in front of the pulpit and led devotion, singing congregational songs that sounded as if our church was in mourning. The deacons talked slowly. The deaconesses moved slowly. The choir sung slowly. The pastor even started preaching slowly.

By the time the offering dish was passed around, it felt good just be able to move. There were so many of us best-friend relatives sitting next to each other, we barely had elbow room to pass the round, wooden offering plate, which was lined on the bottom with red velvet.

Grandma gave us a nickel every Sunday just before the offering. She'd take a clean white handkerchief from the big leather purse that sat on her lap and untied the corner holding the change. It crossed my mind more than once to try to get four cents change from a nickel when the plate came around and Grandma wasn't looking, but I never got up the nerve to try.

It was all I could do to stay awake until the choir entered through the double doors at the back of the church and marched down the aisle. That always perked me up. I loved any kind of music, so I'd sit up straight as soon as they appeared. I smiled at my aunt Lula Mae when she passed us, wearing a bright yellow robe with a white collar that hung down her chest. I was so proud of her.

Grandma's only daughter, Lula Mae was a member of the pastor's chorus and always led the procession of middle-aged women and men, some heads held high, others lowered, their faces barely visible. Aunt Lula Mae also served as the church announcement clerk and as an usher. Grandma's face glowed every time her daughter stood up—dressed to the hilt—to read the church calendar of activities, thank-you cards from bereaved families, and other information related to Trinity Baptist Church.

But there were so many things about church that I didn't understand. Why did Rev. Whittington hum after every sentence he spoke? Why did we pray to Jesus, yet worship God? And why did Rev. Whittington start off speaking just above a whisper, but before his sermon was over, whoop and holler so loudly that sometimes his voice turned hoarse? Everything he said meant nothing to me because I didn't understand it.

Before the service ended, Grandma almost always got "happy." It embarrassed most of us best-friend relatives, so we sat there staring straight ahead, hoping it would soon end. Grandma's "Amens" would grow louder and louder. She'd rock back and forth, clap her hands, and throw her arms in the air. When Grandma really got carried away, she'd start stomping her feet.

"Thank-you, Jesus! Thank-you, Lord. You're a mighty good God. You're a mighty good God indeed," she'd shout, sometimes raising her glasses and wiping tears from her eyes with her handkerchief.

An usher or two always rushed to Grandma's side and dutifully fanned her face until the shouting subsided. Often there would be a chain reaction, where one person would get happy, then another and another. It appeared to be the strangest thing to me. After church had ended one Sunday, and Grandma and I were sitting on her porch, I asked her about it.

"Grandma, why do you be crying in church?" I timidly asked.

"Honey," she said, with so much conviction in her voice. "When I look back over the years and see how far God has brought me, and how good God has been to me, I get so full that I can't do nothing but shout. Those are tears of joy, child."

Sunday school didn't last as long as church, so I liked it better. The smaller classes gave us a chance to talk and ask questions. I understood our lessons, like

Jonah being swallowed by a whale and Daniel being thrown in the lion's den, a lot better than the half-hour sermons preached by Rev. Whittington during worship services.

Sunday school also felt less intimidating to me than church. There were kids my age, and we got to know each other better. It was interesting to find out that some of their families were nontraditional, like ours. One girl was being raised by her father. Her mother died in childbirth. She was a brassy, nice-looking girl who talked fast and flirted with too many of the boys as far as I was concerned. But I felt sorry for her not having a mother. I couldn't imagine not having one, even though I wished mine were a little nicer.

Another girl was being raised by her grandparents. Her mother lived in New York and came to see her two or three times a year. There was nothing that stood out about the girl except that she was tall, slender, and light skinned, with short hair that was always pressed and tightly curled. But her grandparents adored her. I often saw them gazing at her, the way Grandma and my momma's parents sometimes looked at me.

There was one boy who wore the nicest clothes and had the curliest hair and lightest skin of anyone in our Sunday school class. I thought he was so cute. His father was the only black foreman in one of the large factories and made good money. His mother stayed home to care for him and his younger sister, whom we seldom saw outside of their house, except at church.

Trinity Baptist held its Sunday school picnic every July at Ella Sharpe Park. Church officials served us hot dogs and hamburgers, along with baked beans and potato salad. We drank lemonade and Kool-Aid, and finished our meals off with a big slice of watermelon and a dip of homemade ice cream in a cone.

Ella Sharpe Park was beautiful and consisted of more than five hundred acres of land on Jackson's south side. Donated by a woman who died long before I was born, the huge park provided us with ample room to spread out and explore our surroundings. Everyone loved the monkey house, except me. It smelled. Somebody said that monkeys used to live there, but I never saw any in the large cemented area that was six feet below ground and made up of caves and rocks. The son of the factory foreman jumped down into the area every year and walked around, even though there was a big black and white sign that read: "DO NOT GO BEYOND THIS POINT."

TRINITY BAPTIST CHURCH was founded by a mulatto former slave and had a building program from as far back as I could remember. Members placed donations in a shoebox, located in the small vestibule, week after week. Following worship services, members stood outside in front of the church and talked for ten or fifteen minutes. There were hugs, instructions on church etiquette, and questions about how well I was doing in school. Seldom did a Sunday go by when someone didn't comment on how small I was for my age. I hated that.

The busty women's tight hugs nearly smothered me. The men shook my skinny hands so hard they sometimes hurt. We'd stand there patiently waiting for Grandma to make her rounds with her friends, before we all climbed back into Aunt Lula Mae's shiny new Oldsmobile and rode home.

One Sunday, during the eleven o'clock service, I decided to officially join church. I was nine years-old. Grandma and I had talked a lot about getting baptized, and to be honest, I did it for her more than anything else. The only thing I understood about becoming a Christian was that I was expected to be a nicer, happier person. I could live with that. The scariest part for me was being dipped backward in cold water. I shuddered at the thought of my face being underwater —split second or not.

It was a sunny June morning when I eased up from the pew, trembling knees and all, and headed to the front of the church, where two empty wooden chairs sat facing the congregation. The moment I began shuffling in my seat, Grandma started crying and shouting, making me even more nervous. But I was determined to become a candidate for baptism, and believing that water emersion would be at a later date.

My back to the pulpit, I squeezed my way along the pews, crowded with smiling adults nodding their heads approvingly. The girl in my Sunday school class being raised by her grandparents joined me at the front of the church. She sat in the other vacant chair.

On the way home, I was sitting in the backseat of Aunt Lula Mae's car when Grandma told me that I would be getting baptized that same evening. The thought of being dipped in water, with all eyes on me, made me extremely nervous.

—— ⁊ ——

GRANDMA TREATED ME like royalty, knowing I was getting baptized that night. She served me fried pork chops, lima beans, mashed potatoes and gravy, cornbread, and peach cobbler. She and Mother didn't believe in cooking anything but down-home meals, "soul food."

Grandma took care of everything for my baptism. She got me a swimming cap from somewhere to keep my near-shoulder-length pressed-and-curled hair from getting wet. The cap didn't work, and my hair got wet during the split-second dip in the baptismal pool, located behind the pulpit. I walked away from church service that night with nappy hair.

I started off doing pretty good at being a Christian. Whenever my temper got the best of me, I'd remember Grandma's urgings to be more "Christ-like," and stopped whatever I was doing—like hollering at my brothers and sister and bossing them around, behavior that had become a habit with me. I stopped stealing change out of Momma's purse. Her welfare check came the first of the month, and I had gotten in the habit of taking just enough to buy some candy on my way to school. I avoided arguments with my best-friend cousins and schoolmates, and didn't get in a single fight for over four months, a record for me. Before that, it seemed as if I was battling someone every month or two due to my quick temper and poor self-esteem.

The "new and improved" me lasted about three weeks. I still prayed before going to bed each night and had perfect attendance in church and Sunday school. But I had expected God to zap me with some magical power that would make me do the right things, even *enjoy* going to church, but that didn't happen, which puzzled me.

❧ RAISING JASMINE

My mom and dad were so opposite of each other that I often wondered how they ever met but was too afraid to ask. Our family kept lots of secrets.

Momma was born in Ethel, Mississippi, a tiny rural community with fewer than five hundred people. Her family relocated to Michigan when she was seven years old because her father, a former sharecropper, came seeking a medical opinion about a stomach ailment and ended up finding a better-paying job up north.

Daddy was a "city boy" to his heart. Raised primarily by his mother, his father was shot and killed in Chicago before I was born, a victim of mistaken identity or gangster ties. No one knew for sure, and relatives seldom spoke of him.

Momma was a very private person who seldom talked and spent too much time alone in her bedroom. She didn't make friends easily, but had several close ones, most of whom she'd known since their school days.

Daddy always had a crowd with him—even when he came to pick me up, something that irked Momma to no end. People gravitated toward my dad. He was the life of any party and told great stories that kept everyone cracking up laughing, including me.

Momma was conservative. She wore dresses and skirts and blouses that left no lasting memory of color or style. About once a year Momma "went out." She'd wash, press, and curl her thick, black hair, which hung just above her shoulders, then slip into her nicest outfit, usually a skirt and sweater. Momma would pat cinnamon-powdered makeup on her face and line her eyebrows with a black eyebrow pencil. She'd smooth lots of burgundy lipstick on her lips that easily chapped, like mine. After dabbing on some perfume and clipping gold earrings on her ears, Momma would ride with one of her female friends to Leake's Lounge, one of only three black night spots in Jackson at that time.

I can remember standing in the bedroom doorway, watching Momma's appearance transform from matron-like to gorgeous right before my eyes. She'd smile and talk while getting ready, happy to get away from life's hardships for a few hours. I was always excited for her and wanted Momma to have some fun.

My dad wore loud-colored Hawaiian print shirts year round and stuck a straw hat on his head in the summers. He wore a long wool coat in the winter that hung sloppily off of his shoulders. Rather than button it up, he would hold it together with his hands, probably out of habit. Momma called it "trifling." Daddy was a workaholic during the week and a hard-core partier on the weekends. He told me that he and his drinking buddies partied from the time they got off work on Friday afternoons until late Sunday nights.

"Honey, we couldn't wait to hit the highway," he'd boast, his bottom lip curling under the top one. "We'd try to hit every party this side of the Ohio River."

I remember watching him on Friday nights as he stood in front of the bathroom mirror for an hour and a half, washing his dry but curly hair. He'd rub Vitalis through it to give it a nice sheen. I loved the smell. His shaving seemed a little off the mark, because he always had tiny spots of blood on his smiling face when he finished. Sometimes, my dad used pieces of toilet paper as mini bandages, and they were still stuck to his face by dried blood when he finished.

Both my parents were extremely independent, one of the few things they had in common. Momma did day work but never owned a car. She'd walk or catch the bus when she had to go anywhere, often refusing rides even from people she knew. Although we had little, she didn't like borrowing anything unless it was absolutely necessary. Sometimes being hungry wasn't even enough.

"Borrowing things, especially money, causes people to fall out," she reminded me over and over again.

Momma moved away from home at sixteen when she married, and she never moved back again. She seemed to have the will of a thousand men, a characteristic that easily intimidated people.

Daddy quit school in the eighth grade to help provide for his mother and two younger siblings. He landed a factory job at General Motors a few years later, telling officials he was seventeen. He was really only fifteen. I used to think Daddy was rich because he always seemed to have money—completely the opposite of our household back in Jackson.

When I was a young child, my dad lived with his mother. I started out calling her "Grandma" until I heard everyone else calling her "Big Ma." My paternal grandmother, whose skin was so fair she looked white, became "Big Ma" to me, too. She and Daddy lived in a big, two-story house on Michigan Street, near the Buick factory where he worked. There was a trapdoor in their kitchen that led to an underground apartment. Daddy took his female friends there in order to have some privacy. Sometimes he didn't come out all weekend.

Living in Flint during the summers was lonely for me, mainly because most people around me were grown. I had to find things to occupy my time, like sitting on their front steps every afternoon at three to count the new cars that passed, fresh off Buick's assembly line. I used to pick out the flashiest-colored ones and pretend they were mine. I loved bright colors.

Every time I visited Daddy he'd teach me the newest dance steps. I'd return home to Jackson and teach them to my siblings, demanding that they pay close attention. I bossed my sisters and brothers around a lot. Often, I'd sketch the dance steps out on brown butcher paper, with footprints indicating the moves.

We'd go over each dance until I was satisfied that they had it down pat. Dancing didn't seem to interest Momma. I only saw her dance a few times in my entire life, but she wore the biggest smile when she did, swaying to the music and snapping her fingers. I loved to see Momma happy, but those times were few and far between.

— ❧ —

I WAS ALWAYS too afraid to ask questions about Momma and Daddy. All I knew was that Momma ended up pregnant and was only fifteen years old. My Daddy was twenty-one. I was an adult when he finally told me that my grandfather had him arrested for statutory rape, and the judge gave him an ultimatum—marry Momma or go to prison. The two soon married and moved to Flint and lived with Big Ma for a short while.

Daddy admitted to not being a very good husband. He said he was too young and wild at the time.

"One night your momma told me that if I stayed out all night one more time, she was leaving. That Friday, I got off work, put on my glad rags, and spent the whole weekend in Ohio partying. By the time I got back home that Sunday night, Malena was gone and never came back," he said.

But I was Daddy's only child, and he visited often, almost always bearing gifts. There wasn't anything that he wouldn't do for me, and I knew it—completely the opposite of my life at home with Momma, where I felt like just one of six mouths to feed.

Yet every time Daddy appeared, I'd cry, begging and pleading with Momma not to make me go back to Flint with him. He always came with a car full of friends, all of them just as loud and boisterous as he was. They scared me. He scared me. Every time he appeared I felt like a stranger had come to take me away from my family. And because Daddy often spoke of wanting to raise me himself in order to provide me with a better life, I always feared that once gone, I'd never see my "real" family again.

One time Momma took me to Flint and left me. I must have sensed something because I refused to let her out of my sight all day. By nightfall, she had coaxed me into walking around the corner to a movie theater with Daddy's younger sister, Jada, and her boyfriend. Each of them held one of my hands, but I remembered looking back toward the house, just in time to see Momma hurrying into a cab that sped off.

"You couldn't possibly remember that! You were only eighteen months old," Momma snapped one time when I brought the incident up.

That surprised me because I vividly remembered running down the sidewalk in the dark, chasing the cab and screaming for Momma not to leave me. They never stopped.

I cried myself to sleep that night and woke up before dawn the next day in an unfamiliar bedroom, darkened by pulled shades. The only sounds I heard were birds chirping outside the window and an alarm clock ticking on the dresser.

———— ❧ ————

ONE TIME DADDY visited in the middle of the night, something not unusual for him because of his weekend partying. I woke up after hearing his voice coming from the living room. Afraid that he came to take me back to Flint with him, I pretended to be asleep. A few minutes later he crept into the bedroom and gently shook me several times and whispered my name so he wouldn't wake up the other kids. I didn't move a muscle and kept my eyes closed so tight they hurt. Daddy lifted up one of my braids.

"Her hair sure is growing," he said, before pulling back the blankets that covered me. "She's getting a little taller, but she's still skinny as a razor."

Daddy covered me back up and tiptoed out of the bedroom. I breathed a sigh of relief when I heard him telling Momma that he had to go, and that she'd receive her child support check on Monday. I heard our front door open, then close. Straining to listen, I heard his car engine start up and then fade into the night as he drove away.

Over time, I learned to pick up cues that Daddy was coming. Whenever Momma bought me new underwear and a few pair of summer shorts and blouses without buying anything for my sisters and brothers, I knew something was up. Even washing and hot-combing my hair without doing Lisa's and Penny's was a sure sign that Daddy was on the way. Consequently, I lived with a certain amount of nervousness, especially around summer vacation time, knowing that Daddy could walk through the door any time and take me away.

Once I was outside playing hopscotch with my cousins Arlene and Robin when Daddy caught me off guard. Hearing music from a radio blaring, I looked up and saw Daddy's 1954 pink and gray Chevrolet pull up in our driveway, full of people laughing and talking loudly. I started crying right there and ran to Grandma's house, hoping she'd step in and stop Momma and Daddy from making me go back to Flint with him.

"Malena ain't got no business making you go with Eugene if you don't want to," Grandma said. "I never did believe in making chil'ren go with folks—kin or no kin—when they was afraid of 'em. Some kids just don't take to folks quick as others. I don't know what's wrong with Malena and Eugene. Young folks these days ain't got a lick of sense."

Grandma walked me back home and told me to stay outside while she went inside to talk to Momma and Daddy.

It wasn't long before Daddy came out of the house, stooped down and kissed me on the forehead, said his good-byes, and left—loud friends and all. Grandma came out of the house a few minutes later, but walked right by me without saying anything. That was unusual.

I got up relieved and trotted around the corner to Deyo alley, where most of the kids in the neighborhood—including my siblings and best-friend cousins—were playing kickball. I joined in and soon forgot about my earlier ordeal. We had been playing about half an hour when Momma called my name from our front door. I trotted back home to see what she wanted.

"Come walk up to Matthews Ice Cream Store with me, Jasmine," she said calmly.

I was thrilled. Momma and I seldom did anything together, so going to the ice cream store made me feel so special it was almost overwhelming. She didn't talk much as we strolled up to Michigan Avenue, but that was okay. Just being with her by myself was good enough for me. Happy, I chattered enough for both of us.

A man dressed in white pants, shirt, and hat took our order. I asked for watermelon-flavored ice cream in a cone. Momma ordered a pint of it to take back to my sisters and brothers. She paid the cashier, and within minutes we were walking back across the black-topped parking lot, me licking my five-cent ice cream cone with a big smile on my face and feeling pretty darn important.

Suddenly someone swept me off my feet. And before I realized what was happening, Daddy was carrying me kicking and screaming to his car, its engine still running. Despite my struggling as if my life depended on it, he managed to wrestle me into the vehicle. During the encounter, I accidentally hit him in the face. He grabbed both my wrists and, squeezing them tightly, stared me straight in the face.

"Don't you ever hit me again. Do you hear me? I'm your daddy, and don't you ever forget it. This is the first time my child ever hit me, and I'm never gonna forget this day as long as I live."

Daddy looked more hurt than angry. I felt ashamed. His words shook me up enough to take some of the wind out of my struggle, enabling him to plop me into the backseat and lap of Margaret, his friend since childhood. She always rode down to Jackson with Daddy. Years later I realized that he must have brought her so that I wouldn't have to ride back in a car full of men.

Margaret moved me from the door while Daddy closed it. Then he hustled up to the driver's side, climbed in, and drove off. Still crying, I wiggled away from Margaret and scrambled into the rear window just in time to see Momma hurrying back across Michigan Avenue. She never looked back.

I spent some holidays with Daddy, too. One Christmas Eve Daddy and I rode around Flint until the stores closed, looking for a wedding doll I wanted. Another Christmas I thought Daddy had forgotten to buy me a present. As soon as we arrived at his apartment, I got down on my knees under his aluminum Christmas tree that had a rotating wheel casting blue, green, yellow, and red lights on its branches. One by one I read the name on each colorfully wrapped gift. After examining all of them, I let out the biggest "Whaah!"

"You didn't buy me nothing! You forgot about me. Ain't none of those presents under the tree got my name on 'em," I cried, feeling more and more sorry for myself as the drama unfolded, but enjoying the attention. Daddy talked until even I got tired of crying, trying to convince me that he had bought me a gift.

"Look here, Jasmine, I keep telling you I got you something. Daddy didn't forget you. Your gift is just too big to fit under the tree," he kept saying, looking more and more uneasy.

I cried so long that Daddy took me downstairs to his brother's apartment. Four years younger than Daddy, Uncle Darius lived with his wife in the same apartment house on Page Street. They didn't know I heard Daddy whispering on the telephone before we left, so I knew they were up to something. Sure enough, Uncle Darius stepped into his bedroom and returned carrying a small package with my name on it, amateurishly wrapped with Christmas paper.

I stopped crying, but was still whimpering as I tore open the gift. It was a package of white handkerchiefs—*men's* white handkerchiefs. I held my disappointment until we got back to our apartment. Then I cried louder than ever.

Daddy couldn't stand seeing me unhappy and hurt, so he eventually agreed to take me back into his bedroom closet and show me my Christmas gift. It was a shiny blue English Racer bike, something I had wanted for more than a year. After climbing into bed that night, I lay in the dark, unable to sleep.

"I wish I hadn't seen my Christmas present. Now I've spoiled everything," I thought.

✳ MOTHER AND DADDY

"If you ever stop acting like you don't have no sense, you gon grow up to be somebody," my grandfather told me one day, with an almost whimsical smile on his coconut shell–colored face. I never exactly knew what "be somebody" meant, but liked how our grandparents stuck by me no matter what.

Daddy, my grandfather, served as our surrogate father, trudging in and out of our house, sometimes several times a week, delivering messages from Grandma, his mother, and giving Momma rides to take care of business matters. He'd drive Momma to work whenever she missed the bus or didn't have money, and he transported us back and forth to doctors' appointments and the health clinic for shots. Daddy tried to attend at least one school activity per year and did anything else he could to help make life easier for us.

My grandfather was pastor of a small church in Adrian, Michigan, and stayed on the highway a lot, driving back and forth, sometimes several times a week, caring for his congregation. Daddy wasn't one of those fire-and-brimstone preachers. His voice was soft, gentle, and filled with compassion. My grandfather could sing, too, a family trait that skipped me.

Every summer Daddy took my siblings and me to the Goodyear picnic with his family, even though he had four young people still living at home, including three teenagers. The picnic, held at Lake Lansing amusement park in East Lansing, Michigan, was the major event of the summer for Jackson, and nearly everyone in town went. Every year I worried that Daddy wouldn't be able to get enough tickets or have enough room in his car for us, or be able to find somebody who did. That never happened. When we grew too big for Daddy to pack everyone in his blue and white Chrysler, he'd arrange for another family member to take some of us. Every adult man in our family worked at Goodyear.

I was very young when my grandfather caught his hand in some equipment on the job at the plant. Years later he chuckled when telling me about it.

"Ole Jim Donaldson was working right alongside me when it happened. I knew I was in trouble as soon as my hand got caught. I just kept saying to ole Jim, 'Flip the switch. Just flip the switch off.' Jim was a white fella I'd known for years, and for a few seconds he just stood there frozen stiff and crying and saying, 'I can't do it, George. I'm scared it'll do more damage to ya.' It took some calm talking on my part, but I finally got my ole friend to flip the switch, and I was able to pull my hand loose," my grandfather said.

Doctors managed to save Daddy's thumb, but he lost all his fingers on his left hand. He spent several months in Chicago in a rehabilitation facility and came home with his left hand looking like a balled fist that was covered with skin and felt soft and mushy.

Daddy seemed comfortable with having only a thumb, but I was overly protective of him, especially when little kids asked him why his hand looked so funny. I'd give them the evil eye, hoping to discourage any more questions, then sit on my grandfather's lap and hug him.

— ‰ —

"MOTHER" WAS MY angel. Mother also helped us out by sending care packages with Daddy whenever he dropped by our house. The grease-stained brown paper bags he carried almost always contained day-old fried chicken or pork chops, with black-eyed peas, lima or string beans, green peas, mashed potatoes, or macaroni and cheese. Early in the week, Mother sent pound cake or sweet potato pie, left over from Sunday's dinner and wrapped in aluminum foil badly wrinkled from previous use. She baked cornbread every day, and was sometimes teased by other family members. I could tell it hurt her feelings by the sound in her voice when she told me. I hated when family members said hurtful things to my grandmother. Later, as an adult, I would have told a few of them off if it hadn't been for Mother's urgings.

"Don't say nothing, Jasmine. It's all right. I just want to keep unity in the family," she'd say.

Mother often accompanied Daddy when he stopped by our house. Dressed in long sleeves, despite the weather, she'd ease in a few minutes after him, having scanned the yard and porch to see what things were out of place. If it was chilly, Mother wore a bandana on her head, tied under her chin. One day she came through the door behind Daddy and stood talking to Momma, while slowly turning her head to check out our surroundings—something she did in all her adult children's homes.

"Malena Helen, why don't you keep those shoes put up out of the middle of the floor?" she asked, eyeing a pair of scuffed saddle oxfords lying in the living room, on our gray and white linoleum floor.

Mother's comment made Momma mad.

"Mother, now don't you start," she snapped. "I ain't picking up after no kids big enough to pick up after themselves. These kids ain't no babies. I was gon see just how long those shoes were gonna lay there before somebody moved them. I get so tired of yelling at these hard-headed kids, I don't know what to do."

Still staring at the shoes with half-worn heels, Mother batted her big brown cat eyes and patiently waited until Momma stopped fussing. Her hands clasped on top of one another and a small black purse dangling from her forearm, Mother spoke again, never raising her voice.

"Well, Malena, you never know when company might drop by. Seems to me you'd want to say something to them. They're children. Maybe they'd learn to pick up after themselves if they were taught."

—— ☙ ——

THE PERFECT CHRISTIAN in my book, Mother attended church every Sunday and urged her children and grandchildren to do the same. Mother never drank, cussed, or smoked. "And it wasn't because I didn't have the opportunity. It was because I didn't have the desire," she'd say firmly.

My grandmother never raised her voice to anyone. Her harshest discipline was "mauling our heads," something we found amusing as small children. Mother would ball up her tiny fist and rub it furiously against the back of our heads. She only did it once or twice for reasons I can't remember, but Albert and I found it hard to keep from laughing at her

Mother came from a long line of believers. Her father served as superintendent of the Sunday school at Shady Grove Missionary Baptist Church in French Camp, Mississippi, for fifty-six years, never missing a Sunday or a National Baptist Convention during his tenure. Mother volunteered to serve as Sunday school secretary at sixteen years old and faithfully served for sixteen years, resigning in 1941 because her husband and young family were relocating to Michigan.

—— ☙ ——

MOTHER STOOD OVER her stove cooking dinner one hot, sticky summer afternoon, as I tried to scratch my thigh without her noticing. While rubbing, my
green sundress rose up too far, and Mother spotted them. Sores. Tiny pus-filled
bumps. Scabs.

"Jasmine, what's that up there on your leg?" she asked, her eyebrows raised
and eyes batting as she rushed across the kitchen floor to where I was standing.

"I don't know," I replied, hanging my head in shame.

"You don't know?" she asked, while raising my dress to get a better look.

"Has Malena seen this?"

"No."

"She hasn't? Why not?"

"Cause I didn't want to tell her."

"Why?"

"I don't know."

The truth was, I had been too embarrassed and a little afraid to tell Momma
about the nasty-looking sores that were spreading down my thighs. Fearing she'd
get mad at me, I knew the last thing Momma needed was a sick or afflicted child.
Yet I was relieved that Mother found out because I had been scared dealing with it
alone for the past few weeks.

My grandmother called Momma on the telephone and told her about the
"sores running up and down Jasmine's thighs." Momma wasn't mad and got
me in to see a doctor the next day. He diagnosed the sores as impetigo, a highly
contagious condition, and instructed me to wash the area several times a day with
Dial soap, then rub Neosporin ointment on it.

"Don't put bandages or anything like that on it. The air helps it heal," the
doctor said. Within a week, the sores had gone away.

— ❧ —

EVERY FALL MOTHER led a family ritual—canning. We were the youngest generation and would harvest pears and apples from the trees and vegetables from the
backyard garden. Momma and her siblings did the peeling and cutting. Mother
did all the cooking in huge pots that spewed steam from under their clanking
tops and filled the house with the sweet aroma of fresh-cooked fruit.

Mother filled dozens of large and small Mason jars with the fruit and
vegetables, then stored them on wooden shelves in a small dark room in her
basement. Every time we visited, she'd send a jar or two home with us. We ate

preserves and homemade biscuits all winter, but I liked her canned apples and tomatoes the best.

— ℯ —

MOMMA USED TO SAY we had some "Asian blood" somewhere in our ancestry because most of those on Mother's side of the family had small body frames and facial structures that resembled Asians, including big brown eyes that slanted upward. I used to believe it, but wondered how Asians ever ended up in rural Mississippi.

Mother's family was raised on a forty-acre farm in French Camp, Mississippi, living off the land. My grandparents met one day when Mother was walking across the field in Gladys, Mississippi, headed home after teaching in a one-room schoolhouse.

"She was so calm and peaceful," my grandfather said, glowing like a newly-wed as a smile spread across his face. "I'd never seen a person like that before. I said to myself right then, 'I'm gon marry that girl,' and by the year's end, I had."

🌸 ALBERT <u>AND</u> ME

"I got up enough nerve to ask my dad to let Albert spend the summer with me in Flint when I was nine years old. "There's nobody for me to play with," I said during one of our telephone conversations. Daddy did most things I asked, and readily agreed.

He came to pick us up late one sunny afternoon accompanied by his new wife, Charlene. We had been on the highway about half an hour when Albert's stomach started growling.

"Umm hungry," he announced loudly.

Charlene told us we'd eat as soon as we got to their apartment. Albert repeated himself two or three more times before Charlene spoke again

"I know . . . let's play a game," she said. "Look at the clouds and tell me what you see."

"I see a car," I said, pointing to the white fluffy clouds that decorated the blue sky. Charlene saw a horse. Albert was the last to speak.

"I see a big plate of *fried chicken*," he stuttered.

Daddy and Charlene laughed for five minutes.

During our summer stay in Flint, Albert and I visited some of Daddy's friends and relatives every day. Everyone was kind and talked to Albert, asking him questions like, "Are you as smart as Jasmine in school?" or "Do you like school, too?"

Daddy liked bragging to his family and friends about my getting straight As in school. Albert always got Cs and Ds in school and never lied about it. Part of the reason I was motivated to do well in school was Daddy. He often sent me a dollar for every A on my report card and fifty cents for every B. I never got a B in elementary school.

Momma also contributed to my success in school by requiring me to write Daddy regularly. Even before I learned to print, she'd write letters for me, and I'd copy them, not knowing what they said.

I never knew what to make of Daddy's friends' comments about my appearance.

"Eugene, that girl looks like you spit her out. You sho can't deny her."

I failed to see any resemblance. Daddy's skin was several shades lighter than my caramel complexion. At a glance, people sometimes mistook him for white, something he boasted about every so often. Momma had to straighten my hair, which hung just above my shoulders. Daddy's dark brown hair, tinged with red, was naturally wavy with tiny curls around the back from ear to ear. We shared some of the same interests, like music and dancing and talking a lot. I tended to talk only around friends and family. Daddy talked to anyone, anywhere.

Daddy and Charlene treated us royally during our summer stay in Flint. We went on picnics, visited Flint's amusement park, shopped for school clothes, and met new friends. Albert and I were good company for each other during our two-month stay because there were no young people our age to play with.

I'll never forget the night the four of us sat parked in a car at the drive-in theater and Albert asked, "Eugene, are you my daddy?"

The chatter and laughing stopped. Daddy glanced at Charlene. She stared back. Then after an uncomfortable pause, he said, "Yes."

Albert beamed with pride. I did, too.

Momma never talked about Albert's daddy. His name was Gary Steward. The only thing I remembered about him was that he sent Momma and me some satin pajamas one time while he served overseas in the army. Momma kept a picture of him, dressed in his military uniform, tucked away in an overnight case under her bed. Albert and I never talked about his dad. No one else in the family did either.

✳ ROUGHING IT

lbert, get up! You need to make a fire. It's cold in this house. The rest of you kids better get up outta those beds, too. You bet' not be late for school this morning."

We woke up to Momma's yelling every morning. I'd snuggle deeper under one of Mother's hand-made quilts while Albert got up from his roll-away bed, located in the dining room, and trudged out the back door and down the steps to the furnace in the basement.

Still drowsy, Albert picked up two or three pieces of wood and several lumps of coal before tossing them into a furnace about one-third the size of our entire "Michigan" basement. They were called Michigan basements because of their dirt floors and cement-block walls. After tearing a piece of a brown paper bag and twisting it as tightly as he could, my brother would strike a match to light the paper, which quickly became a torch. Some mornings Albert got the fire started right away. Other times it took several tries before the flames in the furnace stayed lit. I felt sorry for Albert, having to get up earlier than the rest of us every morning to get a fire started. Lying under those quilts many mornings, I'd think to myself, "When I grow up, I'm gonna live in a house where the heat comes on by itself, like the rest of my friends' houses do."

— ❧ —

I WAS A TOMBOY and wanted to go everywhere Albert and his two friends June Bug and Teko went. June Bug was the boy who had attacked me in the library. Teko lived two blocks over on Plymouth Street and was an only child. Sometimes the trio didn't want me hanging around them, but I did anyway.

One time the four of us walked several miles to go tadpole hunting in a pond on the edge of town. I ignored the boys' warnings not to get in the water, took my shoes off, and stepped in anyway. Always trying to outdo everyone else, I was determined to catch the most tadpoles in the blue Maxwell House coffee can, half filled with water, that I held in my hands. I waded toward a group of rocks located near the middle of the muddy water. Suddenly I felt a sharp pain. Then the water where I stood started surfacing red.

"Oh my goodness. I think something done bit me. Albert . . . somebody come over here quick."

As it turned out, I had stepped on a piece of glass. My foot hurt and bled so badly that Albert and June Bug had to help me home by letting me hop on one foot while holding on to their shoulders. My brother stuttered and fussed at me all the way home for not listening to their warnings. Momma hollered at me, calling me "hardheaded." She washed the deep, two-inch cut with peroxide, then put some mercurochrome on it before bandaging my foot.

— ❧ —

MY FIRST EXPERIENCE with racism was when I was eight years old and involved a young, single white woman named Deana. She was a neighbor who lived kitty-corner from us on Page Avenue and who often invited us to her apartment. Albert and I loved going to her place because she treated us nicely and had lots of interesting things that we had never seen before, like the black eight ball on her living-room table. We'd rub it over and over, reading our fortunes and believing them to be true.

One day we were sitting in her apartment when the landlord walked in, his face snarled and twisted as he eyed my brother and me. He took Deana in another room, and I could tell by the tone of his voice that he was angry.

"We don't allow niggers in our homes. I won't stand for it. You'd better tell them to leave right now. And I don't ever want to see them in here again or else you'll have to move," he said.

They lowered their voices, and I heard an exchange of words, but couldn't understand what they said. When our friend entered the room again, she looked embarrassed and waited until the landlord had left to tell us what we had already heard. But Deana was feisty and not about to give in. She told us to still come see her, only we'd have to sneak in after dark.

We did, and got away with it for a few weeks, but Deana's landlord caught us coming out of her apartment one evening. I was so scared that I didn't go back again. A few weeks later I walked out my front door one morning and saw a pickup truck, filled with Deana's belongings, driving away. We never saw or heard from our friend again.

——— ॐ ———

"WHITE PEOPLE DOWN south make black people say, 'Yes ma'am' and 'No ma'am' and 'Yes sir' and 'No sir.' And if you don't, they can whip you or even hang you. And your parents can't do nothing about it," June Bug told Albert and me in early August 1959.

It scared the heck out of me. My grandparents were taking my brother, my cousin Debra, their daughter Valerie, and me with them on their yearly two-week vacation to French Camp, Mississippi, to visit my grandmother's parents. The first out-of-state trip for Albert and me, I had been looking forward to it all summer until hearing June Bug's warning about white people down south.

I was considered to be the family rebel by many relatives because I spoke my mind if I strongly disagreed with something—even at ten years old. The idea of strangers whipping me for not saying what they wanted seemed absurd.

"I ain't saying that to no white people. My own momma don't make me say stuff like that. How's somebody else gonna make me do it?" I said, unnerved by the thought.

The next day I walked up to Mother's house and asked her if it was true. Her gentle facial expression turned serious as the words came from my mouth. I even detected a hint of embarrassment.

"You and Albert just watch your mouths down south and stay close to Daddy and me," she said. "Ya'll let us worry about that."

Her response bothered me, and let me know there was some truth to June Bug's words. It dampened my enthusiasm about the trip, but I wasn't about to back out. Albert, Debra, and I had been hearing about Mississippi and our great-grandparents all of our lives and wanted to spend time with them. We had dozens of cousins down there we'd never met. And I loved the idea of being with my grandparents for two weeks.

We pulled out of Jackson before dawn one August morning, the trunk loaded with luggage and care packages of fried chicken, homemade biscuits, macaroni and cheese, and sweet potato pie stacked on the backseat floor. Debra, Albert, Valerie, and I laughed, talked, and sang a lot, which helped keep my mind off of white people down south until we stopped to get gas in Nashville, Tennessee. Scared, I got out and stretched my legs right next to the car. Everyone else went inside to use the restrooms.

An hour later, as my grandfather was speeding down the highway, I asked him to stop along the side of the road so that I could relieve myself.

"Jasmine, why in the name of heaven didn't you go when we were at the gas station?" he asked, looking bewildered. I reluctantly told him the truth.

"Cause I'm scared I might forget to say 'Yes ma'am' and 'No ma'am' and 'Yes sir' and 'No sir' to these white people down here. And they might get mad and whip me. Daddy, how can white people be whipping other people's kids anyway?"

Daddy got quiet and exited the highway. After finding a secluded spot for me, he spoke as I climbed back inside the car.

"Jasmine, Granddaddy gon tell you something, and he don't want you ever to forget it as long as you live," he said, locking eyes with mine. "Ain't nobody gon ever do harm to you and I know about it. I'll hurt somebody first," he said, his voice quiet and calm as always. That made me feel a little better, but I still avoided white people in the South as much as possible.

The drive to Mississippi took thirteen hours, and we stayed with our maternal great-grandparents, whom we called Grandma Linnie and "Papa." His real name was John Edgar Carter. Her full name was Mary Linnie Gregory Carter. Both in their late seventies, the couple still worked their forty-acre farm alone—milking cows, feeding and plucking chickens, planting crops, and chopping wood. Their only toilet was an outhouse located about twenty yards behind the big wooden home. Rural Mississippi was so dark at night that we couldn't see our hands in front of our faces. Valerie had been there many times before, so she was used to going to the outhouse. Albert, Debra, and I were too scared to walk back there in the dark alone—especially after Grandma Linnie and Papa warned us about a fox that had been lurking around the chicken coop.

Our great-grandparents got up before dawn every morning. Papa hauled water from a well dug in their front yard. Grandma Linnie collected fresh eggs from the chicken coop. By the time we woke up, breakfast was on the table, along with a big pitcher of iced tea.

Word of our visit spread fast in the tiny community, so all of our relatives—cousins, aunts, and uncles—stopped by to see us. One cousin rode up on a beautiful brown and white horse and gave us riding lessons. Another cousin took us to a small stream located across the dirt road in our great-grandparents' pasture. The stream was so cool and clear that we drank from it with cupped hands, then took off our shoes and waded in the water. It was as if we had gone fifty years back in time.

"I didn't know people still lived like this," I kept saying. "This reminds me of the log cabin days I read about in school."

My favorite chore was chopping wood with Papa. He'd help me hold the ax and instruct me on where to chop.

"Now Jasmine, this is dangerous. Don't try this by yourself. You hear me chile?" he said.

I said "yes," but was hardheaded. The first time I found myself alone near the woodpile, I picked up the ax, lifted it over my shoulder, and it came down on my baby toe. It bled so badly that I had to tell somebody. Grandma Linnie patched me up, but forbade me from ever touching the ax again.

Albert liked chasing chickens around the house, which sat on cement blocks and looked like a version of the Beverly Hillbillies' first home, only five times larger. Grandma Linnie warned him about that more than once, saying it made the chickens nervous, causing them not to lay eggs. Albert was hardheaded, too. One morning I was sitting on the porch talking to Valerie and Debra when we saw Albert chasing a hen around the back of the house. Next thing we knew, Albert was running back with the chicken chasing him.

Valerie spent lots of time talking to our older female cousins. Each of them was responsible for combing our hair every day. Sometimes they'd come to us. Other times we went to their homes. It was the first time I'd ever seen homes with windows but no glass in them, and walls made of cardboard boxes, the advertising still readable from the inside.

Debra didn't like anything about Mississippi. One night we were lying in our bed, which was so high off the ground we had to help each other climb in. The house was still and quiet. Debra whispered that she wanted to go home.

"It smells down here," she said, and broke down crying.

"We're staying on a farm, Debra. I bet all farms smell. I don't like the smell either. But just think of how bad everybody else would feel, including Mother and Daddy, if they knew how unhappy you were. Everybody is trying to be so nice to us," I whispered to her in the dark. Her crying stopped, but her overall behavior worsened. Our relatives started calling her "bad."

The family gathered on the porch in the evening to talk and listen to the sounds of the night. Crickets sang. Frogs croaked. And even the bells around the cows' necks rattled in the distance. We sipped on iced tea and listened to the grown-ups talk.

THE FIGHT I'D NEVER FORGET

Fourth grade was my favorite year in elementary school because Valerie and I were in the same class. Our teacher, Mrs. Carter, taught a split classroom, fourth and fifth grades, that year.

I was so proud of Valerie because she was very popular and a great singer. She knew everybody in town and across the state, or so it seemed. Mother and Daddy, her parents, were active in Baptist church work through various organizations at the local, state, and national levels, enabling my young aunt to travel lots of places and meet lots of people.

One damp, chilly April afternoon Mrs. Carter asked me to stay after school and help clean chalkboard erasers. I enjoyed doing things like that for my teachers. Patting the oblong erasers against the side of the brick building, I created designs on the wall, as the white dust flew in my face.

Ordinarily I walked home with Valerie and Robin, but they had gone by the time I was finished. Not used to walking home alone, I trotted to get there faster. Halfway home, I heard a crowd shouting.

"Get her, Valerie!"

"Don't let her do that to you, Gail!"

My casual trot turned into a sprint. Breathless by the time I reached the group of shouting schoolmates, I pushed and shoved my way through the screaming and cheering onlookers, only to catch a glimpse of my aunt Valerie tussling in the mud with a girl named Gail Blackwell.

Everyone on the East Side knew of the Blackwell family. They had thirteen kids and lived kitty-corner from Grandma on Deyo Street. Neighbors said that

Mr. Blackwell was so mean that he'd even whip his kids for bringing home the wrong item from the store. Their house was almost always dark inside. According to neighbors, Mr. Blackwell didn't allow his family to burn lights without his permission. They said that the man was so cheap, he didn't allow his nine daughters, most of whom were teenagers, to straighten their hair because using the burners on the stove would make his gas bill go up. Kids often teased the Blackwell girls for wearing thick nappy braids and ponytails at a time when everyone else got their hair straightened with a hot comb.

The boys in the Blackwell family suffered just as much ridicule as the girls. Their father used a bowl as a guide to cut their hair, creating a perfect line all the way around their heads just above their ears. Their haircuts reminded me of Moe's on the old television comedy The Three Stooges.

One of the Blackwell kids got in a fight nearly every month, and usually won. When parents complained to the Blackwells about "your child beat up mine," the couple showed no hesitation in defending their children.

"We teach our kids to take up for each other. If they don't, they know they got a good beating coming when they get home," a neighbor once quoted the parents as saying.

My heart pounded and my steps coincided with Valerie's and Gail's movements as I watched them scuffling on the ground. My aunt, who was just as frail as I was, finally scrambled on top of Gail. That's when Kathy, Gail's sister, jumped in. I did, too.

Before I knew it, someone climbed on my back. My knees hit the ground before I fell face down in the mud. Helpless and unable to see, I still had the nerve to try to reach backward and grab one of the Blackwell sisters. My aunt and cousins disappeared. The two sisters hit and punched me in the back and head with their fists until I heard a familiar voice.

"Now you wait just a minute there! Let my grandbaby up outta that mud," my grandfather shouted, rushing over to the crowd, now silenced and shuffling backward.

I was never so glad to hear my grandfather's voice in my entire life. Daddy pulled Gail off of me with his one good hand. He brushed the dirt and mud from my hair and clothes, as everyone scattered. My face scratched and flushed, I spit mud, which felt like grit, from my mouth. My grandfather drove me home, fussing and swearing he'd go to jail if anyone ever did that to me again. Momma fussed at me.

"Girl, you ain't got a bit of sense. You're gonna jump in somebody else's fight. Then they gon run off and leave you, claiming they all went to go get Daddy," she said.

Sitting on a chair at the kitchen table, tears dripped into my lap while my head hung low. I wiped my runny nose and dabbed my sore and swollen eyes with balled-up toilet tissue, still whimpering from my butt kicking.

"I mean don't you *ever* jump in somebody else's fight again," Momma continued, madder at my cousins and aunt than at me. "I don't care who it is. If they mess around and get their behinds beat—so be it. You see what they thought of you, don't you? Sometimes I think you don't know how to use the sense God gave you, Jasmine."

Sometimes when Momma went on and on, I tried to get the last word. This time I said nothing. My face and runny nose burned, they were so raw from scratches and mucus.

Momma quit fussing sooner than I expected. And my mouth was so sore that she had to spend her last quarter to buy me a can of Campbell's chicken noodle soup to eat for dinner. She and the rest of the family ate leftover hot dogs and pork and beans. Momma even had to throw my only coat away, it was so muddy and tattered.

I cried most of the night. And every time I thought of my three closest relatives outside of my immediate family—the ones with whom I played ball and jacks, and shot marbles with on our wooden porch floors most days; the ones who felt like sisters to me, rather than two first cousins and an aunt; the ones who were my best friends and had been a part of my life for as long as I could remember—running off leaving me to fight the two Blackwell sisters by myself, I cried so hard my whole body shook.

❧ ICE SKATING

The wind whipped against my face like a razor strap. My feet felt frozen and numb. Tears clouded my vision as I stared at the throngs of ice skaters at Loomis Park one late Saturday afternoon in mid-February. None of the white, cheery faces looked familiar. My mind started racing.

"They must have left me," I thought. "I only went into the clubhouse to warm up by the fireplace for a little while. Where could Arlene and Robin be?"

Trudging through the snow, my boots were so heavy I felt as if my feet were made of lead. I checked the women's restrooms. My watery eyes scoured the hilly landscape. Another hour passed, and I still couldn't find my cousins.

The snowfall became heavier, blurring my vision and filling my red rubber boots again. My feet grew numb, and my uncovered hands stiffened from the cold air and snow that powdered the scenery white.

"It's getting late, and Momma said to be home before the street light comes on. I'm gon get another whipping," I thought, while squinting to see through the veil of gray created by the increased snowfall.

Crunching footsteps in frozen snow behind me snapped my attention back to my surroundings.

"Is something wrong?" a gentle voice asked.

I turned and saw a tall woman through the heavy snowfall. She was handsomely dressed in a green plaid wool jacket, with earmuffs and mittens that matched.

I nodded my head yes.

"I think my cousins are gone home," I said.

"Did you come with them?"

"Uh huh."

"What's your cousins' names?"

"Arlene and Robin Collins," I said, my voice quivering, my body starting to visibly shake.

The woman stooped down to my eye level. She reached for my hands, and I pulled back a little and buried them deeper inside my coat pocket.

"My hands are cold," I said, making an excuse for not letting her touch me. She smiled gently.

"Did you lose your mittens?"

"I don't have none."

"Honey, what's your name?" the woman asked.

"Jasmine Armstead."

"Well I'm pleased to meet you, Jasmine. My name is Susan Crandall. You can call me Susan. Do you mind telling me where you live, Jasmine?"

"I live at 214 Page Avenue."

The woman straightened back up and looked toward that direction.

"That's not too far from here. But Michigan Avenue is a busy street. It might be a little dangerous for a little girl like you to try to cross alone. Would you like for me to give you a ride home?"

I searched her face for a few seconds to make sure she didn't look like the kidnappers Grandma always warned me about. Being kidnapped was one of my biggest fears as a child.

My face stiffened from the cold and made it hard to move my lips. So I nodded my head yes. The ice skates I carried were tied together by their boot strings and hung over my frail shoulder. Every time I moved, they bumped some part of my bony chest. We walked about fifty feet to the parking lot, leaving two sets of footprints behind us. Susan unlocked the passenger's side of her 1959 Buick before walking around, opening the other door, and sliding in under the steering wheel. I slowly climbed in, still shaking from the cold. Chills shot through my body so hard that I nearly left my seat for a second.

"It only takes a minute to warm up," Susan said, as she turned the key and started the engine. Feeling a bit uneasy, I nodded my head, then turned and stared out the window. It was my first time riding in the front seat of a car.

"So Jasmine, how long have you been ice-skating?" she asked, breaking the silence.

"I think about two years. Arlene and Robin started coming here first."

"Two years? How old are you?"

"I'm ten years old, but everybody thinks I'm seven or eight."

"And who's Arlene and Robin? Your sisters?"

"No. My cousins . . . my *first* cousins. They live up the street from me. They come ice-skating nearly every Saturday morning. I just started coming with them."

"Did you all get separated or something?"

"I think so. I got cold and went inside the clubhouse to get warm. And when I came back out, I couldn't find them nowhere."

"I'm sorry. But don't worry. You'll be home in a minute."

My uneasiness was letting up. Instead of looking out the side window, I turned my head and stared ahead, occasionally glancing at Susan.

"Those are some nice skates you've got there," she said, looking at the scuffed-up white pair that now rested in my lap.

I squirmed. The skates wiggled, causing one blade to press uncomfortably against my thigh.

"These ain't mine. They're Robin's. She lets me use em."

"Ohhhh, I see," she said, nodding her head. "Where's yours?"

"I don't have any," I replied. "The people at the welfare don't send Momma enough money to buy some ice skates."

"Oh, I see."

"Do you have sisters or brothers, Jasmine?"

"Yes. I got two sisters named Lisa and Penny. Lisa's seven, and Penny is five. They're too little to go ice-skating. I got three brothers. Albert and Terrance don't like ice-skating. They said their hands and feet get too cold. They're younger than me, too. I'm the oldest. My brother Keith is the youngest. Momma always make us baby-sit him. He's only one."

We sat in the car at the corner of Michigan and Page, waiting for the red light to turn green.

"So, what school do you attend, Jasmine?"

"I go to Pleasant Street Elementary and get straight As. I ain't never got *one* B before in my life."

"Well, good for you," she said, looking down at me with a big smile on her face. "That's pretty impressive." I wiggled in my seat and sat up straighter.

Momma was peeking out the living-room window, its curtain drooping because of missing hooks, when we pulled up in front of our house. I quickly climbed out of the car, said "Bye," and hustled into the house.

I didn't get a whipping. Momma just asked me who drove me home. After I told her what happened, she rolled her eyes at me, then went back into her bedroom.

— ℘ —

IT WAS EARLY Saturday morning, and I heard Momma unlock the front door. I was the only one awake. Hearing paper rattling, I eased out of the tiny bedroom that I shared with Lisa and Penny to see what was going on.

"Oh, my goodness!" Momma exclaimed as she pulled a new pair of white ice skates from the box that sat on her lap. She read the card that was taped to the box, then handed it to me.

Dear Jasmine, I thoroughly enjoyed meeting you last Saturday. I went shopping this week and saw these skates and thought of you. I hope you can wear them. I guessed your size. Your friend, Susan.

I felt as if my fairy godmother had just granted me my biggest wish. I couldn't believe it. I felt so fortunate, so special. I kept replaying our conversation in my mind, wondering what made Susan do it.

I must have tried on my gleaming white skates a dozen times while waiting for Arlene and Robin to come pick me up. Momma dared me to walk on our linoleum floors in them, so I sat by the window in a chair with no arms and waited anxiously for my cousins to pick me so that we could go ice-skating again.

— ℘ —

EASTER FOLLOWED a month later on a sunny Sunday morning with blue skies. Our house was filled with chattering young people, all excited about wearing new clothes to church. Someone knocked on the door, and all the commotion in the house stopped.

The four oldest of us bolted to the window to see who it was. Momma unlocked the door and went out onto our glass-enclosed porch and opened the door. It was Susan Crandall again.

This time she carried a huge Easter basket, covered with green cellophane. A pink stuffed bunny sat in the middle with candy Easter eggs and jelly beans around it. Sticking out from the green paper grass was a smaller cellophane package with a chocolate bunny inside.

"Please tell Jasmine Happy Easter for me," she said, smiling, then turned and quickly walked back to her car.

Dressed only in an underslip and panties, I knocked hard on the living-room window and hollered "Thank-you," with the biggest smile this side of sunshine.

"Oh. This is *so* nice of you," Momma said in her proper voice, so sweet that it didn't even sound right coming from her. She came back inside carrying the basket and handed it to me. She looked as bewildered as I did.

Ripping the squelching and crunching cellophane paper off the basket was almost as much fun as eating the candy inside. Taped to the bottom of the basket was another note. *Happy Easter to one of the sweetest girls I've ever met. Your friend, Susan Crandall.*

We never heard from her again.

TOUGHER THAN NAILS

The sweet fragrance of peonies drifted through Grandma's screen door as we sat rocking and watching the people and cars pass early one hot summer evening.

"Your mother was born a slave?" I asked, bewildered. Slavery had seemed so distant—so far in the past.

"Do you remember anything about slavery, Grandma?" I asked.

"No, baby. My mother was just a little child when President Lincoln freed the slaves. And that included my grandmother, Missouri Cheney."

"That's a funny name—Missouri. That was her real first name? Why did her momma name her Missouri?"

"I don't know why her momma did it. I wasn't round to ask. I hadn't been born yet, chile," Grandma said, beginning to sound frustrated. "And Jasmine, it's not pleasing in the Lord's sight to make fun of other people."

"Even their names?"

"Yes, even their names. What may sound funny to you may be a melody to the ear of some other folks," my great-grandmother explained, then resumed her proud look. "Yeah, it was old President Abraham Lincoln who freed the slaves. They called that paper the E-mancipation Proclamation."

"Is that a picture of a slave that's hanging on your dining-room wall, Grandma?" I asked.

"No, chile. That's a famous Negro named George Washington Carver. He invented peanut butter," she replied proudly. "He was so famous they even had him talk on the radio. That's what he was doing when that picture was made—talking on the radio. Umph, umph, umph. Ole George Washington Carver was some kind of Negro man."

We sat and rocked for a while before Grandma hollered back into her house for Mr. Thomas.

"Ah Israel. I need you walk up to Bozak's grocery and bring me back some Epsom salt. I want to soak my feet cause they swelling," she said, slipping off her house shoes to examine her feet.

"All right," he replied, his voice deep, booming, and dragging.

He ended up walking to the A&P supermarket, a fifteen-minute walk away, which made Grandma nervous because he took so long. We were still rocking and talking and waiting on Mr. Thomas when I noticed Grandma's new neighbor across the street come out of her house. Even though she was headed toward the curb, I never dreamed she was coming our way. When Rosalee Chavous sashayed across the street, strutted up Grandma's steps, and rapped on her screen door, I knew something was wrong.

I scrambled from my rocker to let her in, but Grandma started getting up as well.

"Let me get it, Jasmine," she said, placing her hands on the chair's arm and raising her stout body up with a grunt. Grandma waddled stiffly to the door. Lifting the metal hook, she pushed the screen door open so that Rosalee could come in.

"Must be gon storm tonight," Grandma said. "Rosalee, I ain't seen you come cross that street since you moved there nearly a year ago. Come on in and take a seat and tell me what brings you this way."

Grandma turned and waddled back toward her seat.

"No thank-you Mrs. Thomas," Rosalee snapped. "I'd just as soon stand for what I gots to say." Grandma stopped dead in her tracks and turned around to face the woman again.

Wearing a hot pink, flowered sleeveless dress that flowed with the movement of her arms, green flip-flops, and her fingernails and toes polished to match the dress, Rosalee continued.

"Mrs. Thomas, you need to mind your own business. I know that you're the one who's got the police casing my house," the small woman said in a snappy voice. "I've been seeing them riding by here every day, and I know you the one who called 'em."

By this time Rosalee was rolling her neck and had placed her hands on her hips. Grandma's face turn beet red, and her chest swelled up like it did whenever she got really mad. I scooted up to the edge of my rocking chair. My heart pounded.

"What you talking about, Rosalee Chavous? I ain't got no police casing your house," Grandma shot back. "I ain't never called no police on you. And if I did, I sho wouldn't be 'fraid to own up to it."

Still on the edge of my seat, trembling and holding my breath, I wondered what "casing" meant.

"Yes you did!" Rosalee spouted, pointing her finger in Grandma's face. "Ain't nobody called them but you. But let me tell you something. You got one more time to call them and I'm gonna . . ."

Whop!

Grandma had balled up her fist and hit the woman before she got the last words out of her mouth. Rosalee stumbled backward off the steps, grabbing the strawberry blonde wig that had flopped lopsided on her head.

"Ain't nobody gon come up in no house of mine, and go to calling me a liar," Grandma bellowed. "Who do you think you are, coming to my house disrespecting me? Rosalee Chavous, if you don't get on away from my door right now, I'm gonna try my best to bust your head wide open."

Rosalee opened her mouth to say something else, and Grandma balled her fist and raised her arm back to throw another blow. Rosalee ducked and nearly tripped over her own feet trying to get out of Grandma's way. She nearly fell off the step. I immediately jumped up from my chair and grabbed Grandma's flabby arm and began tugging at her.

"No, Grandma—don't," I yelled, trying to pull her from the front porch into the house.

Rosalee hustled back to the street curb, patted her wig, twitched her shoulders a time or two, then headed back across the street as if nothing had happened. At the same time, half a dozen young men of all ages, sizes, and shades of brown and black spilled out of Rosalee's house and into her front yard. Some clutched bottles of beer in their hands and grabbed their crotches. Evidently, they had been watching the whole thing.

"Ooo Rosalee! You let that old woman coldcock you like that? You need to go somewhere and sit yo ass down," they said, laughing and pointing their fingers.

Terrified that Rosalee would come back to try and redeem herself in the eyes of her guests, I raced into the dining room and called Momma. Within minutes, I could hear Momma hollering at Rosalee while I was still inside Grandma's house.

"Rosalee, if you *ever* come over here messing with my grandmother again, I'm gonna come across this street and whip your ass myself," Momma said.

Grandma was still standing on the porch while all this was taking place. Suddenly, she braced herself with both hands on the arm of her rocker, hung her head, and broke down crying and praying out loud, asking God to forgive her for hitting Rosalee. It was the first and only time I ever saw my great-grandmother act ashamed of something she'd done.

Momma was outside still fussing at Rosalee from across the street. The guys who had been "signifying" eased back inside without saying one word to my mother.

Momma walked up and stuck her head in Grandma's front door to make sure everybody was all right. Then she strutted back down the street toward home, her arms slightly bowed from her body like a prizefighter. I had never felt prouder of Momma.

⚜ PLAYING <u>WITH</u> FIRE

Every day I woke up praying that Momma would be in a better mood. Most days I was disappointed. Momma fussed and yelled at us from the time we opened our eyes in the mornings until we crawled into bed at night. I hated it.

"I'm never gonna do my kids like this when I grow up," I thought many mornings, still sleepy-eyed and hearing Momma's fussing in the background.

Some kids said we had the meanest Momma on the East Side. Most knew better than to say it around me because I was very protective of my family. Yet secretly in my heart, I felt it was true. Momma was known for tracking us down. In the summers, we spent most of our waking hours at Rotary playground, located between Deyo and Plymouth streets. Momma would appear at the top of the Plymouth Street hill, her hands on her hips and looking as if she dared anybody to say anything to her. She often carried switches in her hand. After those incidents, I'd stay away from the playground for a few days because everybody knew I'd gotten a whipping. Momma did it so often that kids started warning us when they saw her coming. One time she and Rolland came looking for us. The four oldest of us spotted his car and dashed to a nearby alley, trying to beat them back home. They were waiting at the other end.

"Get your behinds home, right now," Momma yelled from the window on the passenger's side. We ran so fast we almost beat her home.

I got more whippings than anyone in my family, outside of my uncle Samuel. My grandfather broke his arm one time whipping him. The police had picked my uncle up for disturbing the peace and fighting. Daddy had to get up out of his bed and drive down to the police station after one o'clock in the morning to get him. Relatives said the police told my grandfather, "Either you whip him or we will."

Whether it was true or not, Daddy whipped his fifteen-year-old son right there in the police station with them looking on. My grandfather returned home with a broken arm.

Whippings didn't scare me too much until just before I was about to get one. Sometimes Momma threatened to whip all six of us whenever it wasn't clear who had done the misbehaving. I used to volunteer to get my whipping first, just to get it over with. It was easier than watching my sisters and brothers get their whippings, knowing I still had one coming. After several years, I finally realized that I got the worst of it by being first because Momma was stronger when she started. By the time she got to the rest of them, she was winded and tired.

—— ❧ ——

EVERY ONCE IN a while I expected a whipping and didn't get one. Like the time Albert and I broke the glass on the hood of Momma's brand new stove.

It had taken nearly two years for us to convince Momma to let our babysitter, Mrs. Willa Mae, go. We whined and complained (but I never told *anybody* about Mr. Eddie Jones), and looked so pitiful that Momma finally agreed to let me babysit my sisters and brothers. I was in the fifth grade.

Momma had already caught us playing catch in the house while she was getting dressed for work one Saturday morning.

"Are you two nuts?" she asked.

We shook our heads no.

"Jasmine, if you and Albert don't put that ball away, I'm gon break ya'll's neck!" she hollered. My brother handed me the red rubber ball, and I stuck it between cushions of our Early American couch that Momma bought secondhand from somebody who had advertised it in the newspaper.

"And Jasmine, don't you and Albert be playing catch in this house while I'm gone to work. I mean it," she said, eyeing me one last time as she closed the front door behind her.

As soon as Momma disappeared down the street to catch the bus, Albert and I picked up our game of catch where we had left off. We tossed the first two or three softly. But within minutes, we were zinging the ball back and forth, from the kitchen, where Albert stood, to the living room, where I had to lean over our coffee table to catch many of his returns. We were just getting into a groove when Albert missed a fast one. The ball bounced high off the corner of the kitchen table first, then ricocheted like a bullet into the stove that Momma had just bought two weeks earlier. It cracked the glass in the panel, causing the built-in clock to stop running at nine thirteen in the morning.

My brother and I argued all day over whose fault it was. He offered to pay me seventy-five cents he had earned shoveling sidewalks to take the blame. I agreed. By the time Momma came home that afternoon around four thirty, I was ready to take my punishment. I'd even put on an extra pair of pants to lessen the sting. Not wanting Momma to discover the cracked glass in the stove herself, I told her as soon as she took off her brown wool overcoat—only with a slight twist.

"I was sweeping the kitchen floor and set the broom against the wall near the stove. Then I was walking over to the sink to start washing dishes when I accidentally bumped the broom. And it fell and hit the glass on your stove and cracked it, Momma."

Momma rushed into the kitchen to examine the damage. Albert and I shuffled close behind her, bracing ourselves for her wrath.

"Now you mean to try to stand there and tell me that a *broom* did this?" she asked, staring me dead in the eyes.

I looked at Albert. He looked back at me. Then we just stood there in front of Momma with blank looks on our faces. She turned and stormed into her bedroom.

"Ya'll gon mess around, and I'm gon walk off and leave ya'll one of these days and not come back!" I heard her shout from behind her bedroom walls. Those words always scared me terribly. I knew we got on Momma's nerves a lot, and can remember sitting in class worrying sometimes whether Momma would still be there when we returned.

My brother and I stood frozen for several minutes, expecting Momma to emerge from her room with a belt or a switch or something.

Nothing.

No whipping. No shouting. No yelling. No nothing.

— ❧ —

I NEVER SEEMED to measure up to the other students or my peers, but it wasn't for lack of trying. Pleasant Street Elementary School was predominately white, with many of the kids coming from middle-class homes. I'll never forget the time Mother gave me a faded pink dress with thin, dingy white lace that covered the upper half like a vest. I thought the dress was pretty, and pink was my favorite color, so I wore it to school the next day, feeling pretty good about myself.

Midmorning, I noticed the class bully, a female, staring at the dress with a scowl on her face.

"Where'd you get that ole dress from? I know you don't think you look cute, do you? You should have at least had your momma sew up that tear in the back before you put it on," she said, then burst out laughing.

I shrank inside. Having been eager to wear the dress, I hadn't noticed the two-inch gap in the back where the gathered skirt and bodice came together. After school, I rushed home and sewed it with big stitches that caused the skirt to hike up in the back. I continued to wear the dress but never felt the same about it after that day.

✾ JOHNSON STREET

O ur extended family had begun moving away from each other in the spring of 1958 when I was nine years old. Mother and Daddy sold the second home they owned in Jackson to the city, then bought a four-bedroom, two-story house with a nice big kitchen with plenty of cupboards and cabinet space on Tomlinson Street. Several blocks away, it was too far away to just dash in and out like we were used to doing everyday, but their new home was located only a block from our school. We'd drop by on our lunch hours and still walked up to our grandparents' house every weekend to play with our young aunt Valerie.

A few years later my cousins Arlene and Robin moved out of the neighborhood. Their parents bought a lovely two-story home on Pringle Street. I was happy for all of them and spent as much time at their houses as possible.

I wanted to move, too. Everybody in the family but us seemed to be doing better. Momma still worked for the white family that she bragged about all the time. I got so tired of hearing her talk about "Trudy Hamlin did this" and "Dougie Hamlin did that." Anger and resentment started building in me whenever she mentioned their names, even though I had never met them.

"She never brags about her own kids like that," I thought many times. "At least she could be nice to us sometimes. Here she is, doing all this nice stuff for them—cooking and washing and scrubbing their ole floors. Grandma said she needs to do more of that at her own house."

Our family was the last of the original clan to move out of Grandma's rental property in the fall of 1960. Momma found a four-bedroom, two-story house to rent on Johnson Street. The idea of moving excited me so much I couldn't sleep for a week. It didn't matter that I would have to change schools. Though halfway through my sixth-grade year, I was ready to venture out, especially if it meant having a bedroom with a closet of our own. Sure, I wouldn't get to see my cousins as often. But we lived close enough to visit each other after school.

Our new home was a refreshing change from our earlier cramped quarters. The kitchen was huge, with two large wooden cabinets that took up half a wall and smaller cabinets that were below the counter. Everything was painted an ugly lime green.

It didn't matter that our house sat on a dead-end street, two doors from the train tracks. Being eleven years old and growing more curious every day, being farther away from Grandma also had its appeal. I was tired of always worrying if Grandma was on her porch watching.

Johnson Street was one block long, but it exposed us to people and circumstances we had never encountered before. I was walking up the street one afternoon, not long after we had settled in, and one of two men sitting in a car parked alongside the street called me.

"Hey, you—little girl. Come here a minute," the red-eyed man said.

I walked closer to the car and could see the passenger had a quart of beer in a bag sitting on the seat between his legs.

"What you want?" I asked.

"Here. I'm gon give you this dollar cause you got such big pretty brown eyes," he said, smiling so hard his gold teeth in the back of his mouth shined like they had been polished.

"Thank-you," I said, extending my arm to reach the dollar without getting too close to the car. The two men resumed their conversation, and I walked away smiling and thinking, "I never knew I had big pretty eyes."

Then there was the root doctor we called "Mr. Redford." He lived in a storefront apartment building on Johnson Street. Passing his house was necessary if we didn't want to cut through alleys.

A little old dark-skinned man with wiry gray hair and sideburns, Mr. Redford lived alone and kept his blinds closed and lights off. Every so often he'd peek out his large storefront window, but none of us ever saw him outside in the entire five years we lived on the street.

"Momma, what's a root doctor?" I asked one day.

"They make medicine, Jasmine."

"What kind of medicine?"

"I don't know. *Some* kind of medicine," she said, agitation growing in her voice.

"Where does he get it from?"

"Jasmine, my goodness. Don't ask so many questions!"

That made me even more curious about the man. So Halloween night we knocked on his door and hollered, "Trick or treat!" He cracked the door and stuck his head out just enough to drop a miniature package of Life Savers in each of our dingy pillowcases. I tried peeking around him but couldn't see anything but a small table sitting in the middle of the dimly lit room and shelves lined with Mason jars containing stuff that looked like mud and grass.

The youngest married couple who lived on the street was Earl and Harriet Tyler. They lived in the nicest-looking home on the block. I often babysat their seven-year-old daughter and two-year-old son while Mrs. Tyler went out. Neighbors said she was slipping around with another man while her husband worked second shift at a nearby factory. She paid me a dollar an hour and always returned before ten o'clock, an hour before her husband got off work.

I liked Johnson Street. Everything and everybody seemed new and exciting. I missed my classmates, but one classmate who was becoming a good friend, Dara Abrams, lived on the boundary line. She decided to transfer to the same school I had to attend. We enjoyed each other's company just that much.

Dara and I enrolled in Allen School on the same day and were assigned to the same room. For several weeks we told our new classmates we were sisters but had different last names.

"You two sure do look alike," they'd say.

Dara and I would look at each other and smile.

The teachers at Allen School and I didn't hit it off too well. My new sixth-grade teacher, Mrs. Jefferson, was a slightly hunched elderly woman who was close to retiring. She also had been Momma's sixth-grade teacher at Allen School.

Mrs. Jefferson wasn't patient like the teachers at Pleasant School. She wore a forced smile that turned into a scowl at the drop of a hat. Mrs. Jefferson was bossy and tended to snap at me the way Momma did. I didn't like it. So every now and then I'd snap back. Nothing mean or nasty, but just enough to let her know I wasn't going to let her say mean stuff to me and get away with it. Our personalities clashed like cymbals.

To make matters worse, I got into several fights with boys. One teased me, calling me "skinny." Those were fighting words for someone who absolutely hated being thin. I don't remember what the other battles were about, but they all landed me a seat in the office. Teachers sent kids there who got in trouble.

The first time it was embarrassing. I had to sit in a chair at a desk directly across from the opened office door and do homework. That kept me from having to make eye contact with students and teachers who passed. By the third time I was angry and didn't care.

WHEN <u>NO</u> ONE'S <u>WATCHING</u>

M r. Oglethorp was an old man's voice on the telephone. I had never met him, even though Momma started working for him from four to eight thirty in the evenings so she could be home during the day.

He'd call with a squeaky, cracked voice and ask the exact same question every time, the exact same way, "Hello, has Malena left yet?"

"No, she hasn't. She's right here. Hold on just a moment," I'd say as sweetly as I knew how. I didn't want to say or do anything that would jeopardize Momma's job.

Momma would get mad at the ninety-something-year-old man. But she never let him know.

"Now that old man always waits until just before I leave out the door before he calls me wanting something from the store. And he knows good and well that I don't have a car. He's gonna keep on till I get his old, gray ass told," she'd fuss.

I loved Momma working afternoons. She'd either be leaving or gone by the time we got home at quarter to four.

Momma was a great cook and was creative, too. She was the only person I knew who could take welfare pork and gravy, add a little ketchup and onions, and turn it into delicious sloppy joe sandwiches. And I was a fruit-and-vegetable person growing up, and never cared much for meat.

Momma would mix fried bacon with welfare peanut butter and make gourmet sandwiches, cutting them diagonally to make them look good. I think she learned different ways to present food by cooking and preparing meals for the white people she worked for over the years. She fried welfare Spam and put it on toast. She used welfare cheese and butter to make hot grilled-cheese sandwiches. And Momma baked "bakery perfect" cakes with welfare flour, welfare powdered milk and eggs, and welfare butter.

Her chili, made with a tomato soup base, was the best I'd ever eaten. It made our sparsely furnished house smell so good, especially as I came through the door after being outside in the cold. Momma cooked a huge pot of it, making it possible for us to eat chili for several days.

Every once and a while I got tired of Momma's creative foods. Black-eyed peas and cornbread suited me just fine. One of my favorite meals was beans and cornbread, and we usually had plenty of that.

If Momma hadn't cooked when we got home from school, she left a dollar with a note saying to "buy something for dinner." All six of us loved those days. We either had Neapolitan ice cream and pop or potato chips and pop.

There were plenty of things to get into while Momma worked nights. We joined a soccer team at the playground, and when that season ended, some boys I met at Allen School taught me to pitch pennies. We played records and danced after school in the gym some days. The after-school program was called "The Center," and it provided chaperoned activities that included talent shows and costume parties. I loved entering talent shows, even though I couldn't sing a lick. But I won two dance contests, and my friend Dara and I created a skit for my one of my favorite songs at the time, "Kookie, Kookie, Lend Me Your Comb." It was a hit.

Some kids gathered at our house, knowing Momma was working and there were six of us to provide entertainment. We taught each other the latest dances and talked about the hottest singing groups. I knew every word to most songs, and we sang them as a group all the time, even though most of us couldn't carry a tune. I sang flatter than anybody, but no one seemed to mind. We played kickball and softball in the street in front of our house. We had tag-team races to the end of the street and back. A few times we explored the train tracks, even though getting hit by a train was another of my phobias.

Momma said one of my friends had a reputation for "picking up things," and didn't want her coming to our house. I liked the girl and didn't want to believe it until I accompanied her to a store one evening while Momma was working. As we walked to the store she told me that she was going to steal something. I was curious, wanted some candy, and was willing to learn.

"It's real easy," she said. "And I ain't never got caught."

Watching her slip Nestlé Crunches and Milky Ways into her pockets every time the man behind the counter turned his back was fascinating. Two nights later we were back at the store, and I was trying to steal, too. And I succeeded. It became a ritual. We'd walk to the store once or twice a week and steal so much candy that I began giving it away.

——— ℀ ———

JUNE FINALLY ROLLED around, and I was excited about sixth-grade graduation. Most of the girls in my class were talking about wearing nylons for the first time and the styles and the color of the dresses their parents had bought for them. They chattered about going to the hairdresser and which relatives, some from out of town, would be coming to see them graduate.

Momma had already told me she had to work and couldn't attend. And Grandma didn't get out too often except for attending church. Daddy and Mother supported us as much as they could, but parenting their own children and heading the church in Adrian kept them hopping.

So I resigned myself to going to my sixth-grade graduation alone. But I wasn't willing to go looking tacky. I borrowed a dress from Dara. She always wore nice clothes. Her mother and stepfather bought her a couple of new outfits nearly every month. I often borrowed clothes from Dara. Momma didn't believe in that.

"Ain't no telling what people got," she said with disdain when she discovered I was wearing Dara's red sweater and gray box-pleated skirt one day.

My feet were too big to fit into Dara's shoes. So I struck out to a store called Shoe Town one evening after school and stole a pair of black patent-leather pumps to wear to graduation. I got caught. The police took me downtown and called my grandfather because I told them Momma was still at work. Daddy came to pick me up, and thanked the officers for their trouble. We didn't talk much as he drove me back to the house, but he did say that Momma was waiting for us at the house.

Momma snatched me by one arm as soon as I stepped through the front door. I tried to hide behind Daddy, but she pulled me back to her.

"Now wait just a minute," my grandfather said, grabbing Momma's arm and trying to free me.

"Wait a minute nothing! If I don't beat her behind, my name ain't Malena Armstead," she said, pulling her arm away from Daddy so hard he almost lost his balance. My grandfather made no further attempts to stop his daughter. He hurried out the front door just before I grabbed the brown extension cord that Momma held tightly wrapped around her fist.

"If you don't let go of this cord, I'm gonna break your little neck," Momma hollered into my face.

I let go. And Momma went crazy.

"Don't you ever."

Swat.

"Take something."

Swat.

"That doesn't belong to you."

Swat.

"Again."

Swat.

"I'll be damned."

Swat.

"If you gonna be out stealing."

Swat.

"While I'm out scrubbing floors."

Swat.

"And breaking my neck."

Swat.

"To feed y'all."

WHERE THE BOYS ARE

I first started noticing boys when I entered East Junior High School. Before that I had liked a few, one of them named Ronald Patterson. He and his family lived above the mortuary, three doors up from us. He and I wrote notes back and forth to each other, and every once in a while we kissed. The notes always said the same thing, "I love you. Do you love me? Yes or no. Please check one." I didn't like kissing, for fear of getting germs. I even refused to eat or drink after anyone, so French kissing was out of the question.

Ronald was a likable boy with average looks and lips so full that the lower one drooped. Back then, we made fun of people with big lips, but I liked Ronald. He faithfully checked the "yes" box in my love notes and often walked me to school. Some of my peers had already started experimenting with sex, but Ronald never brought the subject up. I liked him for that, too.

Several weeks after Ronald and I started "going together," I admitted to my cousins that we didn't even tongue kiss. They laughed and teased me.

"That ain't kissing. That's what they call smooching," they teased. "Jasmine, you act just like some old woman. You keep on and we gonna nickname you, 'old folks'." They eventually starting calling me that, but I didn't mind. In fact, I kind of liked it for some reason.

People often described me as "different." I hated the word and never understood what being different meant. The last thing I wanted to be was different. I longed to be like everybody else so badly that I started trying to be somebody—anybody—else. I wanted to be the girl that all the boys tried to go with and all the girls envied.

The truth was that I was uncomfortable talking to boys. Whenever they were around, I sat quietly while Valerie, my cousins, and girlfriends carried on long conversations with them. They always seemed to know just what to say. I didn't.

My cousin Debra called it being "self-conscious," something we both suffered from. I hated most things about me, especially my bony legs and crooked teeth. My hair, which hung just above my shoulders, wasn't long enough or straight enough. I wanted to be several shades lighter and twenty pounds heavier.

Displeased with her body also, Debra stood five feet ten inches tall. Kids at school often teased her, calling her "long tall Sally" and "pop eyes" because her large eyes bulged from their sockets. Her hair was shorter and coarser than mine, and Debra walked slumped over, as if trying to appear shorter.

I loved my cousin and was quite protective of her. Our mothers were fraternal twin sisters, which provided an even more special bond between us. Her mother, my aunt Mary, and stepfather, Richard Miller, lived on the south side of town. But Debra and I talked on the telephone every day—sometimes two or three times a day.

Kids teased and picked on Debra a lot. She'd call me up, sometimes crying, telling me the mean things kids at school had said to her. One time I got so mad that I called two of them on the telephone and cussed them out.

"If you ever call my cousin out of her name again, I'm gon come over on the South Side and kick your ass," I hollered into the phone.

What I didn't know is that one of them had their mother get on the other end of the telephone and listen. She called Momma later and told her.

"If anybody does any ass whipping, it's gonna be me," Momma said angrily. "Jasmine, you better not ever let me hear of you doing something like that again, or you and me gon tangle."

I listened, eyes wide and mouth poked out, while Momma continued her tirade.

"You're gon run up in the wrong person's face one of these days, and somebody's gonna take hold to your little behind and turn you every way but loose," she said.

I wasn't worried about it. By then I had at least a dozen fights under my belt and didn't back down from anybody. I didn't dare tell Momma that though.

It hurt me to know that Debra got picked on so much at school. She and I had the closest relationship of any of my cousins, even though she lived the farthest away. We had so much in common. Both of us were the oldest, and Debra also had a younger sibling with a different father. Her sister, Racine, was four years younger and so outgoing that few family members seemed to pay much attention to Debra.

My cousin got good grades in school, bringing home mostly Bs. But Debra was too hard on herself whenever she got a C on her report card. Debra and I had common interests—everything from politics to the Detroit Tigers baseball team and family matters. Debra wanted John Kennedy to win the 1960 presidential election. She said Kennedy was cute. I rooted for Richard Nixon because he looked more fatherly. Neither of us understood their politics, but that didn't matter. Whenever we got together on the weekends, we'd perform self-choreographed cheers, promoting our favorite candidate. It was friendly competition at its best.

Both of us were passionate about the Detroit Tigers. Momma watched Tiger baseball from the time she bought our first television, with rounded-screen sides, back around 1957. Her knowledge of the game impressed me. At first televised games bored me. But after sitting through a number of them with Momma, I also became an avid fan. By the early 1960s Debra and I often watched the games while talking on the telephone together and discussed each play as it occurred. We knew all the individual and team stats. My cousin adored right fielder Rocky Colavito. My favorite player was Tiger first baseman Norman Cash, dubbed "Stormin' Norman."

Debra and I loved school and frequently discussed our assignments over the telephone. We seemed to be the only ones in our family who liked talking about our classes and teachers. Both of us also felt misunderstood. I was considered the "wild child" of the family. It hurt me one time when a relative told another that Momma couldn't do anything with me. As far as I was concerned, Momma was doing a pretty good job of holding her own when it came to me.

A few family members whispered to each other that "Debra was a little 'slow.'" She and I surmised that school officials had prompted that thinking when they held her back in the kindergarten another year. Aunt Mary went along with it, but Debra never understood why. Neither did I. As it turned out, next to me, Debra got the best grades in our family.

—— ❧ ——

AUNT CYNTHIA and her family were the envy of the family when it came to material possessions and good looks. They changed cars every few years, had nice furniture, and had lots of books to read. I loved sitting on their living-room floor reading fairy tales and encyclopedias. Sometimes Aunt Cynthia didn't want me around, and I could tell. She and Uncle Jack, her husband, argued a lot. And when she got mad at him, she got mad at me and everybody else around her.

"It's time for you to go home, Jasmine," she'd snap. I'd just get up and go.

Aunt Louise was six years younger than Momma and bragged about my cousin Robin's big legs and hour glass figure all the time. She even started referring to her as "Miss Foxy." Robin was pretty and made everything she wore look better. With a picture-perfect smile, chocolate skin, and long hair, my cousin caught the attention of most males. Her personality left a lot to be desired, but nobody seemed to notice that but me.

I also wanted to be called shapely and foxy. All my peers had developed breasts several years before me. One day I stuffed some toilet paper in my bosom to make mine look big. Later that day I went to visit Grandma, forgetting about the tissue and my busty appearance.

"Jasmine, what's that there you got in your bosom?" she asked, stretching her neck to get a better look, tilting her head at different angles, her eyes fixed on my chest.

I stood there too embarrassed and scared to say anything.

"Now you know better than to do something like that," she snapped. "You gwone home and get that mess outta your bosom. And don't you do that no more. You hear me?"

I nodded, my head hung. Ashamed, I stayed away from Grandma's house for an entire day, which was highly unusual for me.

✳ OUT OF NOWHERE

"Jasmine . . . Albert . . . Lisa . . . Terrance . . . Penny and Keith ya'll better get out of that bed!"

I snuggled farther down under the blankets. Sleepless nights were common for me growing up. But one time I woke up in the middle of the night to a terrible aching in my right ankle. It kept me up the rest of the night.

I listened to the bed springs squeaking in my brothers' bedroom, knowing it would take Albert about ten minutes to get the furnace fire lit. So I lay there wondering what was wrong with my foot. Albert lit the fire, but the chill was still in the air when I forced myself from under the covers. Heading toward the bathroom, my ankle felt so weak and painful that I limped slightly. Athletic and prone to being clumsy, no one thought much about it that day, including me.

The pain worsened the next day. Day three, there was redness and swelling. Two weeks later the swelling and pain caused a severe limp. My science teacher, an older gray-haired white male, even started calling me Chester, after the character on the western television drama *Gunsmoke*. I'd force a grin and limp to my next class.

One night I cried so much from the pain that Momma took me to Foote Hospital by cab when she got off work. They diagnosed my problem as an infection in my foot. We made another trip to the hospital's emergency room two weeks later when my condition continued to deteriorate. Again, infection in my foot, the doctor said. When the swelling and pain moved to my knees and I was unable to walk, Momma made an appointment to see a bone and joint specialist.

It was a cool, dreary morning when my grandfather drove us to the doctor's office. By then I was unable to walk, and Daddy picked me up and carried me from our sofa to his car. Sitting in the waiting room, I cried because of pain and fear. The nurse finally called us back to the examining room, and I tried to walk. The pain was so great that my legs gave out, and I dropped toward the floor before my grandfather caught me.

"Now just hold on baby. Granddaddy ain't gon let you fall," he said, his voice soft and soothing.

The doctor diagnosed my problem immediately after examining me.

"You need to take this child to the hospital right away. She's suffering from rheumatic fever," I remember him saying.

"Is it all right if we go home to get some things together first?" Momma asked. The doctor hesitated before saying yes. I knew then that rheumatic fever was something serious.

Foote Hospital only had one hospital bed available that day, and it was in the old people's ward. Sick and scared, it didn't matter to me. I just wanted to lie down. Momma helped undress me, then she put me in a gown that tied in the back, revealing my rear end if the two flaps weren't held tightly together.

The large room had five other metal beds. All of them were occupied by elderly white people. Two moaned all night. One of them kept calling for somebody named Cora. Momma had warned me about her soon after we arrived. "You're gonna have some trouble out of that sister," she said with a slight smile on her face and tilting her head toward the old woman's bed.

Most of the patients had visitors during my two-day stay in that ward, except the frail woman who moaned and cried all the time. I felt sorry for her, but dreaded when the nurses' aides came to change her oversize diapers. The room smelled so bad I almost threw up.

My doctor transferred me to the pediatric ward on the third day. Ordinarily the area was for infants to twelve-year-old children. At thirteen, I was still so small that I could fit comfortably into one of their large, metal baby beds. I didn't like the idea but was too sick to protest. Only parents and grandparents could visit patients in the pediatric ward. Momma came to see me each day before going to work. Grandma hobbled up to the hospital a few times. And Daddy and Mother visited me each evening when they were returning from their jobs.

I felt my grandparents' love and concern for me, even though they never came right out and said it and tended not to be touchy-feely types. But with Momma, I wasn't sure. She stood farther away from my bed than did my grandparents, and seldom had much to say other than asking me how I felt. Sometimes she kissed me on my forehead before she left, but I still lay in bed at times wondering if she really even cared about me.

My roommate was a nine-year-old blonde girl who lived in some small, rural community outside of Jackson. The girl had a bone ailment that required her left leg to be in traction during her hospital stay. She acted as if she couldn't get enough attention.

Although her parents drove into town to see her daily, she still listened to every conversation I had with my relatives, usually butting in once or twice. One evening as my grandparents headed out the door, Mother promised to bring me a pack of Juicy Fruit gum when she came again.

"I want some, too," the girl said, almost demandingly.

Mother brought both of us a pack of gum on her next visit. I didn't want her to bring my roommate anything. The girl called the get-well cards my classmates sent "dumb." I figured she was just jealous because no one sent her any. One morning I noticed my roommate staring at me.

"Why is your skin so dirty?" she finally asked.

"It's not dirty. It's brown," I said.

"It sure looks dirty to me. I bet my momma can wash that off you."

"This is my skin color. And it won't wash off," I said, sounding a bit indignant.

Turning my back to her, I pulled the white starched sheets and thin blankets over my head, curled up in a fetal position, and pretended to be asleep. A few minutes later my roommate started reaching for a book that sat on a hospital tray table, just out of her reach. She grunted so much that I peeked to see what she was doing.

"Why don't you just ring the buzzer for a nurse?" I asked from under the blankets, where I had once again retreated to after satisfying my curiosity.

"I don't wanna," she said. "Will you get it for me?"

"No."

"Why not?"

"Cause."

"Cause what?"

"Cause I don't want to," I said.

The truth was that I was still mad at her for calling my skin dirty, but I wasn't about to admit it. So I turned over and pretended to go back to sleep. Suddenly

I heard some bumping, then my roommate screaming. I looked around, and all I saw was her left leg still in traction and her body dangling below, on the other side of the bed.

I pressed the buzzer, calling for a nurse. Hearing all the commotion, several attendants came rushing in the door. They rescued my roommate from her predicament, pampering her and calling her "sweetie" and "darling." After everyone had left the room the nurse's aide who cared for both of us walked over to my bed and stood before me.

"You sure aren't a good babysitter are you, Jasmine?" she snapped.

My feelings were hurt.

Again.

"I'm not here to baby-sit," I replied, then pulled the covers over my head and cried myself to sleep.

— ℀ —

A WEEK LATER I was allowed to use a wheelchair. It was my first time out of bed in ten days. I wheeled myself to the children's playroom and up and down the hallway every chance I got. It was lonely being in the hospital, not being able to see most of my family and friends. I wanted to go home.

Two weeks after I was admitted, the nurses and doctors started talking about letting me go home. The day before my scheduled release, my doctor came in to give me a final examination. I knew the routine well by this time. I raised my hospital gown and let him listen to my chest and back. He moved the stethoscope from place to place, but stopped in one spot and listened longer. Too long. Placing the instrument back around his neck, the doctor told me that I wouldn't be going home.

"You've developed a heart murmur, young lady," he stated in a matter-of-fact way.

I couldn't believe it. I cried and begged and pleaded with him to let me go home. Nothing worked. My doctor ordered complete bed rest for me again. I ended up staying another week.

Grandma was beside herself with worry and called the hospital every day. Momma came to the hospital one day and told me that Grandma wanted me to stay with her when I came home.

"But I don't want to," I said, in a whiny voice.

"Why not? You know Grandma took good care of you when you came home from the hospital after having pneumonia the second time," Momma said. "You need somebody to keep an eye on you while I'm working."

"Grandma won't let me do anything. I mean nothing. She won't even change the channels on the TV. All she's gonna do is make me a pallet on the couch and give me chicken soup and warm Vernor's ginger ale all day. I can do that at home," I said.

I'm sure Momma told Grandma because my great-grandmother never brought the subject up to me.

—— ჲ ——

DR. SIZEMORE DISCHARGED me, but ordered complete bed rest for six months. Being only mid-March 1961, that meant I wouldn't be returning to school that year and would be laid up the entire summer. I was so happy to be home that I was willing to endure that.

Doctors still made house calls in Jackson in the early 1960s. Dr. Sizemore came to see me once a week, listening to my heart and giving me a shot of penicillin in my hip. The injections were very painful and caused my hip to swell. We alternated hips because of it. I dreaded the shots. And by the time the swelling and soreness had gone, it was time for another shot. My bedsores were even more painful. Momma had given me her bedroom downstairs and slept in our room with Lisa and Penny. She bought a slop jar for me because the bathroom was upstairs. A family member would come get the white metal bucket with a black rim every morning and every night. They'd take turns lugging it up the stairwell to the bathroom and emptying its contents in the toilet stool. I never got used to having someone take care of my bodily waste.

—— ჲ ——

THE DOCTOR COMMENTED several times that I was too small and thin for my age. My grandfather heard about it and came to see me with a proposal one day.

"You tell me what kind of food you'll eat, Jasmine, and I'll see to it that you have it every day," he said.

I thought about it a few seconds, then chose chocolate milk. Momma never could afford to buy us the drink, but I liked it better than white milk, especially powdered milk from the state.

My grandfather arranged for the milkman to deliver a quart to our front door every Monday, Wednesday, and Friday. I drank chocolate milk with breakfast, lunch, and dinner. I started giving it to my brothers and sisters. They eventually got tired of it, too. Bottles of chocolate milk, varying in content level, filled our refrigerator to the point that we had little room for anything else. Having gained ten pounds, I finally asked Daddy to stop the deliveries and thanked him.

Summer came, and my condition improved. Sometimes, after Momma went to work, I'd get up to walk slowly around the house. I made my sisters and brothers promise not to tell. But my baby brother, Keith, was a tattletale and usually told anyway.

Valerie, Arlene, and Robin had started going roller-skating on Sunday nights at the Rollatorium in town. Many of those nights I lay in bed imagining how much fun they were having and wishing I were there.

— ❧ —

I STARTED SCHOOL in the fall with everyone else, but still had to get penicillin shots once a week. I'd walk downtown to the doctor's office, located three miles away. He'd poke me in the behind with a hypodermic needle, and I'd be on my way, sore hip and all. Getting so many shots so often, I was always walking a little weird for a few days afterward.

One morning Momma stopped me before I left for school and seemed a little uncomfortable.

"Jasmine, tell Dr. Sizemore that the Crippled Children's Society has agreed to pay for your shots every week," she said quietly. I didn't know who the Crippled Children's Society was, but thought it was nice of them to pay medical bills for someone they didn't even know.

After school, I walked downtown to his office and when called, trudged into the examining room, expecting to get my injection. Instead of a warm smile, the doctor's mouth formed a straight line.

"Jasmine, I can't treat you anymore because your mother owes me money," he said curtly.

Embarrassed for Momma and me, I quickly informed him about the Crippled Children's Society. His thin lips turned upward into a smile for the first time during the visit. I continued getting penicillin shots for another year until I developed an allergic reaction that made me break out with red, itchy patches that covered my face and body before I'd left his office one day. Dr. Sizemore switched to sulfa for another year. My weekly treatments were discontinued after I became allergic to sulfa as well.

EAST JUNIOR HIGH SCHOOL

I thrived off competing against the smartest kids in my classes at school. My classes were identified as Group I, or accelerated. And I stuck right with my classmates, earning As and Bs every six-week marking period just like they did. Everybody thought one girl was a genius. She got straight As and a few A+s on every homework assignment, thus achieving the top ranking of our junior high school class. I admired almost everything about her. She had beautiful handwriting. Her athletic skills were impressive. She always knew the answer to every question and never sought attention. Her looks seemed to be the only thing going against her.

I tried my best to get straight As, too. The closest I came was a 3.83 grade point average once or twice. More often my grade point averaged 3.67. Competing against students at Pleasant Street and Allen schools was one thing. Getting As in junior high school required a great deal more effort because I was competing against the best academic students from at least half a dozen elementary schools. Being a perfectionist, I always did my best. Sometimes it became a stumbling block. I rewrote essay papers three or four times, sometimes for no other reason than I didn't like the way my handwriting looked.

One girl in my class made lovely D's when she wrote her first name, Donna. I started writing mine the same way. I liked the way my young aunt Valerie made her s's, big and bold. I incorporated her s's into my own handwriting style, too. I loved taking a little of something from someone and incorporating it to create my own style, whether it was handwriting, hairdos, clothing, or whatever.

My best white friend was named Janie Rabidoux. We first met in my seventh-grade art class and sat at the same table for an art project one day. From that day on, we became the best of friends. There were seldom any blacks in my elective classes. There were none in my required ones. Janie and I also shared the same Group I English, math, and science classes. We wrote each other notes in school, if time permitted after completing our assignments. We talked on the telephone two or three times a week and often did our homework together during those conversations.

Janie had the most beautiful and interesting handwriting I had ever seen. Each letter was perfectly shaped, the same height and slanted at exactly the same angle. It looked like art. I asked, and she taught me to write r's like hers, improving my handwriting even more.

Janie and I never visited each other's homes, although we knew every member of each other's families. She only had one older brother. Her father worked in an office, but her mother stayed at home. One day Janie suggested that we draw pictures of our houses. I really didn't want to draw mine, because it was old and unattractive, but was curious what her house looked like. So halfheartedly, I drew a picture of a two-story house created from imagination, using crayons. Janie drew hers with meticulous detail, even including doorknobs and smoke coming out of the chimney of a brick bungalow.

My friend wore the whitest socks and cleanest shoes I'd ever seen. Every dress and skirt and blouse set she wore was pressed to perfection. With tomboyish looks and shoulder-length, dishwater blonde hair and dark-rimmed glasses, Janie wasn't anything spectacular to look at, but she was smart, athletic, and nice to me. I admired those qualities in her a lot.

Most of the black kids were in the "dumb room," as they called it—"they" being all the other kids. School officials called it Group III. The teacher was a black man who was a devout Christian, well respected in the community, and a team player with a magnificent singing voice. The only times he appeared on the school stage were during assemblies to sing the national anthem.

My cousins and aunt didn't discuss school too much. Valerie never cared for studying. We nieces always said she was just there to socialize. Arlene was a good student and made the honor roll a time or two. Robin seldom talked about her grades. My cousins and aunt were all in Group II.

I wanted to be with them. They seemed to be having all the fun while I studied hard in classes with white kids. The only time I'd see my cousins and aunt was during music class or in the halls.

The civil rights movement was in full swing, but no one ever made any racial remarks around me. Discussion about race never even came up, except the day my Girl's Choir teacher raised the issue. It was fairly well known around school that I liked to dance and was pretty good at it. Our choir instructor asked another female student and me to do a few of the popular dances for the class, like the Monkey and the Fish and the Mashed Potato. We were delighted.

He put on some music in the sound room, and we danced for ten minutes, grinning from ear to ear the whole time. The class even clapped to the music beat, and the more they clapped the harder we danced. We all had a good ole time—until the music ended and the lecture began.

"Negroes in this country dance like people in Africa," I remember him saying.

This was the early 1960s when nobody, nowhere, wanted to be associated with Africa, especially me. Embarrassed and hurt, I cried right there in class. The other black students were also disappointed in our teacher, but none of them took it as hard as I did. I felt used and humiliated.

The discussion of the civil rights movement never came up in any of my classes in the early 1960s, even though it was picking up steam in other parts of the country. I heard bits and pieces about the lunch counter sit-ins and protest marches in the South on the evening news, but those things seemed a million miles away.

The classes in which I was the only black student were challenging and interesting to me. I had to work hard to keep up, but I did my homework most evenings, before going anywhere else. I thrived on the competition with my classmates. But I was becoming more and more lonely for my "running buddies," as we called each other.

Robin and Monica, a non-relative and close friend, were in Group II classes. There were blacks in all of their classes. I got tired of being the only black student in mine. I wanted somebody to laugh and talk with who looked and acted like me.

In eighth grade I stayed in my biology and Latin classes long enough to see that there were no blacks, as usual, and to realize that my classes weren't getting any easier. I trudged back and forth to my counselor's office several times trying to convince him to transfer me out of the two classes because they were too hard for me.

"You can do it, Jasmine. You're a very bright girl," my counselor said, barely giving me eye contact. "If you really try hard enough, you'll do just fine."

Undaunted, I made several more trips to his office for the same reason. My perseverance eventually paid off. Four weeks into the semester, my counselor agreed to transfer me. I was placed in a science class that had three other black students. And I switched from Latin to Spanish. There were two other blacks in the class and one Mexican girl who appeared older than everyone else.

—— ❧ ——

MY EIGHTH-GRADE geography teacher, Mr. Godfrey, was a former military man, obsessed with war. He talked about atomic bombs nearly every day. He told us everything we ever wanted to know about radiation and how it killed more people than the atomic explosion itself.

"Radiation causes people to vomit and lose their hair," he'd say, too many times for my comfort.

East Junior High held air-raid drills once a month, along with regular fire and tornado drills. We'd duck under our desks for the air-raid drills. We lined up at the door with the teacher at the head of the line and walked to the nearest exit leading outside for fire drills. Fire drills were exciting, but I liked tornado drills the most. We'd go to the basement into designated rooms for them. They felt like hideouts. And I always did like hiding out.

Mr. Godfrey even passed out detailed information on how to build fallout shelters. I don't know how many times he told us that the walls had to be at least thirty-six inches thick, then we'd have to stack sandbags against the walls because radiation couldn't penetrate sand. He listed supplies we'd need, such as canned meats and nonperishable foods and water.

For a student like me, whose single-parent mother could barely afford to keep a roof over our head, the idea of building and supplying a fallout shelter was out of the question. That was another thing about school. It seemed totally separate from my real life. The only time the two crossed was when I did homework each night at home.

The talk of war had me worried. Really, really worried. I don't ever remember mentioning it to anyone outside of school, but I had to figure out a plan for my family just in case the United States and Russia did go to war. So I asked the teacher where his fallout shelter was located. His reaction made me feel even worse.

"Oh no, Jasmine, you never tell people where your shelter is!" he said, frowning and shaking his head. "They would be the first ones at your door if war ever came. And scared people do scary things."

I had never thought about that.

A serious-faced man with average looks and thick, dark hair that he wore parted down one side, our geography teacher even showed us actual film footage taken during World War II. Sometimes our parents' signature was required because some of the scenes were so gory. Momma always signed them, but I didn't always turn them in, especially after seeing footage of Jewish babies being thrown up in the air and used for target practice and human skeletons piled up like garbage, their gold teeth extracted by the Nazis.

The Cuban missile crisis took place the same year and became the center of conversation in most of my classes. Sensing a growing concern among my teachers, I read our local newspaper every day, trying to keep up with the international event. My science teacher provided us with an update each day. The day of the showdown, I'll never forget what he said before we left class.

"We may not be seeing each other again, or at least for a while, because we may be at war by tomorrow."

That terrified me—until school ended that day. That's where the separation between school and home was so pronounced. None of my relatives or people in our neighborhood talked about the possibility of war, at least not around me.

❧ AUNT LULA MAE

I knew something was wrong when I came home and saw that Momma hadn't left for work. She was sitting on the couch in the living room with the telephone receiver in her hand. Instead of the usual stoic look on her face, it appeared unfamiliarly humble. Her eyes were red and swollen with traces of dried tears down her cheeks.

"What's the matter, Momma?" I asked, closing the door behind me, my heart pounding wildly.

"Aunt Lula Mae had a stroke. She's in intensive care at the hospital," she replied.

"Where's Grandma?"

"At the hospital with her."

Aunt Lula Mae, Grandma's only daughter, had collapsed while reading the obituary at a close friend's funeral earlier that afternoon on October 10, 1961. Grandma had gone with her and saw the whole thing. An ambulance rushed Aunt Lula Mae to Foote Hospital, but Momma said she was in a coma.

Family members were taking turns sitting at the hospital with Grandma at Aunt Lula Mae's bedside. Momma had gone to the hospital when she got the news. She was scheduled to go back around one o'clock in the morning to relieve Aunt Cynthia.

"I wanna go, too," I said. Momma said no.

The next morning, Grandma called me before I left for school, crying.

"Lula Mae ain't doing too good," she said, struggling to get the words out of her mouth. I tried to console her, then rushed into Momma's bedroom and told her, as soon as we had hung up.

"You know Grandma," Momma said. "She tends to exaggerate. She's always making things seem worse than they really are. Aunt Lula Mae was doing about the same when I left there at four o'clock this morning."

Momma's comments relieved me, so I finished getting ready for school. But I couldn't shake images of Aunt Lula Mae lying in a hospital bed and Grandma sitting beside her, worried to death. Momma's three-hour shift at Aunt Lula Mae's bedside was scheduled to start at one o'clock that next morning. I heard Momma standing at the door waiting for Aunt Cynthia to pick her up as I lay in bed, unable to sleep. The telephone rang.

"Oh no!" Momma hollered so loudly it woke up everybody in the house. We all knew what had happened.

The first thing that crossed my mind was Grandma. She had congestive heart failure and was always talking about not being around to see us graduate. I found out later that my great-grandmother got so upset about the death of her only daughter that doctors had to sedate her and hospitalize her overnight.

The days leading up to the funeral, my cousins and I sat on Grandma's porch listening to her lying in bed crying, day and night. We said little to anyone or each other. Relatives and friends traipsed in and out of her house, bringing food and sharing memories as they sat with the family awhile. My grandfather hid every picture he could find of his sister because Grandma couldn't bear to see them. She'd burst out crying about anything that brought a memory of her daughter. It was my first experience with losing a family member who was so closely involved in my life.

Details of Aunt Lula Mae's death slowly trickled down to us through the older family members. They said Aunt Lula Mae had been singing in the choir and stood to read her friend's obituary when she was stricken. She tried to get up two or three times before fainting and falling to the floor.

"Every time Lula Mae tried to stand up, she shook her head with a strange look on her face," I heard an elderly friend of the family say. "Your Grandma Beanie sensed something was wrong and stood up and started hollering for somebody to help Lula Mae. It was sad. Real sad."

Aunt Lula Mae had been a seamstress at the Elaine Shop, an expensive women's store in town, and knew lots of people. She worked for the church at the local, state, and national levels and served as everything from usher to church clerk at Trinity Baptist. Her funeral was moved at the last minute to a large Methodist church down the street from ours because so many people were expected to attend. And they did.

The church was so packed with people that even with chairs in the aisles, some had to stand out in the vestibule. The rest was a blur for me, except for one thing. A distant cousin by marriage who was adopted, my age, and hung around us sometimes at school cried harder than any of us. And I mean we all cried. Until the funeral, the distant cousin had been stoic and didn't talk much about Aunt Lula Mae's death.

Grandma was as limp as a rag doll when they took her up to view the body for the last time. Daddy held her up on one side. Uncle David, her baby brother, had her other arm.

❋ CHRISTMAS

The navy blue stretch pants were so tight I had to wiggle my frail body to get them up over my waist. The ten pounds I had gained while convalescing from rheumatic fever were long gone, but with three pairs of pants on, no one could tell. My long arms made the sleeves on my wool coat fit just above the wrist. Squeezing an orange knit cap on my head caused my forehead to wrinkle and my eyes to squint. The brown ball on top made me look like a girl all bundled up for the snow. I still liked hanging around boys, but never wanted to be mistaken for one. Covering both hands with old socks that didn't match, I walked out the door with Lisa, Robin, Valerie, Albert, and Monica, to start our annual Christmas caroling.

"I'll take them off as soon as somebody comes to the door," I thought, excited about our annual money-making adventure.

My sister Lisa could sing, so we always put her in the middle of the front row. Robin, my cousin, stood beside her, along with my friend and former Page Avenue neighbor, Monica. Valerie, my young aunt, was the best singer and most confident of the group, so she could stand anywhere she wanted as long as Albert and I stayed in the back. Neither of us could carry a tune, and knew it.

We'd trudge through the snow, practicing as we headed to the all-white neighborhoods that had street names like Joy and Sweet and Pleasant. Four short blocks from our neighborhood, the houses on the all-white streets looked as nice as their street names sounded.

We got good at selecting the houses. Lisa would knock on the door or ring the doorbell. As soon as we sensed someone was coming, we'd strike up a chorus of "Silent Night" or "Oh Come All Ye Faithful." The people loved it. They broke out in broad smiles and often sent for others in the house to share in the holiday surprise.

I loved peeking inside their homes. All of them looked warmer and more inviting than ours. Some had fireplaces with lots of books on the shelves. Sometimes a cat was perched on the back of the sofa. Other times the pets purred softly, rubbing their owner's leg as we sang. The houses looked as neat as those I'd seen on television. I used to imagine what it would be like to live in a nice home, like those on Joy, Sweet, and Pleasant streets.

Other homes were littered with children's toys, shoes, newspapers, and other clutter. Harried mothers answered the doors, a screaming baby in one arm, a cooking utensil in the other. Seeing the different people and their households always fascinated me.

Two weeks before Christmas in 1962, we earned fifty-seven dollars caroling one Friday night. We all went shopping for gifts the next morning. With my cut of seven dollars and some change, I bought gifts for everyone in our immediate family and Grandma.

Christmas was my favorite holiday. I loved the festivity and kindness that people displayed toward each other during the season. Christmas also had some advantages for underprivileged kids like us. Several organizations always donated boxes of toys and food. At least one group always invited us to their annual Christmas party for poor kids. A bus or someone would pick us up and drive us to the big event, held in the armory or some other large facility. We'd sing Christmas carols and feast off of turkey and dressing and all the fixings. The parties were highlighted by a visit from Santa Claus, bearing gifts. Albert and I got good at knowing which organization's Santa Claus gave the best presents.

Momma always bought us at least one thing we asked for. One year I got a baking set. The next year a portable tape recorder. But Christmas of 1962 brought an unexpected surprise. Momma called me into her bedroom around nine o'clock Christmas Eve and closed the door. Her face looked worried, which made my stomach start to knot.

"Jasmine, I couldn't afford to get you anything for Christmas this year, but this," she said slowly, then handed me a record album by Chubby Checker.

"I didn't have much money this time," she continued, "And since you're the oldest, I thought you'd understand if I got gifts for the younger kids now and bought you something after Christmas."

I didn't understand but tried hard not to appear disappointed. My eyes burned from tears welling up, but I fought them back, biting my trembling lip. That night before I climbed into bed, I prayed that the whole thing was a ploy by Momma to throw me off. "Besides, I don't even like Chubby Checker, especially after he married that white woman," I thought, lying in bed in the dark.

I woke up to find out that Momma really didn't have any money.

✾ LIFE ON THE RUN

Grandma sat on her porch, rocking and staring into space every day. She was taking Aunt Lula Mae's death pretty hard. I tried to visit her every day right after school got out. But we didn't talk much. We didn't laugh. We didn't do much of anything but look out the windows, the only sounds coming from the furnace cutting on and off and Mr. Thomas piddling around in the house.

Although Daddy had removed his sister's pictures off the television and the curved-edged oak dresser in Grandma's bedroom, she still ran across one every so often while going through papers and old mementos. Grandma would burst out crying.

I didn't know what to do the first few times it happened, but eventually started easing up from my rocker and inching my way over to her.

"You'll be all right Grandma. You're gonna be all right," I'd say, patting her back and rubbing her shoulders. It seemed as if an eternity passed before my great-grandmother would stop crying. Secretly, I often wondered if anything would ever be the same again.

— ৡ —

"JASMINE, YOU MAKE me sick. That boy's got a *baby*," Momma said to me one day when she discovered I liked James Moore. He was eighteen year old. I hadn't quite turned fourteen.

James had moved from Lansing to live with his aunt and uncle, who lived around the corner from us on Teneyck Street. After dropping out of school and fathering a son, James decided to move to Jackson to get a fresh start. Momma dared me to see him again.

"You're always running behind some ole thug," she said with disgust.

What Momma didn't know was that none of the "decent" boys wanted to be bothered with me. I didn't engage in sex, and in my opinion, I was skinny, unattractive, and poor.

Robin, Valerie, and Arlene seemed to always catch the attention of the boys who came from good homes. I attracted either the "squares" or those who were streetwise.

James was streetwise, but was kind and considerate to me. Age didn't matter to him or me. We were simply good friends. Most evenings around seven o'clock, he'd stop by on his way from work at a local restaurant. Momma got home around eight thirty. We spent our time sitting on our front steps talking. Sometimes he sang to me in his nice, high-pitched voice. Both of us wished that life wasn't so difficult.

James left about thirty minutes before Momma was due home, giving me ample time to make sure the house and kitchen were in order. If Momma asked me if James had been over, I told her the truth. When she didn't ask, I didn't tell. The more adamant Momma became about trying to keep us apart, the more determined I became to see James. He treated me better than any boy I had known. He acted proud of me and often boasted to his hometown buddies when they came around. And he never once asked for sex.

— ॐ —

ONE FRIDAY NIGHT in October 1963 a friend named Carla Gamble and I went to a football game at Jackson High School. The high school hadn't won a game in three straight years, but that really didn't matter. High school football games were social events for us, attracting hundreds of people of every age, race, and socioeconomic background. The games, held behind the school at Withington Stadium, also provided an excellent opportunity to meet members of the opposite sex.

Carla was a year older than me and much more streetwise. I looked at her as kind of like a big sister. Bold and brutally honest, Carla kept me laughing, and sometimes wishing for a little of her courage, especially when it came to guys. She and her sister, Trina, had lots of boyfriends both in and out of town. Sometimes they even spent the night.

"Girl, Momma and Daddy tried, to keep me and my dude from doing it," she told me with the biggest grin on her face one day, referring to her newest boyfriend from Lansing. "They made him sleep on the couch. I waited just as good until everybody went to bed, then sneaked downstairs and got me a little bit."

Carla and I met in junior high school when her family moved to our neighborhood from the South Side. Momma never cared for her, although she never came out and said it. I got the impression she thought my friend was a bad influence on me. She was probably right, but Carla looked out for me at school and on the playgrounds better than anyone ever had. She stood ready to fight anyone who dared do anything to me. And it seemed every year there was always a bully pushing my buttons.

Tall and broad shouldered, Carla was an attractive female, with honey brown skin and a freckled face. She wore her jet black hair combed back in a ponytail and didn't seem to care much for clothes. Blue jeans and a buttoned-down shirt were her trademark.

Carla's self-deprecating humor kept me laughing, and her boldness tended to stir up trouble. But my sistah friend could back her tough talk up. I liked that.

The night of Jackson high's game, Carla mentioned that she was expecting a visit from some guys from out of town. There were several females on the East Side who seemed to know every young man who stepped inside Jackson's city limits, and Carla and Trina Gamble were two of them.

Our hometown team was wrapping up their latest loss of the season when three dudes in their late teens and early twenties showed up as the crowd streamed out of the stadium. Carla greeted them with hugs and kisses on the cheeks. I stood and waited for her to introduce us, which she did. Afterward, we all climbed in their nice shiny car and rode around town for a while. Around ten thirty, I asked to be dropped off at home.

"Aw, come on, Jasmine. We getting ready to ride over to Parkside. There's supposed to be a party out there at the high school," Carla said. "These guys done come all the way from Ypsilanti to hang out a while. Come go with us. We'll get you back home before it gets too late."

I thought for a few seconds. Momma had given me an eleven o'clock curfew. She and I had been bumping heads more and more often. I hated my turbulent relationship with Momma and wanted to try to do the right thing for a change. Plus, a little voice inside of me kept saying, "You better go home."

"Naw Carla," I said. "There's a quarter party next week, and I sure don't wanna be on a punishment for it. I heard it's gonna be jumping."

—— ॐ ——

MOMMA WOKE ME up about five o'clock the next morning and called me downstairs with an urgency in her voice.

"I thought you told me you were with Carla Gamble last night?" she said, her eyes widened with concern.

"I was."

"Well, Carla got shot in the head last night. I just heard it on the news on the radio."

"Is she dead?" I asked, holding my breath and feeling faint.

"No. But they had to rush her to the University Hospital in Ann Arbor. They said the doctors operated on her overnight. She's in critical condition."

My first reaction was to throw on some clothes and run several blocks over to Carla's house. But Momma stopped me, saying it was too early. So I got ready for school, then stopped on my way to East Junior High. Carla's older sister, Trina, was sitting on the couch at their house when I got there.

"Girl, Carla's doing okay now," she said, looking tired and relieved. "You know Carla. Ain't nothing gon keep her crazy butt down too long."

I felt so much better.

As it turned out, two young men from our hometown had followed the car we were in, shortly after I had been dropped off. Jackson had been engaged in an ongoing rivalry with several other mid-Michigan cities, and Ypsilanti was one of them. Young black males from Jackson often tangled with out-of-towners about dating local women. Females sometimes did the same thing.

The guys in Carla's car pulled over and started getting out. Someone from Jackson fired a gun just as Carla exited the car. The bullet ricocheted off the car door and struck her between the eyes. Her male friends jumped back in their car and rushed Carla to the hospital. It took doctors four hours to place a metal plate around the bullet, which was lodged in her brain in a location too dangerous to try to move.

— ⸎ —

I TOOK UP a collection at school for Carla. Every student asked, black or white, gave. Most already had heard about their schoolmate getting shot. It was all over the newspaper, television, and radio. The issue even started a war of words in the local newspaper when some parents wrote opinion pieces assailing Carla's parents for allowing their fifteen-year-old daughter to be out that time of morning with "a car full of males." Carla's peers supported her overwhelmingly.

I learned how fast the brain heals when Carla got out of the hospital just over a week after being shot. I rushed over to see her as soon as school was out. It surprised me to find her sitting up on a pallet on the couch, chatting with her family, a large white bandage wrapped around her head.

"Girl, I was hoping you'd stop by here on your way home," Carla said, her smile a mile wide. "Come here. I wanna show you something."

I had expected Carla to be sad faced and quiet after such a traumatic incident, but she was just the opposite. My friend nearly hopped off the couch and hurried to the stairway, urging me to follow. She disappeared up the steps before I reached the top. The next thing I knew, Carla stepped out of the bathroom with her bandages removed. Her head was shaven bald. Black stitches crisscrossed her forehead where doctors had operated.

"How do I look?" she asked with her familiar mischievous grin. Stunned, having never seen a female with her hair shaven off before, I stammered a bit at first.

"Ah . . . you look . . . okay," I said, trying to hold myself together.

"Aw girl, you're just lying!" Carla laughed. "You know you're scared to death."

"No I wasn't. I was just taken aback," I said, with a sheepish grin.

WHEN EVERYTHING CHANGED

The clock on the classroom wall said two fifteen when I scrambled to my seat and took a pencil out of my purse. I'd been studying for the big civics test for at least half an hour every night. Our teacher, Mr. Smith, constantly reminded us that the test grades represented 60 percent of our grade for the first marking period of my ninth-grade year at East Junior High.

Expecting the teacher to pass out the test, I was surprised when the fair-haired man announced he would read the questions. Feeling confident, I was halfway through the test when our principal, Mr. Fobbs, tapped on the classroom door. I liked sitting in the front row and spotted him through the glass in the door. The principal's pale, blotchy face looked ghostlike when he walked in. His expression reminded me of my fourth-grade teacher's face the time a classmate's mother died and she had to send the girl home from school.

I held my breath and watched as the principal fumbled with a small stack of notes. He peeled one off and handed it to Mr. Smith. I stared at my teacher's face, waiting for a reaction. His color left immediately. His expression reflected the principal's. After a few uncomfortable glances between the two middle-aged men, the principal quickly walked back out the door. I kept thinking, "The United States and Russia must have gone to war."

By now the entire class was still, realizing something was wrong

"I have an important announcement to make, but I'm not going to make it until after our test," he said slowly.

I thought about atomic bombs. Radioactive fallout. Not having a fallout shelter and not knowing anyone who did. Concentrating on the test was nearly impossible, but I did my best. The teacher quickly collected the tests, then returned to his desk. It was clear that he was trying to maintain his composure but losing the struggle. He took just enough time for me to scare myself into a near panic.

"John F. Kennedy, our president of the United States, was shot and killed in Dallas, Texas, this afternoon," he announced softly.

My classmates and I gasped.

"And having to ask you students the last question on the test was one of the hardest things I've ever had to do in my life," he said, his lips trembling almost as badly as his hands.

The question was, "Who is the vice president of the United States?"

Everything everywhere was eerily quiet. I walked trancelike to my locker right after class was dismissed. No locker doors slammed. No books plunked on hall floors. No chattering voices anticipating the weekend. Everywhere I looked, faces were as solemn as mine. No one knew what to say or what to do. It was the quietest walk home from school I would ever have.

— ❧ —

FROM THE TIME we got home, my eyes were glued to our television for the entire weekend. I saw live coverage of Lee Harvey Oswald getting shot in the basement of the Dallas County jail. It was the first live killing ever televised. During the funeral, I watched John Kennedy Jr. salute as his dad's coffin passed him. I was in love with the handsome little guy from that day on.

Debra kept calling me, crying. We must have talked a couple dozen times that weekend. I wished that Kennedy had been my favorite candidate, too.

✿ WILDFIRE

oshua Campbell had the most innocent-looking hazel eyes and relaxed walk I'd ever seen. His copper brown skin and plaid shirt and blue jeans gave him the appearance of a lumberjack. He was another cousin from Mississippi who had moved to Jackson after graduating from high school. Five had come before him. I didn't remember Joshua when we vacationed on Papa and Grandma Linnie's farm down south. But he remembered me.

It was sometime in the summer of 1964 when Joshua arrived in town. I was spending my summer vacation in Flint with my dad and his family. Robin and Debra wrote me several times, saying our "new cousin" couldn't wait to see me again. I saw him and still didn't recognize him.

"Maybe it's because there were so many of you. Now how many brothers and sisters do you have?" I asked, smiling, charmed by his innocence and humility.

My relationship with Joshua grew so close so fast that some family members started whispering. We didn't care. If anything, I got a kick out of those who talked because I knew they were wrong. Joshua lived around the corner from us, with his brother and sister-in-law, a five-minute walk away. He landed a restaurant job shortly after relocating to Jackson.

My cousin called me every day—sometimes several times a day. Everybody got tired of answering the phone, including me, sometimes. Joshua worked second shift, so he didn't come by until Fridays, which was also the day he got paid. My second cousin almost always gave me at least twenty dollars spending money every week. A hard worker, he earned over a hundred dollars per paycheck.

For my sixteenth birthday, Joshua bought me a twelve-inch birthday cake—white on white with red roses, my favorite. Sometimes we rode around in his old

1959 Pontiac, talking for hours. We talked about his job, my school, our families, their relationships, boyfriends, girlfriends, our fears and insecurities. My favorite topics of discussion were parties and the latest dances and songs. Joshua listened but eventually always wanted to talk about me.

"I've been thinking about you all these years," he said to me one day. "I looked forward to seeing you again."

At first it was kind of flattering and cute. But eventually Joshua started storming out the door when my boyfriends called or stopped by. He'd get quiet whenever I mentioned the names of guys I was seeing. My heart wanted to keep seeing my cousin. He was honest and fun to be around. But my mind told me to put some distance between us because things had gone too far.

Joshua and I kissed a lot. Sometimes things got passionate. But I never allowed myself to go all the way with him, mainly because he was my cousin, and partly because I figured he was too country and probably wouldn't know what to do. As if I would.

I really liked Joshua, but didn't love him the way he wanted. I couldn't. I tried explaining myself to him countless times, but he refused to listen.

"Down home, cousins marry cousins all the time," he told me one day, as we rode around town in another old car he'd recently bought.

He cited examples, one being his older sister and her husband. That was news to me. So I went home and asked Momma. She raised her eyebrows at me.

"Yeah Jasmine, that's true. But you should of told Joshua that people in the North don't do things like that," she chuckled.

— ❧ —

ROBIN, VALERIE, MONICA, and I used to sneak out of town to see our boyfriends every chance we got. The four of us had beaus in Albion, Ann Arbor, Lansing, and Battle Creek—all at the same time. We were serious about every one of them, especially when they were in town.

Every weekend Valerie, Robin, Monica, and I spent at least one afternoon riding around town in a flashy new car with two or three guys who came visiting from out of town. It was a status symbol of sorts.

Joshua didn't like my behavior, and told me so more than once. Being sixteen and just getting a taste of freedom, the last thing I wanted was my cousin who wanted me for himself. I got tired of him preaching to me about messing around with other guys. I also got tired of slipping around, afraid of hurting Joshua's feelings. It felt as if we were going together. And in some twisted way, I guess we were—without the sex.

I wanted out of the relationship. Joshua was my cousin, and there was no way we could be lovers. Less than a year after we met, Joshua was calling me so much it became annoying. His sad hazel eyes no longer made me feel sorry for him. I sensed jealousy and resentment during our conversations.

Thinking he just needed to meet some other nice girls, I arranged a double date between Joshua and Monica. My on-again, off-again boyfriend Marcell, from Jackson, planned everything. We caught a movie, then rode around town. We even rode out to Ella Sharpe Park and smooched for a while. Everyone laughed and talked and appeared to have a good time. A few weeks later Joshua admitted that he didn't like me setting him up with anyone.

"I don't want Monica. I want you," he said.

✻ ALL <u>ABOUT</u> ME

My ninth-grade graduation was held the first week of June 1963. Daddy drove down from Flint to attend. It was the first time I remember my dad attending anything related to my school, even though he always stressed the importance of getting a good education.

Early in the afternoon he accompanied Momma to our school assembly. I was one of thirty-seven students recognized as a three-year honor student. Sitting in the middle row to the right of the audience, I was one of only three black students on stage. Much to my surprise, that really impressed Daddy. He boasted to his friends and family about me being the only black recognized from that day on. The first few times he said it, I tried correcting him. After that, I kept quiet, not wanting to burst my dad's bubble.

I felt so proud to have both my mother and father sitting together at the program, even though things had changed dramatically between him and me over the past four years. His visits were fewer and farther between. Sometimes I went weeks, maybe months, forgetting that I even had a father. Forgetting about him made me feel guilty and ashamed.

"No one should forget they have a father," I'd think to myself.

Daddy's visits slacked off after he started remarrying. By the time my ninth-grade graduation rolled around, my dad was on his third wife. He had three daughters and two sons by her and a daughter by wife number two. Being his only child until I was eight years old, I had a hard time accepting all the new people in his life. I never said anything about it, but really resented them and him.

"Daddy's so busy trying to raise all those kids in Flint, that he don't have time for me no more," I used to think. "Don't none of them look like him. They don't look like his wife either. I don't know who those funny-looking kids look like."

Daddy never stayed around very long. Once the afternoon program and graduation ceremony were over, he headed back to Flint. I felt proud he'd come and learned more about my accomplishments over the past three years.

I'd worked on the school newspaper called the *East Echo* as part of my ninth-grade English class. I loved writing stories about things happening around school, then seeing my byline in the monthly publication. I received lots of compliments and laughs about my gossip column. I realized for the first time that my writing interested people.

I served as a cheerleader for the varsity basketball team, along with two other black females. They also had good grades, one of the requirements, so I convinced them to try out. The three of us practiced at my house every evening after school for three weeks while Momma was working. All three of us made the squad and were the first black cheerleaders in the school's sixty-plus-year history.

—— ❧ ——

"STRIKE THREE," the umpire standing behind me yelled, balling his fist, then jerking his elbow towards the ground and lifting his leg, almost simultaneously.

Most people leaped to their feet. They clapped. They cheered. They slapped each other's back and gave each other "skin." Car horns honked in the alley that connected Plymouth and Deyo streets.

Ball games were a big thing at Rotary playground. I played softball from the time I was seven. My start was a total fluke. Some older teenage girls needed a center fielder. Someone saw me walking across the playground, heading home, and volunteered me. They gave me a black softball glove, and the next thing I knew I was standing in the grass in center field. I'd never played a softball game on Rotary playground before in my life.

Eventually a batter hit a ball high in the air. It arced toward me. Afraid it would pop me in my head, I stuck my glove out, palm up, and caught it. More accurately, it fell in. My teammates couldn't believe it. I couldn't believe it. Word spread around the playground within days. Many smiled and whispered about my catch when I walked by. I ended up with a reputation for being a good softball player before I ever learned the game.

That was seven years earlier. I'd gone from a center fielder to pitcher and was pretty good, if I had to say so myself. The championship on the line, I took a deep breath and tuned out the crowd. Rotary playground was leading by one run, and it was the bottom of the sixth, the last inning. One more out, and Rotary playground would beat our cross town rival, Exchange playground, and clinch the girls' softball championship for the second summer in a row.

The next player marched to home plate, swinging her bat like she was going to win the game single-handedly. Her name was Candi Johnson. She was tall, pretty, and a power hitter. I knew Candi. She had invited me to her parents' split-level home on the South Side on more than one occasion. Their house was beautiful. I invited her to our house only once, ashamed of our two-story, late-nineteenth-century home.

But houses didn't matter on the ball field. It was all about the game.

I stared at Monica's brown catcher's mitt. She pounded it several times with her small fist.

"Hey batter, batter. Hey batter, batter. You can't hit," she chattered. "Put it right across the plate, Jasmine. You can do it!"

I stepped forward with my left foot. Nearly at the same time, I swung my arm around and threw an underhanded pitch that was the prettiest of the entire game in my opinion.

Crack! The ball sailed high into the air over first base. Carla Gamble, our first baseman for the past three years, ran under it. She put her arm to her forehead to block the sun. The ball nicked her glove as it fell to the ground in foul territory. I went into a tirade.

"Carla, if you'd kept your eye on the ball, we would've had three outs," I yelled, glaring at her like I was a madwoman. "Why don't you wake up and pay attention?"

Carla and I had already been in one fight, a year earlier, just a few years after she was shot. It was about a softball game, too. Young people on the East Side fought each other quite often, averaging about two fights a month. We'd come to blows about baseball and softball. Four square and tetherball. Checkers. Records and eight-track tapes. People playing the dozen, and everything else. Sometimes we made up within weeks. Sometimes it took a few weeks. But I never heard of anyone our age, on the East Side, who fell out and stayed mad at one another for more than four months. Underneath all that fussing and fighting, the people who lived on the East Side grew up as one big happy family.

But when it came down to playing softball, especially a championship game, nothing else mattered. I expected every member of our team to make their play, *effectively*. Know where the ball was at all times. Call for fly balls to keep from running into each other. Stop the lead runner. And imagine the upcoming play *before* the batter hits the ball. Real simple.

I wound up and let another one go.

"Strike two," the umpire yelled, pulling his arm from inside his blue, padded chest protector and using his white fist to accentuate the call.

The crowd had already been standing on their feet. They jumped up and down. Laughing. Screaming. Hugging everybody near them. I focused on the batter.

"Two strikes everybody," I hollered, looking around the bases to make sure everyone was in place and alert. "Catcher, if you drop the ball on the third strike, pick it up and tag the batter."

Monica nodded.

I took my step, then threw the ball, never taking my eyes off the catcher's mitt. Monica snagged it.

"Strike three. You're out!" the empire shouted, exaggerating his fist and leg move even more.

Team members dashed up to me, jumping on my back and knocking me to the ground. A sea of hands patted my head, my back, my legs, and every other part of my torso, yelling and screaming, thrilled that we had won.

"That girl walked off that softball field as if she was Mickey Mantle," I heard one man whisper to another when I finally left the field. I loved the way he'd said it, but also knew that Mickey Mantle was a center fielder for the New York Yankees, not a pitcher.

The crowd was thinning out when the city's recreation director, Ms. Madelyn, called my name. A slender woman with short blonde hair, she stood leaning with her back against her black car, her arms folded across her chest. Even her feet were crossed.

"You played a good game today, Jasmine, as usual," Ms. Madelyn said. "But you tend to be a little bit hard on your teammates. You can't expect everybody to play the way you want them to. Now can you?"

I wanted to say, "Of course I do. If I can do it. They can too."

But I didn't. I slowly shook my head, instead.

"You've got quite a temper there, young lady. That's something only you can correct. You have so much going for you, Jasmine. It would be a shame if you don't use it to your advantage."

—— ҉ ——

FALL CAME, and Momma and I walked home from school together nearly every evening. She attended night school at Jackson High. I helped tutor adults who couldn't read or write. I never realized there were so many illiterate grown-ups, most of them white or from other countries. I'd heard of a few adults in my family who couldn't read or write, but even that was a well-kept secret until I was in my teens.

Momma and I walked the same way home every night, straight through downtown. There were more lights and people. I enjoyed walking and talking with Momma, even though I did most of the talking.

One night we stopped at a drugstore so that Momma could get a prescription filled. The pharmacist completed the order, then handed Momma the medicine bottle. She looked at it. She looked at him.

"Where's the information that's supposed to be on the bottle?" she asked, surprise written all over her face.

"It's the same medication you've been taking. Just keep taking it the same way," he said, a bit too snippy for Momma and me.

"I want the information on the label. It's against the law to leave it off," she said.

The pharmacist turned around and walked away. Momma held the medicine bottle and stared at the man for several seconds. I looked at Momma's face and felt so sorry for her I wanted to cry. Her eyes were dark and steely, but deeper inside, they looked helpless. I wanted to butt in the dispute and call him a few names, but I didn't want to make things any worse.

"Come on Jasmine. Let's get out of this man's store before I say something that I'll regret later," she said. We stormed out together.

Another time Momma and I had just walked past Kresge's five-and-dime store when five girls from the South Side walked out through the glass doors. Most were my age. I knew their faces, but wasn't sure about names. They were from the snooty crowd and had little to do with me.

I smiled limply, threw up my hand, and kept on walking. The five girls walked so close behind us, they nearly stepped on my heels. They laughed. They snickered. I even heard them mention my name several times. Momma did, too.

"Don't say anything to them, Jasmine. Just keep on walking. And don't look back," Momma said quietly and looking straight ahead.

I wanted to take them all on. They thought they were better than me, and I knew it. I saw it in their eyes at dances. I saw it in their body language whenever they did say something to me. I'd seen them talking to some of my cousins. They had even invited Robin and Arlene into their homes. It made me jealous.

"Now I know these girls aren't crazy enough to follow me and my momma home," I thought, doing everything I could to keep from turning around and going crazy on them.

But I followed Momma's instructions and kept walking. The girls turned right on Francis Street near the Otsego Hotel. We walked the rest of the way home in the chilly night air, stepping up our pace the closer we got to home.

— ę —

I WAS GLAD to get home from school the next day. I had Tuesdays off. On those evenings, Momma usually caught the city bus. Sometimes she walked home by herself. I didn't like that at all.

Hustling upstairs and rambling through my closet and drawers, I pulled out a pair of denim blue jeans and a faded gray sweatshirt. I tossed them on the bed, then unbuttoned the back of my mustard and black plaid dress. I crossed my arms at the hem and pulled it over my head. I hated wearing dresses. Schools still had dress codes back then. No pants or slacks for girls. That was all I knew.

I stuck one skinny leg in a pant leg. Then the other. I pulled the sweatshirt over my head, then combed my hair back into a ponytail.

I called Valerie. My aunt could do just about anything she wanted. If anybody could go with me, she could.

"Girl, I'm getting ready to go over to the South Side and raise some hell this evening," I said, glad to finally be letting off some steam.

"Why? What happened?" she asked in her usual dramatic way.

I told her the whole story.

"Now there's nothing I can do about that ole crazy white man at the drugstore. I decided to leave that one alone. But those hussies over there on the South Side? If I don't hunt them down and kick their asses, my name ain't Jasmine Armstead," I said.

"Now, Cool, me and you can't whip no five girls," Valerie said. "But you know me, I'll *go*."

We laughed. "I'll go" was an inside joke between us best-friend relatives. Valerie had said those words to her father, who had tracked her down in Battle Creek after she ran away from home, the first time. We used that line a thousand times in all kinds of crazy circumstances and cracked up laughing every time.

Carla Gamble and a second cousin, Betty King, who lived down the street from us, were my only other "aces" who were able to drop everything and join us for the rumble. They sounded almost as mad as I was when I'd finished telling them what had happened the previous evening. My little posse also disliked stuck-up South Side girls. They always acted as if they were better than the four of us.

"Those heffas had the nerve to whisper and snicker about me in front of my own momma. There's no way I'm gonna let them get away with disrespecting me and my momma like that. I bet they won't do it again. Those hussies got a good ass kicking coming," I fussed.

The four of us teamed up outside my house, all dressed in blue jeans and sweatshirts. We called them our fighting duds. We walked to the South Side, asking everybody we knew, until we found out where one of the ringleaders lived. It was dark by the time I marched up to her door, a nice two-story home with a big glass-enclosed porch. The girl who had been the mouthiest and was twice my size lived there. I wanted her. Bad.

The big girl answered the door, something I didn't expect. Seeing her nonchalant attitude at my impromptu visit to her home threw me off my stride for a split second. The next second I was back on.

"I came over here to finish what you and the rest of your group started yesterday when I was walking home with my mother," I said, just loud enough so that no one inside her house could hear.

Big Girl smirked. She took a several steps back, then reached inside the house and slipped a jacket off a wooden banister near the door, without taking her eyes off of me. The girl walked back outside to her porch as if I'd just invited her out to play.

Daddy's lessons in defending myself came in handy over the years more times than I could count. Rule number one. If I knew for sure that a fight was imminent, try to get the first lick in. The element of surprise was a powerful weapon.

I clocked Big Girl in the head as soon as we faced off. I didn't have time to argue anyway, we had others on our hit list. Valerie, Carla, and Betty stepped back, according to the plan we'd developed while walking south. Each of us would take on at least one. And there'd be only one-on-one fights, unless someone else jumped in.

Big Girl was heavy but not quick on her feet. I put her in a headlock and flipped her to the ground so fast she looked stunned. Like most of my opponents,

Big Girl discovered that I was much tougher than I appeared. She talked and acted tougher than she really was. The fight barely lasted three minutes.

By the time people came running out of her house, the four of us were running down the street. We looked for the next girl, a short, bossy little something who lived on Francis Street.

Betty marched up to her house. We stood on the sidewalk and watched. Miss Bossy played the piano and led the choir at Trinity Baptist. None of us could stand her. Only three years older than me, Miss Bossy always treated us as if we were little kids in church. She looked old to be only eighteen. She dressed even older.

No one answered the door, but just as we were walking away, Miss Bossy pulled up in her driveway. Betty met her as she exited the car.

"I heard that you followed my cousin halfway home yesterday. Now what was that ya'll were whispering about Jasmine behind her back?" she asked, her hands on her hips, a violation of fighting rule number two: always be prepared.

Miss Bossy wanted to argue.

"Look, I don't give a darn what Jasmine Armstead came back and told you. We were minding our own business yesterday and just happened to be walking in back of them. Nobody mentioned Jasmine's name," she said defiantly.

"Look, we can stand here and argue about what happened until the cows come home," I interrupted. "I know what you did. And I know what I heard. Ya'll must not know me as well as you think. Because I don't play," I said, stepping up in Miss Bossy's face.

Valerie and Carla pulled me back. Then Betty smacked the girl in the face. They tumbled to the ground before I realized what had happened.

People came running from everywhere. Word had already spread that some East Side girls had come to the South Side to fight. A few porch lights clicked on. Several young people dribbled out of houses. Even Big Girl and her family came racing up to Francis Street. Everyone gathered around the tussle, but nobody intervened. It was one of the quietest fights I'd ever seen.

Minutes later a police car pulled up. Everybody scattered. A longtime friend of Momma's named Doris Fowler opened her screen door and beckoned us with her hand. The four of us darted for her house.

"Go inside and hide. Quick!" she whispered as we rushed by her, stooping to stay out of sight.

Carla hid in the bathroom. Valerie ducked next to the couch. Betty and I crouched in the closet corner, near the front door, and heard every word of Doris's brief conversation with the officer.

"No. I didn't see any girls run this way," she told the man. "I saw a crowd of kids running all over the place, but none of them came over here."

The policeman left. We stayed another half hour until we felt the coast was clear, then thanked Mrs. Fowler for letting us hide in her house.

"I didn't even know you lived on Francis Street. I never knew where you lived after you moved from the East Side," I said to the woman, stepping out to the glass-enclosed front porch.

"Well, I know you girls. I know your mothers. And anytime ya'll came all the way cross town to kick some asses, there was no doubt in my mind that those girls had it coming," she said softly and closed her screen door behind us.

✽ BUSTING LOOSE

My grandparents' house was my favorite place to spend the night, even though we didn't do many sleepovers when we were young. Momma didn't believe in kids staying away from home at night.

"I'll keep my kids at home, and I want other folks to do the same," she said, the few times we dared to ask.

I was fourteen or fifteen when Momma started taking a weekend train trip to Chicago once a year. They were the only vacations I ever knew her to take. We had a host of cousins on Mother's side of the family living in the Windy City. Seleta, Momma's first cousin, was her best friend, next to Aunt Cynthia. Momma and Seleta talked on the telephone about once a month. They eventually started visiting each other whenever possible. Both women seemed like the black sheep of their respective nuclear families. They were single-parent mothers, had several kids apiece, and didn't like other people telling them what to do. I figured that was why they were so close.

Momma gave us two options for places to stay while she visited Cousin Seleta. We could stay with an adult cousin and her husband or with Mother. Albert chose our adult cousins most times because they cooked chitterlings for him. The smell of them made me throw up. Chitterlings were one of the few soul foods that Mother didn't cook or eat.

I always chose to stay with Mother and Daddy. They knew how to treat guests, especially their grandchildren. We ate full-course meals. Played outside later. Slept in big, warm, comfortable beds topped with hand-sewn quilts. And woke up every morning to the smell of breakfast on the stove.

Staying out later at night provided many opportunities for mischief. Robin and Arlene lived only a block away from our grandparents, so we often teamed up for one of our favorite pranks. We called it "raiding."

We'd sneak into the neighbors' backyards after dark and dump their metal trashcans all over their well-kept backyard lawns. The neighborhood was predominately white and mostly of Polish descent. A predesignated person threw the trashcan. The clanking against the ground was our signal to run. On a good night, we'd hit three backyards.

Other nights we traipsed to the corner tavern after dark to buy candy and swipe cherry and apple pies from a small back-window ledge. Kids couldn't come inside the bar and were required to go to the rear door.

After stealing the pie, which had been set out to cool, we had the nerve to sit on a nearby hill, behind the place, and eat it with our hands.

— ℛ —

"GIRL, YOU LOOK like a man with those bushy eyebrows. Come here and let me arch them for you," Valerie quipped, staring at me with a one-edge razor blade in her bony hand and a huge grin on her dark brown face.

"But I heard that once you start messing with your eyebrows, you have to keep it up," I protested. "And I don't know a thing about plucking eyebrows and know even less about using a razor."

Valerie's eyebrows were sleek and arched over her big brown eyes like a movie star's. My aunt had been shaping her eyebrows and wearing makeup for a couple of years.

Valerie was only ten months older than me but took pride in telling people that she was my aunt. Valerie knew more people than the rest of us combined and seldom missed a jumping party. She also traveled a lot. Our grandparents took her everywhere with them—church; vacations; annual trips to French Camp, Mississippi, to visit her grandparents; even Chain Lake District meetings, the Wolverine State Conference, and the National Baptist Conventions, where she met boatloads of young people.

At sixteen, Valerie was much more comfortable with people than I was. My aunt tended to be the life of every party. I loved being around her. I didn't worry about people looking at me as much whenever Valerie was around.

Valerie was as skinny as I was, but it didn't seem to bother her. I hated being thin. My legs looked like baseball bats—only bowed. Some of Valerie's friends started calling her Skinny Doogan. None of us kinfolk ever called her that, and I hated when other people did. But Valerie didn't seem to mind, so I kept my thoughts to myself.

My aunt looked glamorous, especially in makeup. Valerie's thick, bushy hair hung past her shoulders and flipped up on the ends. She favored Diana Ross, the lead singer of Motown's Supremes—big eyes and a broad, toothy smile and all. Valerie could sing, too, and knew it. We teased our aunt a lot about flipping her hair and acting like Diana Ross.

—— ❧ ——

I WAS FIFTEEN when I finally let Valerie arch my eyebrows for the first time. Momma had gone to Chicago, and we were staying with our grandparents.

Valerie and I were getting dressed for a backyard "going back to school party" that my aunt Mary was giving her daughter, Debra. Aunt Mary was Momma's fraternal twin. Valerie washed my hair in mineral oil, a clear, greasy substance that made my thin, dark brown hair look thicker, shinier, and coal black. My young aunt smoothed liquid makeup evenly across my face, then lined my lower eyelids with eyebrow pencil and painted my lips with soft, red lipstick. I looked in the mirror and smiled.

Valerie loaned me a pair of black stretch pants and a red buttoned-down cotton blouse. She looked me over one more time before we headed out the door and said, "You look kind a cute, Cool." The word "Cool" had become a term of endearment that all of us best-friend relatives often used when addressing each other, particularly if we were going to say something sensitive.

At the party, I did my usual thing—stand in a corner somewhere and look stupid. Valerie disappeared in a crowd of chattering teenagers as soon as we arrived. Trying to appear as if I were enjoying myself, I felt awkward and out of place. Most of my cousin Debra's guests lived on the South Side, so many of their faces were unfamiliar to me.

I didn't notice this good-looking guy approaching me until he asked me my name. I stammered and somehow finally got it out. He kept staring at my face. I looked down to keep from feeling so self-conscious.

"Your face is so pretty. You look just like a doll," he said.

I smiled but had no idea what to say. He smiled back. We stood around having small talk for about ten minutes. It was the first time any guy who was considered popular showed any interest in me. When he asked for my telephone number, I was sold on arched eyebrows, mineral oil and makeup.

✾ CHAD BUCHANAN

Chad Buchanan was a good-looking white boy with thick, dark, curly hair and an all-American smile and big dimples. He was one of the most popular boys at school. We had never said a word to each other until the summer of 1965.

Debra and I were walking from Rotary playground just before dark. An unfamiliar car pulled up alongside us as we strolled down the street next to the curb. There were two white guys inside. Chad Buchanan was one of them.

"Hey, do you know where Carla Gamble lives?" he asked, his big brown eyes peering up at me from inside the car.

I pranced up to the vehicle smiling. I gave them directions and ended up in a conversation with Chad.

"Would the two of you like to take a ride with us?" he asked after about ten minutes.

I broke my neck getting in the car. Debra followed my lead, but cautiously. I climbed in the backseat. Chad came back there with me. Debra climbed up front with a guy named Kit Giroux. A chubby, red-cheeked guy, Kit had a quart of beer with a bag wrapped around it sitting between his thighs on the seat.

A six-pack of beer stuck out from under the back of the front seat on the driver's side. Chad pulled it out, struggled to get two cans loose, then passed them forward. He smiled at me, popped the tops, then handed one to me. I took it and smiled back.

Warming up to each other was no problem, particularly after I drank one beer. This was my chance to act hip and cool. Nobody would know but Debra. And I knew my cousin wouldn't tell anybody. Though not good at it, I even had the nerve to flirt.

We cruised the black neighborhoods of the east and south sides of the city. We even stopped in Leake's Lounge parking lot, long enough to drink another beer. My chest stuck out. I wanted everybody in town to know that a white boy showed some interest in me, even though a lot of black guys didn't.

It was ten thirty when Chad suggested going to Ella Sharp Park. I had a curfew of eleven, and it was pitch black outside. But I agreed to go, knowing that a lot of teenagers went to the park to make out. Kit parked his car off the side of the road in a heavily wooded area that he seemed very familiar with. The two guys took some blankets out of the trunk, and each couple went separate ways.

I lost my virginity that night. Shocked and stunned by what was happening to me, I cried, "No stop! Please let me up."

He did. Immediately. The ride back was quiet. Chad let me out at the corner near my house, and stuck his head out the window to ask if he could see me again. I said "yes," and darted down the street with Debra right behind me

"What's wrong Jasmine?" she kept asking. "What happened?"

I didn't want to talk about it and said nothing—until my cousin gasped.

"Oh my God! Jasmine, you're bleeding. There's blood on the back of your pants."

I sped up, Debra still on my tail.

"Did you and Chad *do* something?" my cousin asked, breathing hard but keeping up.

"Yeah. But don't ever tell *nobody*."

"But what if Aunt Malena sees that blood on the back of your pants?" she asked.

"I don't know. Just follow close behind me when I walk through the door. If we can get to the stairway, I can make it upstairs without Momma seeing me," I said, terrified that I was bleeding, and not sure why.

Getting past Momma was easier than we expected. She was in her bedroom with the door closed. Debra and I hollered, "We're home," then quietly scrambled up the stairs. I ducked into the bathroom. Debra, who was spending the night with me, quickly undressed and climbed in bed. Lisa and Penny slept with Momma that night so that Debra and I would have enough room. My sisters loved sleeping with Momma. Momma seemed to like it as well.

Debra and I lay in bed that night, talking about the night's event. Embarrassed and ashamed, I told my cousin everything. She and Kit had just talked, which made me feel even worse. I felt so dirty and unclean. I took a bath and soaked in water, but nothing helped the physical pain for two more days. The mental and emotional pain lasted much longer. Losing my virginity at fifteen years old was something I'd have to deal with for the rest of my life.

✿ JACKSON HIGH SCHOOL

J
ackson High School looked huge to me. I never had any sense of direction, so finding my classes the first few weeks proved to be my most difficult and frustrating task.

My second major challenge in high school was lunch money. It wasn't cool to bring sack lunches in the 1960s. Peers thought those who did were poor. I talked to my homeroom teacher, Mrs. Godfrey, about a student job. She referred me to a white-haired woman who supervised the cafeteria. In exchange for a hot lunch everyday, the woman gave me a job working in a storage room turned snack shop located directly across from the lunchroom. I loved it.

Valerie was in the eleventh grade and had established a reputation as a fantastic singer. I loved to hear her sing. I admired my young aunt's popularity and wished I was half that well liked. I was still kind of stiff around guys I didn't know. People seldom commented on my looks, so I had to rely on my own perception. And it wasn't good. I don't know what I thought. But whatever it was, I didn't like it.

A few days after I started working, Valerie applied for a job and was hired. So instead of being together in an elective class, we worked together for an hour in the little snack room. I often teased my aunt about getting the job, because I knew our grandparents made sure Valerie had lunch money every day.

"Girl, you know you just took this job cause you want to be getting in everybody's business," I'd say. My aunt never denied it.

Valerie and I were closing the shop one afternoon when she noticed an unfamiliar young black male walking down the empty hallway. Wearing a waist-length dark green leather jacket, he was a clean-cut, good-looking guy with golden brown skin and freckles on his large, puffy nose. Valerie called him over to our counter, shouting, "Hey you! Come here."

He slowly walked over to where we stood.

"What's your name?" she said, half demanding, half flirting, and showing her big white teeth.

"Michael Fuller," he replied politely.

"You go to school here now?" Valerie continued. I stood quietly and watched my aunt at work.

"No. I'm a student at Jackson Junior College downtown," he said, smiling at her, then glancing at me.

Valerie asked him so many questions that I was embarrassed. He was on a break between classes that afternoon. He didn't have a girlfriend. He drove his own car. He lived at home with his parents and had one sister.

"And what's *your* name?" he asked, turning to me and catching me somewhat off guard.

"Jasmine Armstead," I said, trying to appear as confident as my aunt.

"Hey, I'm the one who called you over here," Valerie jokingly protested. "What you doing talking to my niece?"

Michael blushed. I did, too. Our eyes met again. The three of us talked for ten more minutes before he had to leave for his next class. Michael turned to me before walking away and asked if he could call me sometime.

"Sure," I said, then wrote my phone number on a piece of notebook paper and handed it to him. Never dreaming he'd call, I heard from him that same night, which floored me. I couldn't figure out what he saw in me.

— ❧ —

MICHAEL PLANNED to be a lawyer one day and work in some large city.

"Big cities scare me," I told him during one of our conversations. "I'm more of a small town girl."

I didn't have a clue as to what to do after graduation. I just knew that I didn't want to be a secretary. Many black girls at Jackson High School were directed down that career path. I liked writing and drawing. But no one ever advised me what to do with my interests. And I never asked.

Within weeks, I introduced Michael to Momma. She liked him. I could see it in her face when he reached to shake her hand. Momma even started letting me go to dances and parties more often, as long as Michael took me. He never kept me out past midnight, and always walked me to the door. He came inside whenever he picked me up and made sure he spoke to Momma.

Most guys who came to see me simply pulled up in front of our house and blew their car horn.

"I wish you would run out that door," Momma would say. "If they ain't got sense enough to get out and come inside, you better not take your behind out of this house."

Michael, who was nearly nineteen, turned out to be almost too nice. Less than two months after we met, he helped paint my bedroom when my family moved from Johnson to Plymouth Street. A few months later he started driving fifteen minutes out of his way to pick me up for school in the mornings. Michael bought me a bottle of Chanel No. 5 for my sixteenth birthday, February 2. It was the only gift I received. He also bought me a heart-shaped box of chocolates on Valentine's Day. I shared the candy with my sisters and brothers, then placed the empty box on the ledge over my bedroom door for decoration. The box looked so nice that I started collecting them.

Michael and I hugged and kissed a lot. I didn't like his kisses because they felt too sticky. We rode around town in his small red and white Chevy, talking, even more. I enjoyed that. It would have been easy to have sex with Michael every day. Momma and his parents trusted us just that much. But we only made love once. I liked Michael. I believed he loved me. And that made me nervous. Deep down inside, I didn't feel worthy of his attention and love, so I started seeing other guys.

✿ SPINNING

Still dressed in the clothes she wore to night school, a pair of brown elastic-waist pants and a white turtlenecked sweater, Momma exited her bedroom and strolled past me, rolling her eyes and not saying a word. I hated Momma's silent treatment. I'd rather that she would cuss me out or whip me than act as if I didn't exist. I had a knack for rubbing Momma the wrong way, so I stepped aside, trying my best to stay out of her path. My plans were to go to a waistline party that night, and I didn't want to do anything that might set Momma off.

I hurried into our small, green ceramic bathroom, where paint was peeling from the ceiling and the face bowl faucet had been dripping for nearly a month. I closed the door behind me and twisted the round metal knob on our claw-footed bathtub. Adjusting the water temperature, I half filled the deep white tub with really warm water. Then I squeezed a crumpled tube of Colgate toothpaste that was almost empty and brushed my teeth. I rinsed my mouth, then gargled with a bottle of Listerine stashed in back of the small wooden cabinet underneath our sink, the drain circled with a rust stain.

Lisa, Terrance, Penny, and Keith were watching television in the sitting room, an area between the living room and kitchen. I heard Momma fussing loudly in her bedroom on the other side of the bathroom wall. I soaped my face towel and tried not to listen.

"Now I wonder where Albert is," she fussed. "Him and Gloria Bennett's son left out here right after they came home from school. And here it is almost eight o'clock. Ain't no telling what they're doing out there in the streets. That boy is gonna mess around and make me break his darn neck one of these days."

That was my clue to get out of the house quickly. I was just getting off of a punishment. It was supposed to be for a month, but Momma had given me clemency after three weeks. I'd caught her in a rare mood earlier in the week. She was smiling. So I casually started talking about the upcoming waistline party on Friday night. Momma didn't roll her eyes, sigh loudly, or frown, which gave me enough nerve to ask if I could go.

"Please, Momma. I promise I'll get home on time this time," I begged in the sweetest voice possible, my eyes big and pitiful.

It worked. But Momma gave me her marching orders.

"Jasmine, you better have your behind home by midnight. I know you. Your little ass don't believe fat meat is greasy. Now, you can try me if you want to," she'd warned.

I immediately called Monica and made plans to meet at her house at eight the night of the party. We'd known each other since fifth grade. Her parents moved across the street from us on Page Avenue one summer from Mobile, Alabama. The family of seven had seemed a bit country at first, but before the summer ended we were sharing secrets and were as close as sisters.

The clock on the stove said seven fifteen when I rushed out of the bathroom. A towel wrapped around me, I hurried through the house and up the steps with my back still wet. Our bedroom didn't have a warm-air register, due to a mistake when previous owners remodeled the house, so my body shivered as I rambled through our scratched and nicked chest of drawers, trying to find underwear and nylons.

I plopped on the full-size bed I shared with my two sisters. The bed was so old that the metal springs punctured the thin mattress and scratched me during my sleep every now and then. I rubbed off-brand lotion on my body from face to feet. I greased my long hammertoes with Vaseline, making sure to smooth away all the ashy spots. I stood up and was slipping into my burgundy stretch pants when the sound of footsteps came from the stairway.

"Jasmine, Momma wants you," my ten-year-old sister, Lisa, hollered from the end of the hall. "She wanna know whose party you're going to."

"It's a waistline party on Milwaukee Street," I hollered back. "It's the one I told her about earlier this week. The Debbies are giving it."

Lisa trotted back downstairs.

I quickened my pace, pulling a pink mohair sweater over my head, which caused two of my pink hair rollers to fall out of my hair to the floor and roll under the bed. Not bothering to get them, I reached inside the closet and picked up my black pointed-toed pumps with an open heel from a corner. I pried both of them on, pinching my fingers in the process, then stood up and viewed my reflection in our window. The only mirror was on the medicine cabinet in the bathroom, and I wasn't going anywhere near Momma's bedroom again.

"Jasmine!" Lisa yelled up the steps, "Momma said who are the Debbies?"

"It's a club of snobby girls who think they're cute. I think the name is short for debutante, whatever that means," I hollered back while snatching the remaining rollers from my hair.

Lisa appeared in my doorway. Her face nearly dark as coffee, she furrowed her eyebrows.

"If they're so stuck up and you don't like the Debbies, then why are you going?" my little sister said softly, her small almond eyes widened, her nose spread across her face.

"Stop asking so many questions," I snapped, nosing closer to the window, combing and patting my hair into a bouffant hairstyle. Lisa trotted back downstairs.

I had just gripped the tarnishing brass front-door knob when Lisa called my name again. She was back in her favorite spot on the floor, two feet from the front of the television, when I peeked over my shoulder at her.

"Momma said she don't wanna have to come looking for you," she said, glancing up at me, then gluing her eyes back to the TV.

"Tell her she won't have to. I promise," I said, then quickly closed the door behind me and trotted around to Monica's house.

— ⸙ —

MONICA AND I walked down the Plymouth Street hill to the corner of East Avenue and stood under the big weeping willow tree, hoping that somebody would come along and give us a ride south. They always did. We had been standing in the cool autumn air for several minutes when a dark brown 1964 Buick Riviera with a cream-colored vinyl top pulled up. It was headed south. We hurried up to the passengers' side, and Albert rolled down the window. Maurice Washington, his best friend, was driving.

"Who's car ya'll got?" I asked my fourteen-year-old brother.

"It's Maurice's uncle Jimmy's new car," Albert stuttered.

"My uncle lets me drive a lot," Maurice added quickly. "I'm taking it back to him now. He lives on Stanley Street. Hop in."

The two of us scrambled into the backseat, glad to be off our feet. I preferred being barefoot to shoes any day, but wore flats outside the house, except when I was trying to be cute. I'd bought the fancy pumps that were killing my feet with my last paycheck of the summer. Albert and I had taken jobs working for the Neighborhood Youth Corps, a federally funded work program for disadvantaged teens.

"Albert, Momma's looking for you. She said she ain't seen you all day. And she's mad," I said, slipping off my shoes and rubbing my toes.

"She is?" he said, his voice changing from jovial to worried.

My brother turned and leaned over the cream-colored vinyl seat. He stretched his tall, lanky body toward me, his mouth close to my ear, as if he was going to whisper. But he spoke really loudly.

"What'd you tell her?" he asked, his voice a little slurred.

"Albert! Have you been drinking?" I asked my younger brother, pulling my head back so I didn't have to smell his breath. "Boy, if Momma finds out, she's gonna hit the ceiling. No. She's gonna kill you!"

"She won't know if you don't tell on him," Maurice said, turning his head around to look at me. I leaned forward and turned his head back around with my hand.

"Keep your eyes on the road. That's all we need is to get in an accident and get killed. Momma will kill us both for sure then," I said, straight-faced and serious as a heart attack.

Everybody cracked up laughing. It took me a second to realize the absurdity of my comment. I laughed until tears rolled down my face.

Maurice had driven a quarter mile down the street to the railroad tracks, and everyone was still laughing. Red lights started flashing. Bells started ringing. The black and white guard rail, installed after three people were killed by trains in two separate accidents, slowly lowered and bounced lightly before locking into place.

"That's gonna be a long-ass train. And it's got the nerve to be moving slow. We'll be here all night," Monica said. "I know that *somebody's* got some beer in this car, cause I can smell it. Let's pop some tops and get this party on the road while we wait."

"Right on with the right on," Maurice said, looking at me out of the corner of his eye.

He pulled out a six-pack of Schlitz malt liquor. Two were conspicuously missing. Maurice popped the top on one, then turned and handed it to us.

"Here, ya'll can split this one," he said to Monica and me. "Me and Albert will knock this one out."

Albert burst out laughing. Then he raised and looked at me in the backseat. I must have had the strangest look on my face because my brother laughed even harder.

"Y-Y-Ya'll must not know Jasmine. She ain't gonna drink after *nobody*. She won't even drink after us. And we're her own sisters and brothers," he said, all eyes on me, and my brother loving every minute of it.

"That's right," I said sheepishly. I was just glad that my brother told them before I did.

"Jasmine, you remember that time Momma got mad at you cause she asked for a swig of your orange Nehi pop," he continued, chuckling as he talked. "And you told Momma, 'You can have it.' Momma looked like she could have knocked you upside your head, Jasmine. Didn't she, Jasmine? D-D-Didn't she?"

"Aw, forget you Albert," I said playfully, throwing my hand up at him. "You're always trying to front somebody off. You sure are bold. All I know is that you better stop by a store to buy something for your breath before you go home. It smells like you've been drinking all day. And please go straight home. I don't want Momma mad when I come in tonight."

Maurice handed two cans of Schlitz, still dripping with mist, over the seat. I reached for one. Monica took the other. Tops popped. Fizz squirted in Monica's face, and a little got on the front of my sweater. I looked at her, rolled my eyes, pretending to be mad, then started wiping it off with my hand. The four of us drank beer and listened to the radio while waiting for the boxcars to pass.

— ❧ —

CARS OF ALL MAKES, models, and sizes were parked up and down Milwaukee Street. My heart started beating fast. I bobbed my head and popped my fingers. I couldn't get out of the car fast enough, opening the door before it completely stopped. Stumbling out, I remembered my shoes as soon as my feet hit the cool, damp ground.

"Wait! My shoes," I hollered as Maurice started the engine and pulled off. He heard me and stopped the car.

High-stepping on the damp grass and cool cement, I hurried to the car. Albert leaned over the seat and unlocked the back door. I opened it and grabbed my shoes from the floor, then quickly limped back to the curb, waving good-bye to my brother and his friend while trying to put my shoes on at the same time.

My pumps back on my feet, I trotted, trying to catch up with Monica. I liked hanging out with her. Next to family, she was my best friend. Monica knew how to talk to guys and attracted them like flypaper. Slender faced with pretty cinnamon brown skin, the girl was built like a "brick house." I used to secretly debate who had the best figure, Monica or my cousin Robin. Both looked good in anything they wore.

I could see shadows of teenagers dancing to the Motown sound through the windows of the gray, two-story house with aluminum siding. Monica was already in line and halfway to the porch, popping her pretty petite fingers by the time I hurried up to the steps and scooted behind her, cutting in front of several people and couples. I smiled. A few smiled back. It took five minutes before we reached the lit glass-enclosed porch, where two teenage females stood, measuring waists and collecting money.

A tall, fair-complexioned girl wearing dark green slacks and a pastel green mohair sweater measured each person's waist. Bangs hanging in her eyes and wavy black hair draped along her shoulders, she seemed friendlier with the guys than with the females. I watched her carefully wrap the seamstress tape around the belly of an overweight guy, her long fingernails neatly polished and shaped. A sparkling bracelet hung loosely from her wrist, which was so pale I could see greenish veins running up them like tree branches. A tiny diamond ring twinkled on the finger of her right hand. She made me sick.

Miss Mohair Sweater whispered something to her partner, who was dressed in a nice two-piece purple pantsuit with a tunic top. Her white blouse, with long, pointed white collars, made her look sharp as a tack. But her nametag hung lopsided on the jacket. Miss Tunic Top sported a "bad" short haircut that looked as if she'd just left the barbershop. Both females wore tags that read "Debbies Club Member" in bold black letters on a white background. Their first and last names were in smaller print, under it.

Miss Tunic Top's gold hoop earrings were a bit larger than silver dollars and gave her a bold, exciting look. I liked her style. She was the shorter of the two and collected the money. I watched her discreetly take the big guy's money and smile at him as he huffed and puffed through the door. Miss Tunic Top took up too much time trying to count people's money for me.

Monica and I never cared for members of the Debbies Club. They acted too snooty. The only reason we were attending their waistline party is because we had arranged to meet two guys from Grand Rapids there.

Monica stepped up to Miss Mohair Sweater, who stood on one side of the doorway that led from the porch to the house. My sistah friend raised her arms to get measured, and her black and red contoured blouse hiked up, revealing more of her hourglass figure. Monica looked so good that some girls turned up their noses and looked the other way.

Monica was so cool. While the girl measured her waist, she turned around slowly, giving everybody a better look and appearing to be bored to death.

"Nineteen cents," Miss Tunic Top said dryly, looking down her nose at Monica. Then me.

Monica reached her dainty hands into her brown and beige balloon purse, pulled two dimes from an inside zipped pocket, then gently handed them to the girl at the door. Miss Tunic Top's gold bangle bracelets jangled as she fiddled in the small shoebox, looking for a penny. She tilted the box from one side to the other until she found one, then handed it to Monica as if my friend had the plague.

That was all I needed.

I didn't raise my arms. I barely spread them from my sides. I wanted the snobby Debbie Club member to work for every penny.

"Twenty-one cents," Miss Tunic Top said, loud enough for everyone nearby to hear. It was bad enough that I was skinny as a toothpick, but now everybody knew I had a pudgy stomach, too.

I cut my eyes at both females. Then I felt for two dimes in the change compartment of my pink billfold that my dad had bought me. It was hard trying to hand her two dimes and a penny while hiding my chipped and unpolished fingernails. Earlier that day, I'd picked my nails so low that they bled. A nervous habit.

I quickly dropped the coins into Miss Tunic Top's hands and sauntered into the house, exaggerating every move.

Waistline parties were popular in the mid-1960s. Young people and clubs earned up to forty dollars a party, charging guests a penny for every inch of their waist. Most parties were held on the South Side, where many blacks who were "better off" lived. They seldom let East Side folks forget it either.

South Side girls couldn't stand me. I'd confront one of them in a hot minute, especially if I thought they were intentionally slighting me. Fighting gave me an illusion of respect that I couldn't get in most other places. But deep down inside, I felt terribly inadequate and hopelessly underprivileged, except when it came to one thing.

"They might have more material things. But I've got more brains," I'd tell myself, even though no one seemed to care much about that.

The waistline party was packed. Couples sat squashed together on a thick-armed, black leather sofa, trying to smooch and gazing in each other's eyes. Others were on the polished oak dance floor, cool jerking, bopping, and doing the cha-cha.

Monica and I edged our way to the dining room, hoping to find some space to sit down. There wasn't any. Young males leaned or stood against the walls, rapping to their honeys. A few strolled back and forth through the crowded house, holding their high-waist pants with one hand and swinging the other back and forth. Processed hair. Afros as big as watermelons. Thin gold chains around their necks. Polished white teeth and fresh breath.

The wallflowers sat around the edges of the room. Arms folded. Hands rested in their laps. I hated whenever I had to sit and watch others dance. Dancing was too much a part of my spirit. It made me feel free and alive. But offers to dance from local guys were few and far between.

Weaving our way through the throng, Monica and I made it over to a big glass punch bowl, centered on the dining room table. A guy with pretty brown skin and thick, wavy, processed hair pulled Monica over as soon as we got there. I persevered on. Alone. Separating two white paper cups from a stack at one end of the table, I filled them nearly full of the Kool-Aid and Sprite with sliced lemons mixture.

Glancing up for a second, I noticed three club members whispering and elbowing each other and eyeing me. I was ready to go right then.

I picked up the two cups of punch and squeezed back through the crowded room, looking for my running buddy. Red beverage splashed on my hands each time someone bumped my elbow. I found Monica sitting on the steps leading upstairs. She was chatting with the foxy guy with processed hair.

"I'm leaving. I'm getting out of here before somebody really ticks me off and I have to show my behind in here," I said, handing Monica one of the paper cups. "I thought for sure those guys from Grand Rapids would have gotten here by now."

"Just be cool now, Jasmine. They said they were coming," Monica said softly, her hand motioning me to settle down. "Let's wait another half hour. And if they aren't here by then, we can leave."

A half hour passed, and no sign of our invited guests. Monica had several offers to dance and accepted a few. I got several glances from the opposite sex, but none of the boys invited me to the dance floor. So while Monica "boo-ga-looed," with most of the good-looking guys, I stood by myself with a fake smile on my face.

"Maybe they think I'm too rough. I've been in more fights than most girls around here," I thought while standing there, feeling more and more uneasy. "Or maybe they think I'm too poor. It's probably both."

I never could figure Jackson guys out. They'd throw quick smiles my way, but seldom approached me. Years later a guy would admit that he and others thought I was stuck up in high school. That blew my mind.

Monica swished her tail off the dance floor, smiling softly and batting her long eyelashes at a guy neither of us knew. We were just about ready to go home when the guys from Grand Rapids walked through the front door.

Most eyes in the room followed them as they strolled up to us. My beau, Peter Burton, had a huge smile on his cocoa brown face and was dressed in a two-piece tan walking suit, with pointed-toe shoes to match.

"Hey Jasmine, what's happening?" he said, looking around, flashing his pearly whites with a small gap between his two front teeth. "People are cramped like sardines in here. You want to stick around and dance or go for a ride?"

"Go for a ride," Monica and I both said eagerly at the same time. We looked at each other and burst out laughing.

— ε —

PARKED ON A dead-end street, the only sounds were loud breathing in the back-seat of the car. I scooted closer to Peter. We sat in the front seat listening to my favorite song, "Baby I Need Your Loving," by the Four Tops, on his eight-track cassette player.

"Did I ever tell you that I used to live on this street?" I asked a bit too loudly.

The hard breathing in the back stopped.

"We used to stay right there," I continued, pointing to the house, second to the end. "I don't think I ever got over having to leave Pleasant School. I loved Pleasant School."

"Jasmine, can we talk about that some other time?" Peter whispered in my ear, and giving me a look I had grown to recognize. "Baby, don't you want to get to know me better?"

"Of course I do," I replied. "Where do we start? When did you first start driving?"

Reggie sighed loudly in the backseat. I could hear him and Monica rustling to sit up.

"Man, can't you take care of your babe?" he said, slightly agitated. "What are ya'll doing up there? I know you've got bucket seats—but damn!"

"I'm talking to my lady, square," Peter replied softly and gazing at me. "That's why I like her. She's different."

I glanced at Peter and smiled. He knew me better than I thought. Juggling several different dudes from several different cities sometimes made it hard to remember who knew what about me.

"When's the last time ya'll have been skating here?" I asked, looking at Peter, then turning to Reggie in the backseat, hoping I hadn't spoiled their evening.

"It's been a while," Reggie replied, with resignation in his voice. "These Jackson dudes don't like us coming to town. They get all jealous and go to wanting to 'thump.' And Reggie Woods ain't got time to be boxing nobody. I'm a lover, not a fighter."

"I know what you mean," Monica said. "I ain't gon get dusty for nobody either."

I didn't say a word. Fighting had become a part of my blood.

"Damn baby, your eyes are as big as headlights," Reggie suddenly said to me, catching me totally off guard. I was hurt and embarrassed.

"You've got the nerve. Your eyes are big, too. And they're popped eyes, on top of it," I shot back.

"Okay, ya'll, I've got some Boone's Farm apple wine in the trunk," Peter said. "Ya'll want a drink?"

I looked at the clock on the dashboard. Eleven thirty.

"I'll take a drink, but I've got to be home by twelve. My momma's been ticked off at me for weeks about staying out too late," I said.

——— ℯ ———

"YOU THINK YOU'RE slick, you little hussy," Momma yelled with rage in her eyes. "James Moore called here tonight asking for you. I know you put him up to doing it. You just wanted to see if I had gone to bed yet."

James Moore was the guy from Lansing who had the one-year-old son. He and I still went together but hadn't seen each other in a month.

"I don't know what you're talking about Momma. I ain't seen James. Last

I knew, he'd gone back to Lansing to live. I didn't even know he was in town, Momma. I'm telling you the truth. I swear I didn't put him up to calling here," I said pleadingly.

Momma didn't believe me and had obviously made up her mind to whip me long before I had gotten home. And I was on time. She reached for a thick, leather belt, which hung over the back of the rocking chair in our middle room, and whipped me until she got tired.

I was so hurt and so mad. Yes, I had been staying out too late. But this time I was knocking on our door five minutes *before* midnight. And yes, I had been with some guys, but not James. And nothing sexual happened. We didn't hurt anybody or anything. I drank half a cup of wine and came home.

Every swat Momma gave me hurt ten times worse because she was whipping me for something I didn't do. It felt as if Momma unleashed sixteen years of frustration on me, calling me all kinds of "lying wenches" and "lying little hussies." I stood there and took it with tears streaming down my face. Each time the belt came down on me, I flinched but refused to make a sound.

Sixteen years of anger, bitterness, and frustration had built up in me also. After a nearly ten-minute whipping, I couldn't hold my tongue any longer. I waited until she had finished and had laid the belt down on the couch, then told her what I thought.

"I'm sixteen years old, and you're still whipping me like I'm some child," I yelled at her as she strolled toward the kitchen, trying to catch her breath. "And this time you're whipping me for something I really didn't do. I'm sick of it! That's it. I'm not taking no more whippings from you!"

Momma stopped and took a few deep breaths. Then she calmly picked up the telephone and started dialing numbers. She was still staring at me when my dad answered the other end.

"You're daughter just got through telling me that she wasn't taking no more whippings. So I suggest you come get her right now before I kill her," she said, emotionless.

Daddy was at our house in less than three hours. I was sitting in the living room, bags packed and all, waiting on him at four thirty in the morning. I stood up. My dad walked up to me, looking tired and wearing a disheveled Hawaiian shirt. Standing toe to toe, Daddy looked me straight in the eye and spoke almost as calmly as Momma had.

"You're crazier than I thought," he said, his voice full of indignation. "Even I know better than to tell your momma something like you said tonight. And I'm a grown-ass man."

I wiped away tears with my bare hands and said nothing. I knew better. Daddy could argue until the cows came home. Half an hour later we were on the highway, headed back to Flint. Daddy lectured me all the way, implying that I was staying out late at night to have sex. I quietly told him my side of the story. I even admitted the times I'd had been intimate. He still didn't quite believe me.

"Well, let me tell you something, young lady," he said, giving me a quick glance. "If your *weren't* out having sex at three o'clock in the morning, you *should've* been. Ain't a damn thing in the streets at that time of the morning but people who are up to no good or who are looking for a woman to screw. I'm a man and I know."

— ❧ —

"MALES HAVE TWO types of girlfriends—one they can sleep with anytime they want and one they take home to Momma. And the one they take home to Momma is the one they respect and will probably end up marrying," Daddy told me during one of his late-night lectures.

He told me he was "schooling" me about men. I got so tired of hearing him that I began to think the man was obsessed. Living with him wasn't as great as I'd thought. Daddy didn't like any of the males who came to visit me. They were guys I'd met in Jackson who lived in Flint. They'd driven down to see me and my best-friend cousins and running buddies on numerous occasions. My dad would sit in the living room with his arms folded and watch every move we made while squirming and rolling his eyes.

"I shouldn't have to tell no respectable young man to take his hat off in my house," Daddy barked after one visit.

My guests usually left after a short while. I would have too, given the way Daddy treated them all. One day I discovered that Daddy had been reading my mail. That was something Momma never did. He followed me to school several times without me knowing and even spoke to a police officer about his problem child. I felt that everyone was really overreacting.

One night my dad challenged me. He swore that James Moore, the guy with the baby, cared nothing about me except for what he could get.

"But he ain't getting nothing, Daddy. We've never done anything. You can ask him," I said, weary from our nightly debates.

"I'm gonna do better than that," he snapped. "I'm going to prove to you just how little Mr. James Moore really thinks of you."

My dad sent the guy a Western Union telegram. He insisted I stand right there with him in the drugstore when he did it. The message read: *Please come to Flint. It's an emergency. I need you. Love, Jasmine.*

"Now we'll see how long it takes for you to hear from him," Daddy said, fuming because James had sent me money for a bus ticket back to Jackson. He had found out by reading another of my letters.

James never showed up. He didn't call or write. A week later Daddy was still grinning and saying, "I told you so."

I was hurt and angry at my dad *and* James. But Daddy proved his point. The guy didn't love me enough to respond, regardless of whether we were having sex or not. I never felt the same about James again.

Christmas vacation came, and I caught the bus back to Jackson to visit. I never returned to Flint to live as a teenager.

ALBERT SMELLED LIKE ALCOHOL

Albert came home around midnight and flopped down in the living-room chair with his brown winter coat still on. It was Tuesday. Our curfew was nine o'clock on school nights. I stopped doing my homework in front of the television and watched Momma saunter over to where Albert sat. She stood over him. He stared into space.

"Albert, have you been drinking?" she asked, with the familiar edge in her voice.

My brother sat silently looking straight ahead. Momma repeated herself two or three times. She got the same response. Momma leaned over and smelled his breath.

Smack!

She slapped him upside his head so hard that everybody in the house stopped what they were doing. Albert started rising up slowly out of his chair. He glared at Momma with dark brown eyes that made me nervous. It made Momma uneasy, too. It was written all over her face.

"No, Albert. Don't do it, Albert," I kept thinking to myself, prepared to intervene.

No one breathed for several seconds. It seemed like an eternity. My brother finally slumped back into his chair and hung his head. Momma walked away.

— ৽ —

I DON'T KNOW when Albert lost interest in school, but the kids used to tease him about being in the "dumb room." They knew better than to say anything bad about any of my relatives around me. I had a short fuse when it came to my kin.

About a third of the black males at East Junior High were placed in Group III classes. The back of our report cards indicated that Group III meant slow learners. Most classes were predominately black, and students had been tracked from one grade to the next. By high school, most of the black males in Group III had become more interested in skipping school, drinking Boone's Farm apple wine, and having run-ins with the law than learning.

One day I ran into my brother just outside his high school counselor's office. His face torn up, he appeared troubled about something.

"Jasmine, you know what that man just asked me? He gon ask me if I ever thought of dropping out of school," he stuttered.

I felt sorry for my brother, but had no idea what to do. Struggling with my own teenage issues, I could barely help myself. As children, I felt I had all the answers for my sisters and brothers. I called all the shots as well. If I wanted to play school, everybody played school. If I wanted to play restaurant or house, Lisa, Albert, Penny, Terrance, and Keith knew better than to object—even though most of them had always been taller and bigger than me.

By sixth grade Albert had me by half a foot. His size made it tougher for me to get my way. Before that, if he refused to go along with my plans, we'd battle.

"Y'all better cut that mess out before I come in there and whip the shit out of both of you," Momma would holler from her bedroom, usually while our arms were locked around each other's necks.

We eventually learned to fight quietly. Sometimes we battled for five or ten minutes without making a sound. But Albert continued to grow bigger and stronger than me, until I had to resort to pinching and biting. He hated that and always gave up, complaining that wasn't "fighting fair." I was thirteen when I began choosing my battles much more carefully with my younger brother. By sixteen, we didn't fight at all.

✤ THE OTHER SIDE OF BLUES

"I can't wait for Michael's mother to meet you," a woman walked up to me and said after church service one Sunday afternoon. "My sister-in-law said that all Michael talks about is Jasmine, Jasmine, Jasmine."

That did it. I wasn't about to meet Michael's mother. We were getting far too close for my comfort. I started going to parties with my running buddies again instead of spending time with him. That seemed to increase the tension between Momma and me, although she seldom involved herself in my relationships with the opposite sex.

"College boys are too square," I remember telling her one day after listening to her fuss about my "hoodlum boyfriends."

One night Michael came to visit me. I didn't want to be bothered. After an hour or so of us sitting together on the couch, I couldn't take any more. Michael was stroking my hands and gazing deep into my eyes as if to somehow revive my feelings, which were all but gone. His touch had begun to annoy me. Even his conversation had started sounding dull and boring.

"Michael, I just want to be friends from now on," I said firmly, after listening to his favorite song by Dionne Warwick, "A Message to Michael." We must have listened to it a dozen times. He appeared to have tears in his eyes when he left. I closed the door behind him and gave a sigh of relief, not noticing that Momma had been watching.

"Jasmine, what did you say to Michael? That boy looked like he was crying when he left here."

"I told him the truth," I said, beginning to resent Momma's affection for him.

"You make me sick!" she snapped. "Now if Michael was one of those hoodlums out there in the streets, you'd be all up in his face. But that's all right, sister. Cause you'll learn. You'll learn."

— ๛ —

ONE SATURDAY NIGHT Monica and I caught a ride to a waistline party on the south side of town. Momma was at night school and had no idea I was going. My impulsive nature got me in more trouble than I'd like, especially as a teenager.

"Tell Momma that I left with Michael," I told my sisters and brothers, knowing she'd be okay with that. I hadn't seen or talked to Michael in two days.

The party was jumping. Good-looking guys from out of town and driving snazzy cars were all over the place. Monica knew two overdressed dudes from Battle Creek. She strolled over to them with me right behind her. She introduced me, and the four of us chatted. They eventually invited us to go riding.

Jackson may have had plenty of good-looking women, but the city fell down when it came to places for black teenagers to go. So after several ten-minute trips from one side of town to the other, and circling "the corner" half a dozen times, the two guys suggested riding back to Battle Creek with them. It was eleven thirty, and I wasn't sure how mad Momma would be when I got home anyway. So I agreed to go.

They took us straight to one of their apartments, I didn't even know whose. With no input from Monica and me—or at least from me—we split up and went to separate bedrooms and were supposed to have sex. I still had no idea what to do in bed, so I just kissed and let him do his thing. He got mad.

"What's the matter with me?" he asked, suddenly rising up from the bed. "I ain't good enough for you or what?"

He snatched his glasses off the table and threw them against the bedroom wall. I had no idea what he was talking about and was too afraid to ask. We didn't say much to each other the rest of the night, which left me wondering why I ever came. We arrived back in Jackson around four o'clock in the morning. I knew Momma was going to wear me out.

"So what are you gonna do?" Monica asked, as we sat in the apartment of a female friend, trying to figure out our next move.

The friend was Momma's age, but young people hung out there a lot. We'd asked the guys from Battle Creek to drop us off there. I was too afraid to go home.

"I'm tired of getting whippings and getting put on punishments," I thought, wishing I'd made better choices the night before.

We decided to run away. We'd go somewhere and never have to live by rules again. It seemed to be our only recourse at the time. We knew that a Greyhound bus ride to Albion, seventeen miles away, cost only seventy-five cents. We'd made the trip a number of times over the past year.

"All we got to do," I said, "is get out to the bus station," which was located on the outskirts of town.

Fearing someone would see us if we struck out walking, I called Michael. He agreed to come take us, but didn't sound happy. I refused to tell him what caused me to stay out so late. Sensing he was mad at me, I didn't care. All I wanted to do was get to the bus station. When he turned down Plymouth Street where I lived, I started yelling.

"Where are you taking me?"

He didn't say anything.

I started screaming at him, demanding that he stop and let us out. Monica was in the backseat, agreeing, and poised to jump out at the first opportunity. He pulled up in front of my house, and I spotted Momma standing on the porch with her hands on her hips.

I tried grabbing the car door to jump out, but Michael was quick. He snatched my wrist and squeezed it tightly. I wrestled with him, trying to free myself. The look in his eyes and the strength of his grip told me that he was madder than I realized.

"Let go of me, Michael. What are you doing? You know I'm never gonna forgive you for this."

His face was expressionless.

We tussled in the car for a second or two, as he tried to shift the car into park. Monica jumped out and ran up the hill toward home. Michael, unable to hold me and get out of the car at the same time, let go of my wrist momentarily. I jumped out and broke out running down the Plymouth Street hill, with no idea where I was going. I just wanted to go the opposite direction of Momma. Michael ran me down and dragged me back, kicking and screaming all the way.

"That's all right Michael," Momma hollered, poking her head out the screen door. "Let her go!"

Then she yelled at me.

"And Jasmine, you *better* not run."

Michael let go, and I took off running again. This time he caught me and grabbed me around my waist. I put up a heck of a struggle, but Michael carried me back to the house. Up the steps and onto the enclosed porch we went before he set me down, two feet from Momma. She and I stood face to face. Momma thanked Michael for his troubles, and marched behind me into the house.

"Why'd you do it Jasmine?" she asked, her voice not angry or accusatory.

I sensed a hint of compassion, which was so surprising that it was a little unsettling.

She put me on a punishment for a month, but let me off after two-and-a-half weeks.

— ℈ —

THE SECOND TIME I ran away the consequences were a lot more serious. This time I was minding my own business, doing homework, when Natasha Grimes, a neighbor and occasional running buddy, knocked on our door. She was crying.

"My momma just put me out, Jasmine. I kept telling you she was going to do it."

Natasha and her mother had been having some run-ins. Some of the things she told me her mother said were hard to believe. Half of it I didn't—until the night we ran away.

Now I had absolutely no reason to leave home. Momma and I had been getting along pretty good, relatively speaking. I had advised Natasha to ignore her mother's comments.

"That's what I do sometimes, just to keep from arguing," I explained.

According to Natasha, that didn't work. Her coat in hand, Natasha told me the whole story.

"When my momma started yelling and screaming at me, I did what you said, Jasmine. I went in my room and lay across my bed. But Momma kept calling me names anyway. And when she came into my bedroom with my coat and threw it on me, saying, 'Get out of my house,' I knew I had to go," Natasha said, crying uncontrollably.

I decided to go with her. Momma was at night school. I put my homework away, grabbed my coat, and we started walking down Plymouth Street—going to the South Side, of course. Less than two blocks from my house, a guy we barely knew offered us a ride. It was a chilly October night so we were thrilled to get into a warm car.

We rode around talking for an hour or so and told him Natasha's whole story. He offered to let us stay at his apartment. Now this man looked a little older than Momma, so I knew something was up. But both of us were hungry and tired.

"There's a second bedroom upstairs," he said, smiling. "I'm going on up to bed. You two just make yourselves comfortable."

"Don't you go up those stairs, girl," I told Natasha when she decided to go to bed. "I don't trust him. I'm gonna sleep right here in this chair."

She did, too.

Just before daylight the man was standing over me with the angriest look on his face. He spoke, staring directly at me.

"I bet this was your idea, wasn't it?"

I just looked at him.

"Get your coats and get the hell out of my house!" he said. "I try to help you out and give you a place to sleep, and you're going to act like this. Get out right now and take your little friend with you."

It was so cold and chilly that morning that we ended up sitting in a twenty-four-hour laundry to keep warm. Daylight came and we struck out walking, with no idea where to go or what to do. Another male we vaguely knew stopped and offered us ride. We told him everything.

We spent the entire day at his house, watching people come and go. The place was nasty and had very little furniture. The things going on in the shabby, two-story house on Russell Street fascinated me. People were drinking and smoking everywhere. A few couples lay in bedrooms with the doors wide open, smooching on beds that were stripped of everything except the mattress.

We stayed half the day, long enough to bum enough money for a bus ticket to Albion, again. Damon Edwards, one of my most devoted boyfriends, lived there. Damon drove his little black Corvair to my house nearly every day after getting off work at Cornings. He loved jazz. Momma did, too. So they hit it off almost as quickly as she and Michael had. His visits slacked up after we had words about me seeing other guys. But I figured he'd still welcome Natasha and me with open arms. That wasn't quite the way things went.

We sat on Damon's steps in the cold for five hours, waiting for him to come home. He worked swing shifts, and a neighbor said he probably wouldn't get off until midnight. Sitting there, huddled up, hungry, and nearly freezing to death, I kept asking myself, "Why did you do this, Jasmine? Why?"

Damon agreed to let us stay at his apartment, reluctantly. Natasha slept on the couch. I slept with Damon. He wanted to have sex, so I did, even though I was exhausted from being on the run for more than twenty-four hours. I fell asleep right afterward. The next thing I knew, a flashlight was shining through the window against his bedroom walls.

I jumped out of bed, the room still dark, and dashed over to the window. Standing on the sidewalk outside was a policeman, with Natasha's mother and stepfather right beside him. I ducked and rushed to the living room and tapped Natasha. Damon sat straight up in the bed, looking scared to death.

"The police is outside with your parents," I whispered to Natasha in the dark. "Quick, get under the bed."

We scurried back into the room and hid under Damon's bed. He answered the door. I could hear voices talking, but couldn't tell what they were saying.

"Stay down," I whispered to Natasha, as we lay under the bed, our heads turned sideways because the springs were so low.

"Okay. Get up. Let's go. Which one are you?" a male voice said. I opened my eyes and saw a white police officer lying on the floor, looking dead in my face.

Dressed in a pair of Damon's briefs and a T-shirt, I scooted out from under the bed. I had bathed and put on some of his clothes as soon as we had settled into his apartment.

The policeman didn't see Natasha, who was still hiding under the bed. He asked where she was, and I started stammering.

"Here I am," she said, wiggling her way from under the bed, face down. By then her mother had come inside.

We didn't have time to get anything, not even my dirty clothes, before we were marched out the front door. Outside, Natasha's mother thanked the policeman, then gave us the evil eye. I whispered and asked the officer if he could take me home.

"Jackson County is out of my jurisdiction," he replied.

No sooner had the man pulled away and we had climbed into the backseat of Natasha's parents' car, her mother started beating my friend with her fists, stretching all over the seat. She called Natasha names I'd never heard any mother call her child. I cowered in the corner of the seat, not believing what was happening. The woman cussed, screamed, and carried on so that by the time a policeman on the highway pulled us over, I jumped out of the car and ran and hid behind him.

"Everyone get out of the car," he ordered. Everyone did.

The officer eyed a toy gun lying on the backseat of the car, then pulled Natasha and me aside. He asked several questions.

"Please, can you give me a ride home? I'm too scared to ride back with her," I said, pointing my head toward the mother. He couldn't either.

We climbed back into the car, and the woman went berserk. She pounded Natasha mercilessly while I pressed up against the seat, trying to go through it.

"Ain't no telling what y'all been doing with that boy. You could have been prostituting for all we know!" she screamed.

I thought the woman was losing her mind and practically ran through our front door when we arrived home. She came behind me, smiling and acting as if everything had gone "peachy smooth." A transformed person, just that quickly. I didn't say a word—until she left. Then I told Momma exactly what the woman had said to me.

"Well, I'm sure as hell through with her," Momma said.

She and the woman had been close acquaintances before we ran away. But when Momma said something, a person could just about put money on it. And so it was. They had little to do with each other after that.

✺ JUNIOR PROM

L ooking in the bathroom mirror, I lightly patted my bouffant hairdo, turning
my head from one side to the other, admiring my appearance. Not a strand
out of place. My makeup looked perfect, and Valerie had loaned me the pink
bridesmaid's dress she'd worn in Arlene's wedding. Robin planned to wear hers,
too. We were excited about dressing alike for our junior prom.

My date, Charles Wallace, was from Flint. Tall and slender, his smooth brown
skin and stylish clothes always made him appear as if he had just stepped out of
a fashion magazine. Some of my friends said Charles and I looked like sister and
brother, probably because we both had high cheekbones, were the same complexion, and wore serious looks on our faces.

I met Charles through some mutual friends who had been driving down from
Flint on the weekends. We hit it off right away. We talked and smooched the first
day. We spent hours talking on the telephone several nights a week and saw each
other at least one weekend a month. Charles was fun loving, independent, and
handsome as all get out. I was feeling pretty good about myself—dating a man
who worked at General Motors, owned a nice car, and had his own apartment.
The only thing I didn't tell Momma was that he was twenty-one years old. I was
seventeen.

Momma planned to throw me an "after party" the night of the prom. It was
the first time she'd shown any real interest in my high school activities. My home
life and love life were on the right track for a change.

Charles called me every night the week leading up to the Saturday night
prom. During our last conversation before the prom, he asked me something I
had managed to avoid talking about up until then.

"Are you going to give me some after the prom?" he quietly asked.

"Maybe," I answered coyly, knowing good and well that engaging in sex on my junior prom night was a strong possibility. That was probably one of the reasons he agreed to be my date.

— ❧ —

THE PROM WAS a big letdown. I had envisioned dancing and finger popping and just having a good ole time. Everyone was standing by the wall, whispering and talking to their dates. A few weren't even doing that. No one danced, probably because the music sounded like a cross between the Big Band sound and elevator music. I didn't recognize a single song. The music was by white performers. The majority of students and all the chaperones were white. I felt as if we had landed on another planet. Everyone was polite to each other, but few ventured outside of their own little cliques.

People from Flint knew how to party, so I was slightly embarrassed by our high school "event of the year." But Charles didn't seem to mind. He was the perfect gentleman. An hour and a half after we arrived, I suggested leaving early. We had planned to drive to Ann Arbor, a forty-five-minute drive away, for dinner, then return to Jackson for my after party.

We were heading toward the highway when Charles stopped at a motel room he had rented earlier that evening. He had planned to spend the night in Jackson rather than drive back to Flint after my party. I sat in the car while he took some belongings inside. A few minutes later Charles appeared in the door.

"Jasmine, I left my cummerbund in the car. I think it's in the backseat. Can you get it for me please?" he said.

Knowing that going inside was risky, I did it anyway. I had every reason to trust Charles. Besides, I'd decided that we'd probably have sex, but it would have to be after my party.

The minute I walked through the door and we came face to face, he pulled me up to his chest, then hugged and kissed me. We ended up on the bed. And by the time I started resisting and saying "no," things had gone too far.

I was quiet afterward and asked Charles to take me home. He put up no argument and reassured me that everything was okay. I listened and believed him.

We walked into my house, and it was packed with classmates and friends.

"Where in the world have you been?" Momma asked, her voice agitated, her eyes piercing.

"It took us a long time to get seats at the restaurant in Ann Arbor," I mumbled, guilt written all over my face.

Momma cut her eyes at me, then hurried back into the kitchen without saying another word. The truth was, we never made it to dinner. We didn't have time.

—— ℀ ——

CHARLES CONTINUED to call me two or three times a week. I never brought up what had happened at the motel on prom night, and he didn't either—until my period didn't come the next month.

"How do I know I've been the only one?" Charles casually asked when I told him.

"Because I haven't had sex with that many guys in my whole life. And you were the first one in a long time."

The other end of the telephone was silent.

"Do you believe me?" I gently asked.

"Yeah . . . I guess so."

Charles's question hurt me. Suspecting I was pregnant was scary enough, but having him question his paternity made things twice as bad.

My insecurity returned. Charles's telephone calls dwindled to none, and for the first time I started calling him. Most times no one answered. When he did, Charles acted distant, not saying much.

It all came to a head one hot summer night at the skating rink. My cousin Debra rushed in and whispered to me that Charles was parked out front with another girl. I couldn't get my white, high-top roller skates off fast enough. Rushing up to a 1965 greenish blue Buick Impala with Flint license plates, I snatched open the car door.

"Get out," I demanded, glaring at the girl and ready to pounce. "What do you think you're doing with my boyfriend? Has he told you about us?"

She looked at Charles. He glanced at me as if I were a pest. He rose up and whispered something to the driver, then the girl. She pulled the door closed, scratching my leg in the process, then they drove off. I stood there, hurt and humiliated in front of all my peers. I was devastated.

I don't remember telling Momma about me being pregnant. But I know I did. I remember hearing her tell Aunt Cynthia on the telephone.

Three weeks later I ended up in the hospital having a miscarriage. A little more than two months pregnant, I hadn't seen or heard from Charles since the incident outside the skating rink. He still came to Jackson because Debra saw his car on the South Side more than once. She called and told me every time. The Sunday I was admitted to the hospital, Debra saw him again. She told him about me. I was so glad to hear his voice when he called my hospital room.

"I'll be up there to see you just as soon as I make one more stop," he said softly. I never saw or heard from Charles again.

Family members never mentioned me being pregnant. Even when Mother and Daddy came to see me, the subject never came up. My dad drove down from Flint during my brief hospital stay, too. I overheard him and Momma talking.

"Jasmine didn't need no baby, anyway," she said.

I got out of the hospital, licked my wounds, and kept on stepping.

❋ CORDELL WALKER

"Next," I hollered, sitting on top of the green picnic table at Rotary playground one hot summer afternoon in 1966. Dressed in yellow Bermuda shorts and a sleeveless, yellow-print blouse with a white collar, I waited my turn, along with a dozen other young people. Most were older teenage males wanting to take on the reigning king. I never tried to master Ping-Pong like I did most things. I played because it polished my reflexes.

Barely an hour had passed when I noticed a guy from high school glimpsing at me. I flirtatiously smiled back. Leaning against a shanty post, his arms folded across his chest, Cordell Walker reminded me of a tanned Paul Newman.

Three years older than me, Cordell had just graduated from high school. He had returned to get his diploma after dropping out for a few years. I never cared for his tough-guy image. It reminded me of a bully. And bullies and I never hit it off. But sitting on the picnic table that hot day in July, I decided to take a closer look at Cordell.

He was definitely the right color—high yellow. He was the right height, about five foot eleven. His hair was wavy, and he had pretty white teeth. When he smiled, his small dimples showed. And I loved his hazel green eyes.

"If his clothes weren't so wrinkled and matched better, and he combed his hair, he'd make a decent-looking catch," I thought, still exchanging goo-goo eyes with my prospective beau.

This was several weeks after my miscarriage, and I was feeling pretty rejected, although I tried not to show it. Starving for a male's attention, I threw a flirtatious smile his way, batting my big brown eyes and swinging my tanned legs. Our eyes showed interest every time they met.

Cordell finally swaggered over to the picnic table, and by the time my turn came to play Ping-Pong, he and I were carrying on a full-blown conversation. I became even more interested in him after discovering he was dating the female art director. She came to Rotary playground on Tuesdays and Thursdays to teach arts and crafts.

"I didn't think he had it in him. She must know something I don't," I thought.

I started watching them interact. She seemed comfortable with his loud laughter and crass speech, so I worked at getting past them, too. The more I saw him and her together, the more I wanted Cordell for myself.

"Girls are always taking my men. I'm gonna start doing the same thing to them," I thought.

A senior in college and very nice dresser, the art director was four years older than me. She presented a formidable challenge, but I wasn't worried. She was slightly overweight and walked around the playground like Miss Goody Two-shoes, treating most young people with little regard, including me. The more I was around her, the easier it was to dislike her. And before the summer had ended, Cordell and I were seeing each other on a regular basis. He'd dumped Miss Goody Two-shoes for me.

— ҩ —

"I GOT MY LETTER today," Cordell said on the telephone one night, then laughed with his usual cockiness.

"What letter?" I asked, smiling, while twisting the curly telephone receiver cord around my forefinger.

"The one that starts off, 'Greetings, this is Uncle Sam,'" he replied, as if getting drafted into the United States Army was no big deal. It was September 1966, and the Vietnam War was escalating.

I was scared for Cordell. Several high school graduates I knew were already fighting in Vietnam. One had been killed. Another was missing. Now my boyfriend received orders to report at the National Guard Armory on October 20, less than two months away.

Every time I thought about it, I got heartsick. Cordell and I had been dating for three months, and our relationship was just beginning to blossom. I had avoided having sex with him, even though he asked often. I still wasn't comfortable with sex. I really didn't know what to do in bed and, more important, feared getting pregnant again.

"When are you going to give it up?" he asked time and time again. "You sure know how to hurt a man."

I made up every excuse imaginable. I'm on my period. I don't believe in doing it in cars. It's past my curfew. My momma will be home from work any minute—anything to keep Cordell at a safe distance sexually. It worked.

Cordell, as crude as he was, brought a refreshing change to my wounded love life. His sculpted body and tough-guy image made me feel safe. And I needed to feel protected.

✿ DIVISIONS

Momma was sitting in the middle room, watching the six o'clock news on television, when I told her my plans for the evening.

"Monica's father is gonna give us a ride back up to the high school for the Viking Show rehearsal," I said, glancing at the television after an angry black man's voice caught my attention. The Viking Show was Jackson High School's annual talent event. Monica, Robin, Valerie, Carla Gamble, and I made it every year, dancing.

"If white America doesn't come around, black America is gonna burn it down!" shouted the twenty-something-year-old angry black man, wearing sunglasses and a goatee.

"Now that's what I'm talking about," I said to Momma, who was sitting on the couch with the newspaper spread out beside her. "I'm tired of seeing those black people down south getting beat up by the police. They're getting water hosed and bitten by police dogs like they aren't even human."

Momma disagreed.

"Humph! That fella's got something wrong with him. He must be crazy," she said. "All he's gonna do is mess around and get a whole lot of people killed, talking that junk."

Like my dad, I could never turn down the opportunity for a good debate. So I strolled back into the living room and sat down in the rocking chair next to Momma.

"But what do you expect those black people down there to do? Just keep letting the police and those crazy white people beat them to death? Those people look like me and you. Grandma and Mother and Daddy. Would you want somebody treating them like that?" I asked.

Momma was unmoved.

"They talking about integration. Humph! I don't want to live nowhere where people don't want me," she replied, looking toward the television and away from me.

"But Momma, those white people are getting ridiculous. They're lynching and killing people just because they don't want black people sitting beside them in restaurants and don't want black kids going to their lily-white schools. We do it up here in the North. And I like it. How come they can't just try it down there? That just doesn't make any sense to me," I said, my frustration turning to anger.

"Well, that's those folks' problem. I've got enough of my own to worry about," Momma said, turning her attention back to the newspaper.

"But it's our problem, too. I still get mad every time me and Daddy have to go to the back door to pick up Mother from work. Their dog don't even have to go to the back door. I hate that. This is 1966," I said, lowering my voice when the angry man appeared on television again. The caption under him read "H. Rap Brown."

"All I can say is that H. Rap Brown sure is fine," I exclaimed. "Now he's speaking for me and a whole lot of other teenagers I know. That guy knows what it's gonna take."

Momma turned the pages of the newspaper, rattling them too loudly for me. My eyes were still glued to the television.

"I thought you said you had to be at Monica's house at six thirty, Jasmine. It's almost quarter after six. And here you are sitting and listening to that mess."

"I'm going—right now. But all I've got to say is that if somebody hits me, there ain't no way I'm gonna turn the other cheek like that Martin Luther King is saying. I'm gonna hit them right back. Look at what they're doing to him. White people hate that man. I know a lot of people my age who don't like him either," I said, staring at Momma, who was trying to ignore me.

"All right now, little sister," Momma said. She addressed me as "sister" whenever I frustrated her, or when she was about to impart a bit of wisdom or cuss me out.

"You keep on talking that crap. Somebody's gonna take hold to your behind one of these days, and turn your little ass every way but loose," she said.

— ✤ —

RACIAL TENSION and riots spread across the country in 1966 and finally erupted in Jackson. I witnessed police brutality for the first time that year. My best-friend relatives and I had attended a dance one Saturday night, held at a local community center on the South Side. Midway through the evening police stormed the building looking for someone. It wasn't clear who they were looking for.

Fifteen-year-old Maurice, my brother's best friend, mouthed off at the police for interrupting our dance. One officer struck him in the head with his nightstick, knocking Maurice unconscious. It happened so quickly that I never saw the encounter. But I did see Maurice, lying on the hardwood dance floor, out cold.

People panicked, pushing and shoving—some screaming, others crying—while the police ordered everyone to stay back. They even refused to let Maurice's mother, Floradeen, who was serving as one of the chaperones, come near her son for several minutes. It made me so angry. An ambulance finally arrived and rushed him to the hospital. Maurice was released several hours later, but the damage had been done. My perception of the police went from protectors to oppressors in one night.

The local newspaper ran a front-page story that Sunday. The following day, Jackson's city commissioners met for their regular Monday night session. An outraged black community packed the place. The tension in the commissioners' chamber was suffocating. One black person after another addressed the all-white city group, who sat stoically one minute, then whispered and passed notes the next.

More than fifty young people and adults left the meeting feeling more powerless than ever. Teenagers spilled out into the quiet downtown streets and started throwing rocks. The huge plate-glass window near the door of city hall shattered, raining glass on the steps and lawn below. The angry crowd kept shouting, "No justice. No peace!" They stormed downtown Jackson, with me close behind, breaking out windows and tossing trashcans. Litter was everywhere.

I didn't break any windows, but was right in the thick of things. I was too chicken to break out any windows. Momma had already threatened to put me in the juvenile home too many times for me to chance getting caught. The revolt felt good though. For a few brief hours, I felt empowered. Sooner or later somebody was going to have to listen.

THE WALKER FAMILY MATTERS

"Man, don't change that channel. I was watching my favorite show. I just left the room to make me a sandwich and take a piss," fifteen-year-old Monty said.

"Fuck that! You move, you lose," Cordell's oldest brother, Hilliard, shot back. Everyone called him Hitchie.

The two brothers shoved and elbowed each other in front of the chipped and scratched console television for several seconds before Mrs. Walker hollered from her bedroom, adjacent to the living room.

"All right, ya'll better cut that noise out before I call Dennis," she threatened.

Their voices lowered, but the arguing and jostling continued. I feared there'd be an all-out fight.

"Ya'll keep it up and I'm gonna have Dennis put all ya'll's asses out in the street," Mrs. Walker yelled, her voice filled with agitation. "You niggahs ought to be ashamed of yourselves—old grown-ass men acting like babies."

That was when Cordell stepped in.

"Wait a minute. Don't ya'll see my woman sitting here?" Cordell said, taking his arm from around my shoulders and rising from the sagging couch covered with a faded brown throw. "You're acting like a bunch of fucking fools."

Third to the oldest, but the tallest, Cordell stepped over the small, rickety coffee table, first with one long leg, then the other. Two more steps and he was pushing his brothers apart. Dressed in a black sleeveless T-shirt and secondhand pants that sagged off his narrow hips and perky butt, Cordell had to grab his older brother and confront him face to face.

"Look man, you been drinking too much Schlitz tonight. Can't you be man enough to give it a break? You know you can kick his ass. So what's the deal?" Cordell said, sneaking a peek at me during a moment of complete silence.

That was the first of many arguments and fights among the Walker brothers, even though the five of them loved each other like crazy. Everyone knew that if an outsider were foolish enough to fight one, he'd eventually have to fight them all. But despite that bond, the Walker brothers couldn't get along to save their lives.

Hitchie, the sharpest dressing of the guys, lived in and out of Benton Harbor and talked more shit than anybody I knew. He was funny, too. Hitchie could watch the saddest movie and make a joke out of it. He was twenty-six, high yellow, and called himself a lady's man.

Simon was twenty-three and wanted to be a woman. Looking like a white man wearing a big black Afro, Simon was a macho man one month, then he would arch his eyebrows the next. His behavior frequently frightened and disappointed his mother and angered his four brothers, who often taunted him and teased him about being a "sissy." Simon was almost too pretty to be a man.

He was also the family militant. Simon loved his fellow black people. Sporting colorful dashikis with turtlenecked tops, he busied himself organizing protest groups and marches. Simon dated only coal black women and often served as the voice of Jackson's young black community. Smart as a whip, Simon could stand up to any argument—especially about the oppression of black people. What really seemed to unnerve the white community is that Simon carried himself with the dignity of a Muslim and had the heart of a lion.

Jonathon was twenty years old and more quiet and reserved than the rest. He wore a big Afro, too, and smiled a lot. Jonathon was the only brother who had facial hair, sporting a thick mustache and goatee. He had a little more color to him, his skin the color of wheat. Jonathan smoked cigarettes, drank beer, and dropped out of school at age fifteen and never held an honest job in his life. But his niche was fixing cars. There was always a car jacked up on blocks in the Walkers' driveway. Sometimes two or three. People paid Jonathon hundreds of dollars to repair their cars. Whenever he got low on money, he'd string a light up in their shabby garage behind their house and work on automobiles all night.

Monty, the youngest, hadn't attended school in more than a year. Fifteen years old and spoiled rotten, Monty was the meanest *young* man I'd ever known. The first time I saw him was several years earlier. Our girls' softball team from Rotary playground was playing Lyons, a team from the North Side. We were in the middle of the game when Monty came riding across the field on a bike, chasing a little girl who appeared to be about nine years old. That child looked terrified and was running for her life. The more she zigzagged to avoid the bike's front tire, the harder Monty peddled. An adult finally stopped the game and chastised the little brat, while a few other grown-ups comforted the scared little girl.

—— ҂ ——

MOMMA DIDN'T LIKE me hanging around the Walkers' house, but didn't fuss as much as she did in the past. Struggling to feed six kids, working full time, and attending Jackson Community College, it was all Momma could do to keep the younger ones in line. I figured she'd given up on me.

Spending my free time at the Walkers' house was a whole new experience for me. It was fun and exciting, just the opposite of my mundane home life. Instead of partying or dancing, as I'd done in the past, I sat cuddled up next to Cordell on their sofa, watching television and drinking a glass or two of beer or wine. I learned to play cards. I learned to pour beer in a glass without getting too much foam. I cussed more and spent less time on my homework, causing my grades to slip.

"I don't believe in sitting up playing cards and gambling with my own kids," Momma snapped one night as I prepared for the Walker family's Friday night card party.

Momma didn't believe in pierced ears either. She said they made females look cheap. I loved pierced ears. Everyone was getting theirs done. I finally snuck out and had a fourteen-year-old-girl pierce mine, then walked around with my hair covering the white thread in my ears for weeks, afraid Momma would see it. I had just turned sixteen.

Momma didn't believe in saying much to our friends either. "Young kids go to thinking they can disrespect you, when you sit around talking and joking with them too much," she'd said one day.

"Momma's got it all wrong. I don't know where she gets her ideas from," I thought, wrapping a thin pink ribbon around my head and tying a nice neat bow just above my bangs. "There's nothing wrong with playing cards with your kids. Momma just don't like anybody and swears that everything I do is wrong."

—— ҂ ——

A FEW MONTHS later Debra and Monica started hanging out at the Walkers' house with me. Robin and Valerie refused to go. They didn't like the Walker family but never admitted it to me.

Debra hooked up with Hitchie, but didn't get caught up in his rap. She found his conversation as amusing as I did. They smooched and drank a little, but that was it. Their romance lasted about a month.

Monica was in it for the free drinks. There was always a six-pack of beer and a bottle of wine waiting for us. She admired Simon, but kept her distance.

"He sure is a fine. But that brother is too militant for me," she said. "I sure wouldn't want to run into him in a dark alley if I was a white person."

We partied hearty at the Walkers' house every weekend. Debra and Monica never played cards. I did. I also helped sell food. The Walkers sold fried chicken and fish sandwiches for a $1.50. Beer cost a buck. The "house cut" usually amounted to $300 or $400 for an all-nighter. Most of the card players were local relatives and a few stragglers who heard about the Friday night card parties.

The closer it got to Cordell reporting for the army, the more pressure he applied for sex. We had plenty of opportunities, but I was never ready to let my guard down until a few weeks before Cordell had to leave.

"You gon give your man some before he goes to Nam?" he asked one night when everyone else was asleep.

Prepared to go all the way, I didn't want my boyfriend going to the army, and probably war, without at least sealing our relationship with sex. I still didn't know beans about doing it. Something was missing from my sexual encounters, and I didn't know what it was. I found out later that it was the climax.

Cordell cut off all the lights in the house, and we tiptoed into a small room, off from the dining room. A curtain divided the alcove-like area from the rest of the house. A roll-away bed was situated just inside. We kissed. We hugged. We had sex.

✤ LEAVING ME

The National Guard Armory felt chilly at six o'clock one October morning in 1966. The room looked like a huge warehouse crowded with young draftees and their sad-faced girlfriends and parents. Cordell and I stood in a corner talking about the things we'd done together the past summer. We avoided any conversation about the army. The Greyhound buses that would take the young men to Detroit was parked outside two large, glass double doors, their engines running. Each time one of the doors opened, the sounds of the roaring engines rushed in, constantly reminding me of our impending separation. The predawn mood was as solemn as I had imagined.

Feeling like an abandoned child, I still tried to appear upbeat for Cordell's sake. It wasn't easy. Whenever quietness fell upon our conversation, it felt as if we were wasting precious time. Silence had always made me uncomfortable.

"You don't have to wait on me," Cordell said, his hazel eyes darting around the room.

"Do you want me to wait?" I asked.

"That's up to you."

"Okay," I said softly, trying to hide my disappointment.

I wanted Cordell to ask me to wait. I wanted him to tell me he loved me, but my dude wasn't the mushy type. So we kept our conversation light by talking about our families and the weather.

"Cordell, you be careful," I kept saying, my arms folded across my chest and looking at the gray tile floor. "I'll write as soon as you send me an address"

"We'll see. I won't hold my breath waiting on the mail," he replied, and for a split second he had the saddest look on his face.

"Hey, there's my man Gary Banks," Cordell said, smiling and perking back up. "Uncle Sam got you, too?"

They slapped each other's hand, giving "skin." It quickly became obvious that Cordell was tickled to have a familiar face inducted into the army with him because he was still grinning and slapping the dark-skinned young man on the back long after his buddy had stopped. Gary Banks had been standing by himself.

"Where's his family?" I whispered to Cordell after Gary excused himself to the restroom.

"His mother died when he was thirteen or fourteen," Cordell replied. "His older sister was raising them last I knew. She must have been taking care of at least four of her sisters and brothers. I don't know nothing about his old man."

A loud, stern, male voice came over the speaker system.

"All United States Army inductees are to report to the Greyhound buses immediately," the voice announced.

The three of us glanced at each other, then strolled out the doors and stood a few feet from the roaring buses. I stood on my toes and kissed Cordell's lips. His face flushed, he turned and hurried to the metal steps of the bus. Gary scurried behind him, saying "bye" over his shoulder.

I didn't stand around like some people who watched the buses pull off, crying and throwing kisses. Saying good-bye had been too painful already. I turned and quickly walked away into the early morning darkness and headed to school.

— ℰ —

CORDELL CAME HOME on a thirty-day leave for Christmas. Afterward, he was going to Fort Polk, Louisiana, for advanced infantry training, his next step before Vietnam.

He and Gary Banks had ended up being bunkmates during their six weeks of basic training in Fort Knox, Kentucky. I had hoped they'd remain together, but that didn't happen. Gary was being deployed to Alaska. Deep down inside, I felt a bit envious and often wondered how decisions were made to send some people to safer areas while others went to fight wars.

It all appeared so arbitrary and unfair.

"The only ones fighting in Vietnam are blacks, browns, and poor people," I thought and heard many times.

Wanting to spend as much time with Cordell as possible, I'd rush home after school and change into a pair of slacks, do half my homework, then catch a ride over to Cordell's. His old car had conked out the week before he got his draft papers.

Gary was always there when I arrived, or on his way. Not having parents, I figured he was lonely and wanted to spend time with friends. With average looks and height, Gary did more listening and laughing than talking. His broad smile and big white teeth lit up his somber face in an instant.

"He's such a nice guy," I thought. "I'm sure glad that Cordell has a friend like him."

We drank so much beer and Boone's Farm apple wine every night that I often went home a little tipsy. We watched television, played cards, and joked around nearly every time we got together. Since my boyfriend was going to war, I made up my mind to oblige him whenever he asked for sex. We ended up in bed five or six times before he left.

"If it means me getting pregnant, then so be it," I thought. "I really don't have any plans after graduating. And besides, Dr. Sizemore should have given me a prescription for birth control pills, like I asked."

I had asked the doctor for the pills a few weeks after my miscarriage. His face turned beet red, and he looked at me like I was crazy.

"I most certainly will not! Jasmine, you are not married," he snapped.

So I took my chances, secretly hoping that I would get pregnant with Cordell's baby. He was light skinned and good looking. I wanted a baby who looked just like him.

✣ COUNTDOWN

itting in the television room rocking chair, my stomach in knots, I started counting, "One, two, three, four. . . ."

"I'll count to 50, then go in Momma's room and tell her I'm two-and-a-half-months pregnant," I thought. After reaching 50, I decided to count to 100. One hundred came, and I upped it to 150. Then 200. By the time I had counted to 300, there was no more getting around it. I had to tell her.

Dr. Sizemore had confirmed it two weeks earlier. My best-friend cousin Robin and my best-friend aunt Valerie already had a leg up on me. Robin was nearly five months pregnant and was completing school at home. Valerie had quit school, married, and given birth to a baby boy in November 1966. Now it was my turn to break the news about me.

"The last thing I want is for Momma to hear it from someone else in the family," I thought, my heart pounding a hundred times a minute. My palms even got wet, and I never used to sweat.

Staring at her white, painted bedroom door, I tried getting up several times, but my body wouldn't obey. Terrance, Lisa, Penny, and Keith were upstairs. Albert was hanging out with Maurice. It was the perfect time to tell Momma, but getting up the nerve was another matter.

My mind and body finally in sync, I slowly forced myself up from the cushioned blue rocker. I took baby steps across the cool beige linoleum floor, barefooted and trembling. I lightly tapped on the closed door right away, fearing I'd chicken out if I didn't.

"Come in," Momma said, with the familiar edge in her voice.

She was lying in bed with books sprawled around her, studying for a nurse's exam at the community college. Having earned her high school diploma at night school, she was studying nursing at Jackson Community College.

I eased through the door, expecting Momma to be in one of her moods. She surprised me by smiling softly. Her calm and relaxed appearance made me feel even worse. But I was determined to tell her.

"What is it, Jasmine?" she asked, looking up at me, the lamp beside her bed shining in her face.

"Momma, I'm two-and-a-half-months pregnant," I said, spitting the words out of my mouth as if they were on fire.

She looked at me. There was no tension in her face. No evil looks or rolling eyes. She didn't even act surprised.

"Does Cordell know?" she asked, her voice never changing.

"Yeah. I wrote him and told him. We're gonna get married when he comes back home in May," I quickly added.

Momma looked down, turned the page of her book, and started reading again. I turned and quietly walked out of the room. Thinking the toughest part was over, a few weeks later I started having morning sickness. After three weeks and no letup, I started skipping classes and going to Valerie's apartment to sleep. She had a second baby due.

I'd noticed a change in my young aunt after she tied the knot. She didn't joke and smile as much. She stayed home all the time, taking care of her son, cooking and watching TV with her extremely quiet and withdrawn husband.

"All he does is go to work, come home, and sit in front of that television all night," Valerie complained as I lay in her son's twin bed, trying to get some sleep. "I get tired of looking at him. I get tired of sitting up in this ole apartment. I wish I'd never gotten married."

I felt sorry for my aunt, but could only offer an ear. My stomach was poking out, my breasts were leaking and staining my clothes, and I was growing tired of school.

— ❧ —

ONE CLOUDY MORNING I was sitting on the hard, worn steps inside Jackson High School, leaning to the side to let students pass by while trying to make up my mind whether to skip school. It would be my fourth time in two weeks. I'd never skipped a day in my life until I got pregnant. The decision was made for me when I looked up and saw my twelfth-grade counselor, Mr. Tinsley, approaching.

"Jasmine Armstead, you're just the person I've been looking for. I'd like to see you in my office for a few minutes," he said, with a big phony smile on his face.

I smelled trouble. Following him back to his office, I suspected he'd heard I was pregnant. He didn't say a word until closing the door behind us.

"How have you been feeling lately?" he asked as soon as we sat down.

"I'm fine."

"Are you seeing a doctor right now?" he asked, leaning back in his chair, expressionless, and wearing a crew-cut hairstyle and a light blue buttoned-down shirt.

"No."

"Are you sure about that?" he asked, skepticism written all over his face.

"Yes. I'm sure," I replied, feeling the heat but determined to play dumb.

"Well, I guess we'll just have to go and have a talk with your mother because I don't think you're telling me the truth," he said, his tone never changing.

He rose from his chair and reached for his gray flannel sports coat, hanging on a stand-alone wooden coat rack. I watched him put one arm in a sleeve, then the other.

"Okay . . . wait. Yes, I *am* seeing a doctor. I'm four-and-a-half-months pregnant," I blurted out, hoping to change his mind about taking me home.

He insisted on it and called Momma. I sat quietly on the front passenger's side the entire two-mile trip. Momma met us at the door, faking a smile and never looking at me. The three of us strolled into the living room and sat down, with plenty of space between us, on our brown, three-piece curved sofa.

"Jasmine has acknowledged that she's expecting a baby. She said you are already aware of it. Is that correct?" he asked, smiling but looking uneasy.

"Yes. I know," Momma said, never looking my way.

"Well, the policy of Jackson public schools prohibits students who are pregnant from attending school. Now, in Jasmine's case, she won't have to worry about the next five weeks of classes," he continued, as if I weren't even in the room. "Her grades are sound enough for her to graduate without having to do any homework. We will send her diploma in the mail, shortly after the graduation ceremony."

"But can't I at least take part in the ceremony?" I asked weakly, thinking that my above-average grades carried some weight. "We'll be wearing robes, so no one will be able to tell."

"Oh no!" Mr. Tinsley exclaimed, his eyes wide and eyebrows raised. "Why, allowing you to walk across stage would be only advertising it."

I gave up right then. I didn't say anything else throughout the rest of the conversation and only half listened. Mr. Tinsley finally left, and I went upstairs and climbed in bed to try to get some sleep.

✽ BABY'S COMING

"Cordell and I can get married, and I can stay home and take care of the baby while he works. Then we can be a *real* family," I thought one morning, lying in bed listening to my sisters and brothers scramble to get ready for school.

There was one slight problem. Cordell and I had never talked about getting married. He assured me he'd take care of the baby, but I had lied to Momma. The word "marriage" had never come up.

"He'll want to marry me once he finds out how faithful I am," I thought, so often it became a belief. "He just needs time to get used to the idea."

I wrote Cordell two or three times a week, detailing my pregnancy and changing appearance. I told him about my doctor's visits, the iron and vitamin pills I took, and everything else that came to mind. The first time the baby kicked, I wrote Cordell the same night. No one else around me seemed to care. I'm sure I mentioned marriage a few times, but didn't want to seem pushy. Pushy people seldom got anywhere with me. Hoping and praying that Cordell would eventually propose to me, I went along with my life as if it had already been sealed.

Being only eighteen, I didn't have a clue about preparing for a baby. My idea of preparation was reading a Dr. Spock book. I saved seventeen dollars in a glass piggy bank and bought a dozen cloth diapers. No one in the family talked about my pregnancy around me. They seldom talked about anybody who was expecting, married or not. Having a baby was a very private matter in our family.

— ๛ —

MY BLACK HAIR looked sandy in the sunlight, thick and lying on my shoulders. My fingernails were long and beautiful for the first time in my life. They looked so good people started asking me if they were fake. My skin glowed, and my face filled out. Motherhood agreed with me.

I wore tent dresses to church to disguise my pregnancy, even though most people already knew. My attendance had dwindled to twice a month, if that. By six-and-a-half months, I couldn't fit into anything and bought my first maternity blouse. It was a brown, orange, black, and white paisley print with a white lace bodice. Even Momma looked surprised when she saw me wearing it. Maternity clothes felt like a rite of passage for me. Most females in our family had traveled the same path. Go to high school. Get pregnant. Drop out.

My gynecologist started giving me iron shots at seven months because I'd become anemic. They hurt, but I never missed an appointment. I still loved watermelon, cherries, and peaches. Cornbread and beans, peas, or greens were my mainstay. Meat still didn't faze me.

Although my stomach was as big as a house, I didn't miss a beat. I went to nearly every party held in Jackson the first two trimesters. Robin, Monica, and I spent my last three months riding around town in a shiny black 1965 Mercury Comet with red vinyl interior and an eight-track tape cassette player. A guy we'd met from down south owned the car. He and his two brothers were some of the sweetest guys we'd ever met. They never cussed. They never complained about Robin and Monica messing with the tape player, which they did a lot. And the subject of sex never came up. The guys were so nice that when my doctor suggested I drink Mogen David wine to help build my blood, they bought me a bottle every week. No strings attached.

—— & ——

SOMETHING WOKE me up. A cramp. The worst I'd ever had. The pain eased up after a few moments, then faded away. It was four fifteen in the morning. I tossed and turned for an hour more, before realizing the cramping was rhythmic and growing stronger. I was in labor, nearly a week overdue.

Quietly creeping downstairs in the dark, I gently pushed open the door to Momma's bedroom.

"I think it's time," I said softly but excited on the inside. "I'm gonna call Robin. She wants to take me to the hospital."

I'm sure Momma said something, but I don't remember what. After closing her door, I waddled back upstairs and dialed Robin's number on our beige phone, mounted on the wall between the boys' bedrooms and ours.

Robin and I grew up like sisters and had become even closer. Both of us pregnant and out of school at the same time, we talked on the telephone every day. She ended up having a drop-dead gorgeous daughter named Maya three months before me. Her baby had skin the color of bread crust and the curliest, thick black hair I'd ever seen. Maya was a living doll, and Robin took care of her newborn as if motherhood was a piece of cake. My cousin gave me hope that I could do the same. She even insisted that I call her when my labor started.

"Now Jasmine, I don't care what time of the day or night it is," Robin reminded me dozens of times. "You be sure to call me. I want to be the one to drive you to the hospital."

I longed for a pretty baby, too. One night I even dreamed that I gave birth to a beautiful baby boy, but it seemed too good to be true. I prayed that my baby would look like Cordell, but feared my child would take after me.

—— ❧ ——

ROBIN ARRIVED at my house fifteen minutes after I called. She drove to the hospital so fast, weaving in and out of cars, that I had to keep saying, "Slow down, Robin. Slow down." Smiling and chattering all the way to the emergency room, my cousin was more excited than I was. I was getting nervous and just wanted to get the whole thing over.

My labor lasted sixteen hours. Sixteen long, excruciatingly painful hours. The pain became so unbearable that I started begging for an oxygen mask, crying, "I can't breathe. I can't breathe!"

A doctor finally gave me a spinal block, deadening everything from my waist down. It was strange to pat my legs and barely feel anything. Several times I thought, "Wouldn't this be awful if my legs stayed like this?" But the spinal block eliminated the pain. That mattered most.

The delivery was a foggy experience. Like a dream. Lying on the delivery table, my legs up in stirrups, I remember seeing a cold, sterile room, with a stainless steel basin and bright lights overhead. Nurses and assistants stirred everywhere.

I dozed off. The next thing I knew, the doctor was placing my baby on my chest, announcing, "It's a boy," with a smile on his face.

The first thing I noticed was that he looked just like his daddy. He even had Cordell's scowl between his tiny, squinting eyes. Andre Cordell Armstead had skin as smooth as peaches and cream and was the prettiest newborn I'd ever seen. Almost too pretty to be a boy, like his uncle Simon. My baby had thin, black, straight hair that was slicked on a perfectly shaped head with mucus and blood. With his clinched fists the size of walnuts, my baby slowly turned his head to me and blinked a few times while lying next to me. I fell in love with the little guy instantly. Seconds later a nurse wrapped him in a white blanket and whisked him away to the nursery.

I bet I walked wide-legged to the nursery dozens of times, pressing my forehead to the window, watching my newborn son. It was hard to believe that one minute I was just a teenager and the next minute a mother.

❧ <u>REAL</u> TIME

I climbed out of Arlene's navy blue and white 1965 Chevy Corvair carrying my baby in one arm and a plastic bag containing a twenty-four-hour supply of Pampers, baby formula and bottles, and my purse in the other. Arlene, who was on her lunch hour from her secretarial job, carried the overnight case I borrowed from Momma and a second bag of baby supplies.

Struggling up the sidewalk, I stepped onto our cracked cement steps, then moved aside and asked Arlene to knock on the door. My hands were too full. She knocked and knocked. No one answered. I sat my bags on the steps, then fumbled through my purse for the door key.

"Momma must be in class," I told my cousin while unlocking the door. "She's giving me her downstairs bedroom and moving upstairs with Lisa and Penny. I really think she's trying to help."

The house was cool, dark, and quiet as we headed toward my new bedroom. Secretly, I was disappointed that no one was home to greet me. I was exhausted. Nervous. Bordering on depression. I opened the door to my new bedroom. The twin-size bed was stripped. No sheets. No blankets. No pillows. Just a bare mattress and boxed springs. I wanted to cry.

The kitchen sink was filled with dirty dishes. The floor needed mopping. Clothes were scattered in the TV room, and the whole house smelled closed up.

"I'm too tired to do anything, and my stitches are burning and hurting so much I can barely walk," I said, dumping my bags on the bed.

I unbundled my newborn and placed him gently into the white wicker bassinet Robin had loaned me. I had put yellow and white striped sheets and matching receiving blankets on it days before my delivery. Thank God.

Arlene helped me make the bed. Always upbeat and smiling, my older cousin put everything away for me. I supervised from the bed, my eyes glistening. Suddenly it hit me.

"I don't have hardly anything," I said, letting the tears flow. "Not even bottles and formula. When this stuff the hospital gave me runs out, my baby won't have anything to eat."

Arlene looked surprised. I was embarrassed. Too busy hanging out and partying during my pregnancy, I never gave much thought to anything but how light skinned and cute my baby might be because of his father.

Reality slapped me in the face. I was responsible for another human being's life. If I didn't have food, my baby wouldn't eat. If I didn't have diapers, my baby wouldn't get changed. I needed a heat lamp for my stitches. I needed a diaper pail and bottle sterilizers. I needed baby bottles, one-piece pajamas, T-shirts, and socks. I felt overwhelmed.

"Don't worry Jasmine," Arlene said as she headed out the front door. "I'll stop back by when I get off work at five."

I didn't know what it meant but knew my cousin would help me whatever way she could. Arlene reminded me of Mother, gentle spirited and able to get along with most people. Arlene and I had grown even closer over the past year because her husband was in Vietnam, too. We had spent our summer consoling each other by going to drive-in movies and talking about how happy we'd be when our dudes would be back home.

My cousin returned after work, just as she had promised. She'd bought me a sterilizer set, two-dozen cloth diapers, and a week's supply of Enfamil formula. I was so appreciative and relieved.

"Use this to buy some other things you'll need," she said, handing me a crisp twenty-dollar bill. "And don't worry Jasmine. Just hang in there. Everything is gonna be all right. You'll see."

THE HOOK UP

The mailman handed me a white envelope with red and blue markings around the edges. I knew it was from Cordell. He had been sending me sixty-dollar postal money orders every two weeks ever since Andre's birth. I quickly took the letter to my bedroom and plopped on the bed. Ripping the envelope open, I began reading and absorbing every word he wrote. It had become an important part of my routine.

Cordell wrote about the war and how miserable he felt, sleeping in muddy trenches with heavy rainfall. He talked of trampling through thick jungle, not knowing friend from foe. He wrote about our baby, urging me to take good care of his "boy."

Usually he sent black-and-white pictures taken with a Polaroid camera. My scrapbook was filled with them. But this time there were none. I read on. Halfway through the letter, my dude popped the question, catching me by surprise. I can't remember what he said, but it wasn't very romantic. He signed his marriage proposal letter "over and out."

— ❧ —

I APPROACHED IMPENDING married life with the same lack of planning as the birth of our son. I just wanted Cordell to marry me. We'd figure out the rest later. Writing each other faithfully, we never discussed a single issue related to married life. I didn't know his favorite foods, his plans for the future—except to get a job—or his expectations of me.

To me, getting married meant getting away from Momma. It meant being able to have sex and not feel guilty or ashamed. Marrying, to me, meant I'd cook meals for my family every day, and we'd sit around the table at dinnertime and eat.

We'd go to the drive-in movies together. Laugh, talk, and live happily ever after —like the people in one of my favorite television shows, Father Knows Best. The things I worried most about being married were undressing in front of Cordell and using the toilet while he was around.

Reaction to the news of us getting married was mixed. My best-friend relatives were happy and excited for me, even though they had little to do with Cordell. Arlene offered to let us hold the ceremony at her house. Marrying in a church never crossed my mind.

"Girl, I'm so jealous," my cousin Debra admitted, looking at me sideways and smirking. "Now you don't have to worry about nothing. You got a husband."

I felt the same way.

Janie Rabidoux and I still talked on the telephone every so often. My former classmate landed an office job at Goodyear and kept me updated on school friends and herself.

"Janie, me and Cordell Walker are getting married," I said to her on the phone one afternoon. Her comments surprised me.

"Jasmine, don't you think he's a little bit too rough for you?" she immediately asked.

"Cordell has been good to me and my baby," I said, trying not to sound offended, even though I was. "He's not like most people think, at all. He's the most responsible person in his whole family, outside of his father. You just don't know Cordell like I do."

The silence on the other end told me that my friend was not convinced. I was hurt and disappointed. My best white friend didn't seem happy about me getting married—knowing I was a young, single mother.

"She's beginning to sound just like the rest of them," I thought, meaning white people. "I don't think I'll call her anymore."

Being 1968, it was easy for black and white teenagers from different worlds to drift apart. I never felt any racial animosity toward Janie. Nor do I believe she ever held any against me. Best friends throughout junior and senior high, after that telephone conversation we gradually went separate ways.

☙ <u>THE</u> LAST STRAW

I t was around eight o'clock at night, and everyone was home. Momma was talking on the kitchen phone to Mrs. Baldwin, Monica's mother and one of her closest friends. The rest of us—except Albert, who was upstairs–were in the middle room watching a show on the new console TV Momma had bought. I sat on the sofa.

Andre sat in my lap, and Lisa knelt on the floor beside us, playing peek-a-boo with him. Trying to outdo his sister, Terrance scooted out of the rocking chair and got on his knees, too. He started spinning around on the floor in front of us and making weird noises. Andre belly laughed, quickly turning his head from Lisa to Terrance, his cheeks bulging from baby fat.

Suddenly, the words "News Bulletin," in big white letters, flashed across the television screen. Stepping over my ten-year-old brother, with Andre dangling sideways in one arm, I rushed to turn up the volume. My finger to my mouth, I signaled everyone to be quiet. Seconds later, a newsman appeared behind a desk and announced that Dr. Martin Luther King Jr. had been shot. Our collective gasp was so loud that Albert came rushing downstairs to see what was going on.

I turned the volume up louder. Minutes later another news bulletin.

"Dr. Martin Luther King Jr. has just been pronounced dead from a sniper's gunshot wound to the head. There are no suspects in custody," Walter Cronkite said.

Another collective gasp. Momma rushed back to the phone. My sisters and brothers looked at me. I handed Andre to Penny, then jumped up and started pacing the floor, wanting to do something, but not sure what.

"I'll bet it was the KKK or some other crazy white person," I fumed, staring at my family in disbelief. Rage surfaced within me. Although I'd never been a follower of Dr. King or believed in his nonviolent philosophy, I felt slapped in the face and spat upon.

"See Momma, that's exactly what I'm talking about," I said. "Here, Martin Luther King preached nonviolence, and look what happened to him. That's why I say, 'Hit me and I'm gonna try to hit you back even harder.'"

—— ℯ ——

MORNING COULDN'T GET here fast enough. Unable to sleep, I climbed out of bed earlier than usual, bathed and dressed. Standing on our front porch by eleven o'clock, I looked up and down the street, mad as hell. Carla soon came walking briskly over the hill, her long arms swinging with each stride. I joined her on the sidewalk in front of our house, and the first thing from her lips was Dr. King's assassination.

"Girl, I'm on my way to a meeting on the South Side right now," she said, visibly pumped. "I heard that there's some people over there who are supposed to do something. These white folks done gone a little too damn far now. I'm ready to raise a whole lot of hell. Wanna go with me and check it out?"

"I'm game," I said eagerly, always a sucker for adventure. "Walk on down the street, and I'll catch up with you."

I dashed back into the house and quietly bribed Lisa with two dollars to watch Andre for a few hours. Then I eased back out the door without Momma seeing me. Carla was waiting a few doors down the street and putting out a cigarette when I caught up with her. We struck out walking across town, hoping to catch a ride on the corner of Plymouth and East Avenue. No such luck. We ended up walking all the way, but didn't mind because the sun was shining and the skies were clear blue.

We had no problem finding the Moore Street address. The small, two-story frame house, situated on a slight hill, appeared quiet. No cars. No signs. No angry crowd of people gathered outside, which I had hoped for.

We marched up to the door and knocked anyway. Seconds later, a muscle-bound, thirty-something-year-old bald-headed guy appeared. Wearing a small, gold hoop earring and a white T-shirt, he looked like a bronze Mr. Clean. He clicked the lock, cracked the screen door, then spoke through an opening, barely six inches wide.

"Who ya'll looking for?" he asked in a deep, smooth voice, his face barely visible.

"We heard there's a meeting. It's supposed to have something to do with the assassination," Carla said boldly, stepping up to the landing of the wooden steps. Her five-foot-nine stature blocked part of my view.

"How'd ya'll get here?" the man asked, sticking his head farther out the door and looking up and down the street.

"We walked," both of us said at the same time.

We laughed. He didn't. The clean-shaven man glowered at us for several seconds. I stepped farther behind Carla and peeked around at him.

"Wait a minute," he said after several seconds of thought, then closed the aluminum door and disappeared back into the house.

Carla and I exchanged wide-eyed looks. I was ready to go. Gangster-looking people scared me. But Carla was tough, not easily intimidated. That was one of the reasons I liked her. Seconds later Mr. Clean returned, rubbing the side of his face with the back of his fingers. His mouth was turned into a half smile.

"Come on through," he said, taking one more look up and down the street before swinging the door open.

Carla led the way. We tromped into the house and found it full of people, quietly whispering among themselves. Most looked older and unfamiliar to me. We searched for a spot where we could sit or stand and wait for the meeting to start. After a couple of hours, I began worrying about my baby.

"Carla, what time is it?" I whispered, sitting Indian style on the floor in a corner of the kitchen, other people standing over my head and bumping me.

"It's almost two thirty," she replied, looking at her wristwatch that had a black leather band.

"Girl, I've got to go. I was only supposed to be gone a few hours. We've been here since noon, and nothing's happened yet," I said, looking at the faces and feeling more uncomfortable by the minute.

Carla had two kids, a three-year-old son and a daughter who had recently turned one. Married and separated, she had moved back home with her parents. They kept her kids a lot even though they had nine of their own.

"Yeah, let's book," my friend replied, raising her tall frame from the floor. We inched our way through the packed living room and over to the front door where two men stood. They appeared to be guarding the entrance.

"We've got to go. We've got babies at home. And our mommas are gonna kill us if we don't get back like we said," Carla said flippantly.

I eagerly nodded my head.

"Nobody's leaving this joint till nightfall," the lighter-skinned guy replied flatly. "We've got business to take care of when it gets dark, and we ain't go' have no fuckups."

Shocked by his comment, Carla and I looked at each other, turned around, and marched back to our spot without saying a word. This time we stood. I wanted to be able to see.

Around three o'clock the light-skinned man, one of the ringleaders, made his way to the center of the living room and spoke. He laid out a plan that didn't seem to surprise anyone in the house, except Carla and me.

"We're gonna wait till dark, then couple up. Then we're gonna walk down Jackson Street to town. If anybody asks, we're a group of men taking our ladies to the movies. And smile a lot. White folks like black folks who smile a lot. Now, don't do anything until I give the signal," he said, raising a big silver whistle that hung around his slender neck.

A surge of adrenalin rushed through my nineteen-year-old body. I quit worrying about my baby. We were going to do something about Dr. King's assassination. We were going to let white people know that we weren't taking it anymore. Our voices were about to be heard. I just didn't know how, yet.

Dusk came, and people started lining up at the door. Carla and I couldn't figure out why it took so long to get outside—until we got to the front of the line. One guy was handing out Molotov cocktails. Another was passing out bricks.

"Choose one," the Molotov cocktail man said, his eyes daring us to back down.

I hadn't planned on doing any real damage, just whoop and holler it up a bit. But feeling the pressure, I reached for the brick. Carla did, too.

"Stay behind me," Carla whispered, as we strolled down Francis Street with our so-called dates. "When you see me run, you better book, too, cause I'm getting the hell out of here, first chance I get."

That sounded good to me. We shucked and jived nearly all the way. I got a kick out of pretending to be couples. Some played their roles to the hilt, all hugged up and smooching. Others cracked jokes that made everyone laugh. The carnival-like atmosphere attracted attention. Cars passed and white people stared, but I don't remember seeing one police vehicle during our half-hour trek.

By the time we reached downtown, Carla and I had plotted to drop our bricks and run as soon as the signal was given. We figured no one would notice us in the dark and chaos that would ensue. I was mad about Dr. King's assassination, but feared going to jail even more.

Glass started breaking sooner than we expected. Near the back of the crowd, Carla and I couldn't see what was happening ahead of us, but we dropped our bricks almost simultaneously and bolted, her leading and me right behind.

We heard glass breaking and people screaming all over downtown. It sounded terrifying. We dashed into a dark alley. Several white people came running from the opposite direction. Seeing us, they stopped suddenly, stooped down, and huddled against a brick building, then covered their heads, as if shielding themselves from an impending attack. It was a realty check for me. I felt sorry for them and angry at the same time. Sorry because they were so scared. Angry for thinking we'd harm them.

Having no idea what was going on, Carla and I turned and ran back the way we'd come. Unable to keep up with Carla's long strides, I fell once, skinning my knee. Carla stopped long enough to make sure I was okay, then took off running again. We didn't look back until we got to the East Side and split up at Teneyck Street, still panting.

The riot made the headlines of the *Jackson Citizen Patriot* the next day. Several businesses had been set on fire. A few were destroyed. Thousands of dollars in diamond rings and watches were looted from a jewelry store. I didn't know about the jewelry until reading the newspaper the next evening.

"That's why they started the shit early," Carla said later. "Somebody saw that jewelry in the window and threw a damn brick."

Throughout the summer of 1968, people sold diamond rings and watches at bargain prices. I even considered buying our wedding rings hot but didn't have the money. No one was ever arrested for the crimes, but one young man burned his face and arm. He had thrown a Molotov cocktail sideways, splattering gasoline all over his arm.

✿ HOMECOMING

ordell sat outside the small, sandstone bus station, straddling his brown, overstuffed duffel bag and squinting from the sun. Dressed in his green army uniform, my dude looked so good that a person would never guess that he'd just returned from war.

He stood up and smiled when he spotted me climbing out of Arlene's parked car. My cousin had driven me to Ann Arbor to pick him up after he missed his airplane flight. It had been fifteen months since we last saw each other.

Grinning from ear to ear, I strutted across the street. My soon-to-be husband met me on the opposite curb. He wrapped his long arms around my slender neck, pulled me closer, and planted a kiss on my lips. I had fretted over that moment for weeks, unsure of the appropriate thing to do. I was glad he made the first move.

"Where's my boy?" he asked, walking me back to the car.

"I didn't bring him."

"Why not?"

"Because the drive would have made him restless and cranky. I want him to be in a good mood when he sees you for the first time. I told you in my letters that he was a little spoiled."

Hearing Cordell call Andre "my boy" for the first time gave me goose bumps. It felt so good and right. But I worried about Andre's response to a complete stranger. I'd warned Cordell that our son was spoiled. It was the "rotten" that I conveniently left off.

— ҉ —

LISA MET US at the door, carrying our rosy-cheeked eight-month-old son. Andre immediately reached for me, with bright brown eyes and a big smile that only a mother can appreciate.

"Hi there. How's mommy's baby?" I asked, hugging and rocking my son against my chest.

"Let me hold him," Cordell said eagerly.

My heart pounded, and I said a quick prayer. I had imagined that moment a million times, but nothing prepared me for the nervousness I felt. I did not want my baby to cry when Cordell held him for the first time. I wanted everything to be perfect.

"This is your daddy. I've showed you lots of pictures of him. Are you going to be a good boy and let your daddy hold you?" I asked, holding my breath and gently handing Andre to his father.

Cordell's smooth-shaven face broke out in the biggest smile. Andre looked around at everybody. Then he spotted the brass buttons on his daddy's uniform and calmly started playing with them. I looked at Lisa and smiled. My quiet, timid sister smiled back.

Andre tugged at his daddy's brass buttons. He fiddled with a black horse patch, then started scratching its fuzzy fabric, occasionally looking up at his daddy with an angelic stare on his face. That lasted all of one minute. Andre turned his balding little head toward me. He stretched out his chunky little arms. Cordell turned his shoulder and pulled him farther away from me. Our baby started whining. Cordell stepped a few feet farther away. Andre's face turned red. His eyes grew big with fright. The corners of his mouth turned down, his small lips quivered. I couldn't take anymore.

"Here, let me have him," I said, hoping not to offend Cordell but dead set on sparing my baby any unnecessary trauma.

"He just needs a little time to get used to you. That's all," I said, hugging and bouncing Andre until he settled down but never leaving the area just inside the front door. Minutes later I handed him back to Lisa, who hustled Andre to the living room, making it easier for us to leave. Cordell was anxious to see the rest of his family, too.

—— ૱ ——

CORDELL BOUGHT OUR wedding rings within a few days after arriving home. I was pleasantly surprised and reassured that he was serious about getting married.

My grandfather married us in a simple ceremony on Friday, May 11, 1968. I wore my pink floor-length prom dress that Valerie had given me. Cordell looked stunningly handsome in his black suit, bow tie, and top hat. I was thrilled to become his wife.

The ceremony took all of twenty minutes and was attended by family and a few friends. My dad didn't make it, which really disappointed me. It seemed that he was never around for the happy times in my life, only when I got in trouble.

My new husband and I enjoyed about fifteen days of marital bliss, even though we had no home of our own. We slept at Cordell's mother's house at night, then went to be with our son at Momma's during the day. The first meal I cooked for him was a breakfast of round steak and fried potatoes with onions, served with bread and butter. Cordell liked it so much, he had me cook it every morning while home on leave.

✿ ROUND 12

"The honeymoon is over, sister!" Momma snapped, before storming upstairs to her bedroom. Upset because I'd asked my siblings to baby-sit while I walked downtown with Robin, Momma had returned to her usual moody self.

"She was just treating me nice because Cordell was around," I thought while sitting on my bed, tears burning my cheeks.

I resented it. I was a married woman now, and Momma still treated me as if I were a child. No sooner than my husband had left for his final five months of military duty at Fort Hood, Texas, Momma and I started bumping heads again. According to her, I didn't do enough to help around the house and was too busy "ripping and running the streets and dragging Andre from pillar to post." Momma complained about the diaper pail in my bedroom smelling. The dishes weren't washed and dried. In a nutshell, she said that I was lazy and took advantage of everybody in the house.

Momma was partially right. Manual labor was not my thing—never had been. If I could get by, pretending to be preoccupied with my baby, I did. Still partying every Friday or Saturday night, usually with Carla and Monica, I'd put Andre to bed and would ask my sisters and brothers to watch him. They always did. I seldom returned home before one or two o'clock in the morning.

I still took care of my business though. Cordell sent me a check for twelve hundred dollars, the money he'd saved while in Vietnam. I spent most of it on new living-room and bedroom furniture, and arranged for the company to hold it until I found a place to live. Despite our differences, the thought of moving away from Momma still gave me butterflies.

The final blowup came one sunny afternoon when I least suspected it. I was fussing at my sisters and brothers for eating some Jell-O I'd made for Andre.

"I told ya'll that that was all the Jell-O I had. I was gonna give it to Andre with his lunch," I fussed.

Momma almost took my head off.

"Hell, Jasmine, you've got some nerve. You eat up *my* food *all* the time," Momma snapped, before I realized she'd been listening.

Hurt and humiliated, I retreated to my room and cried for an hour. Momma's words only reinforced my feelings that she didn't want me living there anymore. And I resented Momma making me feel guilty for looking out for my child.

"If anybody knows about struggling alone with kids, she should," I thought.

A longtime battle raged underneath it all. Momma always left me in charge whenever she wasn't at home. I had a hard time giving up control when she was. Deep down inside, I didn't trust her decisions. It must have showed many times. Looking back, my distrust probably started after being tricked into Daddy's custody as a toddler and small child.

Tears still streaming down my face, I applied for public housing over the phone a few hours after Momma's harsh comments. The Lord had to be looking out for me, even though I had drifted from the church, because the woman on the other end was very kind and helpful. Plus they had a vacancy.

"Because you are a military wife, your name automatically goes to the top of our waiting list. Otherwise, you'd be looking at a two-year wait," she said.

Less than a month later I had moved into a two-bedroom apartment in the projects, on the south side of Jackson, about two-and-a-half miles away from Momma's house. The housing development was well cared for, and my rent was based on my army allotment check. I paid forty-eight dollars a month, all utilities included.

✿ ON <u>MY</u> OWN

The royal blue, tufted-back sofa with gold brocade and thick arms that softly curved. It was mine. The rectangle, mahogany coffee table with end tables to match and deep drawers that were the perfect place for holding the telephone book, pen, and paper. It was mine. The gold armchair sitting beneath the living-room window on the wall opposite the couch, its velvet upholstery changing shades at the touch of my fingers. It was mine.

Upstairs, a sleek, five-piece bedroom suite made of pecan wood, reddish brown with tiny black specks, furnished the room. It was mine. The six-foot-long dresser with nine drawers, three down and three across, and brass handles that looked like door knockers, clanking against the polished wood, then vibrating to silence when the drawers were opened. It was mine. The wood-framed mirror sitting in the middle and slanted against the off-white walls. The chest of drawers next to the doorway with five wide drawers. The nightstand. The small brass lamp on top. They were all mine.

Previously only owning clothes and toys, I'd look at my house and feel on top of the world. And knowing that everything was paid for made it even better. It was my home. It was Andre's home. It would be Cordell's home, too, when he got out of the army in three months.

———— ⸎ ————

MY MONEY RAN OUT before I could buy a kitchen table and chair set. But Grandma stepped in.

"Gwone down to the secondhand store and pick you out something," she'd said to me on the phone one morning. "Tell ole man Crowder I sent you. Don't spend over forty dollars though. You outta be able to find something that'll last till you get on your feet. You have to crawl before you walk."

Grandma sounded so pleased to help. I'd hoped she'd offer to buy me a new dinette set, but not wanting to hurt her feelings, I traipsed downtown one day and picked out a table and chair set. I hated it. It was used. Everything else in my house was brand new. The purchase sort of reminded me of Grandma's big wooden dining-room set. But Grandma's was in mint condition. This set had seen its best days. Nicks, chips, and scratches were everywhere.

I spent hours trying to spruce it up, splashing furniture stripper in my face, which burned my skin. I sanded so much that my knuckles hurt. I scrubbed the dusty upholstered seats until their beige color started fading. I dragged, tugged, and pulled the heavy furniture onto our tiny backyard patio to do the work. It was just as tough getting it back inside.

Scooting the table under my kitchen window, where yellow and white flowered curtains hung, I still didn't like the way it looked.

"As soon as I get some extra money, I'm gonna buy me a *new* dinette set," I reminded myself every time Andre and I sat down to eat dinner. "I just won't tell Grandma when I do it, and she'll never know."

We ate at the wooden table and chairs for six weeks. During that time, I set my sights on a new dinette set that included a brown oval table and brown and white vinyl-cushioned chairs. I saved every penny possible until reaching my goal. What a feeling!

✳ <u>ALWAYS</u> TOGETHER

Three weeks before Thanksgiving, 1968, Cordell hustled up the sidewalk, wearing an olive Ban-Lon shirt and khaki-colored pants, lugging a large suitcase in one hand, his oversize burlap duffel bag in the other. Grinning as if he'd won the lottery, my husband had received his honorable discharge from the U.S. Army earlier that morning. He was home for good. It had seemed as if the day would never come.

I hurried to the door before Cordell knocked, scooping up Andre in my lanky, thin arms. Our fourteen-month-old, who had been trying to climb on our coffee table, appeared confused. Wearing cocoa brown bibbed overalls and matching turtleneck, Andre looked darling for his daddy's arrival.

I flung the door open with a big smile on my face. Dressed in dark purple pants and a lighter-shade turtleneck, and an off-white vest that looked like basket weave, I wasn't bold enough to initiate a kiss yet. Cordell sensed it and made the first move, bending over and planting his thin lips softly on mine.

Andre pushed his daddy away, saying, "No!" His face scowled. Our son wasn't having any part of our welcome home party.

"You're still a stranger to him. It's been almost five months since he last saw you. Once he gets to know you better, he'll be all right," I told Cordell, whose face looked hurt, but he'd never admit it in a hundred years.

"Hey man, I heard you can walk now," Cordell said, kneeling to eye level of his pouting, curly-haired son. "Let Daddy see you walk."

Our son stepped behind me and grabbed one of my legs so tight his face pressed into my thigh. I tried to gently push our child forward. He resisted. I stepped away from him. He started whining.

"Where'd you get those fancy overalls, man?" Cordell asked, fingering his son's shoulder straps.

Andre pushed his hand away. My stomach tightened when Cordell grabbed his arm and pulled him away from me. Andre batted his small arms and screamed. Our son had never taken to strangers very easily, but I'd never seen him so uncomfortable. It really bothered me. I think it bothered Cordell just as much.

"So, what do you think of our home?" I asked, trying to avoid Andre's pleading brown eyes and talking over his crying.

"I like it. Looks nice. Blue's my favorite color," Cordell replied, bouncing Andre in his arms.

Cordell kissed his little forehead. His son turned away, still crying and reaching wildly for me.

"Arlene helped me pick out most of it," I said, stroking the smooth pattern on the sofa arm. "Remember when I told you we went furniture shopping two nights in a row after she got off work? That was a couple of months ago."

Cordell nodded. Andre cried louder.

"I wanted to get one of those long console stereos, but couldn't afford it. And come to find out, this one has been working out just fine," I said, hurrying over to the gray and white portable Zenith record player in my stocking feet.

"Do you want to listen to some music. I just got the Dells new album, *Stay In My Corner*. I've played that song so many times that I've learned every word," I said, smiling and moving a thick strand of an auburn hair piece that hung in my eye back in place.

"Who'd you say sings it?" Cordell asked, doing his best to talk above Andre's screaming.

"The Dells. They're one of my favorite groups," I said, unable to take my eyes off my son.

I couldn't take it anymore. I reached for my terrified baby. He nearly jumped into my arms. It was the beginning of a long, hard struggle between Andre and his daddy.

—— ～ ——

I PULLED BACK the gold bedspread and white flat sheet on our full-size bed. Andre was tucked in his baby bed, after he'd gone to sleep. Although his bed had been just a few feet away in the bedroom, Andre had been sleeping with me while his dad was in the army. Cordell swore to put a stop to that right away.

My husband stripped down to his briefs, then tiptoed over to the door to click off the ceiling light. Andre whined and turned on his stomach in his bed, but didn't wake up. My husband didn't budge until our son had settled down, then tiptoed back to our bed and climbed in. We snuggled into each other's arms, his warm body firmly pressed against mine. He turned my face toward his. I smiled. He gazed into my eyes, smiling back. Our faces grew nearer. Our noses touched as his lips crushed mine. Heavy breathing was the only sound in the room as I eased my arms around his thick neck.

Knock, knock, knock. Someone rapped on the window of our front door. I jumped up and started scrambling to find my clothes, feeling for them on the hardwood floor in the dark. I didn't want my husband to see me naked.

"Cut the light on, Jasmine," Cordell said, taking a deep breath and swinging one leg along the side of the bed.

"It'll wake up the baby," I whispered, slipping into my flannel housecoat.

More rapping, only louder. I rushed downstairs and peeked out the curtains that hung on the door. It was Cordell's family—everyone but his father, who tended to be shy and reclusive. I twisted the lock and opened the door. The five of them stepped inside, laughing and talking loudly. Cordell bounded down the stairs, and his face lit up as soon as he saw them.

Hitchie stepped through the doorway, laughing with his mouth wide open and accompanied by his mother. He gave Cordell some "skin," then pulled his hand back really quickly. In his other arm and hugged close to his chest were two wine bottles, each with a brown bag twisted around its neck. I knew it was going to be a long night.

"It sure is cold out there," Mrs. Walker said, her shoulders hunched but momentarily letting go of her black coat collar to give Cordell a stiff hug.

She pointed at Hitchie and rolled her eyes. I offered to take her coat, but she shook her head, saying she wanted to warm up first.

Simon swished through the door, with one hand holding his coat together and the other limp at the wrist. He hugged Cordell and patted him on the back. Stepping back, he raised his fist in a Black Power salute and shouted, "Power to the people!"

"It's about time our oppressors let you go," Simon said, looking at his brother out of the corner of his eye, his indignant smirk turning into a smile. "We've got no business over there in the first place. Vietnam is the rich white man's war, and our black brothers are dying on the front lines. Don't get me started."

Simon handed Cordell his jacket, then took a seat on the couch and beckoned me. He knew I loved hearing his viewpoint. We'd had some interesting discussions. He taught me a lot, especially about the Black Muslim movement and the Black Panther Party. My brother-in-law was also a great cook. He taught me to make hot water cornbread, bean pies, and fried fish. Simon also styled hair and kept mine looking "tight."

Simon had visited me several times a week during his brother's military duty. We had a lot in common. Neither of us smoked and seldom drank. We enjoyed the same music and loved to dance. We laughed. We debated. We encouraged and counseled each other. Simon spent more time with Andre than anyone, outside of my immediate family. And I loved the guy like a brother.

Jonathon whizzed through the door and past Cordell, looking down. Cordell tapped him on the back. The older brother turned, facing him again.

"Oh, welcome home," he said, then headed to the kitchen table, cutting a deck of playing cards he held in his hand.

Monty, who had been wiping fingerprints off the door of his girlfriend's new white-on-white Ford Mustang, strolled through the door last. He'd driven his family over to our house and had the car more than she did. And she worked every day.

"That sure is a bad car," I said as he passed through, grinning like he was "the man" and his pants up to his chest. Stroking his young ego almost always chilled him out, for a while anyway.

"Jasmine, cut on some music. Your husband's home from Nam. It's party time!" Hitchie yelled from the kitchen, slamming the white metal cabinet doors in search of drinking glasses.

"Ya'll get out of that girl's kitchen. Can't ya'll see that they were in bed? I bet ya'll were almost sleep, weren't you, Jasmine?" Mrs. Walker asked, sounding as if she didn't believe her own words.

I didn't have the heart to say "yes." Her third-oldest son had come home safely from the war. There definitely was a reason to celebrate.

"I can put up with this noise for a little while. I'm probably making a big deal out of nothing, anyway. And after all, Cordell and I will have the rest of our lives together. I bet they won't even stay that long," I thought, opening the kitchen drawer to find some coasters.

Wrong. They stayed so long that Cordell and I finally dragged ourselves to bed around three in the morning. His family was still downstairs, playing bid whist, spilling wine, and thumping cigarettes everywhere but in the ashtrays. Monty even broke one of my new blue drinking glasses after tossing it in the sink and hitting another glass.

— ❧ —

CORDELL'S MILITARY FATIGUES smelled. His duffel bag smelled. His pictures, slides, projector—everything smelled like nothing I'd ever known. It wasn't the sand and red dirt stuck on the plastic covers of his gray photo albums. I wiped those several times with Lysol disinfectant and bleach. It didn't help.

Washing his clothes several times didn't help. Scrubbing his duffel bag didn't help. Even airing Cordell's belongings in our backyard for three days didn't take the smell away.

I gave up trying to get rid of the odor and stashed everything from overseas behind the water heater in the laundry room, near the back door. I still got whiffs of the stench every now and then. The smell didn't seem to bother Cordell. I could barely touch anything he brought back without becoming nauseated.

One Saturday afternoon June Bug dropped by. He'd gotten home from Vietnam a month after Cordell. I told him about the odor. He asked me to get something that smelled. I rushed to the laundry room and dug out some of Cordell's belongings. June Bug recognized the rank odor before I plopped a photo album in his lap.

"That's the smell of death, Jasmine. Everything in Nam smells like that. It's even in the dirt over there. You'll never be able to get it out," he said, looking serious and shaking his head.

I looked at Cordell, who glanced back at me. He knew exactly what I wanted to do. I started with the clear pages to his photo albums. They got tossed in the morning trash. His army boots and clothes went a few days later. I carried them to a dumpster across the street. Within weeks I'd gotten rid of everything my husband brought back from overseas, including nearly a hundred color slides that Cordell had smuggled back to the States. Many showed mutilated bodies, stacked in piles and thrown in ditches. Some were decapitated. Others had their genitals removed. I was glad to get rid of them because every time we had visitors, Cordell would get them out and provide a slide show.

❧ SECOND <u>TIME</u> AROUND

"I might be sterile," Cordell said to me one night, pulling me closer to him while we lay in bed.

"Why would you think that?" I asked, turning to face my husband, my eyes widened.

"Cause I had a disease in Vietnam."

"What kind of disease?"

"Hepatitis. Remember, I wrote you a letter about it?"

I nodded my head.

"I spent thirty days in a military hospital. The doctors said I probably got it from the swamps or filthy drinking water," Cordell said, as if it were no big deal.

I sat up.

"Did a doctor tell you that hepatitis makes you sterile?"

"They said it could. But nobody really knows for sure. Uncle Sam just sent our black asses overseas with rifles in our hands. I laid in those muddy trenches, soaking wet, many nights, wondering how in the world did I end up over here," he said, his voice trailing, his toes rubbing my leg.

Silence.

"I want you to stop taking birth control pills to see if you get pregnant," he continued after a few seconds, his big hands easing me back down into our warm bed. He kissed my lips. His callous hands explored my body.

"Cordell, I think something's wrong with me, too."

"What?"

"I don't think I know how to have a climax. Simon thought it was strange. He also thought it was weird that we've never said 'I love you' to each other face to face."

"You and my brother been talking a lot, haven't you?" he said with a slight edge in his voice.

"Simon helped me out a lot while you were in Vietnam," I replied. "We can talk about anything, and he'll give me his honest opinion."

"Well, I'm home now. So Simon can keep his nose out of our business. If he didn't switch his ass so much, I'd start to wonder what ya'll got going on."

I turned my back to Cordell again. Offended. Embarrassed. I hadn't intended to talk about Simon. I wanted help with my sexuality. Seconds passed. It seemed like an eternity. Then Cordell wrapped his arms around me.

"I love you, Jasmine. Let's see what we can do about making Andre a baby brother."

— ℛ —

MY FACE FILLED OUT. My caramel-colored skin looked even smoother. My hair grew thick and long again, only this time I sported a big Afro instead of a home-done perm. Three months pregnant, I looked five.

Cordell and I grinned like kids stealing cookies when the gynecologist told me I was expecting. Everything was falling into place. Fast.

My husband had landed a twelve-dollar-an-hour factory job less than a month after being discharged. He worked hard and didn't miss a day. Some weeks he pulled double time. Working five and six days a week, Cordell brought his paycheck home every Thursday night and handed it to me without blinking an eye. I thought I was in seventh heaven.

My fairy tale life lasted long enough for me to get spoiled and pregnant— about four months. One Friday, Cordell didn't come home from work until three o'clock in the morning. I stared out the window for hours wondering, "Where could my husband be?"

"Is he with another woman? Is he hurt? Did he get arrested by the police?" I stood at the living-room window, watching for any sign of Cordell and listening for Andre, who was upstairs sleeping in our bed.

I finally joined him half an hour later. When a car door slammed, I jumped to our bedroom window and peeked out. Voices outside in a car caused my heartbeat to quicken. I rushed down the stairs, praying that Cordell was all right. I was mad as hell when he walked through the door, looked at me, and stomped upstairs.

"Where have you been all night?" I asked, my heart hammering in my chest.

"At the fucking pool room."

"What pool room?"

"The one on the corner of Milwaukee and Biddle."

"Doing what?"

"Playing poker and drinking a few beers."

"Where's your paycheck?"

"I cashed it."

"Why?"

"Cause it's my fucking money."

"Oh, I see. Now it's your money. What about groceries? How are we gonna pay the rent?"

"Fuck the rent."

"Fuck you," I said.

"Fuck you, too," my husband snapped back.

Cordell pulled a crumpled wad of money from his denim blue jeans' pocket and threw it on the nightstand. He undressed and climbed into bed. I slept on the couch. We didn't speak for two days. It killed me. I hated walking around the house without speaking. It reminded me of Momma. I lasted three days. Day four, my anger evaporated into sympathy. Day five, I blamed myself. Day six, I promised myself to try harder. Day seven, we made love again. It was the beginning of an addictive cycle.

"I can't believe you did it again," I cried a few weeks later, indignant and hurt. "What kind of father are you, to keep putting your family through these kind of changes?"

"Aw, that's all you do, Jasmine, is bitch, bitch, bitch."

"We've got a son to take care of and another baby's on the way, Cordell. What do you expect me to do?" I cried.

Cordell stormed out of the house that night, slamming the door so hard its window vibrated. He stayed at his mother's. He didn't come back home until Monday morning, just in time to get ready for work.

T he iron spewed steam. It hissed. Water bubbled softly inside. I was ironing the collar of Cordell's blue denim, long-sleeve work shirt when I looked up at the kitchen wall clock. Resembling a copper teakettle, the clock read two ten. I ironed faster.

"Hey Jasmine. You done with my shirt?" Cordell hollered from the bathroom upstairs.

"Give me five minutes," I hollered back.

I ironed the sleeves. Then across the shoulder area. The front. The back. Momma had taught me the correct way to iron clothes when I was in elementary school.

Factory grease and oil drifted up with steam from the iron. I held my breath. I hated factory smells. I always washed Cordell's work clothes separately and twice. The factory odor and black smudges of oil lingered in the fibers anyway.

"Jasmine. You done with my fucking shirt?" Cordell yelled again.

I hated when he cussed.

I hung Cordell's shirt on the back of a dinette chair, then let the ironing board down, pinching my finger. I ran cold water on it, then peeked in the living room to check on Andre.

He was sitting patiently on his wooden potty chair in front of our twenty-one-inch black-and-white television. He'd been on the potty so long that his bottom had a red circle imprint of the white removable pot on it. We had been trying to potty train him for two weeks. Our son sat on the pot but waited until I put some undershorts and rubber pants on him before peeing. I thought he'd never learn.

Cordell bounded slew-footed down the wooden steps. I discovered shortly after living together that my husband was extremely heavy footed. I never got used to that. Cordell grabbed his shirt from the chair. His thick, wrinkled fingers quickly buttoned it. I grabbed his black metal lunch box from the fridge. I opened the plastic bag holding a pork chop sandwich and pressed my fingers on along the flap, squeezing out the trapped air that remained. I moved his shiny red apple farther in the corner. I placed the package of chocolate Hostess cupcakes on top of the fruit, so that it wouldn't get smashed, then closed the lid and flipped the metal latch back down.

Cordell grabbed his brown all-weather jacket from the sliding-door closet next to the front door. The telephone rang. Cordell picked it up on the third ring.

"Yeah. Okay. I'll just try to get another ride, then," he said politely.

My husband stared at the beige receiver in his hands, then slammed it down on the cradle. His ride stood him up for the second time in two weeks. It was two thirty, and he had to be at work by three.

Cordell called his father. Mr. Walker's truck was down. The cab company estimated a half-hour wait. My husband rushed to the front door and flung it open, looking up and down the street. I noticed that his shirt hung crooked below his jacket.

"Cordell, your shirt looks funny. Let me look at it," I said, running alongside him, reaching for his shirttail.

"I got to get the fuck to work. If I don't put in forty hours, I won't be able to pull a double this week," he said with so much frustration I momentarily debated whether to bother. But I did.

I rebuttoned his shirt. Cordell paced the floor, eyeing the decorative wall clock hanging in our living room. He picked up the telephone. He hung it up. He hit the wall. Andre screamed.

"Don't cry, baby. Daddy's just a little mad. He doesn't want to be late for work," I said, stroking his soft hair and watching my husband snatch open the front door again.

"I'm just gonna strike out walking. Maybe I'll see somebody who's going that way," he said over his shoulder.

I rushed over and kissed him. Andre in my arms, I pushed him closer, hoping he'd also give his daddy a kiss. He didn't.

I watched from our front door as my husband trotted up the street toward the East Side. Whenever a car passed, Cordell would stoop down to see who was driving. The cars never stopped, and he ended up walking all the way.

— ❧ —

THE SOFT, PINK print housecoat nearly wrapped around my frail body twice. The belt was tied in a bow across my protruding stomach. I stepped outside our front door wearing pink sponge hair rollers and a scarf and no shoes. Reaching my hand in the black metal mailbox, I pulled out a narrow brown envelope.

"This looks like something from the military," I thought at first glance.

It wasn't. It was our first income tax refund check. It had come earlier than we had expected in the spring of 1969. My face lit up.

"Now we can finally get us a car," I thought, stumbling through the door, smiling and staring at the envelope. "I know Cordell will be tickled."

Flashbacks. The gambling. The drinking. The late hours in the streets. The heated arguments. Common sense told me to hide the check. Quick!

Money management was never one of my biggest strengths either. I paid my bills on time out of habit, thinking businesses repossessed cars and furniture or cut off electricity and gas the first time a payment was missed. It was the *extra* money that I spent impulsively. I bought new custom-made plastic covers for the couch and chair. I replaced my white ceramic lamps in the living room with blue, glass globe ones that matched my sofa perfectly. Andre got new clothes he quickly outgrew and toys that busied him for all of ten minutes. My red leather jacket had been on sale. Cordell's shirts were a steal, too. Buy one, get one 50 percent off. But we didn't even have a bank account.

"I'm going to hide this check under our mattress. Then tell Cordell about it once we find a car," I thought, nodding my head.

The light blue room-size rug felt warm and soft under my bare feet. I was feeling so good that I wanted to hear some music. Flipping the metal latch, I lifted my stereo's gray polyurethane cover. Clicking the small, black reject switch, the arm slowly moved, lowering itself on one of my favorite LPs, *The Impressions' Greatest Hits*.

I eased down to the shag rug and sat Indian style. I lay my head back against our sofa and read every word on the album cover for the twentieth time since purchasing it several weeks earlier. I closed my eyes, listening to "I'm So Proud," and thought of how lucky we were.

— ❧ —

TRAIPSING THROUGH puddles of water, our shoes' soles were thick with mud from dirt car lots. One car lot. Two. Three. We finally found a car we liked and could afford at the fourth car lot we visited. It was a brown Buick LeSabre. It looked good—my criterion. It ran good—Cordell's criterion. Its tan upholstered seats enabled three people to ride in the front seat—Andre's criterion.

"Mommy, c'mere. C'mere Mommy," Andre said, tugging at my black leather coat with a sense of urgency.

Our son toddled around the car and pointed to several patches of rust around the trunk. His mouth was wide open. Using the end of his brown corduroy coat sleeve, stretching it so hard, I thought he'd choke himself, Andre started furiously rubbing the rust.

We got the biggest kick out of our son's attention to detail and played along with him for a minute or two. Cordell and I both scurried over to our baby boy and pretended to take a closer look.

"Hey man. That's just a little rust. We'll just let that slide this time, okay? But thanks for looking out for your old man," Cordell said, smiling proudly, rubbing his son's head.

I knew Cordell had gotten caught up in the moment when he reached to take Andre's hand. Our son, who still hadn't gotten used to his dad, moved quickly away. Cordell picked his son up under his armpits and hoisted half his body over his broad shoulder. Andre's head hung upside down facing his daddy's back, his face turning beet red.

Arching his back, he whined and reached for me. I decided to let him cry and stepped away.

"I'm not going to let you run to me every time your daddy even looks at you, Andre. You're going on two years old, and almost big enough to carry me," I said, frustration peppered in my voice.

Andre cried so much he fell asleep, slumped between Cordell and me in the front seat of our car after we had transferred the title, bought 1969 license plates, and were driving our first car home.

❧ BABY MAKES FOUR

J ust before daybreak on August 26, 1969, my labor pains started. Cordell was working a double shift and wasn't scheduled to get off until seven. The windup clock on our nightstand next to the bed said five twenty.

I reached for the phone and dialed the shop. I knew the number by heart. Cordell's foreman answered.

"Hello, this is Cordell Walker's wife, Jasmine. Would you please tell him that my contractions have started, and I need him to come home?"

"Sure. I'll let him know right away," the man said, a touch of excitement in his voice.

It was seven thirty when Cordell dragged through the door. I had expected him to be excited. He complained of being tired.

"This baby's coming, and I hadn't packed a thing. I've already called the doctor, and pulled my stuff together in my overnight case while I was waiting on you to come home. When did you get my message?" I asked, trying not to sound as mad and disappointed as I felt.

"I don't know. My foreman told me as soon as you called. I was two hours short of working a double. I wasn't gonna pass that kind of money up. Hell, I bet the baby doesn't come until tomorrow."

"I bet you it comes today," I said, my hands pulling the elastic waist pants away from my stomach to ease the discomfort. "The doctor said my contractions should be five minutes apart before I go to the hospital. Right now, they're about eight minutes apart."

I wanted Cordell to act like the expectant fathers on television, pacing the floor, passing out cigars as he eagerly anticipated his new child's arrival. He wanted to lie down and take a nap until it was time. My husband looked so tired and broken down, I didn't have the heart to say no.

I dressed Andre, then called Momma. She had agreed to keep him so Cordell could work. I fed our son a bowel of oatmeal and toasted him a piece of bread. By the time he'd finished eating, my labor pains were five minutes apart.

Waking Cordell up wasn't easy. I shook him. He flopped his right arm along the side of the bed. I shook him again. He swung so hard I had to step back. Creeping back up to the bed, I shook his shoulders until he opened his glazed-over red eyes.

———— ℛ ————

THE LARGE, ROUND wall clock in my hospital room said nine thirty. My nurse's aide, an older woman from my old East Side neighborhood, took my blood pressure and pulse.

"Your baby's going to be born on my birthday," she said, smiling. "You just relax and take deep breaths when you feel a contraction coming."

Still dressed in grubby, dark blue jeans and a lighter blue denim buttoned-down shirt, Cordell sat slumped in a metal hospital chair, mumbling about being tired. He twisted and turned. His face looked angry and miserable.

"I know he's got to be tired. I couldn't possibly work *one* shift in a factory building tires, let alone two," I thought, watching my husband try to get comfortable.

An hour passed. My labor hadn't progressed. Reluctantly, I suggested that Cordell go home and get some rest. It was only a ten-minute drive.

"I'll call you when the nurse says the baby is ready to come. They said it won't be for a few more hours yet," I said halfheartedly.

Cordell jumped up, kissed me on the forehead, and left. I was so disappointed. Having been in Vietnam for the birth of our first child, this time I had expected him to spend every minute at the hospital, holding my hand, wiping my forehead, and saying how much he loved me.

Two hours later the nurses informed me I had dilated to eight. I called the house. The line was busy. I called again. And again. And again. Each time, I got a busy signal. I finally called my next-door neighbor, another longtime friend from the East Side.

"Linda, will you go knock on our door and wake Cordell up? I'm up here at

Foote Hospital getting ready to have my baby and can't get through to him on the phone," I said, the sedation kicking in.

By the time Cordell walked through my hospital room door an hour later, our new son was sleeping in my arms. Born at 2:25 P.M., we named our son Lamar Elliott Walker.

✤ TRIPPING

I t was our second wedding anniversary, and I walked around the house, crying and feeling sorry for myself. Cordell had stayed out all night, then came home broke, again.

I heard my husband's key turn the lock just after six thirty that morning. The door slowly opened, then closed, before he quietly tiptoed upstairs. Standing a few feet from the bed, he peeled off everything except his underwear, dropping his clothes in a heap on the shiny oak floor. He, pulled back our chenille bedspread and eased into bed, barely making a sound. My back turned to him, I lay there stewing for five minutes, my stomach muscles knotted so hard they ached. I figured he'd lost all his money and suspected he was seeing another woman.

"Who is she? What does she look like? Does she look better than me? Did they do it? Did he like it? Was she better than me in bed?" I wondered, lying on my side next to him, so mad I wanted to scream.

"Who's gonna tell the phone company that our payment will be late again? How are we gonna eat and buy gas for the next week?" I thought, my mind jumping back and forth from jealousy to worry. "I'm so tired of struggling to make ends meet, I don't know what to do. And Cordell makes six and seven hundred dollars a week. That doesn't make any sense."

Cordell still gave me most of the money, when he hadn't gambled it up. But he would ask for it back within a few days to buy gas and snacks during his breaks. I didn't like it, but felt it was his money. He'd worked for it.

"I worked hard to establish good credit. And now that he's home from the army, he's even ruining that," I thought, staring into space and rehearsing what I was going to say when the argument began.

My thoughts were abruptly interrupted by Cordell's loud snoring. That made me madder. I sat up in the bed, cut on the table lamp, then reached over and shook him.

"Cordell, wake up. We've gotta talk. There's some things that we need to get straight right now," I said, trying my best to keep from punching him.

He snored louder.

I shook him again, first with one hand, then both. I shook him so hard that our bed bounced, the pecan headboard bumping against the wall. Cordell's slit eyes popped open. He sat up as if hit by a bolt of lightning—trembling, sweating, and turning his head from side to side with a terrified look on his face.

I knew that wild-eyed look. He was dreaming he was still back in Vietnam. I felt sorry for my husband whenever he woke up scared like that. It happened at least once a month. Usually I'd step back to keep from getting hit and give him ten seconds or so to calm down and get his bearings. This time I waited five—long enough for him to stop swinging.

"You must think I'm crazy. I know you lost all your money gambling again, didn't you?" I screamed, not caring who heard me on the other side of our paper-thin walls.

Cordell's wild, glazed-over eyes started focusing, then blinking. He was becoming aware of his surroundings again.

"You keep on doing this kind of shit to us, and I'm gonna leave your ass," I hollered, my voice hoarse from lack of sleep and screaming. "And when I leave, I'm gonna do just like my momma did my dad. I'm *never* coming back."

Cordell's eyebrows folded into a scowl. His bottom lip rolled under, showing his teeth. His puffy eyes scoured the room, while he scratched and furiously rubbed his smooth, curved shoulders, still trying to shake off the nightmare. His eyes returned to mine with a glare that would have scared a bull.

"Damn it! Is that what you woke me up for, woman?" he yelled, rising from the bed, leaning on one elbow, and looking at me like I was crazy.

"Uh huh! You *must* have lost your check. Or else you would've said 'no' right away. What's wrong with you Cordell, are you crazy or something? Don't you realize what this is doing to our marriage?" I screamed, my voice cracking.

"You're the one who's crazy—you jealous-ass bitch!" he shot back. "You just think I was somewhere fucking some woman. You ain't fooling me with that bullshit about being mad about some money. I make money. Money don't make me."

"I got your jealous-ass bitch all right. Your bitch is out in the street," I yelled, nose to nose.

"Jasmine, you better get the hell out of my face. I'm warning you."

"Or else what? You can't do anything worse than you already have."

Andre wandered into the room, wiping his eyes, yawning and stretching his arms toward me. Cordell leaned forward, naked from the waist up, and yelled at him.

"What did we tell you about climbing out of bed? Boy, you gon break your neck one of these days. You're always crying for your mammy. Get back in bed!"

"Don't you dare take it out on him, just because you messed up. That's why he's scared of you now," I yelled, picking our two-year-old up, who had frozen in his tracks. "You don't even know how to talk to your own son. Let alone your wife."

"He ain't nothing but a momma's boy. But I'm gonna toughen his ass up," Cordell yelled, as I carried Andre back to his bedroom, both of us crying crocodile tears. I had to peel his small hands from around my neck.

"No Mommy. Please," he cried, looking pitiful and clinging to me as if his life depended on it.

I swung his legs back over the rail. I pulled up the side and snapped it into place. Tears dripped down my face and plopped on his mattress as I kissed him on the forehead.

The fighting and name calling resumed as soon as I returned to our bedroom.

"I've given up everything for you. My family. My friends. Everything. I've spent so much time trying to please your crazy-ass family, that I've even ignored my own. And it hasn't done a bit of good. Nearly everybody in your family smiles in my face and talks about me behind my back. And you aren't even man enough to stand up for me."

Cordell threw back the blankets and jumped up from the bed. He grabbed his pants, still lying crumpled in the floor, and began struggling to put them on.

"Those fucking niggahs down on the corner are some cheating bastards," he mumbled to himself, hopping on one leg, the other foot caught in his pants. "I should've quit when I was ahead. That's what I get. I ain't going down there gambling with them no fucking more."

The clock said five minutes after nine. The sun was shining brightly, and car doors slammed outside as people started their day. I felt like the only woman in the world who was mistreated on her anniversary. It hurt like hell. But I still wanted Cordell to stay at home. I hoped we'd fuss and argue until we reached some type of understanding—maybe even make up. But it didn't happen that way.

"And where do you think you're going now?" I asked indignantly, my eyes glaring at him, then his pitiful dance to put on his wrinkled work pants that were covered with so much grease and grime I wondered how he had the nerve to be seen in public. But then Cordell never cared much for clothes or how he looked.

"Jasmine, I ain't gonna stay here and listen to you bitch all day. Fuck you! I'm going to my momma's house, where I can get some sleep."

"I can't believe you," I shouted, tears burning my cheeks. "Here it is our anniversary, and not only do you stay out all night, but you come home smelling like smoke and alcohol, then slide into bed with me, hoping that everything is cool. You must be out of your mind!"

Cordell twisted and shimmied until he got his pants up. My heart pounded so hard, he probably could have heard it, but he was too busy trying to get his arms in the sleeves of his equally greasy and grimy blue denim shirt. Then he stormed out of the bedroom with his socks and shoes in his hand.

"You just want me to sit up under your ass all day," Cordell hollered from the bathroom as he stood peeing with the door opened. "I ain't one of those ole henpecked men those other women in your family got. And I ain't gonna let you turn me into one either. I'm a *man*."

I jumped up out of bed and darted to the bathroom to retaliate face to face. His back turned, Cordell was zipping up his pants just as I reached the door. He turned and with a smirk on his face stepped so close to me I could smell his breath. But I wasn't about to back down.

"I don't consider it being henpecked just because you stay at home and take care of your own family. And *you've* got a lot of nerve talking about somebody's relatives, with all those hoodlums and criminals in your family," I screamed so loudly that Andre woke up again and started crying.

While tending to our son, I heard the front door slam. Hurrying to our bedroom window, with Andre slung on my hip, I watched my husband speed down the street. It scared me. I felt incredibly alone all of a sudden. I just hoped and prayed he'd come back.

He did, about two hours later. We walked around not speaking for another hour, the tension stifling. I kept replaying our arguments over and over in my mind, weighing reasons for and against leaving Cordell.

"Kids need their daddy. A half a daddy is better than none at all. I don't want my kids growing up without a father living in the home, like I did," I thought. "But I'm so unhappy. One minute I think this marriage is gonna work. The next minute I don't know. Is that the way marriage is supposed to be?"

I walked around lifeless and teary eyed. By nightfall, Andre's eyes were as swollen as mine. His nose red and runny, he whined and cried all day. I had to change Lamar's diapers with my two-year-old son hanging on my leg. I couldn't even go to the bathroom without him climbing up in my lap as I sat on the toilet. He stayed so close under me that I almost stumbled over him several times.

Lamar was the complete opposite of his brother. My baby lay in his crib without crying for hours. Sometimes I forgot I even had another child in the house, which shamed me, because he was so quiet and non-demanding.

I started putting the boys in their pajamas about nine o'clock when the telephone rang. Cordell had been sitting in front of the television for hours and answered the phone downstairs at the same time I did upstairs. It was Cassandra, his sister-in-law, who had married Hitchie, several months earlier. We called her Cassie. She wanted us to come over to their house for a drink to celebrate our anniversary. The last thing I wanted to do was sit up with his family that night.

"Aw come on, Jasmine," Cordell said, his voice softening as if trying to make up. "You're always stuck in this house. You need to get out once in a while. That's what's wrong with you. You need to loosen up a little and have some fun."

I wasn't going for it. I wanted to stay home. I wanted my husband to stay home with us but was too stubborn to admit it.

"I just put the boys to sleep," I said. "And I'm not gonna wake them up and take them out in this night air."

Cordell made a few more weak pleas, but I refused. I had undressed, clicked off the overhead light in our bedroom, and crawled into bed before he left the house. Lying there on my side in a fetal position, I thought about all the sacrifices I'd made trying to please him.

"I go around his family more than I do my own now. And they don't care a thing about me anymore," I thought. "I've given up everything for this man. Everything. And look where it's gotten me."

Every now and then a car would pass on the street outside my bedroom window. Its headlights strolled across my walls, the swishing fading gently into the stillness of the late night. I held my breath and listened as each car passed, hoping that one of them would be Cordell, coming home to apologize. Coming back to say he'd seen the light. That everything was going to be okay from now on. But he never came.

Around eleven o'clock the phone rang again. Thinking it was Mother, making a second nightly call, I grabbed the phone in the dark. It was Cassie again.

"Girl, how come you didn't come over here with Cordell?" she asked in an expressionless voice that I almost didn't recognize. "You ain't got no business staying home on your anniversary. Come on over here so we can help celebrate your anniversary before this day is gone. I'll come get you."

"I'm really not in the mood to celebrate, Cassie," I said, trying my best not to sniffle. "The kids have been asleep for a few hours, and I'm in bed, too."

"Aw, girl, come on. Don't be a party pooper," she insisted. "We're just sitting up here talking and drinking and smoking a little weed. Come on now, Jasmine, you've got to come and have at least one drink with us."

"Who's all over there?"

Just me, Hitchie, Jonathon, and Cordell. Don't dress up or anything. Just slip on some clothes. I'll come help get the boys dressed. I'll be there in fifteen minutes."

A part of me wanted to stay home and brood. Another part of me longed to spend time with my husband on our anniversary night, even though we were at odds with each other. I agreed to go.

— ౭ —

EVERYONE WAS SITTING in the dimly lit living room when we entered. I put the boys back to bed in Cassie's room, then quietly tiptoed back out, closing the door behind me. I joined the others in the living room as they sat around talking and listening to music by the Spinners. A strobe light flashed red, yellow, blue, and green reflections on the furniture and walls as the wheel rotated.

Everyone was laughing and talking to one another when I quietly took a seat on the end of the couch next to Cassie and Hitchie. Cordell sat in a brown, overstuffed armchair on the carpeted floor that had a foot of hardwood showing around the walls. Jonathon sat next to him in a kitchen chair.

Cassie, a tall, thin, dark-skinned woman who usually was a big talker, still acted strange to me, but I didn't think much about it. Fifteen minutes after I sat down, she stood up and beckoned me to follow her into the kitchen. I did.

"Here's something that'll relax you," she said, smiling slightly, and opening her polished finger-nailed hand to reveal a tiny purple pill.

"What's that?" I asked.

"It's acid."

"What will it do?"

"It should make you relax, maybe even feel good," she said softly.

The only pills I had taken in the past were those prescribed by my doctor. I didn't even know what acid was. But not wanting to appear square and desperately wanting relief from the foul mood I'd been in all day, I took the pill while she got me a glass of water.

"A pill this little can't do too much to me," I thought, before putting it in my mouth and taking a sip of water. I threw back my head and swallowed. Cassie put the glass away, then we strolled back into the living room with the others, who were still laughing and talking quietly.

Before long, I was laughing and having a good time along with everybody else. Sometimes the laughing got so loud it sounded deafening. Other times I could barely hear. About an hour later I started feeling nervous and scared, but had forgotten about the pill I took. Suddenly everyone in the room started looking as if they were snickering and talking about me—right in front of my face. Their necks stretched like rubber and snaked closer to each other, with everyone whispering and eyeing me. Their heads started swelling like balloons being blown up, then shrank so small I could barely see the features on their faces. My heart pounded.

"Am I losing my mind or what?" I thought, wanting to scream but afraid to say anything.

My eyes darted around the room and became fixed on a large plant sitting on the floor beside the sofa. Suddenly it started growing, with stems sprouting and leaves growing out of one another. Tall trees sprang up in the middle of the living room floor, and before long a jungle had engulfed me.

"Oh my God! What's happening to me?" I screamed, jumping from my seat, swinging my arms and ducking to avoid the dense foliage surrounding me.

The laughing and chattering in the room stopped. Cordell rushed over to me, wide-eyed and concerned.

"Jasmine, what is it? What's the matter?" he asked.

"Get away! Don't come near me," I screamed, still batting and waving my arms in the air.

"What's the matter with you, Jasmine? Tell me," he hollered, his face so close to mine I could smell alcohol and marijuana on his breath.

Cassie came up beside Cordell and stooped down in front of me.

"Jasmine, do you think you're having a bad acid trip?" she asked in a soft voice, her eyes filled with concern.

"What's a bad trip? Maybe . . . I don't know," I cried, shrinking back from everybody. "All I know is that something weird is happening to me."

Cordell's face changed from worried to irritated.

"Aw hell, Jasmine. You can't be doing that kind of shit now. Why do you always have to fuck things up for everybody else? We were having a good time," he fussed.

The angry look on his face made me even more afraid. Cassie kept trying to calm me down, while Cordell paced back and forth ranting about how nothing ever goes right for him. After what seemed like an hour, Cassie suggested that I go lie down in their extra bedroom. I agreed, just to get away from everybody.

Cordell led me to the room, but I refused to let him come in. After sitting on the side of the bed for several minutes, terrified of moving, I lay down and closed my eyes, hoping it was all a bad dream. Suddenly I heard a noise that sounded like paper being balled up. I opened my eyes, looked up, and saw the ceiling appearing to be cracking. Then pieces started falling down on me in slow motion. I covered my head, screamed, and braced myself for the impact, only to have the jagged pieces of ceiling taunt me by lingering inches above my head. At the same time, the bedroom door flew open, and everybody rushed in.

"What's the matter now?" Cordell asked, sounding more frustrated than ever.

Too scared to let any of them near me but terrified to be alone, I kept crying and repeating, "Something's wrong with me. There's something *really* wrong with me."

I saw them exchanging uneasy glances, which made me even more paranoid. It was obvious that none of them knew what to do. So I started begging.

"Please call my cousin Robin. I want to talk to her right now."

Cassie hurried into the kitchen and returned with the telephone. Ordinarily a cool, calm, collected woman, she looked worried—almost desperate. I dialed Robin's number, and she answered after the third ring.

"Hello?" she said, her voice raspy from sleep.

"Hi . . . Robin. . . . This is Jasmine. I need you to come get me. There's something wrong."

"What do you mean something's wrong?" she said, her voice rising in alarm.

"I took some acid. And now I'm seeing things. I want to go home, but I'm too scared to be by myself. Can you come get me?" I said, trying not to sound too hysterical.

"Jasmine, I can't come over there. It's four o'clock in the morning, and my kids are in bed asleep," she said, sounding a little afraid and a little agitated.

That hurt me. I wanted someone from my family with me. Scared to death for me and my babies, I wanted to get away from Cordell's family as soon as possible.

Next, I called my cousin Debra.

"Hi Debra," I said, fighting to sound sane. "I need you to come get me. I'm scared. I took something. Cassie said it was acid. And now I'm seeing things, and I'm scared to death."

"Acid?" she asked. "Isn't that LSD?"

"I don't know. All I know is that I keep seeing weird things."

"Oh my God! Girl, I think acid is LSD," she said. "I read somewhere that that's the stuff that makes people do all kinds of crazy things, like jump off roofs and put their babies in ovens."

My cousin promised to come as soon as she got dressed. A half an hour later Debra was knocking on the front door. She hurried to the bedroom, her hair still in black foam rollers and wearing a black spring coat with sleeves that came just below her long forearms. I felt better just seeing her face.

"Girl, are you okay?" she said, her eyes asking more.

I quickly shook my head no.

"I want to go home," I said, my panic rising again. "The boys are in the other bedroom sleep. Please, Debra, go get them so we can get out of here."

"I'll take you home. Don't worry," Debra said, her voice calm and reassuring.

"Will you stay with me?" I asked, like a child afraid of the dark.

"Of course, girl. You know I will," my cousin said. "Let me get the kids. Cassie's gonna take us to your house."

—— ❧ ——

THE GRAIN IN OUR mahogany coffee table shuffled back and forth, sometimes so fast it shimmered. I was frozen in fear. Debra kept talking to me from upstairs as she put the boys, who were still groggy, back to bed. My body felt heavy, like dead weight, when I finally forced myself to go upstairs to the bathroom.

Something drew me to the mirror of our white medicine cabinet, and to my horror, I saw hair growing on my face. The pores in my skin opened and closed. Every sound, every color, every everything was magnified or distorted in some way.

Andre's lips started swelling. Lamar's eyes grew as big as saucers. My sons' faces became so grotesque that I turned and ran from their bedroom into ours, slamming the door behind me to avoid looking at them. The loud noise woke up Andre, who started whining and calling me. His cries sounded so loud that I cowered in our closet for several minutes until Debra found me. The hallucinations continued throughout the day, and by nine o'clock that night I couldn't take any more.

"Debra, you've got to call my doctor. Tell him what I did. I don't care who knows anymore. I just need someone to help me."

My cousin wasted no time looking up the number and calling Dr. Sizemore, who had taken care of me most of my life. She told him the whole story, and he asked to speak to me.

"So, young lady, what have you gotten yourself into?" he asked in a firm but compassionate voice.

"I took some acid," I said meekly.

"How much did you take?"

"One pill. A real tiny purple one."

"When did you take it?"

"Around midnight last night. I've never taken anything like that before. I didn't know acid was LSD."

"Where'd you get it?"

"From some friends," I said, not wanting to snitch.

"Well Jasmine, you sound pretty coherent to me," Dr. Sizemore said. "What seems to be the problem right now?"

"I'm seeing things. I think I'm hallucinating. Even my kids look like monsters to me. Can you do something?" I asked, almost pleading. "I can't take any more of this. I haven't been able to sleep or anything."

"Yes. There is something we can try," my doctor replied. "I'm going to prescribe a sleeping pill for you. What pharmacy do you want it called in to? And do you have someone who can pick it up?"

"My cousin can."

"Well, the medication is strong and will probably make you sleep for quite a while, so be sure not to take it until you are able to go right to bed. If you're still hallucinating when you wake up, the only thing I can tell you to do is go to the psychiatric ward at the hospital and admit yourself."

My heart fell. I knew of a person who had taken LSD and never recovered from it. All I could think about was the possibility of me ending up the same way.

"And by the way," the doctor said before hanging up, "I prescribe the same bad acid trip thing for all the people who were with you last night."

— ❧ —

DESPITE DEBRA'S constant reassurance, I cried all the way to the drugstore.

"Girl, you'll be okay," she said, glancing at me while trying to keep her eyes on the road. "Shoot, you probably just need some rest. You haven't slept in almost twenty-four hours."

We got back home, and my cousin gave me the pill with a glass of milk before I climbed into bed. Just before three o'clock the next afternoon, I awakened from a seventeen-hour sleep. My first thought was the acid. I sat up and slowly turned my head, looking for any sign of hallucinations. Seeing none, I climbed out of bed, still jittery, and took a peek into the boys' bedroom. Lamar was sleeping peacefully on his back in his baby bed. Smelling like baby lotion and dressed in a turquoise one-piece sleeper, he looked like himself again, chubby cheeks and all. I started downstairs after hearing voices coming from the kitchen.

"Where's Mommy?" Andre asked Debra, who was frying potatoes, his favorite food.

"Here I am, honey," I said, stepping into the kitchen and feeling a little strange, trying to smile for the first time in over two days. Debra and Andre both glanced up with surprised looks on their faces. My cousin's expression quickly changed to a relieved smile.

🌸 BUSTED

"Jasmine, you promise you won't go and jump bad with anybody when I tell you this? Cause you know how *we* are," Carla said on the telephone one morning after I had sat up waiting for my husband all night.

"I promise. Come on out with it, Carla. I can take it," I replied.

"Cordell left the club last night with Beverly Dobson," she said slowly.

"Who is Beverly Dobson?" I asked with indignation.

"Girl, you don't know who Beverly Dobson is?" she asked, sounding surprised. "She's older than us—around my momma or your momma's age. And the biggest whore in Jackson and . . ."

"Well I'll be damned," I said, interrupting her. "I'm sorry. Go ahead, Carla."

"This 'person' told me that Cordell was drunk last night at the club and Beverly was *supposed* to be giving him a ride home."

That was all I needed to hear. Carla told me where the woman lived, right around the corner from Momma. I crept in the boys' bedroom and found them still out like a light. Andre had stayed up until eleven thirty the night before while I rocked him to sleep and talked to Mother on the phone. Figuring they'd sleep another hour at least, I called a cab.

All the way across town, I stared at the rain dripping down the window of the backseat door on the driver's side. In my mind, I called Cordell and Beverly every name I could think of, and couldn't wait to confront them. By the time the cab pulled up in front of a one-story, tiny house that sat close to the street, I was crying. Drying my eyes before getting out of the vehicle, I marched up to the front door and knocked softly. Everything seemed very still at first. I knocked again, and the door eased open.

A light-skinned, gentle-talking woman peeked out the cracked door, smiling.

"Hi, Jasmine. You want to come in? Cordell is sleeping on the couch," she said, wearing a white, silk housecoat, a strand of black wavy hair dangling down her neck from a mussed-up French roll hairdo.

Cordell appeared at the door behind her, looking confused and sleepy. His hair matted on his head and eyes crusty, I wanted to jump on him right then and there.

"No thank-you," I said, glaring at her for a second or two while she struggled to keep smiling.

Holding her housecoat together with both hands, she stepped aside so that Cordell could come out on the small, glass-enclosed front porch with a warped wooden, scuffed-up floor. I could tell Beverly was a good-looking woman in her day. My perception of beauty was still straight black hair and light skin. She had both. It had to be my home training of respecting my elders, because I contained myself in front of Barbara, even though I was about to explode.

"I hope you've got a place to stay," I said to Cordell as he stood there, the tail of his work shirt hanging outside his pants, his eyes looking bloodshot and scared.

My composure even surprised me and must have confused Cordell, because I asked for the car keys, and he quickly dug in his pocket and handed them to me, knowing I'd never driven before except for a six-week driver's training class in the eleventh grade. I walked back out front to our car, opened the door on the driver's side, and climbed in. Not looking back, I stuck the key in the ignition and drove off slowly, with one foot lightly on the gas and the other on the brake, in case I had to make a quick stop.

Rain was pouring down by the time I loaded up the car with as many of Cordell's clothes as I could grab without waking up the kids, then headed slowly back to the East Side. I pulled up at Beverly's house and parked in the same area out front as earlier. Scrambling to get out of the car, I opened the backseat door, grabbed an armful of clothes, socks and underwear dropping everywhere, and threw them into her front yard. I must have dumped two or three loads, rushing like a madwoman, before Cordell or someone else could stop me. I climbed back into the brown beast and slowly drove back home. As far as I knew, the boys never woke up.

❀ WHERE THE HEART IS

The front door was unlocked, but no one answered when I knocked. Gently, I pushed it open. I needed to talk to my grandmother.

"Mother? Daddy? Is anybody home?" I called, peeking through the cracked door.

"I'm upstairs, Jasmine," my grandmother gently called from upstairs.

I found Mother on her knees, looking under the bed in a room she still referred to as Linnie's bedroom. Linnie was my second-youngest aunt and named after our great-grandmother, who still lived in French Camp, Mississippi. Linnie had moved to Baltimore several years earlier.

Stuff was strewn everywhere—on the bed, dresser, and floor. Mother had already searched the old wooden trunk that Albert made her when he was in junior high school, because the wood-planked top was lying on the bed. The trunk's contents—bed linen, towels, doilies, hymnals and other religious books yellowed from age, old letters, post cards, and funeral programs were piled on top of it and scattered everywhere.

"What are you doing Mother?" I asked, knowing she was always looking for something.

"I'm trying to find an old hymnal my mother gave me when I was still living at home," Mother replied, with an embarrassed smile on her heart-shaped face.

"What does it look like?" I asked, getting down on my knees to look under the bed, too. "I came over cause I need to talk to you about something."

Moving quickly for a woman nearing seventy, Mother scrambled to her knees, her black bushy eyebrows jumping. Her eyes grew bigger and started blinking—a sure sign of my grandmother's concern. I knew I had her undivided attention.

"What about?" she said, her eyes penetrating mine. "Is everything all right?"

"No, Mother, everything is going wrong. I'm thinking about leaving Cordell."

My grandmother's eyes blinked faster. She wiped her long, slender hands on the blue-bibbed apron she wore, her golden brown face wrinkled from years of toil.

I hated telling Mother bad news. Everyone in the family knew she worried about us all too much. But my grandmother was the only person I knew who would listen and not take sides.

"You say you're thinking about leaving Cordell? For what?" Mother asked, her eyebrows still jumping, her brown cat eyes still blinking.

"Cause he ain't doing right. He's even gambling his paychecks away."

"You say he is?" she asked.

"Yep. But that's not all, Mother. Cordell stays out all night at least once a month on the weekends. This past weekend I caught him at Barbara Dobson's house. They claimed he slept on the couch."

"Barbara Dobson? What business did he have there?" she asked, her oversize ears sticking out from her head and hearing everything.

"That's exactly what I said, Mother. But you know what? Cordell doesn't even think he's done anything wrong. Neither does his mother. I told Mrs. Walker about it, and she had the nerve to try to defend him."

Mother looked at me without saying anything. Her eyes said she understood. My grandmother never said much, but had a way of conveying empathy like no one else I knew.

"Daddy will be home soon. I need to fix a bite to eat," she said, her eyes on me, still feeling my pain.

We traipsed down the steps and into the kitchen, passing Mother's old piano, which sat in the dining room.

"Now where'd you say you got that piano, Mother? I keep forgetting," I said, stopping to admire the antique.

"A little ole white man sold me that piano for forty dollars back in 1959," she said, her face a bit more relaxed. "He lived in a little bitty old house that sat back off the street at 6301 Page Avenue."

I marveled at my grandmother's memory. She had a house overloaded with furniture and items, most of them given to her. Mother could tell us where every single piece came from, and never threw anything away.

The kitchen was Mother's domain. She seldom ate anybody's cooking but her own, and was so adept in the kitchen that she could whip up a hearty home-cooked meal in less time than it took for ice to freeze. I started setting the table while Mother cut up chicken at the sink, her back turned.

"Now what did that hymnal you were looking for look like?" I asked, while wiping spilled sugar from the center of her table.

"It's about so big," she said, turning around, holding her wet hands six inches apart. Her long, scrawny arms looked like tree branches. "It's a little gray book, with a little girl holding a songbook against her chest on the cover. She was wearing a sun bonnet on her head and some little bitty gloves on her hands."

I smiled.

"Your memory is something else, Mother."

"What does that mean?" she asked sheepishly.

"It means your memory is good. Real good."

Mother's dry lips formed a smile.

"Now Jasmine, what was that you were saying upstairs?" she asked, her eyebrows jumping again.

I took a deep breath, then eyed my grandmother, whose tiny stature belied her remarkable strength.

"I said I might leave Cordell. I want a divorce. What do you think?"

My grandmother stared at me. White flour had floated up to the hair across her forehead, giving the appearance of salt-and-pepper hair. She wiped her long, slender fingers, sticky with chicken flour, on the tail of her apron. Walking over to the table, Mother pulled out a chrome chair with a green vinyl seat and sat down in her usual spot, closest to the stove. I sat down in mine, closet to the window and refrigerator.

"Jasmine, all kids need a father. And you've got two big ole boys to raise. They need a father living in the home," she said, her eyebrows steady and her big brown eyes penetrating.

"But I can't keep putting up with all this crazy stuff Cordell keeps doing, Mother. It's too much. That man will drive me crazy if I let him."

Mother was quiet. Then she stood up and took a few short steps to the stove and picked up the aluminum teakettle with a small dent in the spout. Pouring herself a cup of black coffee, she looked up at me.

"Jasmine, you need to go back to church."

"Mother please," I interrupted. "I really don't feel like hearing that right now."

"You say you don't feel like hearing that right now?" my grandmother repeated, her eyes blinking again.

"Yeah. I get tired of you telling me that. Church is for people who believe in that stuff. Everybody needs something to believe in, I guess. I just happen to be one of those who don't," I said unapologetically.

Mother's mouth flew open, then closed just as quickly. Her eyes grew as big as they could get. She looked as if she couldn't believe what had just come out of my mouth. I almost wished I hadn't said it. But I did and felt relieved.

I held my breath and waited for her response. Surprisingly, none came. Mother quickly reached for her blue and white coffee cup, a piece from a set Debra had given her. After taking a sip, she got up and checked on her cornbread in the oven. I wanted to say something, but couldn't think of anything. My grandmother broke the ice.

"Have you seen Albert today?" Mother asked, catching me off guard with her dramatic change of subject.

I felt so strange. So uncomfortable. I didn't know what her response meant, but it sure unnerved me. But I tried not to show it.

"Yeah. He called me a day or two ago. He sounded okay," I said, wondering where the conversation was going next.

"He came up here and got twenty-five dollars from Daddy yesterday," Mother continued. "He said something about needing it for some treatment program. Do you know what he was talking about?"

"Yeah, I came up here and talked to Daddy the other night while you were at choir practice. Someone told me Albert has been using drugs," I said gently. "I told Daddy."

"Who told you that?" Mother said, her eyebrows nearly leaping off her forehead.

"Debra told me. I promised not to tell anybody where it came from. She said her friend Louella Bush told her. You know Louella and Grover Lyons live together. He's supposed to be a drug user, too, based on what Debra said."

Most members of our family would have kept that secret from Mother. I couldn't. I valued my grandparents' counsel and tried to be as honest and forthright as possible with them. There was something about telling them that made me feel better.

"Daddy said he'd talk to Albert," I said. "So don't worry, Mother. Everything's gonna be okay. Albert listens to Daddy when he won't listen to anybody else."

Our conversation went from one family member to another, but never returned to church. Mother insisted on updates on everybody, so I tried to halfway keep up with the activities of family members around my age. Even though we didn't see each other as much as before, we still talked on the telephone.

My grandmother and I parted that day without saying another word about church. I kept replaying our conversation about the subject as I slowly drove back home. Her reaction to my comments bothered me so much that I told Cordell while lying in bed that night, even though I knew that church and God had never been his "thing."

❧ TIGHTROPE

Hitchie and Jonathon knocked on our door one Friday night, just as I was putting the boys to bed. I trotted back downstairs and saw them snorting white powder through a dollar bill rolled into a straw.

"They paid me twenty dollars to let them get high here," Cordell said, handing me the money. "We can use that to buy gas next week."

I didn't like it but gladly accepted the money. It seemed unimaginable that someone would pay that much money just to get high. I poured myself a glass of Schlitz malt liquor and sat on the sofa and watched. Cordell asked questions. I didn't. I wanted them to hurry up and leave but said nothing to avoid another fight. They stayed until after midnight, when I climbed in bed.

The next weekend the two brothers came again. Same reason. Same pay.

"At least Cordell is staying at home instead of in the streets. If letting his brothers snort that mess at our house is what it takes, then so be it," I thought, not realizing that the white powder was the same substance people shot in their arms. I'd seen it in an antidrug film at school once.

I watched as they used Cordell's driver's license to chop tiny chunks into a consistency like baking powder, then scrape the drug into several half-inch lines. Jonathon borrowed a dollar bill from Cordell and rolled it into a tight little straw. The brothers laughed and talked for hours after snorting the white substance. It seemed to make them feel good and happy. Cordell and I watched the brothers snort for several weeks before curiosity got the best of us.

"I want to try it," my husband said, looking at me.

"I do, too," I replied.

Jonathon smiled. Hitchie passed the album cover, then scraped a line for Cordell and another for me. Cordell took the dollar bill turned straw, put it to his nose, and sniffed until the powdery line disappeared. He passed it to me, and I did the same thing.

A bitter taste drained down the back of my throat a few seconds later, sending a chill through my body. Several minutes later I felt light-headed, then on top of the world.

I laughed hard for the first time in weeks. Cordell and I even gave each other goo-goo eyes and excused ourselves for the night. Spontaneous laughter broke out from his brothers.

"Aw hell, Cordell. You and Jasmine fuck more than anybody I know. Damn man, give it a break," his oldest brother said, grinning from ear to ear, his mouth looking like piano keys, due to missing teeth.

We did stay in bed a lot, but we had only been living together as man and wife for less than two years. I laughed. Never having seen myself as sexual before, I felt downright proud to be viewed otherwise.

Cordell and I made passionate love that night. I felt aggressive, bold enough to try new and different things. Cordell enjoyed every minute. I did, too.

The next morning, I avoided looking at Cordell while cooking breakfast in the kitchen. Whenever his hazel eyes met mine, we smiled sheepishly at each other.

✻ <u>THE</u> WHITE HOUSE

One cool, clear April night in 1970, I was driving down Francis Street, the main drag on Jackson's south side, headed to the grocery store, when a boxy, white, two-story house caught my attention. The stately, well-kept home on the corner of Francis and Robinson streets intrigued me so much that I circled the block more slowly a second time to get a better look.

"If they ever put that house up for sale, I'm gonna try to buy it," I said to myself, coasting by and craning my neck.

Cordell and I had been talking about buying a home but hadn't started looking. I mentioned the house to my husband that night, and from then on drove by it whenever possible, wondering who lived there and how it looked inside. Two months later I spotted a "For Sale" sign posted in the front yard. I couldn't believe it. I drove home and got Cordell.

"This is just like a dream come true," I said as we drove by the house.

Cordell liked the house, too. We contacted the real estate agent listed on the sign and arranged to see it three days later. As soon as we stepped inside the door, both of us wanted it.

The long, glass-enclosed front porch was perfect for sitting and watching the boys play in the small fenced-in yard. There was a small patio in the back and even a gas grill.

The twelve-by-sixteen-foot living room had light gray paneling halfway up the wall. I always wanted a paneled room, and the room was at least twice the size of the one we had. A large, brick fireplace with a gas log was along the wall opposite the front door. A dark oak stairway was a few feet away.

The dining room was just as large, with the same soft gray paneling. A beautiful glass chandelier hung from the white stucco ceiling, and the room had three large windows on the north and east walls. The bright and cheery kitchen had a walk-in pantry on one side and a storage room on the other. Cabinets lined the same wall as the double aluminum sink. It even had a garbage disposal, something I'd never seen before.

None of the three bedrooms were as large as the ones we had, and all were upstairs. But that didn't matter. For a classy home like that, I was willing to sacrifice.

We applied for a veteran's loan because it required no down payment. Our credit was still decent, but we had no money saved. The application was approved within a month.

A middle-aged white couple owned the house and liked us so much they paid the closing costs. We signed papers for an hour, Cordell's handwriting tiny and scrunched, mine big and bold. The couple's new home wasn't ready at closing, so they remained in the house for another month and paid us rent. I could hardly wait to move.

Less than a week after closing on the house, Cordell and I had our biggest blowup yet. I hid his keys, trying to keep him home. He got so mad he hit the wall again.

"That's it. I've had it with your crazy ass, Jasmine. I'm moving back home to Momma's," he said.

I was sickened. Every morning that he was gone, I woke up hoping it was all a bad dream. As soon as reality hit, my stomach sunk.

"And I'm not paying for that house either," he snapped over the telephone a few days after moving out. "If I do, it will be for my momma to live in it and not you."

I'd grown immune to much of Cordell's callousness, but his words still hurt. Worried about his threat, I called our realtor, who reassured me that the contract we signed was binding.

"And VA loans require the applicants to live in the house for at least five years," the real estate agent added.

That was all I needed to hear. My dream home was saved. New life seeped back into my weary body. When I finally turned my focus to my kids, Cordell started coming back around. At first he started slipping over to the house in the middle of the night, not wanting his family to know we were reconciling. I was so glad to be with him that it didn't matter. We made mad passionate love every night. I loved making up, especially after breaking up. That would become addictive, too.

Two weeks after leaving, Cordell moved back home again. Both of us vowed to try harder to make our marriage work.

—— ⚬ ——

ONE OF THE HAPPIEST days of our marriage was a sunny morning in June 1970. We moved into our first house. I couldn't sleep for nights, I was so excited and anxious to put my touches on the home. It was previously decorated in Early American.

I arranged the living room so that the sofa was three or four steps inside the front door, rather than against a wall. People had to walk around it to sit down, like on television. It made our home look sophisticated and unique. I put one end table against the staircase wall. The other faced it on an opposite wall, next to a window that provided a perfect view of the front yard.

We placed our small dinette set in the formal dining room. Our plan was to eventually buy a mahogany dining-room set. My uncle laid down blue wall-to-wall carpeting for us. We bought a used washer and dryer through the want ads in the newspaper. We painted the boys' room blue with white trim, and the kitchen yellow. I bought new misty blue insulated draperies from a catalog. Mother told me I didn't need new drapes, but I wanted them anyway. Mother was much more frugal than I was.

Once everything was in place, Cordell and I lay in front of the fireplace for a few nights, feeling pretty darn good about our accomplishments. Cordell was twenty-four. I was twenty-one.

❧ SURPRISES <u>KEPT</u> COMING

A few weeks after unpacking boxes, moving furniture, and getting the house in order, I started feeling tired and weak. The couch became my bed for several days because I had no energy, doing only what was necessary to care for my family. Nearly three weeks passed before I saw my doctor.

"You're almost three months pregnant," he said after an examination. "No wonder you've been feeling out of it."

I was stunned. That had not been my plan, even though I'd gotten sloppy taking my birth control pills.

"Our marriage has been shaky from the beginning. And I'm barely getting any help with Andre and Lamar. We just bought a new house. I'm just getting Lamar off a bottle and trying to potty train him. The last thing we need is another baby," I thought, driving back home in a daze.

I dreaded telling Cordell, but did as soon as my feet touched the floor. He wasn't happy about it either, but took the news better than I had.

"Just don't bring no bitch babies in here," he said with a sly grin, his hazel eyes sparkling. "You know I don't make nothing but boys."

— ❧ —

TWENTY-FIVE WEEKS into my pregnancy I received a call from Cordell's job. His foreman told me that my husband was being rushed to the hospital by ambulance. Debra, who was visiting me at the time, helped dress the kids. We all loaded in the car and zoomed to the hospital so fast that we arrived before the ambulance. My cousin and I stood nervously waiting in the emergency room until they wheeled Cordell past us on a stretcher.

"Oh my God!" Debra screamed when she saw him. "What's wrong with his face? It looks so gray."

Cordell looked better than I expected, not knowing what had happened. We found out later that he had fallen at work and sprained his back. The gray on his face turned out to be dirt and grease.

— ❧ —

MY HUSBAND had been in the hospital a week when his brothers, Monty, Hitchie, and Jonathon, and their girlfriends dropped by our house around eight o'clock one Tuesday night. Simon had been sentenced to prison for five years for inciting a riot.

Happy to have company, I put on some music, then started dressing the boys for bed.

"Cordell's doing a lot better. I just came from the hospital this evening. I had to hurry back cause Momma was watching the boys," I told them as we took our usual places around the table in the dining room.

Before long, the seven of us were bobbing our heads to our favorite songs, drinking alcohol, and getting our party on. They smoked cigarettes and drank Schlitz Light. I watched, ran my mouth, and sang every song playing on our stereo.

Eventually, Sabrina, Monty's newest girlfriend, started rummaging inside her oversize dark brown purse. The eighteen-year-old pulled out two red capsules folded in toilet tissue and handed them to Monty. He pulled them apart and scraped heroin into eight small white lines on an album cover, then took two sniffs. Wiping his nose and smiling, Monty passed the album to his girlfriend of two months.

Feeling gutsy, I reached for the album, placed the straw up to my nose, and snorted. I don't know why. Call it crazy. Call it irresponsible. Call it stupid. But at the time it seemed quite natural. I had slipped that far from sanity—one quiet step at a time.

A few hours later my seat felt wet. "Oh my goodness. I must be peeing on myself," I thought. "The only thing I've been drinking is water."

Easing up from my chair, I hurried upstairs to the bathroom and sat on the toilet for several minutes. I could hear my guests downstairs laughing while I sat waiting for the dripping to stop. It didn't. Around twelve thirty in the morning, I called my obstetrician.

"You need to go to the hospital," he said, his voice full of sleep. "It sounds as if your placenta could be leaking. That could be dangerous for the baby, Jasmine. Go straight to the maternity ward on the third floor. I'll call the hospital and let them know that you're coming."

That was the last thing I wanted to hear. We had been having fun. I was tired of being alone and had planned to hang with them as long as possible. But reluctantly I followed my doctor's orders.

The three brothers cleared off the table. Their girlfriends straightened up the house while I packed an overnight bag. Then I called Momma.

"Momma, I want to know if you would watch the boys for me if they end up keeping me in the hospital?" I asked, forcing each word from my mouth.

Momma sighed loudly. There was a split second of uneasy silence.

"I guess so, Jasmine," she said, sounding agitated and sleepy.

— ❧ —

THE EXAMINING DOCTOR admitted me immediately, saying my placenta was leaking. A nurse placed me in a semiprivate room with a woman I'd grown up with on the East Side named Jackie Coleman. A year younger than me, Jackie had given birth to a beautiful baby boy with a head full of thick black hair two days earlier.

"Can you believe that we ended up in the same room?" I asked as soon as the nurse's aide got me settled in bed. "Girl, I haven't seen you in months. We've got a whole lot of catching up to do."

Jackie and her boyfriend had been living together for three years, she said. He was a good-looking brown-skinned guy with freckles who drank a lot and stayed in and out of jail. I told her about my problems with Cordell, his gambling, womanizing, and his family, but didn't mention my experimentation with drugs. My old friend and I talked until the sun beamed through the blinds. Around nine thirty a nurse with big, curly red hair came to see me.

"Jasmine, the doctor says your tummy looks bigger than it should be at six-and-a-half months. Are you sure you couldn't be farther along?" she asked before listening to the baby's heartbeat with a stethoscope.

"I'm pretty sure," I said.

She smiled and pressed her hands lightly against my abdomen, saying the doctor had ordered complete bed rest until I took some x-rays.

"If the baby is farther along and big enough, the doctor will probably induce labor. But if you are only twenty-seven weeks, then you're going to have to stay off your feet until you deliver," she said, pulling the white hospital blanket and sheet over my stomach and sliding back the green and white plaid curtain panel that served as a partition.

I thought of the people at my house, particularly Sabrina. I didn't trust her. She and my husband had gotten too chummy for me the weeks leading up to his hospitalization. I thought of Cordell, who was still in the hospital one floor above me. He probably would be discharged in a day or two.

"Ain't no way I'm gonna be laying up here in the hospital having another one of Cordell's babies while he's at home playing house with Sabrina," I thought, lying on my back in my hospital bed, staring at the ceiling.

I thought about my kids. The only babysitters they'd ever had were my siblings and Momma. I had never felt comfortable with anybody else but didn't remember about my childhood and Mr. Eddie Jones. So, being confined to a hospital bed for weeks, maybe months, and expecting Momma to watch my boys was out of the question.

A guy wheeled me down to x-ray about an hour after the nurse left. Two o'clock that afternoon the same nurse popped her head in the doorway again, wearing the biggest smile.

"Jasmine, guess how many babies you're gonna have," she said in a voice too perky for my depressed state of mind.

"How many?" I repeated incredulously, shocked at the thought of having more than one. My next fear was that she was going to say five or six.

"You're carrying twins. Isn't that exciting?" she said as I sat up with my mouth open, my mind trying to absorb it all.

"It sure is," Jackie said, sitting straight up in her bed. I just looked at her.

"How long am I going to have to be here?" I asked meekly.

"It's hard to say right now," the nurse replied. "Of course, the closer you get to your due date, the better chance the babies will have. Your due date is about two months away, right? Around December first?"

I nodded my head. My mind was still stuck on the word "twins."

"Oh well, just try to get comfortable, sweetie. You're probably going to be hanging around here with us for the next several weeks," she said, still smiling.

The redhead pulled her head from inside our door and disappeared down the hall. I waited until the sound of her footsteps faded, then climbed out of bed and closed the door. Jackie chastised me right away.

"Didn't you hear what that nurse just said?" she asked, raising her eyebrows and looking at me like I was crazy. "You're supposed to stay in bed."

I didn't care what that nurse said. I needed to get out of the hospital and go home—the sooner the better.

"There's no way I can stay in this hospital," I said, pacing back and forth at the foot of our beds, imagining what could be taking place at 1002 Robinson Street. "There's way too much crap going on in my life right now. I've got to go home."

"Aren't you scared you gonna hurt yourself?" my former schoolmate asked, her head slowly following my steps.

"I'm more afraid that I'm gonna hurt somebody else if I have to stay up here in this hospital," I said, referring to Cordell and Sabrina.

We both laughed. Jackie and I both had reputations as fighters, even battling each other once as young teens. We ended up becoming good friends, however.

"So what are you gonna name your babies Jasmine?" my roommate asked, her voice settling down.

"The thought of names hasn't even crossed my mind. Isn't that horrible?" I asked, stopping to peek through the blinds at the landscaping and cars in the parking lot below.

"No it ain't girl," Jackie replied. "I didn't give my baby a name until after he was born. I wanted to see what he looked like first. He looked like a Charles. So I named him that."

A few minutes later Jackie managed to coax me back into bed. I picked up the telephone and dialed nine to get an outside line. I called Momma, Mother, Valerie, my older aunts Bernice and Mary, and Grandma.

"Humph!" Momma said when she heard my news.

I quickly ended our conversation and fought back tears before making a call to Mother. My grandmother sounded as if she was smiling. I knew she'd be glad to hear.

Mother loved her grandchildren and great-grandchildren and made no bones about it. The more the merrier.

"Oh yeah? You say you're having twins?" she said, sounding tickled and proud.

I needed that and cried silently during our conversation.

My aunts Bernice and Mary sounded supportive, too, but I wasn't convinced. There were too many silent pauses during our talk. Grandma was dealing with loneliness and said she'd been worried about me.

—— ❧ ——

JACKIE AND I spent the rest of the day talking. We didn't even cut on the television, mounted in a corner of the room, high on a ledge. Around nine o'clock a nurse came in and asked if I needed something to help me sleep. The pill must have done the trick because the next thing I knew it was one forty-five in the morning, and another nurse was shaking me.

"Jasmine . . . Jasmine . . . are you in labor, honey?" she whispered in the dimly lit room.

My head popped up from the pillow. I looked around, dazed and disoriented. Jackie was sitting up in her bed, wide-eyed and clutching a corner of the white sheet against her chin.

"Huh? Labor? I don't know. Why?" I asked, rubbing my eyes, then scratching my arms and wondering where I was.

"Cause you was moaning in your sleep," Jackie blurted out. "You've been doing it for the last hour. I didn't know what was wrong, so I called the nurse."

A pain hit me seconds after she spoke.

"Ugh," I said, grabbing my stomach and arching my back.

The next contraction came two minutes later. The pain made me gasp. The nurse switched on the overhead light, cut off her flashlight, then pulled back layers of white blankets and sheets to examine me. She confirmed that my labor had started and called for assistance. Minutes later our room was buzzing with people—everyone appearing more excited than I was.

I asked for Cordell, saying, "He's here on the sixth floor." Fifteen minutes later a female hospital attendant with short dark hair pushed my husband into my room in a wheelchair. Dressed in hospital pajamas, Cordell smiled when he saw me and waited patiently for the aides to slide me from the bed to a stretcher. Minutes later I was being wheeled down to the delivery room.

"I'll be right here when you come out," Cordell said when we reached our destination. We gave each other a peck on the lips. The next minute I was gone.

The delivery room was cool, gray, and sterile. Unlike my previous two deliveries, I breezed through these. The pain was just as intense, but my labor lasted less than two hours as far as I knew. I closed my eyes on the delivery table. The next thing I knew, the doctor announced that we had twin daughters. Blood surged to my head. My brain stalled. My mouth flew open. My first coherent thought was Cordell.

The doctors and nurses labeled the firstborn Baby A. The second was Baby B. That was all I knew. No one told me how much they weighed, and I didn't ask. Nurses rushed them to incubators so quickly that I never even saw their faces.

Cordell was standing at the door when they wheeled me out of the delivery room. I looked at him. In a weak and reluctant voice, I told him that we had two daughters.

"Both of them are girls?" he asked, sounding as surprised and disappointed as I felt. He just sat there expressionless. I knew I had let my husband down.

—— ❧ ——

BABY A WEIGHED three pounds six ounces and was sixteen inches long. Baby B weighed three pounds two ounces. Her length was fourteen inches. Jackie and I walked down to the nursery about nine o'clock the next night. Her son slept quietly in the main nursery, looking healthy and pink. My twins lay in separate incubators in a special nursery for preemies, behind the main one. Hooked up to all kinds of wires and machines, my babies were so tiny and wrinkled they didn't even look human. Their color was dark red. Lying on their backs, my twins wore nothing but diapers. I wanted to care about them, but couldn't. I wanted to go home.

Cordell's doctor released him from the hospital the day after the babies were born. We never discussed naming them. My husband left those things to me. I was glad.

I named Baby A Kendra, because it sounded ethnic. I named Baby B Kamari for the same reason. Plus they both started with a K.

Cordell visited me twice during my seven-day hospital stay. Mother and Daddy came to see me every evening. Other than that, I spent the last four days sad, worried, and alone.

The day I was discharged, the pediatrician stopped by my hospital room. His words would have shocked and saddened most people. I didn't bat an eye, listening to his dire prognosis for my twins, and didn't ask any questions.

"Mrs. Walker, I suggest you try to not get too attached to the babies because their chances of survival are quite slim," he said carefully.

Kendra had serious respiratory problems, not unusual for premature babies. Her heart occasionally stopped beating, requiring her to be hooked up to a monitor around the clock. Kamari was just too small.

"If they make it, fine. If they don't, that's okay, too. I really don't want any more babies. I'm already dealing with more than I can handle," I thought, packing my belongings to go home.

My grandfather came in and flatly rejected the doctor's negative thinking. He beamed with pride every time he talked about the newest additions to our rapidly growing family.

"Heh, heh, heh. That little bitty baby sho do squirm and wiggle a lot. She just be kicking those little ole legs of hers. Humph! I don't care what those doctors say. Those babies are gon make it. I know they are. Now, *man* can say what he want. But it's *God* who has the last say," he said with more confidence that I cared to muster up.

I nodded my head and forced a smile. Daddy always looked at things from a positive perspective. For me, it was never easy. My mind constantly focused on worst-case scenarios, which kept me zapped of mental and emotional energy. I must have called my house thirty times during my hospital stay.

✳ PARTY <u>LIGHTS</u>

Standing on a chair, I twisted a red light bulb into the dining-room chandelier. I screwed in a blue one. Green. Yellow. I loved using color lights when throwing a party. They made our entire downstairs look festive.

We threw at least one party a month. They were always well attended, mostly by young girls fresh out of high school and a few of my old running buddies like Carla Gamble and Dara Abrams who had recently moved three doors down from us.

It had taken me weeks to learn to smoke. The night Hitchie taught me to inhale a cigarette at a party, I was so excited that I called Momma up and told her. She was not impressed.

"I wouldn't tell nobody that I waited until I was twenty-two years old to start smoking," she said dryly.

"Momma never likes anything I do anyway," I thought before ending our conversation and joining my friends in our dining room, where everyone was sitting around the table smoking, drinking, and getting high.

One night Carla was sitting around our dining-room table partying. The colored bulbs in the chandelier provided a dimly lit room. People drank beer and wine. A few puffed on joints. Weed made me paranoid and sleepy, but every now and then I'd take a few tokes, then get in a corner and conk out. That night I gave it another try.

Paranoia set in, again. I was sitting quietly in a corner and looked up just as Carla's hair caught fire. The girl's hair ignited so quickly that for a split second she appeared to be wearing a hat of fire. Females gasped and screamed. Males rushed to Carla's aid, putting the fire out with their bare hands. The house was suddenly eerily still. Gray smoke swirled and drifted toward the ceiling. Marvin Gaye was singing "What's Going On" on our new console stereo.

We immediately figured out what had happened. Carla had been wearing hair spray, and someone walked behind her. His cigarette got too close to her head, and her hair caught fire.

Fifteen minutes later we were laughing and partying as if nothing had ever happened.

⚜ BABIES MADE SIX

Cordell and I told some drug addicts that we needed baby clothes for our new twin daughters. The next day, June Bug and another guy came to our house with armloads of baby clothes, including pajamas, gowns, T-shirts, and outfits of all colors, styles, and sizes. We paid half price for it all. June Bug and his sidekick started coming by with so many baby clothes that we finally told them we didn't need any more.

Preparing for the babies' homecoming was fun and exciting. We painted the walls of our daughters' bedroom my favorite color, pink. We painted the woodwork white. I hung pink curtains with ruffles around them, then painted a beat-up dresser white and decorated its sides with pink and white flowered contact paper. We bought a white baby bed. We already had a dark walnut one. I bought a room-size pink and white shag rug that covered nearly the entire floor. After finishing the babies' room, I used to stand in the doorway and stare at our accomplishment with pride, hoping my babies would soon be home.

—— ℯ ——

THE TELEPHONE RANG at nine o'clock one Monday morning in late December 1970. It was the nurse I spoke to most mornings when I called every day to check on our babies.

"Mrs. Walker, how would you like to come to the hospital this morning and give Baby A her eleven o'clock feeding?" she asked cheerfully.

I couldn't get dressed fast enough. After quickly bathing and dressing the boys, I left them with their dad and drove to the hospital, alone. I couldn't wait to see one of my babies up close for the first time. By then they had determined they were identical. I parked the car in the hospital lot and hurried up to the third-floor nursery.

My daughter was so tiny I was afraid to hold her. I gently rocked her in my arms in a chair outside the main nursery, examining every inch of her contented face, while smiling and trying to figure out whom she looked like. I decided Kendra favored the Walkers because she was so pretty.

Every morning I hustled to the hospital to feed my baby. She came home with me on the fifth visit. One week later we bought Kamari home, too. She only weighed four pounds fourteen ounces. Kendra had weighed five pounds. Relatives and friends traipsed in and out of our house for weeks. Our phone rang twice as much as usual. Andre and Lamar were so proud, they stood out front announcing to everyone who passed, "Our new baby 'tushters' came home."

A Health Department official visited twice a week, a common practice when mothers had preemies. The nurse weighed them and listened to their lungs and heart. She always asked if I had any questions. I seldom did. I was just glad to see her come and go.

"Be sure to avoid taking the babies around crowds. Preemies have weaker immune systems, which makes them susceptible to respiratory infections," she explained.

I had no problem with that. The nurses' instructions fit right into my lifestyle, which was spinning out of control and rapidly down the path of drug abuse. She gave me the perfect excuse to shield my daughters from our drug-using buddies who frequented our home.

—— ₰ ——

THE TWINS had been home about a month and required feedings every three hours. Each took half an hour to drink four ounces of formula. So I only had two-hour breaks during the night and was exhausted all the time.

One morning I dragged into the bedroom to feed them, and Kendra lay sleeping in her baby bed. But Kamari was gone. I looked under the beds. On the sides of the beds. The closet. Even behind their pink and white dresser.

"Now, I know I haven't gone crazy," I thought, hurrying out of the room to check the hallway.

Then it hit me. Cordell had hurried out of the house about twenty minutes before I'd gone upstairs, headed to his mother's. I called their home. Sure enough, Cordell had smuggled Kamari away from the house under his winter coat.

"I thought he hurried out of here faster than usual," I said to my mother-in-law, relieved that our baby was safe and tickled that Cordell wanted to show off his daughter.

✿ SABRINA

My relationship with the Walker family grew more strained after I put Sabrina out of my house one Saturday morning. I'd caught her and Cordell whispering in a corner of our kitchen. Their backs turned, my husband's big hands gripped her thin upper arm, as if he owned her.

"Where were you last night?" he whispered.

Sabrina tried pulling away. Cordell squeezed her arm so hard she yelped and moved quickly away. She turned and saw me standing less than four feet away. Cordell looked startled. Sabrina acted ashamed and embarrassed.

"What the hell is going on?" I hollered, doing everything in my power to keep from jumping on both of them.

"Here you go with that jealousy shit again," Cordell said, opening the cabinet door, grabbing a coffee cup, then storming out of the kitchen.

I wasn't buying the jealousy bit this time. I was jealous, but I wasn't *crazy*.

"Get out of my house and don't ever come back!" I yelled at Sabrina. "Here I've been trying to help you by letting you spend as much time as you wanted in our home. Then I catch you huddled in a corner with my husband? Get the hell out of my house right now."

Sabrina gathered up her meager belongings, then scurried out of the house without saying anything. I cussed Cordell out and told him to leave, too. He told me to get a job.

"If I do get a job, the first thing I'm gonna do is get the hell out of your life. I promise you one thing, Cordell Walker. If I ever make up my mind to leave your ass, I won't be coming back. I mean that!"

"Good. The only reason I married your black, skinny ass in the first place was because I felt sorry for you."

"Felt sorry for me?" I asked, rolling my neck, my hands on my hip.

"Yeah, I felt sorry for your pitiful ass. You'd already lost one baby," Cordell yelled. "And I heard the guy wouldn't marry your ass. I'm the fool. Your own momma don't even care about your ass. So I tried to be a decent guy. And this is what I get?"

Cordell's words hurt so badly that I cried for two days straight. He swaggered around the house like nothing had happened. He had mentally and emotionally battered me so much over the years that it became easy to end up blaming myself for every argument we had.

—— ❧ ——

SABRINA MOVED IN with Cordell's mother. I figured the family let her do it just to spite me. The girl even started calling my house again, asking for Monty. Every time I heard her voice, I saw red.

"Look, don't call my house anymore," I told Sabrina one afternoon.

"You said not to call your house anymore?" she repeated, as if someone else was nearby and listening.

I could hear Mrs. Walker coaching her in the background. She and I had been barely speaking for weeks. But enough was enough. I slammed down the receiver and bolted toward the front door. On my way out I hollered to Lisa, who had been visiting for about an hour.

"Watch my kids for a minute!" I yelled over my shoulder.

My sister knew me well. She'd heard my telephone conversation and sprinted right behind me.

"No Jasmine. Don't go over there messing with those ole crazy people. They aren't even worth it," she pleaded, staying right on my heels.

My eighteen-year-old sister, who was bigger and taller than me, was still tying to change my mind when I knocked on the Walkers' screen door.

"Come in," sang a chorus from the living room. Mr. Walker came to the screened porch and unhooked the door.

I marched in and headed straight up to Mrs. Walker, who was sitting in the living room with everyone in the family—except Cordell. He was out in the streets somewhere. Seated around the room as if awaiting my arrival, they all looked up at me with smirks on their faces. I wanted to cuss Mrs. Walker out right then and there but knew I'd never live to tell about it.

"Mrs. Walker, I'd appreciate it if you'd quit putting that girl up to calling my house," I said, glaring at her, then at Sabrina, who sat next to her on their old broken-down brown, white, and beige plaid couch.

Mr. Walker was standing nearby and slipped up behind me as I spoke. The tall, quiet man started pushing me toward the door.

"You're gonna have to leave," he said, smiling and shoving me toward the door.

I think one push was harder than he had intended and caused me to stumble backward. He grabbed my arm and gently guided me out the wood-framed entranceway, then stepped onto the front porch with us. Lisa, who was ordinarily quiet and shy, stepped between us and stood toe to toe with the man.

"Don't you *ever* put your hands on my sister again," she said, her deep chocolate face stiff and not batting an eye. Mr. Walker smiled as if the whole thing was comical to him, then strolled back inside the house.

✳ IT HAPPENED

The phone rang just as I was getting the kids ready for bed. It was Grandma. I threw my head back and rolled my eyes.

"I don't feel like talking to her right now," I thought, at the same time trying to sound happy to hear her voice.

"Hi Grandma. How are you?"

"I reckon I'm doing all right. My arthritis been acting up again. How have *you* and *your* family been doing?"

I could hear the loneliness in her voice. I hadn't seen Grandma but once since moving. I even avoided riding down Page Avenue for fear she'd be sitting on her porch and see me. If I did pass her house, I'd look the other way to avoid seeing her. But despite my slights, Grandma still called every now and then to check on me. The silence in the background was deafening.

"Did you go to church Sunday, Grandma?" I asked stiffly, attempting to break the uneasy quietness.

"Yeah. Son come took me," she said, referring to my grandfather. She'd always called him "son."

Silence again.

"So what else you been doing lately Grandma?" I asked, knowing good and well that an eighty-seven-year-old woman with congestive heart failure, arthritis in her knees, and no car couldn't be doing much of anything.

"Jasmine, I ain't seen your babies yet. How old are they now?"

"Eight months old. Grandma, the only reason I haven't brought them over is because the doctors said they shouldn't be around a lot of people until they get bigger and their immune system is stronger or else they might get some kind of respiratory infection. They only look like their four or five months," I said weakly.

Grandma listened to my entire excuse, but the tone of her voice never changed.

"Jasmine, you gon mess round here, and I ain't gon live to see them babies," she said.

I felt like dirt. There was no excuse. The truth was I was too busy running after Cordell and had been snorting heroin two or three times a week. Taking care of two infants and two toddlers, I didn't have time for my great-grandmother anymore.

"Grandma, I'm gonna bring them over Sunday when you get out of church. I promise," I said, cutting my eyes at Andre, who was bouncing on our bed. She said okay but didn't sound convinced.

Grandma sensed things. Always had. She told me that I was pregnant with Andre a month before I knew it. I bounced into her house one day, and Grandma stopped dead in her tracks, looking me up and down.

"Jasmine, you're pregnant! I can tell it in your face," she'd said.

"No I'm not," I quickly replied, knowing I hadn't had my period in over a month.

A few weeks later I found out that Grandma had been right. So, the deeper I sank into drug use, the more I drove past my great-grandmother's house and looked the other way.

Grandma lived alone. Mr. Thomas had died seven years earlier, the victim of a pigeon drop. Con artists came to their home, pretending to be interested in renting an apartment. Mr. Thomas took the couple down to see it and didn't return after four hours. Grandma called Daddy. He called the police. They found my step-great-grandfather wandering along Michigan Avenue, disoriented and confused. Police later concluded that Mr. Thomas had been drugged. The couple had convinced him to draw eight thousand dollars out of the bank. He also took three hundred dollars from the house without Grandma knowing it. She'd said he must have slipped in the back door while she was sitting on the porch.

"Jasmine, they took all of our life savings," she cried to me shortly after it happened. I'd never heard of a pigeon drop before and didn't know what to say.

Police never caught the con artists, and Mr. Thomas never totally recovered from the incident. He became bedridden within weeks, requiring around-the-clock care. It really wore on Grandma—caring for a sick husband and losing their savings, as well. The whole family pitched in and helped. My siblings and I took turns sitting in a chair beside his bed, making sure he didn't try to get up while Grandma went to church and doctors' appointments. He died less than two years later.

I don't remember how our conversation ended the night Grandma called, but I felt guilty for a split second after we'd hung up. The next minute I turned my attention back to my family and heroin.

— ℥ —

IT WAS ELEVEN O'CLOCK Saturday morning. The telephone rang. I was bathing the kids, having plopped all four of them in the tub together. I quickly finished washing Kendra, then grabbed a towel lying on the toilet stool. Rushing to my bedroom, I snatched the phone's receiver, my daughter dangling from my arm, dripping wet.

"Jasmine, there's something wrong with Grandma," my youngest brother Keith said, urgency and fear in his voice.

"Why do you say that? I just talked to her last night."

"Cause there's an ambulance down at her house. I was walking down to the store and saw it. Granddaddy's car was down there, too."

I panicked.

"Go see if you can help her Keith. Hurry!" I screamed into the phone. "Go down there and see what's going on. Then call me right back."

I sprinted back upstairs, still holding Kendra with one arm. I sat her on the toilet with the seat down. I bathed the other kids, assembly-line style. I led the boys to our bedroom where their clothes were laid out on our bed, Kendra sideways in one arm, Kamari in the other.

I smelled smoke. I forgot I'd been frying bacon on the stove before starting their baths.

"Watch your brother and sisters for a minute, Andre," I said, dashing downstairs through the living room and into the dining room.

A flame jumped out of the kitchen doorway. I darted back upstairs and grabbed my babies. I gave my sons eye contact, then told them, "Follow Mommy, real fast."

Andre and Lamar asked a dozen questions as they lagged behind. I didn't answer, racing out the front door, a baby in each arm. I laid the twins in the grass and spotted Christopher Brewer, the father of Robin's kids, walking slew-footed toward us.

"My house is on fire. My boys are still in there!" I yelled, panting and heading back inside.

Christopher ran past me.

Three-year-old Andre was standing on the blue-carpeted living-room floor, barefooted, snotty nosed, and crying. Lamar, who was a few months away from turning two, was halfway back upstairs. Christopher grabbed the boys and took them outside. I called the Fire Department. The truck arrived screaming and honking its horn within minutes.

We stood on the sidewalk watching—the boys in T-shirts and briefs, the twins in diapers and one-piece, pink terry cloth pajamas. My old, flannel night-gown showed too much of my bony knees and was ripped under both arms. I kept a safe distance from gathering neighbors and held my arms close to my sides to hide the tears.

Fifteen minutes after arriving, the firemen signaled it was okay to go back inside. The bacon grease on the stove had caught fire. Our kitchen walls and doorway were singed with black smoke, but the overall damage was limited. The firemen were still talking to me when the telephone rang again.

Keith was crying.

"Jasmine, Grandma's dead," he sobbed.

"Oh my God. No!" I screamed, dropping the telephone as if it were on fire.

I couldn't breathe. I couldn't think. I couldn't even pick the receiver back up. I cried and cried and cried. Grandma wasn't supposed to die like that, in her home, alone, unable to call for help. There were too many of us family members. Her death was too unexpected. I needed to talk to Grandma one more time. I needed to hug her and bury my head in her soft bosom. Tell her I loved her. Tell her I was sorry. Tell her she was right. I needed to apologize for deserting her, and thank her for always remembering me.

Still crying, I finally picked the phone back up and called Cordell. He had gone to his mother's earlier that morning.

"Grandma's dead," I said, sniffing and gasping for air. My husband hurried home.

The next several days were a blur, but I learned every detail of what had happened. Grandma died of a heart attack. Daddy drove by her house that morning and noticed her green shades were still down. He stopped and turned around.

Daddy knocked and knocked on her door.

"When nobody answered after I knocked so hard, I went to taking off the hinges on the front door," my grandfather said, teary eyed.

The Polish next-door neighbor saw Daddy feverishly removing the hinges. He spoke little English, but scampered across the dirt driveway to help. They got inside, and Daddy checked Grandma's bedroom. The elderly neighbor ran to the bathroom.

"Please, George, don't come in here," he hollered to my grandfather in broken English. Daddy ran to the bathroom anyway.

Grandma lay face up on the cold tile. Her flannel nightgown was smoothed out, as if deliberate. She clutched an empty medicine bottle in her hand, the contents scattered on the floor.

"It was as if Momma knew she about to go to meet her Maker and fixed her gown to get ready," Daddy said.

Following her death, the family met at Grandma's house around eleven o'clock every morning. My generation sat on the porch. Momma's siblings kept track of who gave what food in which dish. Mother sat quietly near Daddy. He didn't talk much, which was uncharacteristic of our grandfather. When he did, everyone else sat quietly and listened.

—— ๏ ——

THE RED CROSS informed Albert of Grandma's death. He had been drafted into the army in March 1970 and was deployed to Panama instead of Vietnam. I was glad. We hadn't seen each other much before he left, even though both of us were doing drugs. Albert hung out with an older crowd of addicts who'd been using so long, they looked like dried-up skeletons who were on their last breaths. I was scared of them.

Albert flew home two days before Grandma's funeral. Six feet tall, my brother had put forty pounds on his slender frame. He looked good in his military uniform. Relatives came from all over the country. Aunt Linnie caught a flight from Baltimore. Uncle Billy and his wife and family drove from Hartford, Connecticut.

Hibler's Mortuary, a few doors down from Grandma's house, was still the only black undertaker in town. Tuesday afternoon, thirty or forty family members quietly trekked to the funeral home to view her body for the first time. Elders gathered around Grandma's metallic gray coffin. Some wiped tears. Others nodded gently, saying, "She looks peaceful and asleep." Daddy broke down. It was the first time I'd ever seen my grandfather cry. We all fell apart when he whispered to my great-grandmother, "Momma, I'm the only one left now."

✿ SARAH PARKER

Crawling out of bed one sunny morning, I glanced out my window and noticed a red pickup truck, filled with furniture, parked out front. I watched a middle-aged black man carry two boxes up the steps. A thin boy, who appeared to be in his midteens, dragged behind him, with lamps in both hands.

Minutes later a girl I knew named Sarah Parker pulled up in a car filled with boxes. I unlocked our front door and hurried onto the porch.

"Hey Sarah, are you going to be my new neighbor?" I hollered. She waited for a car to pass before yelling back.

"Girl, if I can get all this stuff in that little bitty ole apartment. Momma and Daddy bought me some of everything," she replied.

"Must be nice," I thought, stepping off our cement steps.

Sarah joined me at the curb. We knew each other, but not well. I'd heard a lot about Sarah through my cousin Debra. They had attended the same high school on the South Side. According to Debra, Sarah's father spoiled her. The girl always wore nice clothes, and her hair stayed sharp. She was definitely somebody I wanted to know better.

"Sarah Parker is a lot of fun to be around," Debra said after I told her about the girl moving across the street from me. "She's always been a little wild and *real* boy crazy, but she's real cool."

I had been wanting some female friends. Most of our visitors were Cordell's family, mainly his brothers and their girlfriends. Robin and I had distanced ourselves from each other. My cousin acted as if she didn't like being around me anymore. I had convinced myself that most of my best-friend relatives were just jealous because I had a husband and nice house.

"They always did think they were better than me," I told Cordell one night while venting about my family. "We always were the black sheep of the family. They don't know how to deal with me, now that I've got just as much as they do."

The five of us female relatives who grew up together had been growing apart. Valerie divorced her husband and lived in the projects with a guy four years her junior. Pregnant with her third child, this one by him, she loved the guy. I never dreamed my young aunt would end up like that. The dude was as charming as a cottage in the woods, but beneath all the glitter he was as mean as all get out. Good looking and whorish, he had begun dabbling in drugs, too. So our paths crossed at the dope house every now and then. Valerie smoked cigarettes and drank a little, but drugs were out of the question. She had returned to being a person who loved having a good time. I was happy for her, despite her young, drug-abusing lover.

Arlene relocated to Virginia and worked as secretary for a law firm near Washington, D.C. The only times we saw each other were at family reunions. I still attended most of them, even though I was abusing drugs, left and right.

Even though we were going our separate ways, Robin and I still talked on the phone occasionally, but our circle of friends had changed dramatically. She ran with a more sedate crowd who sat around smoking cigarettes and brooding about their love lives. They were too boring for me. Action and adventure were more my speed.

Robin worked as a secretary from nine to five. She had three kids and still drove men crazy with her good looks and big legs. She wanted to marry her children's father, but he skipped town with an older woman.

Debra and I were drifting apart, too. All she talked about was getting married someday.

"I'm telling you, Debra. Married life isn't all it's cracked up to be," I warned her countless times.

She refused to listen and started dating an ex-con from Southern Michigan Prison. I don't know how they met, and held my breath on that relationship.

So, Sarah moving across the street was right on time. I was ready for new friends. I thought I was ready for Sarah.

— ❧ —

SARAH LIVED IN OUR neighborhood three weeks before we bumped into each other at the bus stop one morning around eight forty-five. Andre was four, and starting Head Start. Her son was, too. We chatted while waiting for the yellow bus to come, then watched it pull off with both our young sons smiling and waving good-bye in the window. Sarah and I talked a little more when the bus returned at noon. Meeting and talking at the bus stop became our routine for several weeks.

One bright sunshiny morning after our sons' bus had pulled off, Sarah suggested getting high.

"Right now?" I asked with surprise. "Ain't this a little early in the morning to be getting high?"

Sarah rolled her neck. Her head held back, she stared at me for a second.

"Haven't you ever heard that morning highs were the best kind?" she asked, with a big wide grin on her smooth, sable brown face.

"No, I haven't. But I'm game to try anything once," I replied, wanting to sound hip for my new neighbor, who was obviously on the fast track.

Sarah ran home and returned with two pieces of aluminum foil folded into thumbnail-size packages. It was my first time seeing heroin in anything but red capsules. I called Cordell, who had been upstairs sleeping.

"Sarah's got some blow. Want a toot?" I looked up and asked when he appeared in the dining room buttoning up his jeans and bare backed.

Cordell didn't even bother to put on a shirt. We sat around the dining-room table snorting heroin, laughing, and talking. Everything stopped, and we scrambled to take the pieces of foil and album cover off the table when Lamar staggered into the room, rubbing his eyes and asking for Cream of Wheat.

☙ ANYTHING GOES

We had no money one unusually cold, chilly night in June 1971. The babies needed formula and Pampers. There was no food in the house, and Cordell and I needed a fix. We'd sold our mahogany coffee table to a neighbor for forty dollars. The next week we pawned our wedding rings for fifty dollars and never got them back. We'd sold all but one of our televisions and anything else that brought us a little money. The only things coming into our house were shut-off notices for our water and electricity.

"I don't need no man who can't even buy his babies' diapers or put food on the table," I yelled at Cordell the night our daughters were wearing towels for diapers and none of the kids had eaten all day.

"Fuck you, Jasmine. Get your skinny black ass out somewhere and get a job, then. I worked when I could. I can't work with a fucked-up back," he shouted so loudly that I thought the veins in his neck would pop.

Cordell hadn't worked since hurting his back. He sued Goodyear and expected a settlement within three years. I took care of our drug habit by stealing meat from grocery stores and selling it for half price. I'd hustle up twenty dollars, then try to get two dime bags for eighteen. I'd take the few extra dollars and buy food for the kids. They ate McDonald's a lot. Sometimes they didn't eat anything but oatmeal or cold cereal until I got home from boosting, often around ten o'clock at night. I hated coming home to a nasty house, the kids half dressed with dirty faces and a stressed-out husband who needed a fix. I felt so sorry for my children but couldn't help them. I couldn't even help myself.

"I'm the one whose been taking care of your drug habit, so don't try to front me off about getting a job," I yelled at Cordell, who sat next to the living-room window, staring out and rubbing his aching knees.

"Didn't nobody ask you to go out there stealing. You did that on your own," he snapped back.

"Yeah, because I knew you'd lie in the bed all day, complaining about being bogue. I take chances of going to jail every day, just so that you don't have to worry about it. You know that if the police catch your ass doing anything, they will probably send your sorry ass to prison. You're the only one of your brothers who's never been locked up," I yelled back, ready for whatever my husband threw out next.

Four-year-old Andre looked at us, then quietly started upstairs. Arguing made him uncomfortable. He'd go outside, upstairs, or anywhere to get away from our screaming and yelling. Lamar, who started talking early, stuck around trying to mediate. Cordell would get mad at him, too.

"Get your ass back upstairs," he snapped. "I'm the daddy, not you."

Lamar beat it. He climbed the stairs without help, mumbling like a little old man.

"See, there you go again. You get mad at me, then take it out on one of the kids," I hollered. "If you didn't spend so much time at your mother's with those sorry-ass brothers of yours, we'd be a whole lot better off right now."

"I ain't got to stay here and take this shit," Cordell shot back. "I'm getting the hell out of here, and this time I ain't coming back!"

"Go ahead! Leave!" I yelled. "That's what you always do. You were just looking for an excuse. Go on over to your momma's house and stay there. All y'all deserve each other."

Cordell slammed the door behind him and disappeared into the night. I lay in bed for an hour or two afterward, distraught that my kids went to bed hungry. Two thirty in the morning, someone rapped on our front door, sounding like the police. Hurrying down the steps in my panties and bra, I was still trying to put my arm in the sleeve of my old housecoat when I reached the front door.

"Hurry up, Jasmine. Open the door and let me in," Cordell hollered, as if someone were after him.

Still steaming mad, I was ready to cuss him out again through the door. I peeked out the window and saw only Cordell. It was his fists full of money that made me decide to let him in. He hurried through the door and clicked on the overhead light in the dining room. My husband threw two fistfuls of old, one-hundred-dollar bills on the table.

"Oh my God, Cordell, who have you robbed?" I asked, afraid that my nagging had driven my husband to knocking somebody in the head.

"Those junkies have been lying all this time," he said, peeking out the window, panting and trying to catch his breath. "They've been saying that Fort Knox was out there on Race Road. Monty finally told me the truth tonight. The fucking place is right around the corner from us, on Mansion Street."

I was stunned. Fort Knox had become a legend in the drug community. It was an old two-story house with a rock exterior. Several junkies had broken into the place one night, looking for something to steal. They stumbled up on thousands of dollars in cash, hidden in closets and drawers and even lying on a telephone table in the living room. All of the money was in old bills. One longtime drug addict walked away with eighty-one thousand dollars. Another got eighteen thousand. Both were broke a month later. They'd shot most of the money in their arms.

"Me and Monty climbed through a back kitchen window," Cordell said, surprising the heck out of me.

Now, I would shoplift in a hot minute. But Cordell hadn't stolen anything since a teenager. It showed. His face flushed, he paced the floor, peeking out the window and rubbing his arms as he recounted every detail.

"All the furniture was covered with white sheets. It was real dusty—like nobody's lived there for a long time," he said, his slanted eyes wide open, dimples showing.

Cordell said he headed upstairs first and looked in the closet, then under the mattress. Bingo. He pulled out two raggedy brown envelopes filled with old money. I thought I was dreaming.

No one knew where all the money came from or why the older home had been vacant so many years. One story was the owner had died and never believed in banks. Another was that the home once belonged to bootleggers.

It didn't matter to me. I was just happy to have so much money. We put all the fifty-dollar bills in one pile and the hundreds in another.

"Oh my goodness," I said, holding an old crumpled bill up to the light, counting zeros. "This is a thousand-dollar bill. I didn't even know they made them."

Cordell grabbed it from me. He was taking it to his mother for safekeeping.

He also took all the hundreds and gave me the fifties. I hid old fifty-dollar bills behind every picture in the house and even buried a few in the backyard in a soup can. The money totaled sixty-five hundred dollars.

— ℞ —

HEROIN CONSUMED my every thought. It dictated my every move. I'd wake up thinking about drugs and would hit the streets, not knowing where my next fix was coming from. It was a cruel, vicious cycle that enslaved me.

One of my easiest hustles was buying heroin for white drug addicts. Dope dealers seldom sold to them. They didn't trust white people and stuck closely to the street adage: "Beware of a friend of a friend."

My most reliable customer was a short guy named Robert Renchler. Everybody called him "White Bob." He'd come every morning around eleven and wait at our house while I copped. He'd split his twenty-dollar bag with me, which eased my edginess so I could at least concentrate. White Bob and other white customers didn't like Cordell buying their drugs for them. My husband would beat them, giving them quinine—a white, tasteless powder—baking soda, crushed aspirin, or anything else that could pass for heroin.

White addicts seemed to have more money. Consequently, they tended to have bigger drug habits. There was a spoiled little rich kid, well known by every junkie in town. I'd been hearing that his mother drove him to dope houses and sat out front in her car while he used heroin inside. I didn't believe it until I spotted her parked outside a dope house, then ran into her son inside with a needle in his arm.

One day the spoiled little rich kid, a tall, handsome guy with long, dark hair and a serious look on his face, knocked on our door.

"I'll pay you twenty dollars to cop for me," he said sweetly. "I want eighty dollars' worth of dope."

I readily agreed and ran smack dab into the dope dealer who happened to be driving past our house that sunny afternoon. I flagged him down and made the transaction without having to leave my front yard. Happy to get the heroin so soon, the spoiled little rich kid put the packets of dope in his pocket, then tried to renege on paying me.

"You didn't have to do a fucking thing but go out your fucking front door," he said in tone so nasty that I immediately began despising him.

"You said you'd pay me twenty dollars if I bought you some dope," I snapped back. "I did that. Now you owe me twenty dollars."

Ignoring my protests, he opened the front door and started walking out.

"Give my sister her fucking money," Terrance said, who was six-feet tall and glaring at the spoiled spoiled rich kid without blinking an eye.

I had forgotten that my brother had spent the night and had been sleeping in the boys' bedroom. He'd heard us arguing and came downstairs to see what was happening. It couldn't have been more perfect timing. The spoiled rich kid stopped in his tracks. He reached in his pocket and threw a twenty-dollar bill at me. It floated to the ground outside my steps. I walked over, picked up my money, and laughed.

"You black bitch!" he yelled, storming away and climbing into his shiny red GTO.

"Your momma's a black bitch!" I hollered back.

His tires skidded as he drove away.

— ℛ —

IF A PERSON overdosed on heroin, every junkie in town scrambled to get some. High-grade heroin was called "the bomb," and often made users vomit and nod, which was a good thing from their perspective. Heroin made me vomit regardless of the potency. I threw up so much that it became routine. I chalked it up as part of the cost of getting high.

Nodding was the closest thing to overdosing, and every heroin addict loved to do it, including Cordell and me. We sat up in bed at night smoking cigarettes, our heads hung—on the brink of dozing off any minute. By the grace of God, we didn't burn up everything and everybody in the house because we dropped cigarettes in our bed all the time, burning many holes in our sheets and mattress.

When the town was dry, every addict in town gathered in certain locations around town, talking and trying to figure out how to get their hands on some drugs. I'll never forget the poster that hung on the wall of a white guy's house. We'd gone there to buy heroin. Standing in his living room, waiting for him to return with our drugs, I read: "It's easier to get through times when there's dope and no money, than to get through times when there's money and no dope."

"Right on," I thought.

Many times I struck out in pitch-black darkness alone and the middle of the night, in temperatures so cold my feet burned, looking for dope. Often times the only sound I heard was the ice and snow crunching beneath my worn overshoes or the occasional swishing of a passing car.

"There is nothing else in the world that could get me out at this time of the night," I said to myself many times while trudging through the snow.

Cordell and I sometimes sat in cars for hours waiting for the dope man. At one point we drove back and forth to Detroit several times a week, buying drugs from people in places that could have easily been the scene of multiple drug slayings. In the late 1960s and early 1970s, it seemed that every time I looked up, the newspaper and television carried stories about Detroit dope houses being robbed and everyone in them being killed—kids and all.

"What happened to me?" I'd sometimes ask myself. "I can't even remember what it was like not using drugs. It seems as if that was in another lifetime."

I quit on my own two or three times. Each time I started back within days, the urge returned stronger and more fierce than ever. I sought treatment at the local methadone clinic. It gave me a break from the streets but also enabled me to meet new drug contacts when I fell off the wagon. I was never clean for more than a month. Nothing and nobody seemed able to rid me of my demons.

But there was one television commercial that pricked my conscious, causing me to shudder whenever I heard it—the United Negro College Fund motto: "A mind is a terrible things to waste."

⚜ ABUSED AND ABUSING

The twins were fourteen months old when Momma paid her first visit to our new house one Saturday evening in November 1972. We'd been living there for a year and a half. She and her new boyfriend dropped by to see the kids, she said. I suspected she was checking up on us.

I had been out trying to find the dope dealer when Momma arrived. I returned home to find her holding Kendra and steaming mad at me.

"I found these babies upstairs in their beds in the dark while you had your behind out in the street somewhere," she snapped. "Their diapers are soaking wet. I know they're hungry. I bet you haven't fed them all day."

"I did too feed them. They ate before I left," I said, coughing with chills running up and down my back.

I needed a fix. Bad.

"Look Jasmine, you aren't taking care of these babies, and I know it. And I'm not going to sit by and watch you do them like this. If you don't want to take care of them, give them to me. I'll raise them," Momma said, handing Cordell the baby and putting her hands on her hips.

Shaking and coughing, I didn't care what Momma or anybody else thought. My throat felt as if my windpipe was closing. I couldn't stop yawning. My eyes watered. The two ten-cent bags of heroin I squeezed in my hand were calling my name. And Momma was blocking my action. I just wanted her to hurry up and leave.

"Go ahead. Take them. I don't care," I said, still wearing my coat, and hoping she'd be on her way.

Momma stopped at the door. She looked at Cordell. She looked at me.

"If I take them, it's going to have to be legal. We can go downtown Monday morning, and you can sign them over to me," she said.

"That's fine with me," I replied, slinging my black, fake fur coat on the floor of our walk-in closet.

I resented Momma coming to my house and telling me how to raise my kids. We hadn't spoken in weeks, then she popped up unannounced at my house. Edginess set in. I couldn't focus. I couldn't even argue coherently. Momma never sat down and stayed about half an hour. When she let herself out, I figured that was the end of it.

Monday morning, our telephone rang around nine o'clock. It was Momma.

"Are you ready to go downtown?" she asked in an unusually calm voice.

"No. I've changed my mind," I said. "I thought about it over the weekend and decided I don't want to do it."

"Well, you'd better do better than you have been. Or else I'm gonna have those kids taken away from you. And I mean it," she said.

"Okay," I whispered sheepishly and hung up.

It would have been easier to give my kids away. I was struggling to maintain a twenty-dollar-a-day habit and was spending more time in the streets than at home. But I thought about my four kids and how much they needed me. I thought about how much I needed them. They were my only reason for living and kept me somewhat sane. Knowing how unhappy I'd been living under Momma's roof as a child, I wasn't going to put my kids through the same thing.

———— ℀ ————

ONE MORNING Cordell was at his mother's house, and I had been home screaming and hollering at the kids all day. Late that afternoon, I caught the twins trying to stick one of their tiny, stainless steel feeding spoons in an electrical outlet in the dining room. I went off.

I grabbed Kendra, the closest one to me, and starting tearing her little behind up. I kept Cordell's leather belt hanging on the banister just for those occasions, which were too many. I was tired of running after the twins. They were busting the terrible twos wide open and plucking my last nerve.

"You meddle too much. You're hardheaded. If I don't beat your asses, my name ain't Jasmine Walker," I screamed at the top of my voice.

Yelling and threatening to kill them seemed to be the only way to keep the little rascals in check. I whipped my babies twice a day, every day. If a belt wasn't handy, I'd hit them with my hand or sometimes my fist.

"They're just babies," Andre and Lamar would say, looking at their sisters and me with worried faces.

Every time my sons said those words, I'd feel guilty, but not enough to stop. I beat my daughters on their legs and back until they bruised. All my pent-up rage was taken out on the smallest and weakest in the house. I knew it wasn't right. I knew there was something wrong with me. I just didn't know what to do about it.

During my tirade over the electrical socket, Kendra got away. I ran behind her, not letting up with the belt, screaming at both of them like a madwoman. Kendra always made me the maddest. She reminded me too much of Cordell. Plus Kendra bullied her smaller sister so much I had to put them in separate beds. I'd watch Kendra guzzle down her milk, then reach over and snatch her sister's bottle without even looking. Kamari reminded me of myself. She'd look pitiful and would put her thumb in her mouth and suck it, without making a sound. It was like watching Cordell and myself in toddler bodies.

During their whipping, Kendra stayed two steps ahead of me. I swung at her and missed with the belt, then got so mad I used the bottom of my foot to shove her. She lurched forward. Her small legs buckled beneath her body. Kendra fell so awkwardly to the floor that my mind would never erase that image. I knew she was hurt.

My twenty-month-old baby lay on our wall-to-wall blue carpet, crying. Appearing more terrified of me than worried about herself, my baby's big brown eyes begged forgiveness as I rushed to her. It should have been *me* begging *her*.

Every time I tried picking Kendra up, she screamed with pain. I was terrified—scared for what I'd done to my daughter and scared of what would happen to me.

Gently lifting her, I carried her upstairs and lay her in our bed. I wrapped cold towels around her swollen leg. I stroked her hair and forehead. Kendra's eyes were needy, but she no longer acted afraid. I prayed she was getting better, even though I hadn't thought about God in a long time.

"Lord, if you let my baby be all right, I promise I'll never hit her again," I said, closing my eyes while listening to my child whimper.

Ordinarily, if an emergency occurred, I called Cordell home from his mother's. This time I waited until he showed up—two hours later. I told him Kendra fell down the stairs. He knew I was lying.

"Damn it, Jasmine. I keep telling you that you whip these babies too much. Now look what you've done!" he yelled. "This baby's got to go to the hospital. I think you've broke her fucking leg."

I was scared my kids would be taken away from me. I feared going to jail. A year earlier I'd gotten caught stealing a cardigan sweater for Andre to wear his first day of Head Start. The theft landed me in the clink. Being locked up for two or three hours had seemed like an eternity. I cried and carried on so that one inmate scoffed at me, saying, "Hell, I don't know what you're crying for. I've been in here for forty-six days."

"You shut up and leave me alone!" I screamed. "Just shut up!"

This time it seemed certain that jail would become my new home. My family would find out that I beat my kids. It would be in the newspaper. Probably on TV. I wanted to run somewhere and hide. I felt guilty. I felt ashamed. I felt like the scum of the earth.

Cordell took control of the situation while I stood trancelike in a corner, my hand over my mouth. I didn't even go to the hospital with them. I was too scared. I couldn't face anybody after what I'd done. So I stayed at home with the other kids, who had watched the whole incident unfold. As soon as Cordell left with Kendra, I called my grandparents and told them the same lie.

"Kendra fell down the steps and hurt herself," I said tearfully.

Mother and Daddy rushed to the hospital. They stopped and picked up Momma on the way. My beautiful daughter spent three weeks in the children's ward. Her pelvis was broken. Unable to face up to what I'd done, I slipped into her hospital room to visit her only once. It was bad enough being a drug addict. Being a child beater was even worse.

Kendra smiled when I walked into her hospital room. Her leg up in traction, she wore a white cast that covered her body from the waist down, including her right leg and hip. Seeing my daughter in that condition, because of me, was the hardest thing I'd ever had to do. Family members and Rev. Whittington visited Kendra every day, then called me, giving updates. I listened carefully but asked few questions. The guilt was eating me up.

"Why don't you let Kamari come stay with us for a few weeks," my aunt Linnie proposed, adding, "I think you really need a break."

She had temporarily moved back home from Baltimore and was staying with Mother. She and her teenage daughter, Stacia, kept Kamari for a month. I was so glad. I needed the rest. Bad.

After being discharged from the hospital, Kendra spent another two months in the body cast. I even slacked up on my heroin use to care for my injured child but couldn't stop. No one asked me any questions, and I never brought the subject up. Most people probably already knew all the facts.

The day finally came when Kendra's cast would be removed. I met her doctor at the hospital that morning, and he took her into a room to saw it off. I was so happy and relieved to see my baby walk again. But her tiny leg had atrophied, and she limped. It would be a constant reminder for another six months.

Her doctor walked her out of the examining room, holding her tiny hand and eyeing me.

"Keep the area clean and dry, then see me in four weeks," he said, his eyes looking through to my soul. "And let's not have any more of those *accidents*."

I nodded my head and quickly looked away in shame.

❧ BIG LEAGUE

Tired of spending our money on drugs, one time I got really daring. After sharing my plan with Cordell, who was skeptical, I paid a visit to the biggest dope dealer in town. The dubious distinction of "biggest dope dealer" usually changed every three or four months in Jackson, but this dude had been dealing for nearly a year.

Never having met him before, I practiced what to say while knocking on the door of his upstairs apartment on Francis Street. I recognized the person who answered. He was my age. We'd never carried on a conversation before but knew of each other. He turned out to be the dope man's brother. I smiled and flirted a little, while telling him the reason for my visit.

"Wait here," he said with a curious, uneasy grin on his face, then closed the door.

I was still rehearsing my line when he returned, appearing more comfortable. He said his brother had agreed to see me. I followed him through a small kitchen to a dimly lit living room, where he left me standing for several more minutes. When his brother, Lucious Vick, finally appeared, my heart trembled. The guy looked meaner than I expected. The scar down the left side of his face looked as if someone had tried to cut his jaw off. His eyes didn't soften, like some men's did, when I batted mine. But I'd come too far to back down.

Introducing myself, I reached to shake his hand. He seemed slightly amused.

"You've got the best dope in town," I said, not wasting time with small talk. "And I know you're making a lot of money. But I can make you more money than any of your other dealers—and faster, too. I'm very smart, and I know how to take care of business. Ask anyone who knows me."

His expression never changed, but I could tell that he was listening. Holding his attention gave me more courage.

"If you let me deal for you, Lucious, I promise to be loyal and will never be short," I said, making a veiled reference to his current dealers, rumored to not always have all his money when he came for it.

Lucious stared at me the entire time I talked, never blinking an eye. I felt he could see my heart through my eyes.

"I'll get in touch," he said softly, then turned and strolled back down a dim hallway, disappearing into a bedroom. His brother escorted me out.

Three weeks later Cordell and I were sitting at our dining-room table around midnight, broke and brooding over the upcoming Christmas holidays. We both froze when someone knocked at our door. It was Lucious and his brother. They never sat down but stayed long enough to give me five hundred dollars worth of heroin to sell. They explained the arrangement—a seventy/thirty split—and within five minutes they were gone. I peeked out the window and saw nothing but two figures disappear into the dark. No car. Nowhere.

We sold dope for Lucious for three months and found out that drug addicts came from all walks of life. I met an attractive black woman from Ann Arbor who wore business suits and worked for an attorney in Southfield. She'd been strung out for five years.

Mexican Joe sold dope, too. He came to us when his "bag" ran out and vice versa. Woody was a Native American and lived in Lansing. He'd drive forty-two miles every day to buy two half spoons of dope. Woody even stayed with us for a week one time.

Ashley Burrows was a white woman around my age. Less than five feet tall and the mother of three, she was divorced and raising them alone in a nice split-level home in a Jackson suburb. Ashley would drive up in her new 1973 gray Honda Civic, her oldest son, twelve, sitting up front, and the youngest son and daughter, eight and six, in the back. Our kids got along well. They played together in the backyard, in their bedrooms, on the porch, or anywhere else we both deemed safe while we got high. She became my closest friend.

One night Ashley surprised me, dropping by with the new man in her life. He was black, twenty-three years older than her, and one of the biggest dope dealers in town. I was speechless. Rumor had it that the dude wined and dined women, especially white women, until they fell head over heels for him. Then he'd control their every move, often beating them for pleasure. It took several days for me to get up the nerve to tell my friend about the rumors I'd heard, but by then he already had her under his spell. Six months into their relationship, she sold her house in the suburbs, at his order, then rented an apartment in the inner-city projects.

Ashley's man isolated her from her family and friends, including me. Every once in a while I'd stop by their house to buy dope, when we had run out. It also gave me a chance to chat with her for a minute or two. She always looked sad and acted uncomfortable, rushing our conversations as if she was afraid he'd see us talking. One day she came to the door with a black eye and several large bruises on her arms that had begun healing because they were green around the edges. I hated seeing my friend like that.

Ashley stayed with the guy for a little more than two years. She finally left the dude after he broke her arm and manhandled her oldest son, who jumped in and tried to help his mother during one of the attacks. I guess Ashley's parents couldn't take any more. They offered her their bi-level home in another suburb if she left him. Ashley quit the guy for good, and her parents kept their promise. She moved into their bigger and nicer home, and they moved to Florida.

Once Ashley freed herself of the dude, we started visiting each other again. I loved sitting on her oak and brown upholstered Early American living-room sofa, puffing on a joint and watching the fish in her fifty-gallon aquarium. Ashley smoked reefer every day, lighting one up when she woke up in the morning and a last one before going to sleep at night. Weed had always made me paranoid until Ashley schooled me.

"Try taking a blue when you smoke pot," she said. "It'll take the paranoid feeling right away." A blue was a ten-milligram Valium that got its nickname because of its color.

Ashley eventually married a guy who was several years younger than her. His father owned a hardware business, and she slowly drifted back into the white mainstream. Not wanting to complicate her new life, I quit calling and visiting. She did, too.

Then there was the twenty-something-year-old blonde-haired couple who drove into town from a rural community at least twice a month. They almost always brought big spiral suckers for the kids and often watched them while we went to cop. Our kids adored them.

Suddenly they stopped coming. Several months later I found out that the guy had died of a cocaine overdose. I was so hurt. They were a sweet couple who loved having fun.

But life went on. Junkies would overdose and die, and the rest of us wouldn't miss a beat.

Our dope-dealing days came to an abrupt end when Lucious was arrested one night after a domestic dispute. He had two females living with him at the same time. Bad decision. One was twenty. The other was his age, about forty. The three of them got into a big fight, and someone called the police. Lucious landed back in prison for parole violation. He managed to tell the older woman to bring all his guns and rifles to me.

She showed up at my door with weapons in her hand. The rest were in her car. I didn't know what to do. Guns terrified me, especially after Carla got shot when we were teenagers. And with four small, curious children and a hotheaded husband, the last thing I wanted was a couple dozen firearms—including a machine gun—in my house.

I ended up calling Albert's buddy Maurice, who was Lucious's cousin, and asked him to come get the arsenal. He did. Gladly. I never heard from Lucious again. Maurice sold the guns to help pay Lucious's legal expenses.

✾ THE VISION

I was at the lowest point in my life when a voice woke me up before dawn one morning. I sensed something unusual was happening right away. Cordell was sleeping beside me in bed with the most peaceful look on his face. I sat up and shook him even though I wasn't afraid.

Scenes from my life drifted before me in a foggy but gentle light. All of them were sad or difficult experiences. The last scene showed me sitting alone in the front pew of an unfamiliar church, dressed in black, with a hat and veil, as if mourning. I appeared solemn but not sad.

A comforting voice, with deep authority, spoke from somewhere I didn't know. It carried an explicit message: *"Things are going to get worse before they get better. But when it's all said and done, you're going to be very religious."*

In the same instant, something touched me, giving me a split second of peace beyond anything I could ever imagine and would never forget.

— ❧ —

BIRDS CHIRPED in the maple trees outside our bedroom window. Dogs barked in backyards. The sun came up. I turned to Cordell just as he opened his sleepy eyes.

"What's the matter?" he said, yawning and stretching, still on his bare back.

I didn't know how to start telling him but got it out, somehow. I had to. Right then and there. I told my husband everything—the cloudy light, the male voice that spoke with so much authority, and the scenes from my life. I even told Cordell about the peaceful look on his face when I tried to wake him up during the experience. Cordell looked at me like I was crazy.

"I'm serious," I pleaded, hoping he'd take me more seriously.

I felt that something supernatural had happened. I didn't know why. I didn't know who. I didn't understand what it all meant. I just knew that something out of the ordinary and significant had just happened. Something that didn't scare me, but caught my attention and would forever be a part of my memory.

The more I talked, the more uneasy Cordell appeared. Unable to let the subject go, I finally convinced him to walk down the street a few doors to one of my best-friends' house. Dara Abrams was the girl who transferred to Allen Elementary School with me midway through the sixth grade. Dara and her live-in boyfriend had moved three doors down from us about two years earlier. Our old friendship had been rekindled.

It was six o'clock in the morning, and Cordell and I were standing on Dara's front steps, knocking on her door. They were asleep but got up. Dara started giggling when I recounted the story. She always did when excited. Hunching her shoulders and placing her fingertips over her mouth, my friend wanted to hear every detail. I convinced them to walk back to our house to continue our conversation.

Dara's man, Melvin, liked drinking as much as Cordell did. They hit it off the first time we introduced them to each other. Melvin was in his late twenties and always wore the same black wool tam on top of his thick, wooly hair, and was as lazy as he looked. He quickly admitted being too scared to talk about the subject.

"Can't we just leave this one alone?" he asked, straightening his hat and slouching different ways in our blue chair, a cigarette between his fingers, his wrist, limp.

Dara and I sat on the sofa, facing each other. We lit cigarettes and shared an ashtray, then picked up our conversation where we'd left off. Cordell clicked the television channels around four or five times. Finding no shoot-'em-ups at seven o'clock in the morning, he joined our conversation again.

—— ℘ ——

THE KIDS WOKE UP around seven thirty. Lamar came down the stairs first, wearing a dingy T-shirt with red Kool-Aid stains on the front and blue print pajama bottoms. Always the first to wake up in the morning and the last to go to bed at night, Lamar had sleeping problems similar to mine as a child. Cordell took our son into the kitchen to fix him a bowl of cereal.

The more Dara and I talked about my vision, the louder the other kids upstairs got. The twins cried. Someone kept bumping against the walls. The toilet flushed several times. Water started running in the bathroom.

Andre finally came scooting down the steps on his behind and bare backed. Our son slept that way more often than not, like his dad. Yawning and wiping his crusty eyes, my nearly five-year-old son started tuning up to cry. Nothing unusual for him. Our son woke up most mornings with a scowl on his face, like his daddy's, too, and ready to cry at the slightest inconvenience. He was still a little timid around Cordell. As soon as my little man reached the bottom step, he marched right up to me and climbed in my lap.

It was another fifteen minutes before the twins came scooting down the steps. They headed straight to the lower doors of the china cabinet we'd bought with some of the money Cordell stole from "Fort Knox," and started pulling out record albums before Cordell noticed. He took them into the kitchen to feed them, one thrown across each hip, their legs dangling. I continued talking about my "religious experience," even though the term didn't feel exactly right.

Around eleven o'clock there was an unexpected knock at the door. Two brown-skinned women, holding Bibles in their hands and wearing dresses that hung well below their knees, were standing there when I opened it. They appeared to be in their mid to late thirties. Judging by the way they dressed, I figured they were members of a well-known sanctified church in town.

"We were just walking past your house this morning, and the Lord told us to stop in and pray for you today," the shorter one said, with a warm smile on her face, which lacked makeup.

None of us knew what to say for a second or two. Given the conversation we'd been having, I invited them in. Prior to that, the only church people who had graced our door in more than a year were Daddy, Mother, and Rev. Whittington. The pastor of Trinity Baptist often passed by our house, and if he saw Cordell and me playing catch with the kids out front, he'd stop and join the game. It also gave him a chance to remind me of my religious roots.

"Jasmine, now you know you weren't raised like this. Your Grandma Beanie raised you in the church," he'd say, tossing the ball back and forth. I dreaded seeing him coming.

The two women sat down on our sofa and listened quietly as I told them about what had happened to me earlier that morning. Both said it was no coincidence that they stopped by. I was inclined to agree.

"We need to get on our knees and pray for understanding," the taller woman said, already laying her purse down on the sofa and raising her dress slightly to kneel.

Cordell, Dara, and Melvin declined to take part, but I did. On our knees in front of the couch, the two women prayed for me for ten minutes. It seemed like ten hours.

"Now, do you feel any different?" the taller woman asked when finished, looking at me, then my husband and friends, who were sitting around quietly watching.

I told the truth.

"No."

"Then we're just gonna pray some more," the plain-looking woman said with even more conviction.

"Me and my big mouth," I thought.

Her second prayer wasn't as long as the first, which relieved me. Afterward, I hurried them to the door, my body demanding its daily fix. They stopped on the porch momentarily and invited me to a church service being held that night.

"Go ahead Jasmine. I think you should do it," Cordell said, his facial expression had changed from bewildered to almost frightened.

I was shocked. I was even more shocked when my husband offered to go to church with me. I'd never seen Cordell inside a church before, except for Grandma's funeral.

"No thank-you," I said politely, then made up some lame excuse before quickly closing the door behind them. Heroin was calling me.

OVER AND OVER

ordell never returned to his factory job and settled out of court for ten thousand dollars. His lawyer got a third. We had been waiting nearly three years when his lawyer finally called one morning around eleven and said, "Your ship has come in."

We dropped everything. I wanted to go with Cordell to the lawyer's office, but he asked his oldest brother, Hitchie, to take him. I should have known something was up, but didn't.

A few hours after they left, my phone started ringing off the hook. People were calling and asking where Cordell had gotten all the money he was flashing down on the corner and at a popular party store where addicts hung out. I wanted to kill my husband.

I was still awake when he finally showed up around three o'clock in the morning. Cordell had bought a two-year-old black Cadillac with a white vinyl top and a wardrobe of clothes for him *and* me.

"I don't even like black cars. And you don't even buy clothes for yourself, so how are you going to pick out a whole wardrobe for me?" I cried. "And our house payments are three months past due. Our lights and gas have been cut off twice. And here, the first time you get some money in your pocket, you head for the streets."

The next day Cordell caught our mortgage payments up and bought a used white pickup truck that had a stick shift. I could barely drive an automatic. We bought a red battery-operated car for Andre that was large enough to sit in and drive. Lamar got coloring books and a huge, stuffed Cookie Monster, his favorite *Sesame Street* character. The twins got tricycles and coloring books, too.

We took five hundred dollars to Detroit to buy half a gram of heroin to sell, but ended up using most of it during a three-day hiatus. We stayed locked up in the house and got high.

— ℰ —

THREE WEEKS LATER I wrote a check for groceries, and it bounced. We had an even bigger fight.

"You mean to tell me that you've blown all that money already?" I yelled as soon as Cordell walked through the door from his mother's house.

He hemmed and hawed and made up all kinds of excuses, but the bottom line was that we were broke again. Being broke meant I'd have to start stealing again. Never good at boosting, I was terrified of going to jail. One time was more than enough for me. Being broke meant hanging around the pool rooms again, smiling and flirting with old men, hoping they'd win a hand of poker and throw five or ten dollars my way. Being broke meant leaving my kids with their daddy for four to eight hours at a time, knowing that he was more interested in me bringing home his fix than taking care of four active kids.

Drugs had distorted my thinking so much that it became easier and easier to rationalize our behavior, especially when it came to my husband.

"Better me than him," I thought many times. "The police don't like Cordell's family. If he gets caught doing anything, he'll probably do time in jail or prison. Or else he'd start clowning and make somebody have to hurt him or kill him."

Taking responsibility and blame was nothing new for me. I was okay with the role of victim or martyr. I had started taking the blame for things as a kid, so taking the blame as an adult came easy.

— ℰ —

RUMORS WERE FLOATING around the drug circle that Cordell had started shooting up heroin. I refused to believe it.

"Nah. Not as much as Cordell hates needles," I thought the few times the rumor reached my ears.

Cordell denied it from day one.

"If I was doing that, don't you think I'd have some kind of tracks on my arm?" he asked one day, stretching out his arms, palms up, so that I could see. "Does it look like I've got some fucking tracks on me?"

I wouldn't have known a track if I had seen one. Yet Cordell had me convinced he was telling the truth, until the afternoon I stumbled upon him in a far corner of our basement with a hypodermic needle in his arm. I placed my hand over my mouth and screamed. He took several quick steps toward me, his face looking like a scared little boy.

"I'm not hooked Jasmine. I swear I'm not hooked," he said pleadingly.

I ran back upstairs and starting packing. I stuffed clothes, most of them dirty, in paper bags, and used a beat-up old suitcase that Mother had given me several years earlier.

"I can't take any more of this, Cordell. It's too much. Your family. Your gambling. Your women. And now this. It's just too much," I said as he grabbed my shoulders, begging and swearing he'd quit.

I called my aunt Jada in Flint and told her the whole story. She agreed to let the kids and me stay with her for a few days until I figured out what to do. With eighty dollars to my name, I paid a distant cousin twenty dollars to drive the kids and me up to her house.

Aunt Jada and I had always been cool. She was even more streetwise than my dad and loved to party. She had plenty of men and told me anything I wanted to know. I chose my aunt's house because I didn't want to hear my dad or mom say, "I told you so." They had never spoken against Cordell, but they weren't happy with him either.

Being in a new place, the kids were more active than usual. Aunt Jada never complained, although she winced every time one of them came close to knocking something over. It was nerve-racking living in somebody else's house with four small children. I had to watch their every move, fearful they'd break something.

Aunt Jada always had a nice house. My dad's people loved material things. Nice cars. Nice clothes. Nice homes. Nice furniture.

Growing up, I adored my daddy's baby sister. She spoke whatever was on her mind, and if push came to shove, she'd fight. Aunt Jada's brown skin was smooth and pretty, like Uncle Darius's. He was the youngest male, and was a stone fox. Women couldn't take their eyes off of him. Neither could I.

Aunt Jada appeared disappointed when I told her my plans to return home after five days. But she allowed me to make my own decisions. That's what I liked about her and my dad. They would counsel me all along the way, but the final decision was mine.

My kids needed to be in their own house, where they could return to their normal routines. I was proud of how well they adapted to our sudden move. It was my first time realizing how resilient children were.

I thought of Cordell's drug abuse. I thought of the kids. I thought of my life without a father. I thought about Cordell before he started using drugs. Before the army. Before Vietnam.

"This is the time when my husband needs me the most," I thought, while packing up to go back home. "Besides, even Mother is always telling me that children need a father."

Three months after going back to my husband, I started shooting up heroin, too, motivated by two reasons: I wanted the maximum impact of the drug. And I wanted Cordell to feel guilty and responsible for my actions.

"If he had never started doing it, neither would I. That's what he gets."

⚜ SHAMELESS

lbert was honorably discharged from the army after a two-year tour of duty. I didn't tell him about my drug addiction for a month or two, and only after I'd heard that he'd started using again. He had always looked up to me and was shocked and disappointed when I told him. But we eventually started getting high together.

My brother and I still shared a lot of secrets. I even admitted snitching on him to our grandfather several years earlier when I first heard about his drug use. He smirked, then looked really devilish, the way he did when he was going to admit something really shameful.

"Daddy called me up to their house to talk to me about that, Jasmine. You know a junkie ain't *no* good. Daddy gave me twenty-five dollars that day," he stuttered, looking over his eyebrows at me, his eyes big and white. "I told him it would cost twenty-five dollars to get in a drug treatment program. I bought me two dime bags of blow with that money."

We laughed. I think junkies laugh a lot to keep from crying because they are so manipulative and heartless. Addicts would steal from their mommas, something I never did but probably would have given the opportunity. One time I did think about arranging for a relative's house to be burglarized while she was out of town. I had thought about it all day, but couldn't go through with it. I hated myself for even thinking about bringing harm or hurt to any of my kin.

My grandfather saved my behind more than once during my seven years of drug abuse and addiction. I wrote a $180 worth of checks on my personal account when it had been closed for several months. The store wrote me a warning letter.

"I need the money by tomorrow or they're gonna take a warrant out for me," I told Daddy, trying to look and sound as pitiful as possible. He brought me the money the same day with only one bit of advice.

"Go downtown and get that matter taken care of today," my 78-year-old grandfather said. Afraid of going to jail, I did exactly that.

Another time my grandfather was driving by just as I was being pulled over by a police officer on Francis Street, driving our 1962 gold Pontiac with expired plates. Daddy doubled around the block and pulled over to talk to the officer, who knew him and addressed him as "Rev. Brown." Our grandfather knew lots of white people downtown.

The policeman let me go without writing a ticket. But he gave me a stern warning.

"Go straight home and park this car until you get the plates renewed," the middle-aged officer said.

Right.

I was looking for heroin, and nothing or nobody was going to stop me. I rode and rode, running into the same police officer twice more. The second time he pulled me over he threatened to put me in jail if he saw me driving again. The third time, I ditched him before he could stop me. I did what a junkie had once advised when fleeing the police, "Just keep turning corners."

———— ౨ ————

WHEN IT CAME TO drugs and junkies, it was a dog-eat-dog world. Albert stole heroin from Cordell and me on more than one occasion, creating all kind of havoc between the three of us. Another time, my brother stole three hundred dollars out of our bedroom dresser drawer. Albert even set us up to get "beat" once, by selling us an expensive baseball glove, then having its owner, the guy accompanying him, steal it back the same day.

My brother eventually got so strung out that he stuck up a cab driver for fifty dollars, landing him in prison for three-and-a-half to fifteen years. On sentencing day, I was the only person who accompanied Albert in court. Both of us hoped for a miracle, but it wasn't to be.

"You're a menace to society. People like you don't belong on the streets of our community," the gray-haired judge said, leaning forward over his bench, spectacles low on his nose.

My heart pounded as I stared at my brother, feeling helpless and angry. Albert stood at the defendant's table, his head hung and voice low, answering the few questions asked of him with a simple "Yes, Your Honor" or "No, Your Honor."

I was mad at the judge for the things he'd said about my brother. Albert was a kind, sweet person who had a great sense of humor and would give a person his last dime. Heroin changed him. He needed medical help, just like a person with any other disease.

I was mad at Momma for not visiting Albert during his two-month stay in jail before the trial. She and I had a big falling out about that.

"Those white people downtown don't care nothing about Albert. And if they see that his own family doesn't care, they'll send him up for life," I shouted at her one afternoon. "You and I know the *real* Albert. They don't."

Momma didn't go down to the county jail to visit her son, but she started writing and sending him money. I was happy she did that.

After my brother's sentencing, they took him away without letting me even say good-bye. I cried all the way home, feeling sorry for him and fearing I'd be next. Blinded by tears, a song on the radio caught my attention. It was called "Miracles," by the Jefferson Starship. I loved it, and from that day on, every time I heard that song it reminded me of Albert.

Mother and Daddy were down south when Albert got sent to prison. The family always tried to keep bad news from them, especially our grandmother, but Mother almost always knew more than they ever imagined. I made sure of that. But some of her church friends got to her before I did and told her about Albert. Then she dug out the newspaper article and read it. Mother looked up at me with the saddest expression on her face.

"Well, they're mine if they do wrong. And they're mine if they're president," she said softly.

✲ FRESH AIR

Next to early mornings, dusk was my favorite time of day. Cordell and I had gotten our daily fix and were playing "hot box" with the kids on the sidewalk in front of our house. Hot box was a game simulating baseball players being caught between two bases in a rundown. We played the game quite often. All four of the kids loved it.

We had Kendra in a rundown when I threw the ball too high over Cordell's head. He was trotting back from the neighbor's yard with the ball in his dry, ashy hands when an unfamiliar car pulled up in front of our three-bedroom, ranch-style home, rented to us by the city. We had lost our big house on Robinson Street, and I didn't even care.

"This house is getting too big for me to take care of anyway," I said, stripping up the carpet to lay in our city-owned home.

Cordell cut all the copper pipes in the big house and sold them for junk. He got $102.38. We spent most of it on drugs.

It was Jonathon's estranged wife who got out of the car. They married two years after we had and stayed together three. Joyce had two children from an earlier relationship and a daughter by Jonathon.

I used to hate seeing her coming. The girl was downright depressing. She dragged around with a look on her face sadder than mine. A pretty girl, her big dark eyes were always lined with too much eyebrow pencil, giving her the appearance of being a floozy. Our complexions were the same, but we never had much else in common. I hadn't seen the girl since she divorced Jonathan.

Joyce climbed out of a shiny new gold car. I noticed something different about her right away. She was smiling. She helped her three kids out of the vehicle without fussing at any of them. Another *big* difference. She had always snapped at her kids more than I did mine, and they were the same age. Joyce spoke to Cordell as she passed him. He didn't speak back. The Walker family never had anything to do with people who dumped one of them. And Joyce was no exception.

They talked about Joyce like a dog when she left Jonathon. I had never cared for the girl either, so it was easy for me to put my two cents in the conversation. Seeing her coming to my house was totally unexpected.

"I just thought I'd drop by to see how you've been doing, girl," she said, her face radiant. "I've been thinking about you. And the kids. My kids ask about them all the time."

I was touched. Cordell jumped in our beat-up, barely making it, dusty 1962 Mercury. Our Cadillac had been repossessed. Terrance totaled out our Pontiac, and we didn't have insurance. So I bought the green Mercury from my cousin Arlene for forty dollars.

Cordell hollered as he backed out of the paved driveway, "I'm going to Momma's. I'll be back." I watched the Mercury chug down the street, leaving a trail of exhaust fumes.

The kids had run to greet each other. Then my kids hugged Joyce. Her three hugged me. They started playing catch, while my ex-sister-in-law and I strolled into the house.

"Girl, where in the world have you been?" I asked, examining her face, trying to figure out what made her so upbeat and showing all her pretty white teeth.

"I've been around. I just needed to get away from the Walker family. Girl, it's a real trip to see how differently things look when you step back from that family for a little while. I wouldn't wish those folks on anybody," she said, sounding genuine for the first time since I'd known her.

I wondered if it were true. Would I really see things differently without Cordell around? I wanted to leave Cordell so badly I resented him. I resented his family. They resented me.

"People say that women know when they've had enough. I'm probably one of those people who don't have sense enough to know it even if I did. I wish I could leave Cordell like Joyce did Jonathon," I thought, sitting on our sofa, anxious to hear more of her story.

"I joined church. Trinity Baptist, that used to be over on Franklin. The new church is on Prospect Avenue," Joyce said.

"That used to be my church home," I said eagerly. "But I haven't been inside the old church in years. And the only time I stepped inside the new one, was for my cousin Debra's wedding." The thought shamed me.

"Knowing God has changed my whole life," she said, her copper face lit up, her voice calm and peaceful. "For the first time in my life, I know that somebody really loves me for who I am. Not for sex. Not for money. Not for anything. Jesus loves me unconditionally because I'm a child of God. Once I started believing that, things started changing in my life for the better. Now I have faith."

I hung on every word Joyce said. Whatever she had, I wanted it, too. I felt good just being in her company. I knew I was seeing a miracle.

Joyce had a new man, Quinton Turner, who was nineteen. She was twenty-six. Quinton adored Joyce. He called her several times a day from the factory where he worked since graduating from high school. The boy showered Joyce with gifts. New furniture and appliances. New clothes. No more secondhand clothes for her family. Quinton told her, "Never again." Joyce even drove his car every day while he worked.

"He wants to marry me," she said sheepishly. "But his mother isn't happy about our relationship. I really can't blame her. He doesn't have any kids of his own, and I can't have any more. I don't want to tie Quinton down with a family, and he's so young."

Joyce had never been a drinker, druggie, gambler, or smoker. As far as I was concerned, her main problem—outside of having been married to Jonathon—was her personality. Seeing her so kind and gracious really blew my mind.

Joyce strolled to the window and checked on the kids. I wanted some of the peace she had so badly it made me envious. I needed help. Quickly.

We faced eviction again, and had only been living there eighteen months. Cordell owed a loan shark four hundred dollars. I'd almost overdosed twice and ended up in the hospital. I hated my marriage. I hated my life. But most of all I hated being a junkie. Desperate, I absorbed every word my friend spoke.

"Knowing God has helped me to forgive myself. I've done so many things wrong in my life, it's a wonder I'm alive. Just knowing that Jesus has forgiven me really helped me start over. Only this time I'm trying to let Christ lead me. I used to think I needed a man telling me where to go and what to do. Now I know the only thing I needed was God."

Joyce told me that she read the Bible every day. She took her kids to church every Sunday. She even attended Bible study a couple times a month.

"The real test is putting what the scriptures teach into practice every day," she said. "Being a true Christian is a lot of hard work. That's why I have to stay involved in my church, to keep me from getting distracted."

It sounded like too much church for me. But I was desperate and wanted to hear more. I couldn't help staring at Joyce with utter amazement. Never had I seen such a dramatic change in someone's life.

"I try to pray before making big decisions," she continued, radiating an inner beauty that I wanted—badly. Even her golden skin, which was ordinarily oily and bumpy, appeared smoother.

Listening to Joyce and observing her behavior, she had me beginning to think that there just might be something to praying and believing. I told her about the vision I'd had several years earlier, hoping she would provide some explanation. She couldn't but offered reassurance.

"Everything happens for a reason. And the Lord reveals things in his own time. Not ours. If he wants you to do something, he'll let you know what it is at the right time. The Bible says, 'To everything there is a season.' That means there's a right time for everything," she said, her dark eyes twinkling, along with her teeth.

I wanted to believe her. My body and soul craved what she had. I wanted to think and feel the way she did so badly that my insides cried out. I was desperate and didn't mind admitting it to her, even though we'd never been close.

Instead of looking down on me or trying to tell me how messed up I was, Joyce seemed genuinely interested in my well-being. It was such a relief. I had been feeling so alone.

"You should start by praying and reading the Bible," she suggested. "Prayer really does change things."

"But I don't own a Bible. And even if I did, I wouldn't be able to understand it. I never could. I tried when I was a teenager, but it didn't make sense," I said, hoping she had some faster remedy to heal my aching heart and soul.

That's when Joyce told me about the Living Bible. She explained that it was written in everyday language, making it easy for anyone to understand.

"I've got mine in the car," she said with more excitement than I'd ever seen in her, then rushed outside to get it.

Within a few minutes she was trotting across the grass, carrying a black, leather-covered Bible in her petite hands. I watched her finger through the thin pages as if she knew exactly what she was looking for. I was impressed.

"I love reading Proverbs," she said. "It really helps me to deal with everyday stuff. That's probably a good place for you to start reading, too, Jasmine."

She found the book of Proverbs, then handed me the Bible. I felt awkward, having not held a Bible in years, but began randomly scanning the book. The first chapter I stopped at was Proverbs 1:7, which read: "How does a man become wise? The first step is to trust and reverence the Lord."

I found the thought fascinating but still wanted a quick fix. Trusting the Lord didn't seem to be something that I could do right away, nor did I know how. I thumbed through a few more pages and ran upon another scripture, Proverbs 14:13: "Laughter cannot mask a heavy heart. When the laughter ends, the grief remains."

The more I read, the more reality began slapping me in the face. I wanted to learn more. I needed to learn more. Each scripture soothed my aching soul and brought comfort like nothing else had—not even heroin.

"I had no idea that they made a Bible like this. Can I borrow yours for a few days?" I asked, prepared to beg if necessary.

Hesitant at first, Joyce agreed to let me borrow it for three days. She explained that she slept with the Bible over her head in the bookcase headboard of her new bed that Quinton had bought.

"I don't feel comfortable sleeping without it," she said.

I found that even more fascinating. I couldn't imagine anything but drugs meaning that much to me.

—— ℘ ——

CORDELL OWED a local loan shark four hundred dollars. A well-respected man in town, the loan shark quietly loaned money to drug addicts who worked. He charged 40 percent interest rates.

Cordell was apprenticing with a local tool and die maker, earning the minimum on the pay scale. He worked every day, attended four-hour classes at Jackson Community College on Tuesday nights, and was guaranteed a substantial pay raise every six months. My husband didn't miss a day's work, and the loan shark knew it.

Every payday Cordell owed the man almost his entire check. Caught up in a vicious cycle, we'd have to borrow more money from him to feed our drug habits and our kids, in that order. My husband had promised to pay the loan shark the same week we had agreed to pay our rent. The city had already taken us to court and served us with eviction papers. We were two months behind and had until payday to catch up.

"You know we've got to pay our rent, Cordell. They'll put us out if we don't," I said to him, six days straight. "Please don't mess up this time. Please."

My husband just looked at me and never said much back. That worried me.

"You have a family," I pleaded on payday morning before he left for work. "Mr. Porter can wait until next pay day for his money. We need a roof over our heads."

My husband did the opposite. He came home after paying the loan shark and nonchalantly announced that we were moving in with his mother. I thought I'd die.

"I can't believe you decided to pay him over your own family! What kind of man are you, moving your family in with your momma?" I cried.

My husband was unmoved.

"At least I can go home to mine. You couldn't go home even if you wanted to," he shot back. After ripping each other's heart out with words for several hours, we did what we always did—tried to patch things up. Cordell promised we'd move into our own place as soon as our income tax refund check came in early March. It was early November.

❧ MRS. WALKER'S HOUSE

Moving into Cordell's mother's house was the hardest thing I'd ever done in my life. It felt worse than being strung out on drugs because at least I'd had a home. With my head hung and forcing a smile, we trudged through Mrs. Walker's house with belongings that had grown skimpy. Most of our expensive furniture and appliances had been repossessed, sold, or pawned.

Cordell, the kids, and I slept in a nine-by-ten-foot bedroom that Mrs. Walker had prepared several days earlier. I kept the kids holed up in the room for half a day before letting them roam the house. Knowing the Walker family disliked me, I feared they'd take it out on our kids—grandchildren or not.

A week passed. I started easing into the living room to watch television with Cordell and his family. Most times they spoke without looking up. I sat in the same green plaid armchair every time, never feeling comfortable or welcomed. Every time I stepped out of our bedroom, the tension almost suffocated me. I dragged to the bathroom and living room as little as possible. My eyes dimmed. A hole replaced my heart.

Every now and then I'd hear someone snap at my kids for simple things. They stood in front of the television. They took too long in the bathroom. They talked too much. I felt helpless. Paralyzed. Afraid to say anything that might get us put out.

Sometimes two or three days passed before an adult would speak or say anything to me, including Cordell. When they did, their voices dripped with distaste. I cried myself to sleep every night.

— ❧ —

STARTING IN MID-FEBRUARY, every morning I walked out to the front porch and opened the mailbox and peeked in. Nothing for us. I often stuck my hand into the mailbox several times and rubbed the insides, just to make sure.

Cordell kept promising we'd move as soon as our income-tax refund came. It finally arrived one Saturday morning. Cordell bought me a ten-cent bag of dope, then disappeared until the wee hours of the next morning. He'd given me all but a hundred dollars of the money, so I didn't sweat his late-night hours.

One good thing came out of living with the Walkers. It curtailed my drug use tremendously—but not because I'd lost the craving. I had no money and seldom left the house. Too afraid to leave my kids alone with the Walkers, I didn't go anywhere except for occasional trips to the store. I ran into Joyce twice.

"Girl, you look so stressed out. You really need to get away from those people. They'll drive you crazy, Jasmine. I'm telling you," she said, looking at me as if she could feel my pain.

"Where would I go? I've got four kids. Who's gonna want to put up with that?" I asked one day.

"I will. If you ever decide to leave for good, you can come stay up here with me. I've only got two bedrooms, but we can make it work."

"Well, we were supposed to be moving into our own place. And I'm going to make sure that it's real soon. We put away most of our income-tax money, and I've started looking in the want ads already."

"Well, that's up to you," my friend said skeptically. "I think you need to get away from all of them—including Cordell."

I wasn't ready to do that. I'd hid the money in the pocket of an old coat hanging in our bedroom closet and didn't even tell Cordell. I checked the gray coat pocket every morning and every night for three days. The evening of the fourth day, it was gone.

I fingered every inch of the pocket. I grabbed the others, turning them inside out. Nothing. I broke down crying.

"Cordell, please ask your family about the money. Someone had to take it," I begged.

He did. Reluctantly. His parents cussed him out and me, too. The whole family stopped speaking to me all together. I had never felt so desperate and alone in a house full of people in my life.

— ৯ —

CORDELL STOPPED coming home on payday, again. Money he didn't blow on drugs and alcohol, he gambled away at the poolroom. Sometimes I wouldn't see him until well into the night, if at all. We argued constantly, because I refused to let him come home drunk and pick at me without at least cussing him out.

One Friday night Cordell didn't come home on payday, knowing I had no money or food for the kids. After waiting several hours, I swallowed my pride. Easing out of my self-imposed prison, I fixed the kids a plate of food his mother had prepared. Mrs. Walker cooked hearty meals and had the food on the dinner table by noon. She spent the rest of her day watching the soaps on television.

My kids had eaten Mrs. Walker's food many times during our stay. I don't think she really minded, either. But it hurt like hell to feed them not knowing if we'd have money to pay Mrs. Walker fifty dollars a week for rent. I went to bed hungry many times, trying to lessen the load on the rest of the house. That night was no exception.

Weary from constant tension and stress, I made myself a promise not to argue with Cordell, if and when he showed up. I couldn't sleep. Miserably crowded in a twin bed I shared with our daughters, I closed my eyes and practiced what to say to Cordell without so much venom in my heart.

He stumbled into the bedroom around four o'clock in the morning. Clicking on the overhead light, Cordell started talking so loudly it startled me, just as I was drifting off to sleep.

"Get up Jasmine. I wanna talk to you," he said, his speech slurring, his wrinkled clothes smelling like stale cigarette smoke and musk.

I adjusted my eyes to the light and saw Cordell standing over me, glaring. My heart wouldn't let me take any more.

"Look, Cordell. Don't come in here starting that shit with me after you've stayed out all night again," I said. "I don't want to hear a thing you've got to say."

"Oh you don't, huh? Why not? You've got the nerve, you ole jealous-ass bitch. You're just mad cause I wasn't stuck up here in this house under your ass all night. You ain't fooling me," he said, pulling the blankets off of me and the girls, who were cuddled up beside me.

Mr. Walker hollered from his bedroom upstairs.

"All right y'all. It's four o'clock in the morning. I ain't gon have that shit in my house tonight."

I sat up and folded my pillow. I hit it twice. I threw my head back down and closed my eyes, praying he'd leave me alone. Cordell flicked the light switch on and off several times. I sat back up.

"Cordell, will you please stop? You're gonna mess around and wake up these kids."

He mimicked me. Word for word.

"Kiss my ass, woman," he said, snarling his nose at me.

I got him told. But instead of the usual screaming, cussing, and name calling, I threw him for a loop by speaking calmly and rationally.

"I've been kissing your ass for nearly eight years now," I said. "But God knows I'm so tired of doing it, Cordell, I don't know what to do. I'm not gonna . . ."

"Didn't I tell y'all to cut that shit out?" Mr. Walker yelled, his voice sounding as if he was coming down the stairway.

I threw my head back down on the pillow. Tears streamed down my face. I wanted to scream. I wanted to hit Cordell and cuss everybody in his family out. I felt trapped, like a prisoner, only my cell was a small, crowded bedroom on the first floor of the Walkers' home.

My husband staggered across the hall to the bathroom several feet away. He slammed the door. He slammed it again when he came back out. I sat watching in disgust. Cordell crawled into the other twin bed in his socks with the boys. He had removed his shirt and pants. Minutes later, his arms sprawled across Andre's face and Lamar's neck. Both our sons slept just as wildly.

Lying in the dark, I cried so much I had to turn my pillow over twice. I had no fight left in me. My back was against the wall. I felt helpless, worthless, and alone. It was the scariest feeling imaginable.

I crawled back out of bed and quietly knelt beside the bed and started praying. "Please, God. You know I can't take any more. Please help me. I don't know what else to do. I know I haven't lived right. I know I need to get myself together. But Lord, I need your help. I can't do it by myself."

I cried myself into exhaustion. What happened next had to be the work of the Lord because an incredible peace came over me. It reminded me of the touch I'd felt during my vision several years earlier. Climbing back into bed, I felt completely different. No more troubled thoughts. No more anger. No more fear. Just peace and relief.

I lay in bed until daylight pierced the panels of the blue sheer curtains hanging over our bedroom window. I tiptoed in the living room and called Joyce.

"Is that offer you made still good?" I whispered.

"Of course," she replied. "Just tell me when you and the kids are coming."

"Give me until noon," I replied.

—— ℓ ——

"WHAT DO YOU THINK you're doing?" Cordell asked, propped up on his elbows in the small bed.

I didn't look his way and continued struggling to get an oversize box of clothes through our bedroom door.

"I'm leaving."

"Going where?"

"You'll find out soon enough," I said calmly.

He laughed. My husband watched me scuffle with the box and offered no assistance. I dragged the box outside to the car. He slipped into his pants and was sitting bare backed in the living room when I returned inside.

I piled boxes in the trunk and to the roof of our old car. The kids sat on and around them. We drove four blocks to Joyce's upstairs apartment on Greenwood Street, where she and I and our kids carried boxes up fourteen steps. She lived above a party store.

I made four trips back to the Walkers' house and was hauling my last load while most of the family gathered in the living room, pretending to be watching television.

No one said or did anything. They didn't even ask about the kids. Cordell said nothing about using his car.

I had no idea what they were thinking. And didn't care. My mind was fixed on leaving, as if being led by a higher force. I wasn't afraid. I wasn't angry. I was just plain through. I felt unstoppable.

The car packed, I made one last trip back inside the Walkers' house. The kids had sat down on their knees and were watching TV in the living room.

"Give everybody a kiss," I said as we headed out the door. Each kid went to each relative. One by one they hugged and kissed them good-bye.

✻ STARTING OVER

The next three weeks were like paradise. Joyce and I got along great. We spent our days cooking and cleaning while the kids were in school. Quinton called a dozen times a day from work and popped in and out afterward. At night Joyce and I sat around listening to "Car Wash" by Rolls Royce and "Love's in Need of Love" by Stevie Wonder, while the kids sat on the hardwood floor watching TV—all of us in the same small living room. We played the two songs so much that even our kids learned the words and sung them all the time, too.

Our kids played well together. They always had. We kept their toys in the bedroom they shared and would not allow them to bring them outside of it, due to a lack of space. I don't remember them ever disobeying the house rules, even though seven young children had to, at some point. It was as if all of us in the house understood our circumstances and were doing our best to make it work.

Joyce and I took turns cooking, washing dishes, and cleaning house. It was fun to eat each other's cooking, something we'd never done before. Our kids enjoyed spaghetti, fried chicken, pork chops, pot roast, and vegetables and anything else our imagination and food stamps allowed us. I was able to get some of them right away.

Joyce's kids were on a strict bedtime schedule. Mine were used to going whenever they got tired. Her kids were perfect role models. They didn't talk back. They seldom complained. They were so obedient that they acted like little soldiers. My kids rose to the occasion, too. Seven kids shared one bedroom and went to bed at nine o'clock without much of a hassle. When we lived in our own home, I'd have to cuss and yell and beat my kids' behinds to get them to go to sleep nearly every night. My soul was relieved.

The only problem we initially encountered was Cordell. Three days after I moved out, he marched up to Joyce's apartment and banged on the front door. Joyce answered cheerfully, then strolled away when I came.

"I heard you and Joyce are going together," he snarled, looking me straight in the eyes.

I started to close the door in his face but didn't.

"Look Cordell, don't come around here with that mess. I could care less what you've heard. Is that what you came here for?"

I sensed he didn't know what to say. His eyes shifted. He shuffled his feet. He finally asked about the kids.

"They've never been better," I said, trying to act civil.

We exchanged a few more words. I don't remember what they were. But I remember Cordell's troubled face, as if the reality of our break-up had finally begun setting in.

Joyce and I did sleep in the same bed. It felt a bit uncomfortable at first. But after a week or so, I'd convinced myself that there was nothing wrong with it, as long as we didn't touch each other. I slept really close to the edge.

Cordell never bothered us again, but his brothers hassled me a few times. Monty threatened me in the grocery store one day.

"If I ever hear about you messing around on my brother, I'm gonna kick your ass myself," he yelled in front of a crowd.

"And while you're kicking my ass, what do you think I'm gonna be doing? Just standing there? I know you'll whip me, but it won't be easy. I guarantee you that," I shot back.

No more harassment.

Four weeks after moving in, Joyce's landlord called on the phone. Someone told him that another family was living with her.

"Either you get them out of there within a week, or I'm gonna evict every-body—including you," he yelled so loudly that I could hear him across the table where I was sitting.

Joyce wanted to fight the man in court. There was nothing in her lease that prohibited anyone else from living with her. I didn't want to take the chance. I appreciated her loyalty but was not going to be responsible for Joyce and her kids getting put on the street.

I moved back home to Momma's, something I swore I'd never do. Momma wasn't happy about the idea either. But she was willing to give it a try since I had no place else to go. It didn't work. Momma started snapping at the kids and me within hours. A week later I started letting Cordell spend the night. I don't know why. Maybe it was my own way of rebelling against Momma again. Or maybe I thought Cordell could bail me out of my difficult situation because he desperately wanted to reconcile. He'd sneak into the house after Momma left for her third-shift licensed practical nurse job at the hospital. We got away with it for two weeks before our next-door neighbor snitched.

"Miss Agnes told me that she sees Cordell's car in my driveway every night when I leave for work," Momma said in that voice that signaled a battle was brewing.

I stared at her and said nothing.

"Jasmine, you make me sick!" she said disgustedly and stormed away.

I started looking for another place to stay.

—— ❧ ——

GRANDMA'S HOUSE had been abandoned for several years by now. I'd sworn for years I'd never step foot in her house again. Too many memories. Too much guilt. Too much pain.

Being homeless made me reconsider. I walked around the corner to the house and eased through the back door. It was never locked. I peeked inside and saw empty beer and wine bottles strewn everywhere. Smelly garbage littered every room. A pee-stained mattress lay on the dining-room floor, with bottle caps filled with cigarette butts and ashes around it. I'd heard that drunks and homeless people had been staying there.

The last family members to live in the house were my cousin Ronnie Earl, his wife, and their two sons. It had been three years earlier. She divorced him and moved back to Georgia. Ronnie Earl moved back home with his parents but left most of their new furniture in the abandoned house. He covered everything with plastic and stacked it in the living room and bedrooms. Surprisingly, it appeared untouched by intruders.

I looked at the melon-size holes in the walls. There were some under the free-standing old-fashioned kitchen sink. There were holes in the living room and both bedrooms walls. I peeked in the bathroom and saw rust stains in the bathtub, the thick orange crud running from the spout to the drain. There were broken windows. Warped doors. The house was in such a mess that I cried.

—— ❧ ——

THE LARGE ROOM was cold and impersonal, with lots of chairs. Long tables. Longer lines. Sad-faced women and men sat at the Aid to Dependent Children (ADC) office, looking worried and needy. It took me an entire day to see a caseworker. I felt like cattle, waiting to be slaughtered.

It took a few weeks, but I started getting ADC checks for a $283 twice a month. I talked to my grandfather about moving into his mother's house.

"Daddy, I can't afford to pay you any rent right now. But I will, as soon as I get on my feet," I said, sitting in their living room watching the six o'clock news on Channel 7.

"Darling, just take care of those babies," my soft-spoken grandfather said, turning his head toward me. "I know that if there was anybody Momma would want to be living in her house, it would be you."

I bought paint, wallpaper, and a few paintbrushes with my first check. The kids and I started cleaning Grandma's house the same day. We painted and patched the kitchen walls. We put up wallpaper in the living room. We scrubbed the toilet and bathtub so many times my knuckles got raw. Although I was growing more comfortable with being in Grandma's house, the thought of her dying on the bathroom floor still gave me the willies.

——— ₂ ———

LIVING IN GRANDMA'S house turned out to be a deeply spiritual experience for me. Although I still rushed in and out of the bathroom where she had died, I felt protected—by Grandma. Her home had been a refuge in my childhood years and served that same purpose when I became homeless. After Grandma's death, I swore many times to never step foot in her house again, stemming from guilt or fear—probably a combination of the two. Yet the longer I stayed there, the more I felt like Grandma was right there with me. The feeling was reassuring as I lay in bed many nights, tossing and turning and thinking about what to do next.

Within a few weeks, living alone became exciting. I even engaged in a couple of one-night stands and didn't feel one bit bad about it.

"I'm a free woman. I can do anything I want," I thought, knowing good and well that Cordell had better not find out. He was even more jealous than I was.

A relationship that had been simmering under the surface for three years became more intense after I moved into Grandma's house. Jerome Taylor had always flattered me with attention. A tall, slender man who was seven years older than me, he used to flirt with me at gambling parties and the poolroom, saying that I had "bedroom eyes." When I was hospitalized having the twins, he sent me fifty dollars in a card, a complete surprise.

We first started seeing each other when the twins were about a year old. I had started snorting heroin regularly and needed money. Jerome was a big-time numbers man who handled lots of money. It started out being a money thing. He'd loan me fifty dollars at a time. I always paid him back. But it evolved into an intimate relationship where I could unload on him. I talked. He listened. I even admitted being strung out. After spending a few hours in a motel with Jerome, I felt that I could deal with my husband better. Strange but true.

I never had any illusions about a serious relationship with Jerome, nor did I ever seek one. He lived with a woman, and I was still married. Sometimes he got frustrated with me because I'd put him off for months at a time. He tickled me when he started calling me a "once-a-year fucking thing."

"I know your type," he said to me one day. "You like giving a man some just to tease him and let him know what he's missing."

Jerome read me like a book.

— ๛ —

THE HOUSE WAS dim and quiet. Peaceful. The kids were asleep, and I lay awake in my bed, thinking. My drug involvement was lessening and being replaced by church. I wanted to quit using heroin altogether—not for my sake, but for the sake of my kids.

"I owe them that much," I thought, while listening at night to the creaks and settling of Grandma's house, which had to be nearly a hundred years old.

For the first time in my life I didn't mind living alone. I had had some practice at it several years earlier when Cordell spent ninety days in jail for drunk driving. I accomplished so much during that time—painting the kitchen, buying new bedspreads and curtains for our bedroom, and putting up wallpaper. I'll never forget Cordell's first comments when he came home.

"It looks like you don't need me," my husband said sadly, a reaction I never expected.

"Yes, we do need you," I quickly said. "Don't say that. You know how I am. I just wanted to make sure the house was nice and cozy for you when you got out. That's all."

What I didn't realize at the time, however, is that I had gotten a taste of peace and freedom while Cordell served time in jail. I missed him, but it had been easier getting things done without him being around. I never could totally forget the sense of peace I experienced in his absence.

Living alone enabled me to focus more on attending church. Cordell, who was trying like crazy to get back in good with me, offered to let me use his car anytime I wanted, but most times I'd use it only to go back and forth to church. Sometimes Joyce picked us up for worship service. We enjoyed those few hours together. We all sat side by side in the pews—Joyce's three kids, my four, and two adults. It reminded me of my childhood in church when my cousins and I all sat alongside each other.

I had made up my mind to rejoin church after going regularly for a month. Rev. Whittington called it "reinstating my membership." The Sunday I joined, I had squirmed in my seat for several seconds before going forward. Rev. Whittington smiled so broadly I felt unworthy of it. He placed his arms around my shoulders, and I would never forget his words.

"Don't be hanging your head down. You've come back to the Lord. You don't have nothing to be ashamed of. Hold your head up, child."

❧ KEEP ON MOVING

I was combing the girls' hair one Thursday morning when my third cousin Ronnie Earl dropped in on us. I'd never seen him so angry.

"You didn't even ask if you could use my furniture!" he yelled, stalking from room to room, acting as if he hoped to find something wrong with his belongings. There wasn't. I took care of his stuff better than I had my own.

"Ronnie Earl, I swear I won't let the kids tear anything up. I just planned to use it until I got on my feet," I cried, with hot, salty tears streaming down my face and into my mouth.

He was unmoved.

"I'll be damn if you're gonna let your kids piss all over my kids' bunk beds. Me and Josephine might get back together one day. If we don't, I'm gonna sell everything," he said, his face full of rage.

"But you let this stuff sit in here for two or three years, at least. You're lucky all those drunks who were hanging out in here didn't mess your furniture up," I said meekly, knowing that arguing with my cousin, who was eight years older than me, seldom got me anywhere.

"Here you are, a full-grown-ass woman, and got the nerve to drag your kids all over town," he said, his eyes glaring, venom dripping from every word. "I ain't never had no respect for a woman who can't even keep a roof over her kids' heads."

That really, really hurt me. It was the type of low blow that had me wondering if I would ever recover. My cousin swore to return the next day with a pickup truck to get his stuff. I lay in bed praying and crying most of the night. I was sickened at the thought of all the work we had put into Grandma's house, only to have much of the furniture we had been using snatched away. Nothing I did seemed to turn out right.

Sure enough, Ronnie Earl returned the next morning around eleven with another cousin—a third or fourth, I was never sure. He strode past me without saying a word. The other cousin spoke before they started hauling Ronnie Earl's black, white, and beige plaid sofa and loveseat into the pickup truck that was backed up to the front door.

I had just purchased my food stamps the day before, so when Ronnie Earl opened the refrigerator, filled with fresh food, I saw a glimpse of compassion and a tiny bit of embarrassment on his face.

"I guess you can keep the refrigerator until you get another one. I don't want all your food to spoil," he said, not looking my way.

By then I didn't want anything that belonged to him. I just wanted him to leave.

"No. Take everything. Just take everything that's yours and go," I said. My voice cracked a few times, but I was determined to stay strong for my kids, who stood watching with the saddest looks on their faces.

—— ᷔ ——

SITTING IN A nearly empty house, I felt destitute. We had no beds. We had no furniture in the house except an old red sofa that I had placed on the porch because the fur and dye made me itch. I had thrown a small blanket over it, and up until the day Ronnie Earl took his furniture, I had enjoyed sitting on Grandma's porch again, watching the people and cars pass.

The kids and I were sitting on the porch when Momma walked by on her way to work at the hospital, less than a ten-minute walk from her house. She stopped out front to talk, something we had started doing. I hated to tell her about our cousin, but couldn't hide my despair.

"Now Ronnie Earl ain't said a word about that ole stuff or this place the whole time it's been sitting here vacant. And after you get it decent enough to live in again, he's gonna do something like that. That's all right. He still has my lawn mower that he borrowed two weeks ago. I'm gonna call him and tell him I want it back. And he can't get nothing else from me. I'll fix him," she said.

I needed to hear that. I needed Momma to take up for me. I'd been through tough times in the past, but this felt like the killer blow.

"So, what are you going to do now?" she asked with compassion in her voice and pity in her eyes. I had never seen Momma like that before.

"I'm just going to move. I think I'm going to move up to Flint with my dad," I said. "There's no reason for me to stay here anymore. It's just not working out."

I wanted Momma to say, "No Jasmine, please don't do that." I wanted her to beg me to keep the kids closer to the only family they really knew. I wanted her to grab me and hold me and say that everything was going to be all right. Just don't go. But she didn't.

"Well . . . I think that's the best thing, Jasmine. But don't tell Mother. She'll just try to talk you out of it," she said, her voice soft and sad.

That sealed it. I called my dad that night. Four days later he drove down to Jackson in a U-Haul truck to move us. We loaded up all our belongings, which he later joked and said "could have fit in a matchbox," then rode up to Momma's house to say good-bye. It was the saddest day of my life. All of us cried—the kids, me, and Momma.

—— ℯ ——

I SPENT MOST of my free time sleeping my first three weeks in Flint. Sleeping a lot was a symptom of depression, but I didn't know it at the time. The kids and I shared a basement bedroom. The girls slept in the bed with me, and the boys slept on pallets on the floor. They didn't like Flint schools. Neither did I. Their first classrooms consisted of small trailers parked beside a brick school building. They had never attended schools where blacks were the majority, so it was a bit of a culture shock.

Twelve people lived in the three-bedroom, ranch-style home in Beecher District, on the northern outskirts of Flint. Daddy worked third shift at Buick, so he slept during the day. I spent my days cleaning house, cooking dinner, or sleeping, while Charlene, my stepmother, worked and all nine young people went to school.

I enjoyed cooking, but resented washing dishes left the night before and picking up clothes tossed here and there throughout the house. Grateful to have a place to stay, I bit my lip and didn't complain. I felt like Molly the Maid.

It wasn't good enough for my stepmother, who readily admitted not being a good housekeeper herself. She started calling me lazy. Momma used to say the same thing. I never considered myself lazy. Although I preferred working with my mind, rather than with my hands, I tried to do my share.

—— ℯ ——

THE CLEAR BLUE skies deceived us. The chilly September morning forced Charlene and I to step briskly past Daddy's old station wagon, hiked up on cement blocks in their driveway, to their yellow Chevrolet van, parked behind it. Scrambling to get inside the vehicle, both of us rubbed our arms for a few seconds before she turned the key to start the engine. It didn't quite turn over. She tried again. It started up, sputtered once, then purred.

"Your daddy said it's gon snow soon," she said. "I didn't believe it until I stepped outside. Looks like I'm gonna have to get my winter clothes out a little earlier this year."

"Um hum," I said, gazing out the passenger's window.

My mind was on finding a place to stay with only a $100 in my pocket and an income of only $263 a month from ADC. The state had cut my check when I moved in with my dad. We'd been living with Daddy and his family for two months. They charged no rent, and things started out fine. I felt safe, away from the riffraff, memories, and emotional pain associated with Jackson. After a month I started noticing signs all too familiar to five vagabonds—my kids and me.

Everyone in the house began snapping at my kids for one thing or another—not all at the same time or out of malice. It was just ongoing and stressing me. It was bound to happen with a dozen people cramped in a three-bedroom house. I expected friction.

The defining moment came one sunny afternoon after I had a falling out with a friend of their family. My half sister, Carmen, and I went grocery shopping and left my kids in the car with her sixteen-year-old boyfriend. We returned to find them all crying and her boyfriend trying not to smirk.

"He was teasing us and calling us names," Lamar said, his big eyes red and looking hurt.

Now when it came to my kids, I didn't play. I used to tell my best-friend cousins that "I'll whip a bull over my kids," and meant every word. I jumped on a woman twice my size when Andre came in the house crying with scratches on his neck. My six-year-old son told me the grown woman had grabbed him by his neck and fussed at him because he and her son had a small spat. She never did that again.

Another time I took a butt kicking by a sixteen-year-old girl. She'd been teasing Andre and sent him home crying. I watched for that girl for days before running up on her at a local party store.

"I don't appreciate you running up in my face with your junkie ass," she said when I confronted her.

I hated the word "junkie." It hurt me to my heart. I slapped her as hard as my bony hand could. Nine years her senior and strung out on dope, I was no match for the young girl. She turned my pitiful-looking behind every way but loose. Momma said there'd be days like that. I'd met my match.

The one good thing that came out of that butt kicking was that I thought two or three times before running up in another person's face. But even that didn't stop me completely. I was still like a pit bull guarding her pups when it came to my kids.

All four of my kids were laughing and talking in the car with Carmen's boyfriend when we left them. They were all crying when we returned. I gave the boyfriend a piece of my mind, knowing Carmen would go back and tell Daddy. When we got home, Carmen went straight into Daddy's bedroom and closed the door. She came out several minutes later, and my dad called me into his room to ask about the incident. I unapologetically repeated what I'd said to the boyfriend—word for word.

"I told him that he better not ever say another word to my kids or we were gonna to have it out."

Daddy's nose flared. His chest puffed up. His jaws stiffened. He poked out his lip, something he did whenever he got really mad. He stared me in the face, then gave me a look as if he thought I were crazy.

"Well, Jasmine, you know what?" he said, small eyes glaring, his chest looking as if it would explode. "If I was him and I saw your kids about to be run over by a Mack truck, I wouldn't open my mouth and say a word to them."

I felt like Daddy had stuck a dagger in my heart. He could say some mean things when he was angry, but this took the cake. I retreated to my quarters in the basement and cried the rest of the day. I knew it was time for us to move on.

— ॰ —

It was a cool, late Monday afternoon in mid-September when Charlene and I were driving down Coldwater Road. I spotted a row of nice-looking town houses, with two large signs posted on each end of the street. The large, black, bold letters read "Brookfield Terrace." The huge complex had four-unit, stand-alone brick buildings, each with a different facade. One porch had a brick arched doorway. Another had white pillars situated at each end of the porch. A third and fourth had plain brick fronts. All of them looked well kept with manicured lawns.

"Do you mind turning around so I can see if the rental office is open?" I asked my stepmother. "I want to see if they accept applications from people on ADC. I bet they don't. These places look too nice, but I want to at least check and see."

Charlene may not have been the best housekeeper in the world, but as far as I was concerned, she was the best stepmother a person could possibly have.

She counseled me often with an old folks' wisdom that made sense—sometimes more than my dad. She always referred to me as her "daughter," even though I always introduced her as my stepmother.

Charlene turned the van around and drove back to the apartment complex. Our visit proved very productive. The leasing manager was a blonde, outgoing woman who stood no taller than me. She gave us a tour of the sprawling complex and encouraged me to fill out an application.

"I'm separated from my husband and have four kids in school. We're living with my dad right now. But I need to get settled in my own place as soon as possible," I said, praying at the same time.

The rental agent listened. Her eyes appeared sympathetic, giving me confidence even before she spoke.

"We've got some guys just finishing up a three-bedroom unit that was damaged by fire," she replied. "They're touching up the painting right now. We can swing by to look at it if you'd like."

My heart turned cartwheels. My spirit cranked up two notches. We strolled past so many rows of brick buildings, I couldn't even count them. The manager took us around a winding parking lot before we reached the vacant town house, situated in a grassy courtyard. I was sold on the place before going inside.

I silently prayed about it all the way home. The chances of my application being approved didn't seem likely. I had a terrible credit history, but that didn't stop me from praying about it. I prayed before bed that night. I woke up the next morning thinking and praying about that town house. My mind refused to let me think about much else. Every time the telephone rang, I hustled to answer it, praying for a miracle. My prayers were answered three days after filling out the application.

— ℀ —

WE MOVED IN at night to keep the neighbors from knowing. I'd written a check to pay the first month's rent, knowing I had only a hundred dollars in my account, but my ADC check was due to arrive in a few days. I planned to pay the rent with a money order and ask them to tear up the check.

In the still of the night we quietly folded clothes and placed them in dresser drawers. The girls and I washed and dried dishes, trying not to clank them against the wooden shelves we lined with shelf paper. The boys helped put up beds and carried empty boxes to a large green dumpster in the parking lot. We all lent a hand making up beds and moving our dilapidated sofa around several times before deciding where it looked best. My kids didn't complain once. They were just as excited as I was about moving into our own home again. It was our sixth move in ten months.

The kids took their baths after midnight. They put on their pajama tops and bottoms, a rarity, and were asleep within an hour. I tiptoed into both bedrooms and kissed each of their foreheads as they lay asleep in bed. I loved to see their faces when they slept. They looked so peaceful and angelic. I stood over them, my arms across my chest, gently rocking from side to side, savoring the moment.

After taking a shower I soaked in bath water that initially was so hot I shot up out of the tub and had to wait a few minutes for it to cool down. Really warm baths always relaxed me. Aretha Franklin's "Natural Woman" played in the background on my stereo downstairs as I sung along off-key, basking in a feeling of accomplishment and peace in the tub.

I dressed for bed in one of my raggedy cotton gowns, then returned downstairs and lay on the gold shag carpet in our living room, my hands behind my head, listening to "Sarah Smile" by Hall and Oats, "I Can See Clearly Now," by Gladys Knight and the Pips, and "Just My Imagination," featuring Eddie Kendricks of the Temptations. The evening was so quiet and peaceful. I must have thanked the Lord a hundred times that night.

"I'm living in my own place for the first time in my whole life," I thought, smiling contentedly. "No one knows anything about me here but Daddy and his family. I can be anybody I want to be. I can start all over and not have to worry about people judging me by my past."

———— ❧ ————

WE ATE OUR MEALS on a brown and beige tweed oval rug in the middle of the kitchen floor because we had no table or chairs. My kids never complained. Their body language, facial expressions, and constant chatter told me they were just as happy and relieved as I was to be in our own place.

I was sitting on my bed combing Kendra's hair when a security guard rapped on our door Tuesday morning. Pressing my finger to my lips, I signaled for the kids to be quiet. He knocked a while longer, then left a note saying my check had bounced and to contact the rental office right away.

I explained to the kids what I'd done, and we all tiptoed around the house and stooped to stay clear of any windows until the next day when my ADC check arrived.

✿ RECONCILED

Cordell called me every night from Jackson, begging and pleading with me to give him one more chance.

"I miss my family real bad," he said. "I want to be with you and my kids. Now that you're gone, I realize my mistakes. Baby, I know we've tried in the past, but we've never tried starting over in a different city. I'll transfer my job if I have to. Jasmine, I just want you and my family back."

I gave in. Like a fool, I took the man back, even though I was torn between my kids needing a father and my desire to start my life over again without him. Still training in skilled trades, Cordell transferred to a company in Flint without much trouble. In my heart, I knew it was a mistake.

"You must be crazy," Terrance said to me one day when I was visiting Momma for the weekend. His head cocked to one side, my brother cut his eyes at me and spoke with so much disdain in his voice that I wanted to run somewhere and hide, out of shame.

But the decision had been made. All I could do was give it my best shot and pray that things worked out. A month after I agreed to take him back, we all were living together as a family again, only this time in Flint. The first six months were great. I was so glad to have given our marriage another chance.

My dad gave us his old station wagon so Cordell could get back and forth to work. We had once owned two cars, including a Cadillac, and a pickup truck, all at the same time, but lost them due to our heroin habit. I didn't even have a license because of unpaid traffic tickets in Jackson.

"And Jasmine, if I see or hear of you driving this car, I'm gonna take it back," Daddy said to me while handing Cordell the keys.

Daddy didn't know that driving wasn't my thing anyway. And as big as Flint was, compared to Jackson, I had no intentions of driving.

One month after getting the car the drinking and arguments started again, only worse. Every Friday night Cordell would drink Tanqeray and grapefruit juice until he passed out on the living-room floor. I didn't dare try to wake him up because he'd start swinging and screaming, thinking he was still in Vietnam.

"I'm warning you, Cordell. The next time we split up will be the last time. There won't be any more starting over," I yelled at him during a heated argument one Saturday morning. That became my mantra.

Cordell knew I was serious, yet his behavior and attitude worsened, probably because he sensed our marriage was nearing its final days. Things got so bad so quickly that Cordell had begun drinking and cussing the kids and me out every day. I resented it and made no bones about it.

"You've got a lot of nerve to come all the way up here to Flint and go to clowning and making our lives miserable. We've never had this much tension in our house since we moved in," I yelled at him each time we argued.

My Bible helped keep my sanity. It became a constant source of comfort in the midst of my despair. Cordell would walk in the bedroom, and I'd be sitting on the bed, reading and crying. He even started laughing at me each time I picked up my Bible around him. But I just kept praying.

"Lord, please help me. I've made some bad decisions again, and now I don't know what to do. You've brought me this far, Lord, please don't leave me," I prayed.

My faith was the only thing I had.

 # LYDIA

Our kids knew each other several months before I formally met my neighbor Lydia Sutton, who lived in the same building, three doors down. Lydia's oldest son was named Christopher. He was ten years old, the same age as Andre. Her two daughters, RayAnna and Jamilia, looked like twins and were only eleven months apart.

The three of them stopped by our house every morning at eight thirty to pick up my kids for school. They stood quietly at the door, not saying a word unless spoken to. Their behavior impressed me. Noticing that they dressed neatly and their hair was always combed, I began to ask more questions about their mother.

Lydia and I started off simply waving to each other as we came in and out of our front doors. Both homebodies, neither of us did a lot of visiting, and I was preoccupied with marital problems.

My neighbor didn't have the kind of face that made me want to get to know her better. The truth was, she looked downright mean. Hard lines accented her pecan-colored face. Her jawbones looked rigid, and she had deep-set, unforgiving, dark brown eyes.

One day I finally strolled down to her end of the building and knocked on her door. She invited me in for a cup of tea. We hit if off immediately, probably because both of us were so honest about our lives.

"My real momma left me when I was six weeks old. So my grandmamma raised me," Lydia said. "I never even saw my real momma again until I found her in Brooklyn, New York, when I was eighteen years old."

Whenever Lydia, born in North Carolina, spoke of her maternal grandmother, her tough-sounding voice softened, along with the lines on her face. But she despised her mentally ill uncle who had lived with them.

"My ole crazy-ass uncle tormented me and my grandmamma every day when I was growing up. I just knew he was going to kill us. And as crazy as my uncle was, my grandmamma took care of him till the day she died. He got locked up in some crazy house then. That motherfucker died there, too," she said.

"And I thought my childhood was bad," I thought, sipping on a glass of ice water that Lydia set down in front of me on top of a white paper napkin.

I told her about growing up under Momma's roof. It was hard because Albert and I often talked about it, but we never told anybody else.

"My momma's so moody and mean. We can't stay in the same house together more than an hour or two without getting on each other's nerves," I said, my eyes watering. "She's always thought I was fast or something. But I never saw myself that way. I considered myself slow compared to the rest of my friends. We just have never seemed to understand each other."

"The more I hear about your momma, the more she sounds like me," Lydia said after hours and hours of conversation. "I bet I could relate to her."

I'd never noticed it before, but she was right. Lydia often walked around looking hateful and not saying anything to her kids. When she did, it was usually to cuss them out—like Momma. Lydia finally explained why she walked around looking as if there was a chip on her shoulder, even suggesting that Momma may have had the same reason.

"People don't fuck with you when you look mean," she said in her North Carolinian accent. "They're too scared."

I thought I'd die laughing.

Lydia didn't play. She'd cuss her kids out like they were strangers on the street. Sometimes her words made me cringe.

"If ya'll don't cut out all that motherfucking bickering and arguing up those stairs, I'm gonna come up there and start kicking asses," Lydia said on more than one occasion. "I'm telling you the truth. If it's one thing that makes me madder than a motherfucker is sisters and brothers fussing and fighting with each other. I grew up an only child. I ain't used to that bullshit."

Momma cussed, too, but her swear words were limited. She'd get mad and say things like, "You gon make me knock the shit out of you," or "How in the hell am I supposed to do that?" or "Ya'll get on my damned nerves." But I'd never heard her or anybody else in our family use any other cuss words.

So Lydia's foul language took some getting used to, coming from a female. I could sling some cuss words around, too. But I had my limits.

The more time I spent around Lydia, the more she reminded me of Momma. Both kept to themselves too much. Both were also brutally frank. I doubted that either of them knew how harsh they came across to people. And I don't think they really cared.

— ↄ —

LYDIA'S HOUSE became my little getaway for a few hours, especially while Cordell worked and the kids were in school. We both loved to talk and laugh and have fun—something neither of us had done much of in recent months.

Married at sixteen, Lydia quit school in the tenth grade, saying, "Me and school just never agreed." She started looking for her biological mother shortly after her eighteenth birthday. Lydia found her living on the streets of New York, almost homeless.

"By the time I'd spent three or four days with Geneva—that's my real momma's name—I thought to myself, 'I'm sho glad my grandmomma raised me,'" Lydia said during one of my morning visits.

I laughed. Her attitude surprised me. I had imagined she'd be more resentful. I couldn't imagine growing up without Momma, even though we still had trouble seeing eye to eye.

— ↄ —

LYDIA AND I both smoked Kool cigarettes and wanted to quit. I had been smoking for seven years. She had been smoking for twice that long. One of the things that really bonded us and helped cultivate our friendship was that we both also enjoyed smoking weed in the morning.

"I first started smoking weed in the morning when Cordell went to jail for ninety days for drunk driving," I said during one of our initial conversations. "We were still living in Jackson, and smoking helped me deal with things and get a lot of stuff done around the house. By the time he got out, I was smoking weed every day."

Lydia had started smoking around the same time, for the same reason, but she explained it differently.

"Reefer calms my nerves and helps me deal with all the fucking changes that being a broke-ass single woman trying to raise three kids puts you through," she said.

KIDS AND NERVES

"Mom, do you know where my other shoe is?" Kendra asked, her hair combed neatly into ten ponytails with red barrettes clipped half an inch from the ends, matching her red-and-white-checked smock blouse.

It was quarter to eight in the morning. School started in fifteen minutes, and my seven-year-old daughter was still running around the house looking for her belongings.

"Every single morning you've got to run around looking for something. Kendra, if you put that stuff in one place at night, you wouldn't have to worry about looking for it the next morning," I fussed, getting on my knees to help her search.

We looked under both beds. We looked in their bedroom corners. Jaunting downstairs and getting madder by the minute, I looked in the closets, then under the sofa. I finally found the small, brown, tie-up shoe sticking out from under the stove.

"Girl, I'm not gonna keep going through this with you every morning. You don't take care of anything, Kendra. You had the nerve enough to lose a brand-new pair of shoes that I scuffled and got with my little bit of ADC money. Girl, you'll never have anything if you don't learn to value your things."

"I did put my stuff up," Kendra spouted, her mouth poked out and face tightening.

"If you did, then why did I find the shoe on the kitchen floor?" I snapped back.

"Somebody else must have put it there," she said. "Cause I know that I put my shoes . . ."

"Shut up, girl! Just shut your mouth. You know good and well that you didn't put your shoes up. You've never done it before. Why would you start now? And

I'm sick and tired of you always having to get in the last word. Just put that shoe on and get on out that door to school before I break your neck. You're gonna mess around and be late, trying to stand up and argue with me—knowing good and well you're dead wrong."

Our mornings started out that way too many times. If it wasn't Kendra's library book, it was her coat. If it wasn't her socks, it was a note she was supposed to return to her teacher. We bumped heads about everything from bullying her twin sister, who always forgave her sister's transgressions, to refusing to eat food that touched on her plate.

Kendra gave me the blues much more than the other three kids. I worried about our relationship every day and spent many nights crying.

"Lord knows I don't want her to end up being like the Walkers. Maybe I'm taking it out on her because I see so much of them in her. Maybe she's so rebellious because of what I did to her that time," I thought during some of my guilt trips.

The thought frightened me. I did not want my child growing up miserable and unhappy. I wanted Kendra to get along with people, and not to be so argumentative and stubborn.

Despite my daughter's troubling disposition, she was drop-dead gorgeous and growing more so every day. Her light brown skin was still baby smooth and flawless. Her thick, long black hair was wavy and easily straightened with hair grease and water. I loved combing it. Kendra's smile lit up any room. On her good days, my daughter could be as engaging as a student fresh out of charm school. Smart and extremely competitive, my daughter had the potential to be anything she chose. I feared that her testy attitude might be too big of an obstacle to overcome. It never dawned on me that she was just like her mother.

— ⁊ —

KAMARI HAD A LOT of mouth but wouldn't harm a fly. My daughter loved being near me and would sit so close that sometimes I couldn't move my arm to get a cigarette.

"Kamari, will you please give me some air?" I'd ask in frustration. She'd scoot an inch or two away.

But Kamari was my heart and often took a lot of heat from her siblings because of it. I did, too. They'd tease her, calling her "Momma's little angel." Kamari would cry.

Other kids picked on Kamari more than the rest, even though she tried her best to make everybody like her. I also had a few run-ins with neighbors about her.

One boy who lived several buildings away slapped my child one day after he'd join them in our courtyard playing kickball. Kamari ran in the house crying. The kid ran home. I knocked on doors until I found the little brat and confronted him and his momma. We almost started "knocking."

"Jasmine, I keep telling you this ain't Jackson. This is Flint, Michigan," Lydia warned me after the encounter. "Motherfuckers here don't give a damn about shooting or stabbing you about little or nothing, let alone about fussing at one of their bad-ass, stupid-ass kids."

"Hell, my kids ain't going over into their courtyards. These bad-ass kids are coming all the way across the parking lot and starting a lot of mess," I replied, but heeding my friend's advice just the same.

My kids needed me to protect them. And I needed them. I can't say exactly when our interdependency began, but the worse our situation, the closer we became.

The one thing I disliked most about living in such a large housing development was there were so many kids without parental supervision. Some parents worked. Some attended school. But too many didn't seem to be doing much of anything while their kids raised hell in the neighborhood. Too often kids didn't even know where their parents were.

— ℁ —

ANDRE AND LYDIA'S SON, Christopher, hung out together a lot. Christopher was three months older than my Afro-wearing son. Christopher's hair was close cut. The ten-year-olds spent lots of time hunting frogs in the tall weeds nearby. They made slingshots to shoot at birds—unbeknownst to me until years later. They often walked to the corner gas station and got hot ice. They'd put it in a jar of water and watch it bubble and smoke. Both were the quietest in our families and loved watching television.

Lamar was the only one who didn't have a best friend in Lydia's family. All eight families in our courtyard were headed by single mothers, but their kids were either girls or toddler boys. So Lamar tagged along with Andre and his buddy whenever they'd let him.

My eight-year-old was also a fanatic about playing ball. Lamar organized kickball or softball games nearly every day. They'd pick teams and play until the sun went down. Sometimes we had to call them in out of the dark.

"Those kids done played ball in that courtyard so much, they're wearing down the grass," Joyce laughed one sunny afternoon.

Lamar was the brains of the family and corrected everyone's grammar, which drove his sisters and brother crazy. They nicknamed him "Daniel Webster." He tried bossing his sisters around, but they would double team him. Although small and frail for his age, Lamar wasn't the type to back down. I broke up arguments and fights between the three of them constantly.

One time Lamar came home complaining about a boy at school named Brandon, who had been picking on him.

"Mom, if he keeps messing with me, I'm gonna have to fight him," my fifty-five-pound son said.

I couldn't imagine Lamar fighting anybody but his sisters. And even they gave him a run for his money.

"I'd prefer you wouldn't fight, Lamar. But sometimes you run into people who don't understand anything else. If you end up having to fight him, you better try your best to give him everything you got," I said, then prayed the bully would leave my son alone.

Talking to school officials did no good. The problem continued for weeks. One day Lamar came home from school with his shirt torn nearly off his back. The corner of his mouth was bleeding, and his nutmeg-colored face was scratched in several places. It hurt me to my heart to see my mild-mannered son like that.

"Mom, I told you that me and Brandon was gonna fight if he kept picking at me. He was doing it again today. I didn't want to, but I had to fight him," he explained, stuttering like his uncle Albert. My son's eyes were big and apologetic.

I was furious. It took half an hour of calls to find out where the kid lived. Within an hour I was knocking on his front door, steaming. The boy who answered appeared to be twelve or thirteen years old. He was big, dark, and burly.

"I'm looking for Brandon," I said politely, looking past him.

"I'm Brandon," he said even more politely.

I was shocked. The kid was twice my son's size. His parents hadn't gotten home from work yet, but I gave him a piece of my mind anyway.

"If you put your hands on my son again, I'm gonna come back over here with the police. You got that?" I said, feeling proud that my son had stood up to such a big kid.

He nodded. I marched away from his house. Brandon never bothered my son again.

✣ THE FINAL ROUND

One Friday evening in July, Cordell had been drinking since he got off work at four o'clock in the afternoon. He'd bought a pint of gin and grapefruit juice, and by the time I put the kids to bed that night, he was cussing and calling me every name in the book. He kind of scared me, but I wasn't about to let him know it. Around ten o'clock he stormed out of the house. I heard the car door slam and the engine start up before he sped away. I was so relieved. I got on my knees and said a prayer.

"Lord, please don't let Cordell come back here clowning tonight. Wherever he is, please sober him up. Whatever is troubling him, please ease his mind, Lord, cause I don't know what else to do. Please bring peace back into my life," I prayed.

A part of me hoped my husband wouldn't come back. But he didn't know all the whores in town, like he did in Jackson, so I knew he'd return sooner or later.

Sure enough, around midnight I heard someone banging on my door so hard it startled me out of my sleep. After scrambling to my knees in my bed and perching myself at the window ledge of my bedroom, I pressed my forehead against the pane but was unable to see. So I hollered.

"Who is it?"

"It's Jerome Taylor."

I recognized Cordell's voice immediately.

"Awww shit," I thought. "This man is getting ready to raise hell tonight."

Jerome and I had carried on an affair for several years while living in Jackson. Cordell had never suspected a thing until one night when we bumped into Jerome coming out of the club.

"Jasmine, you and that niggah is fucking. I can tell by the way he looks at you," Cordell said as soon as we climbed into our car.

I played it off.

"I'm not thinking about you, Cordell," I said playfully, smiling and waving his thoughts away with my hands. To my surprise, my husband didn't press the subject any further that night. But from then on Cordell threw Jerome's name up in my face every once in a while, just to see my reaction. I don't think he ever really believed that I would ever "creep" on him.

Cordell was still banging on the front door with his fist when I hurried downstairs and swung it open, the hot, humid night air hitting me in the face. Cordell glared at me, then staggered inside, smelling like a distillery. Cussing and spitting, he called me every tramp and whore in the book. I realized right away that my husband was out of control, so I kept my mouth closed and turned to go back upstairs. Cordell grabbed my shoulder and dug his long, thick, wrinkled fingers with bitten-down nails into my flesh.

"Stop, Cordell. You're hurting me," I said, too afraid to look into his blood-shot eyes.

He squeezed harder. I pulled away. Before realizing what had happened, Cordell hit me in the back of my head so hard I fell to the floor, bumping the side of my face on the carpet. Dazed, I tried to get up, but he knocked me back down to the floor with his fist. I tried crawling away. He kicked me back down on my stomach so hard my face slammed against the floor again.

"Come back here, bitch. I'm not through with you. Get ready for a good ass whipping tonight. I been wanting to do this for a long time," he said, his speech slurred and wearing a weird smile on his flushed face.

"Stop, Cordell. You've been drinking too much. You don't know what you're doing. You're going to hurt me," I pleaded.

He socked me in the mouth with his fist. I tasted blood. Every time I tried to get up from the floor, he knocked or kicked me back down harder. He grabbed my collar and swung me before letting go. I slammed into the sofa, head first, then slumped in front of it on the floor.

"Stop it, Cordell. You're hurting me. Somebody help me!" I screamed, trying to crawl away.

His glazed eyes terrified me. He panted and slobbered so much he had to wipe it away with his dirty hands.

"Shut up," he said, then hit me again. I tried climbing to my feet, but he shoved me into the wall, head first, before I could stand up.

"Oh my God. He's going to kill me," I kept thinking.

We had been in our share of fights before. But none like this. I'd never feared for my life before. I struggled to get up, crying and begging and praying for someone to intervene. The noise and commotion woke up the kids. They came charging down the steps screaming and crying.

"No! Stop Daddy! Please don't hurt Momma. Please, Daddy, don't," they cried.

He stopped beating me and ordered them back upstairs. They refused to go. He started trying to round the four of them up. They ran in different directions, forcing him to chase them. I scrambled to my feet and darted out the front door.

The night was pitch black, and the court was unusually quiet as I ran scream-ing and crying down the sidewalk to Lydia's house. I banged on her door.

"Lydia, somebody, please let me in. Please, somebody, open the door!" I begged.

The night had never been more quiet. No lights flicked on anywhere. No one answered the door. Looking back over my shoulder, I kept banging until Cordell grabbed me from behind by my neck and dragged me back to our place in the crook of his arm. I kicked and fought all the way, but he easily muscled me up the front steps, then shoved me through the front door, which was still open. Plunging forward, I stumbled uncontrollably for several steps before hitting the floor again.

"Please, Cordell, I don't deserve this," I cried.

He kept coming. My eyes begged for my life. His eyes chilled my bones.

"No Daddy. Stop. Please don't hurt Momma," I heard the kids crying as they banged on the door upstairs. Their father had barricaded them in the girls' bedroom.

He kept punching me in the back with his fist. I cowered in the middle of the living-room floor, protecting my head with my arms. The kids came rushing down the steps again and started grabbing at their dad's muscular arms. He snatched them away with relative ease. They tried dragging me away from him. That failed. They climbed on top of me to protect my body from their father's blows. Dazed, I started getting up again.

"Stay down, Mom," Andre whispered in my ear. "Stay down."

I'll never forget the fear in my son's brown eyes when I raised my head and looked helplessly at him through a fog. In the next instant, a stomp from Cordell's foot slammed me back against the floor. I lay still and pretended to be unconscious.

One by one, Cordell pulled the kids off me while they struggled to cling to any part of my body or nightgown. He dragged our children, kicking and screaming, back upstairs. As soon as Cordell was out of sight, I bolted to the kitchen and pulled open the cabinet drawer so hard that the silverware clanked against each other. Frantically feeling for a knife with one hand, and trying to dial "O" with the other, my trim-line phone slipped off the kitchen counter and dangled in midair by its cord.

"This is the operator. May I help you?" a woman's voice on the other end said.

A blow to the back of my head sent me slumping to the floor. The next thing I heard were men's voices arguing above me as I lay in a heap on the cold, gray-tiled kitchen floor.

"Why don't you hit me like you hit your wife?" an unfamiliar male voice yelled.

Still groggy, I raised my head and saw a pair of brown pants with a shiny stripe up the leg. It was a sheriff's deputy. I broke down crying hysterically.

"Would you like me to send for an ambulance, ma'am?" the middle-aged deputy asked, stooping to one knee and tilting his head to see my face as I lay sobbing on the kitchen floor.

I shook my head. My legs, still wobbly, gave out on me when I tried to get up, but the officer caught me and helped me to my feet.

"I'm sure sorry I didn't see any of this assault," he said, giving Cordell the evil eye. "Cause I could have locked this guy up right now. I'm gonna go back and write up the police report tonight. And lady, you be sure to go down to the prosecutor's office first thing Monday morning and take out a warrant on this guy. If it's one thing I can't stand, it's a wife beater."

His face flushed. Veins bulged in his neck.

"Are you sure you're all right, ma'am?" the deputy asked again.

"I'm sure," I said, my eyes searching the room for Cordell, fearing he would come after me again.

"Is there someplace you can go and stay tonight?" the officer asked. "I'll be glad to give you a ride. You shouldn't stay here."

"You go to hell!" Cordell yelled at the officer. "You got a lot of nerve to come in my house and tell my wife to leave me. You kiss my ass and go to hell."

The officer turned and took a few steps toward Cordell. I scooted along behind him, using his body as my shield. The two men engaged in a brief argument that got so heated the kids started screaming from upstairs. The officer turned away.

"Do you want me to take you some place or not? I'm not gonna stand here and argue with this guy. He's a nut case," the tall, uniformed man said.

"I'll call my dad and see if we can go over there," I quickly replied.

At that moment I noticed my four wide-eyed children standing near the bottom landing of the stairway, their faces worried but saying nothing.

"I'm okay, kids. Really. But I need you to hurry upstairs and put some clothes on. We're going to Granddaddy Eugene's house."

They scurried upstairs, and I rushed to the kitchen, not taking my eyes off Cordell. Grabbing the phone, I dialed my dad's number. He answered after the first ring, sounding half asleep.

"Daddy, Cordell jumped on me tonight," I sobbed. "A policeman is here right now, and I need a place to stay. Can I come over there for a while? This officer said he'll bring me."

Silence.

"Ah . . . yeah. Come on," he said, sounding irritated, like Momma.

Scared and desperate, I ignored the reservation in his voice, even though his initial silence hurt me. The officer stood waiting in front of the couch as I scurried upstairs like a scared rabbit. I grabbed toothbrushes from the metal medicine cabinet and snatched clothes from our chest of drawers, not paying any attention to what matched. Downstairs, I heard the policeman and Cordell exchanging words.

"I don't need no bitch like her no way," my husband sneered. "She better get the fuck out of here before I kick her ass again."

"You try that mister, and I guarantee you'll spend your weekend, if not longer, in jail," the officer shot back.

I sped up, opening and closing drawers so fast clothes hung out of most of them. The kids finished dressing and hurried into my bedroom. We all practically ran back down the steps, our feet sounding like a mini stampede.

"You ready?" the officer asked, sounding agitated.

I nodded my head and never took my eyes off of Cordell as I sidestepped around the deputy and ushered the kids out the front door. The officer followed us. Although it was mid-July, by the time we were riding down Coldwater Road, I was shivering so hard I could barely talk.

Coldwater Road seemed longer and lonelier that night. I sat in the backseat in the dark, trembling and crying the entire ten-minute drive. The deputy cussed and fussed the whole way.

"Lady, you get rid of that bum! That guy's crazy. You don't need anybody who treats you like that."

I cried harder, sniffling and saying, "I will. I will."

The officer pulled up in Daddy's driveway, and we piled out of his cruiser. Daddy flicked on the kitchen light and opened the side door. I thanked the deputy without looking him in the face. The kids yelled "thank-you" over their shoulders as they scurried into Daddy's house.

Telling Daddy about the assault was almost as bad as the beating. He ripped into me for not "killing the son of a bitch." I cried harder, shaking my head as he fussed.

"No, Daddy. I just can't take somebody's life. That's just not in me," I said, hoping for a little more compassion and understanding.

"I don't know where you get that shit from," he snapped. "If it had been any of my other daughters, that son of a bitch would be lying in the morgue right now. Don't you know that women don't have to take that bullshit no more. Honey, you had the perfect alibi. That bastard was beating your ass. You blew it."

My body felt lifeless as I listened to Daddy rant and rave. I felt like an object that nobody wanted.

— ℞ —

TOSSING AND TURNING on Daddy's sofa, I didn't get a wink of sleep. Every time I thought of how close Cordell and I came to killing each other, I shuddered and broke down crying again. By the time I had decided my next move, birds were chirping and dawn was easing through the window blinds.

"I've gotta get my place back. My kids need their *own* home," I kept thinking.

"Why should we keep suffering because of Cordell? Forget that, I'm getting my place back, no matter what."

Daddy sighed with frustration when I told him my plan. He drove us back to Brookfield Terrace around seven o'clock, not saying much. He parked a few doors away from my house, then turned the engine off and stared at me, just as I reached to open the car door.

"What are you going to do when he comes back? Because he *will* be back. You know that don't you?" he asked, struggling to contain his anger.

I didn't have answers. My plan was to play it by ear. My dad took another deep breath, then opened his glove compartment and pulled out the biggest gun I'd ever seen—not that I'd seen many up close.

"Take this. And if that niggah comes back here messing with you again, you can shoot right through the door. You don't even have to open it up."

Clicking the lock off and on, Daddy then gave me a sixty-second lesson on gun safety. He had me try it a few times. My heart hit a new low.

"Is this what eleven years of marriage has come down to?" I thought. "What if my kids see me do something to their father? What if I go to jail? What would happen to my kids?"

I knew Cordell would be back. He also knew that I was defenseless. So I reached for the gun and carefully placed it in my beat-up black purse before waking the kids, who had all fallen asleep again during the drive. They looked so tired.

"When we get out of this van, I want all of you to run as fast as you can to Lydia's house. Don't stop for anything," I whispered before exiting the car.

— ҽ —

WE SCOOTED DOWN the sidewalk in a line and ducked down when passing our house. After gathering on the concrete landing of Lydia's front steps, I quietly tapped on her door. Within seconds, she pulled back a panel of her kitchen curtains and peeked out. I heard the brass knob rattle furiously before the lock clicked and the door swung open.

"Girl, are you all right?" Lydia asked, quickly closing the door behind us. "Was that your daddy who just let you out?"

"Yeah, that was him," I said softly, my lip hurting and swollen from one of Cordell's blows.

"I figured that's where you stayed last night," she continued. "I was just sitting here smoking a cigarette and drinking a cup of tea, and thinking about all that bullshit that happened last night. Girl, that blew my mind. I haven't been able to sleep yet."

Her hair still in rollers and wearing a faded pink cotton housecoat, Lydia pulled the belt tighter around her narrow waist. Then she gave me a look I'd never seen in the four months we'd been friends. Compassion. For a split second, neither of us knew what to say. Then she abruptly started directing my kids upstairs, where hers were still asleep.

"Andre, you and Lamar can go get in the bed with Christopher. And the twins can sleep with RayAnna and Jamilia. I know ya'll still tired," she said, pointing toward the steps.

All four of them traipsed quietly up the stairwell while Lydia and I stood silently watching. We heard the bedroom doors close, then headed to the kitchen. I pulled out the dinette chair in my usual spot, nearest the door and window. It always gave me a good view of the courtyard where the kids played. I could also see my front door. Lydia took her usual seat at the opposite end of the table.

We had spent many hours around the brown Formica-topped table over the past few months. I'd walk down to her place whenever I needed to get out of the house and vent—especially about Cordell. Lydia came to know nearly every detail of our rocky marriage. She shared hers with me. But even as good friends, it was hard facing her after what my husband had done to me the night before. Really hard.

"You sure you're all right?" she asked again after we sat down.

Humiliated and ashamed, I nodded my head.

"Want some tea or orange juice?" she asked casually.

"Tea," I said, wiping my eyes with my fingers.

Lydia pushed her metal dinette chair back and strolled over to the stove. Her furry, white house slippers swished across the tile floor with each step. She took a cup, a saucer, and a box of off-brand tea bags from one of her dark wood-veneered cabinets, then dragged her way back and set them on the table in front of me. Yawning and with dark circles around her dark brown eyes, my friend returned to the stove to pick up her copper teakettle, which had started whistling. Using a blue potholder trimmed in white, she filled my melamine cup with water that sent curls of steam up to my face. I aimlessly pulled a tea bag from the box and dipped it in the water a few times, before laying the bag across the rim.

"Girl, I ain't gon tell no lie. I thought I'd seen some shit in my days. But I ain't never seen no shit like what happened in Brookfield Terrace last night," she said slowly, refilling her cup and glancing at me.

Finding words was difficult, but I needed to talk to someone who'd understand. I needed somebody who wasn't going to judge or criticize me. I needed somebody to listen.

"I've never been through anything like that before, either," I said quietly, and feeling helpless and alone. "I've been telling you that Cordell was deep. After all he did to me and my kids last night, he's probably lying up in our house right now, sleeping."

"Girl, that motherfucker ain't deep. That stupid motherfucker is *crazy*," Lydia said abruptly. "Cordell Walker is lucky the police didn't shoot his retarded ass last night. I heard him whooping and hollering and you screaming and the kids crying all the way down here. I just knew I'd be reading about his ass on the front page of the Flint Journal this morning."

"You sound just like my daddy. He's mad cause I didn't kill Cordell," I said, my mind wandering back to the night before. "Lord knows that he had me so terrified that I would have tried if he hadn't stopped me."

I shuddered again.

I had sensed a breakup was coming because the tension had been building in our house by the hour. I prayed every day that if and when that day came, no one would get hurt. And despite the beating I took, which was worse than anything I could have imagined, I honestly felt relieved that it ended with no one being dead.

Lydia dogged Cordell, calling him everything from a stupid-ass, carnival-looking motherfucker, to a sick, retarded son of a bitch. I listened and cried.

"Don't think I'm crying cause of what you're saying or because we broke up," I sobbed, dabbing my eyes and nose with tissue from a black and white, or "Brand X," box my friend handed me. "I'm crying because I know it's really over this time."

It was like losing a loved one. I mourned the nearly twelve years we'd had together, feeling like they were wasted. It was one of the strangest and saddest, yet most liberating feelings I'd ever had.

Lydia picked up her red leather cigarette case and unsnapped it. Thumping a package of Kool menthols across her forefinger, two cigarettes slid out of the ragged opening. She took one out, then handed the green and white package to me. I pulled one out, then handed it back.

"You know Peaches, the girl who lives across the court from you?" she asked, picking up a yellow cigarette lighter and flicking it several times before it lit.

"The girl with long black hair who looks like an Indian?" I asked.

"Yeah. That's her, with her dizzy, pill-taking ass. Her real name is Zandra, but everyone calls her Peaches. She called me last night, asking should she call the police. I told her, 'Hell, I'd done called them twice already.' We wondered what the hell was taking them so long. And Mrs. Moore, the woman with the four girls who live next door to you, she called them twice, too. Then she called me."

Lydia took a long drag off her cigarette, then gulped, a noise she always made when smoking. She blew a plume of gray smoke from her mouth before speaking again.

"Humph! After what I saw last night, I'm scared of Cordell Walker's ass, too. Aren't you scared he gon come back? Cause he will bring his stupid ass back. You know that don't you?"

I unzipped my overstuffed purse, wrinkled from wear, and showed her the gun. I was too scared to touch it—let alone take it out. My friend showed no reaction, which surprised me. It seemed as if everybody wanted Cordell dead but me. I just wanted him out of my life.

"Well, at least your daddy gave you something to protect yourself," she said. "Cause you know you gotta think about your kids. They *need* their momma. That's why I didn't open that door last night. I didn't want Cordell Walker running up in here. If something happens to me, my kids wouldn't have nobody."

It hurt to learn that my friend had heard my pleas and chose not to open her door the night before. I understood her point and might have done the same thing, had the situation been reversed. But I doubted it. All that didn't matter now. No one got seriously hurt, and she was there for me at that moment. I closed my eyes and thanked God.

An hour into our conversation RayAnna, Lydia's oldest daughter, entered the kitchen, wiping her eyes and whining. Her brother wouldn't let her watch her favorite cartoon show.

"RayAnna, don't you see that me and Jasmine are talking?" Lydia asked the seven-year-old, whose ponytails stuck out of a red paisley scarf that was sliding off her head and tied in the back.

RayAnna batted her eyes, but said nothing.

"Take your black ass back up those stairs, RayAnna. And you tell Christopher that I said to take turns watching that motherfucking TV. Ya'll don't want me coming up there," she said, eyeing her child, her words dragging with a heavy southern accent.

RayAnna turned and hurried back upstairs. Lydia took another drag off her cigarette. She again glanced out the kitchen window, which extended a few inches past her table. She mashed her cigarette in a round aluminum ashtray, then got up and started frying bacon.

"Let me get their breakfast on the stove. I can see the other kids coming down here any minute looking like they ain't ate in years," she said.

Lydia always made sure her kids had a healthy breakfast—orange juice, eggs, sausage, and toast and all. Mine barely got cold cereal most mornings. But I made up my mind that morning to change all that. With Cordell no longer in the picture, I could focus on being a better parent. I loved my kids and wanted to give them a decent shot at life, if nothing else. I saw this as my chance.

My whole thought process started changing. It was the Lord preparing me. Instead of fearing being alone, I looked forward to its possibilities. My survival instincts were kicking in.

Cordell had talked about going down to Jackson that morning to see his family for the weekend. I prayed he was still going.

"If Cordell leaves the house, me and my kids are going home. And I'm gonna lock his ass out," I announced after mulling the plan around in my head for a while. "That's our house. I'm the one who moved up here and struggled to put a roof over my kids' heads again. And he thinks I'm gonna let him lay up there while we are out here in the streets again? No way. No way," I cried.

— ℀ —

LYDIA AND I had sat at her kitchen table talking for over two hours. RayAnna trudged back downstairs complaining about the television again.

"RayAnna, take your ass back upstairs before I get up from here and kick it," Lydia shouted from the back of her throat.

Dressed in blue and white print pajamas, her deep-brown-skinned daughter quickly disappeared back up the steps. Lydia's tough talk to her kids sometimes made me feel uncomfortable, though I could say some pretty mean things to mine at the drop of a hat. But her tough love worked. They never gave her any lip around me.

"Christopher can eat all these pork chops by himself," Lydia said, pulling a frosted package from the freezer compartment of her brown refrigerator. "I hope this is enough meat for dinner. It's the middle of the month, and I've spent most of my food stamps."

Click. Click. Click. My mind went to my empty kitchen cabinets. Ordinarily, I went shopping Saturday mornings after Cordell gave me grocery money. He hadn't given me one penny this time. I had no money and no food.

"Oh my God! What am I going to do about feeding my kids?" I said, feeling overwhelmed again. "There's no food in our house."

"Girl, I haven't seen a niggah man yet who's gonna leave your ass with some money. That's too much like right," Lydia said, taking her seat back at the table after placing the meat in a large bowl of warm water. "But don't worry bout that. I'll talk to some of the females in our courtyard today. I told you we've all been down that road. Cause we've all been through changes trying to feed our kids. And we're still ain't finished yet."

I wanted to ask for clarification, but didn't. I was too ashamed. Did she mean our neighbors would bring us food or what? It was hard enough to admit not having anything to eat. I didn't want to harp on the subject. So I just left it in God's hands, knowing that he had been faithful up to that point.

The Lord gave me the strength to leave Cordell the first time at his mother's house and had been watching over me even when I didn't realize it. He had provided us with the house of my dreams. He had kept my crazy behind out of jail when I was doping and running the streets. The Lord helped me to stop using drugs, gradually, minimizing my physical discomfort. He placed people like Joyce and Lydia in my path. Through his grace and mercy, my application for Brookfield Terrace was approved. His word comforted me during the six months of reconciliation with Cordell. Then he kept us from killing each other when it didn't work out.

Lydia and I talked for hours, with me crying off and on the whole time. I felt sorry for myself. I felt sorry for my kids. They deserved better, and I knew it.

My friend told me more about her challenges as a single parent. It didn't sound easy by any stretch of the imagination. She had been living on state assistance in one state or another since her seven-year marriage ended. Her husband remarried and half paid his child support. Lydia budgeted every penny. She paid her bills on time and sometimes didn't know where her next meal was coming from. Yet she seemed okay.

"If she can do it, I can, too," I thought, absorbing every word that came from her darkened lips. Lydia would be my friend *and* my secret mentor.

— ℀ —

Lydia and I took turns pulling back her kitchen curtains to peek at my front door. About eleven o'clock Cordell came bouncing out of our house and up the sidewalk to his car. He climbed into his money green 1968 Chevy Impala that he'd bought a few months earlier, started the engine, then sped off.

I waited about fifteen minutes, wanting to be sure he didn't come back. Then the kids and I sprinted up the sidewalk to our house and rushed inside.

"Go upstairs and lock all the windows," I told them while twisting the brass lock on the front door until it clicked. "I'll get the ones down here."

The kids disappeared up the steps. I locked every window downstairs, then rushed upstairs to check the other ones. They were all secure. I had no idea what my kids did after that, but I flopped on the bed, my heart still racing, and stared at the ceiling while trying to figure out my next move. I was so thankful to be back in our own home. For me, it was the first and most important step.

❧ <u>SUNDAY</u> SADNESS

The sun's rays slit through the panels of the brown sheer curtains that hung on our living-room window, warming my face as I slept on the brown-and-white-striped sofa. A rustling nearby caused me to pop my head up and look around, still half asleep.

"Lamar, what are you doing up so early?" I asked softly.

His small, cocoa brown hands looked rusty and rested on the arm of the corduroy sofa. His dimpled smile was gone, replaced by a solemn, more penetrating stare from his oversize dark brown eyes. It was much too serious a look for an eight-year-old child. He broke his silence after a moment.

"Mom, I don't love Daddy no more. And I don't never want him to live with us again," he said, stepping around the couch to face me.

My soul gasped. Pulling my son closer to me, I hugged and squeezed him as tightly as possible without saying a word. Guilt consumed me. Why hadn't I done more to protect my children from seeing such an ugly side of life? How would I ever make it up to them? Was it too late? How much damage had already been done?

The tenseness in my son's frail body relaxed. Our embrace melted, and he turned to go back upstairs. He stopped after a few steps and turned and faced me again.

"Mom, do you *really* think we can make it by ourselves?" he asked, his eyes searching my face.

Tears stung my eyes and rolled down my cheeks. After taking a deep breath, I spoke in a soft but firm voice.

"Honey, there's no doubt in my mind that we're gonna make it. I know we're going to make it because we've got God on our on side. *He's* gonna help us make it."

Lamar glanced into my eyes one more time, then trudged back upstairs to bed. More determined than ever, I had no idea how we were going to make it. I just knew that we had to.

— ๛ —

MY KIDS HADN'T eaten all day. Ordinarily, I cooked my biggest dinner of the week on Sundays, but we had nothing.

"I promise I'll get you something to eat before the day is out," I told them every half hour, but had no idea what or how. I had checked every inch of every cabinet in the kitchen. Nothing. The only things in the brown refrigerator were a jar of mayonnaise and half a stick of margarine.

I was desperate. My kids' eyes looked hungry, although the children tried not to complain. But I could tell. Any mother could. Having to watch my children's drawn faces and stifled gestures, yet pretending that everything was okay, was more than I could bear.

What kind of mother was I anyway? Mothers were supposed to be able to provide for their children.

I couldn't leave the house and go looking for food because Cordell may have come back. And even if I did, where would I go? Whom would I ask? And for what?

Every minute that passed made me more nervous. Our whole world seemed to rest on Lydia's vague comment about "getting with the other women in the courtyard."

One o'clock. Two o'clock. Three. Four.

About a quarter to five, I considered calling Lydia up and casually mentioning the subject of food, hoping to trigger her memory, but didn't. My heart couldn't take another rejection. She had her own problems to worry about. The last thing I wanted to do was put more pressure on her. So I slipped into my bedroom, knelt down on my knees, and prayed some more.

Around quarter to seven, just as I had begun to lose hope, Lydia knocked on my door, accompanied by three other single females who lived in our court. They all carried dishes of food, some in brown paper bags, some covered with aluminum foil.

The kids rushed downstairs when they heard our voices. Seeing food, their faces lit up immediately. So did mine. They eagerly washed their hands, then sat down at the table with the biggest smiles on their faces. I was so grateful.

The four females busily positioned the food on the table, smiling but not saying much. My heart sang. There were black-eyed peas and cornbread—my favorite—macaroni and cheese, peach cobbler, and iced tea. They called it "sweet tea." I must have thanked them twenty times before they left, and they didn't stick around long. I got the feeling they wanted to let us eat in peace.

Escorting them to the door, I was still thanking them and fighting back tears.

"Girl, don't mention it," Lydia said. "I'm telling you the truth, if it weren't for somebody helping me, only the good Lord knows where I'd be right now. The way we see it here in this court, we're all in the same boat—single women trying to raise our kids the best way we know how."

— ❧ —

OUR STOMACHS FILLED, the kids talked more and even laughed a little. The dullness in their eyes and the strain in their faces had disappeared. The chattering and bickering of four school-aged children replaced the uneasy quiet that had consumed our home for the past day and a half. Seeing my kids perk up made me feel better.

The temperature outside had hovered in the mid 90s for a week. Our apartment was even hotter because we kept the windows and doors locked, fearing Cordell would return. The kids endured the sweatbox for as long as they could.

"Mom, can we go outside and play for just a little while?" Lamar pleaded as I stood over the kitchen sink, washing dishes and silently thanking God for my neighbors.

I looked down at my son. His green cut-off denims hung off his small waist, his long fingers twisted the end of his white T-shirt.

"I wish you could go outside, but you can't," I said, hoping not to go into a lot of detail.

"But it's too hot in here. I'm sweating. I can't breathe," he replied.

"Lamar, please. You know that we've got to be looking out for your dad. I'm too scared, honey," I said, trying to hurry the conversation.

"But all the other kids are outside," my son insisted, his eyes big and forehead glistening. "We'll be careful. Can't we just go outside for a little while, Mom? Huh?"

The sound of children laughing and playing in the grassy courtyard outside our living-room window made me feel even more guilty. I explained our predicament several times, but they kept begging, with Lamar speaking up the most.

I finally gave in after noticing my four children, foreheads pressed to the glass, gazing out the windows at neighborhood kids, including Lydia's, playing kickball out front.

"Okay kids, you can go out, but you can't leave this court no matter what. Do you hear me?" I said, eyeing each one, who stared back without blinking. "I want y'all to stay where I can see you at all times. And if you even think you see your dad or his car, I want you to beat it inside this house as fast as you can."

Four small heads nodded eagerly, like puppies waiting for their meal. Grinning and their tanned faces glistening from sweat, they broke for the door no quicker than I'd finished my mini lecture and slammed it behind them.

I pulled back the living-room curtain and watched them race across the sidewalk outside our door and onto the grass. The twins usually dressed alike, but not that day. I hadn't been to the laundry. Kendra wore red elastic-waist shorts and a red and white striped tank top. She had combed her hair into four ponytails. Two hung alongside her face. The other two lay against her back.

Kamari, who would wear whatever she put her hands on first—like her daddy and oldest brother—wore a blue denim, sleeveless blouse that was stretched around her neck and hung loosely off one shoulder. Her lime green shorts had already been worn once that week and had a big round spot of dirt on her behind.

Andre's navy blue cut-offs and brown, short-sleeve, buttoned-down shirt were badly in need of ironing. My sons' Afros were nearly twice the size of their heads, and all four of the kids needed shoes.

I watched them huddle with their playmates. Then they divided up the new players. A few minutes later my kids were yelling, laughing, and contesting plays like everybody else.

Tears filled my eyes. I blinked, and they dripped down my face.

"They act like little prisoners just let out of jail," I thought. "This whole thing is so unfair."

I stood watching them for several minutes before returning to the kitchen to sweep the floor. I was just beginning to relax about them being outside when the kids bolted through the front door yelling.

"Mom, here comes Daddy! He just pulled up in the parking lot!"

My heart pounded. I dropped the broom and dashed to the door, slammed it shut, and bolted the lock. Trembling, I turned back around, facing the kids, and was horrified. Lamar wasn't there.

"Where's Lamar?" I yelled at the three of them.

"He didn't come in yet. He was running after the ball, near the parking lot," Andre yelled back, with fright in his eyes.

I pulled back the sheers at the living-room window and saw Cordell strutting up the front steps holding Lamar's hand, grinning, with his chest stuck out.

"Open the door, Jasmine. Lamar wants to come inside," my estranged husband said in an unusually lighthearted voice.

I dashed into the kitchen and grabbed the telephone off the counter and dialed "O" to get the operator.

"I need the police right away. This is an emergency," I said, losing all sense of calm in front of my kids. My voice trembled. My insides shook as I urged the operator to hurry.

I stretched the phone cord as close to the front door as possible. I wasn't about to let Cordell out of my sight with my son. Seeing Lamar standing outside the door—no sparkle in his big brown eyes, his head hung and shoulders slumped—tore at my soul.

"Lamar," I called. "Are you all right?"

He glanced up at me with watery eyes. My legs got weak and my head spun so fast I almost fainted. Shoving the telephone into my oldest son's hand, I told him to give the police our address.

"Tell them to get here quick! It's a matter of life and death," I said, darting to the stairway and skipping steps on the way up.

I dropped to my knees beside my bed and squeezed my hand between the mattress and box springs. My fingers found the gun. Afraid to look at it, I grabbed the weapon and bolted back down the steps. By this time, Andre was talking to a police officer on the phone. I grabbed it and began yelling into the receiver.

"This is Jasmine Walker at 1312 Laurel Lane. My husband's got our eight-year-old son outside my front door, and I'm afraid of what he's gonna do to him."

"Just calm down, ma'am," the man on the other end said. "What do you think your husband's going to do to your son?"

"I don't know. I don't know," I cried. "I just know that he wants me to let him in this house, and I'm not gonna do that. I'm too scared of him. He'll try to hurt me again."

"We've got someone on the way right now, ma'am," the cool, calm voice said. "Now I want you to stay on the line and talk to me until the officer gets there. You sound pretty shaken up."

"I am shaken up! My husband beat me up the other night. Now he's come back, and he's got my son out there with him. But God knows that if he even looks like he's gonna leave here with my son, I'll kill him. I swear I'll kill him!"

Cordell disappeared from my sight while I was talking to the officer. I dropped the telephone and rushed to the window. Pressing my forehead against it, I caught a glimpse of my estranged husband walking away from the building. Lamar was nowhere in sight.

"Don't you take Lamar away from here Cordell. I'm warning you!" I hollered so loudly my last words faded into a hoarse shrill.

Cordell turned and shouted back. "I'm giving you thirty seconds to open this door, or I gonna take the motherfucker off the hinges."

I glanced down at the gun in my hand for the first time. I scanned the room to see where the kids were. Andre stood near the stairway, stone faced with quiet terror in his eyes. He tended to withdraw when scared or worried. Kendra stood halfway between us, her eyes wide and teary. Staring at me, she said nothing. I looked at Kamari, who stood nearest to the living-room closet under the stairway. The minute our eyes met, her mouth turned down. Her pug nose flattened, then she let out a howl that usually made her sister and brothers mad.

"You kids get upstairs—quick!" I yelled. They scrambled for the stairway as if they could read my mind.

I stared at the pearl-handle gun, and suddenly things seemed to switch to slow motion. Lying my head against the brown front door, I prayed.

"Lord, you know I don't want to have to shoot this man. Please help me. I can't let him hurt my baby. You know I can't. Oh God, please help me."

The sound of something scratching the door startled me. I scrambled back to the window, only to see Cordell on his knees with a screwdriver. When something metal clanked against the cement, I realized he had gotten a hinge off the door.

My heart pounded so hard I could hear it. Shuffling back behind the door, I closed my eyes and raised the gun, which felt heavier than ever. Both hands on the trigger and handle, I placed the nose directly against the door. In the same instant, I heard a loud, unfamiliar voice coming from outside.

"What seems to be the problem?" asked a male voice with a thick southern accent.

My eyes popped open. I scrambled to the window and saw a tall African American sheriff's deputy standing behind Cordell. Lamar stood silently a few feet away.

"This ole crazy woman won't let me in my house to get my clothes," Cordell snapped.

Tears streamed down my face.

"Thank-you, Lord," I said, rushing to stuff the gun underneath a pillow on my sofa.

The officer started rapping loudly on the door.

"Open up. It's the police," he hollered sternly.

"But I'm scared he'll beat me up again like he did the other night," I hollered back.

"He says he lives here ma'am, so I'm afraid you're gonna have to let him in."

My mind raced faster than my hammering heart. This was the one opportunity to get Cordell out of my house.

"He's just saying he wants his clothes. I don't believe him. He can't stay here anymore. I'll only let him in to get his things if you promise to stay with us until he leaves."

The officer once more asked Cordell what his intentions were, then agreed to stay until he got his things and left. I swung the door open, and my husband stormed past me, rolling his eyes and stomping up the stairs. Lamar stepped inside the door next, looking weary and confused. I grabbed him and hugged his limp little body as tightly as I could. His sisters and brother bounded downstairs, and we did a group hug, something we had started soon after moving to Flint.

I forgot about the officer until he walked past us and over to the bottom of the steps. He looked upstairs impatiently. The kids and I stood quietly, waiting until their father had finished carrying piles of clothes, some dangling from his arms, outside to his car. It took four trips. I sent the kids back up to their rooms while their father headed to the basement.

Twenty minutes had passed and the stoic-faced, good-looking officer began pacing past the stairwell to the basement.

"You better hurry it up. I ain't got all day," he hollered down the steps.

He eventually went down to the basement, too. I heard arguing but couldn't understand what they were saying and backed away, not wanting to know. Their voices grew louder, but all I could hear was Cordell calling me every name in the book.

"I ought to go up there and kick her ass again right now," he shouted loudly enough for me to hear. "All this bullshit she's putting me through. I ought to just kick her ass and pay the fine."

"Naw, now that's where you're wrong, mister," the officer replied flatly, his southern accent even heavier than Lydia's. "You won't be just paying a fine. You hit her around me, and you're going to jail."

If Cordell was trying to intimidate me, he did a good job. Every time he surfaced from the basement carrying boxes out to the car, I cowered in a kitchen corner, trying to avoid looking his way. Every now and then he and the deputy exchanged words, each time more heated. I listened but missed a lot, trying to stay as far away from Cordell as possible.

It took about forty-five long minutes for him to load everything into his car. His last trip out the door, he turned back and glared at me. I glanced his way, then inched closer to the officer, who quickly followed him out the door.

"Take care of yourself," the man in uniform said, looking back before closing the door behind him.

"Thank-you," I replied.

— ઢ —

"GIRL, WHAT HAPPENED?" Lydia asked as soon as I answered the telephone.

Cordell and the deputy had been gone about twenty minutes, long enough for me to slip out of my clothes and lay my head against my pillow for a few minutes, weary and exhausted.

"The same ole thing," I said, fighting back tears and wondering how much more could any person take.

My lips trembling, I told her the whole story. Lydia listened quietly, giving an occasional "uh huh" or "umph umph umph" to let me know she empathized.

"See, now a niggah like Cordell would make me have to kill his stupid ass. I'm like your daddy now. Cordell's ass is *supposed* to be lying in somebody's morgue right now."

Thinking of how close we'd already come to killing each other made me shudder. I thought about all the stories that had been running in the *Flint Journal*. Week after week, it seemed, I had been reading about women or girlfriends being gunned down or stabbed by their husbands or significant others. The stories felt like omens. I could actually see my obituary in my mind. I had never been so scared from one moment to the next in all my life.

"Well, you know how to dial my number if you need me," my neighbor said, after we had analyzed my latest ordeal from every way possible.

"Like I told you before," she continued, gulping from a drag off her cigarette, "I ain't never been no fighter. Now, I'll talk shit in a minute, but I ain't looking to try and fight nobody—especially some crazy motherfucker like Cordell. But I *will* call the police on his big, tall, sorry ass—then watch them carry his retarded ass off to jail."

After crying until my stomach muscles were sore, I craved to laugh but couldn't. My eyes dark and sunken, I hadn't slept well in weeks. My hair, which had begun looking better after seven years of neglect, looked like a matted mess of soft black wire.

Lydia and I talked for more than an hour. Every so often, one of the kids would stick their head in my bedroom, their faces filled with concern. I'd nod my head and mouth the words, "I'm okay." They'd smile faintly, then close the door. None of us knew what to expect next.

—— ✿ ——

THE NUMBERS OF my alarm clock radio said ten fifteen by the time I pulled back the covers on my bed and climbed in for the night. Curled in a fetal position with the blankets over my head, I must have drifted off to sleep.

Around midnight the phone rang. My fingers felt up and down the base of the lamp next to my bed for the switch. I clicked it on, then sat up and picked up the receiver.

"Hello?"

No one responded.

I repeated myself.

Still no answer.

I listened for a second or two. Then hung up.

I turned back over with the light still on. The telephone rang again.

"Hello?" I said, hoping the person on the other end had forgotten who they were calling the first time it rang. I did that myself sometimes.

Silence.

Instead of hanging up, I listened carefully and heard muffled sounds of people talking and a television in the background. Nothing was audible, and none of the voices were familiar. I hung up again. Within seconds the phone rang for the third time. By the fourth time, I was convinced it was Cordell making the calls.

"Listen, Cordell," I said, hoping that by calling his name, he'd feel exposed and stop calling out of fear I'd report it to the police. "You're gonna wake up the kids. Will you please quit calling here?"

The prank calls continued. Every time I hung the phone up, it rang again within minutes. I tried taking the receiver off the hook. It began making a noise that sounded like a cross between a busy signal and a fire engine. I placed the receiver back on the base of the phone after two or three minutes of that noise.

My phone wasn't a plug in, and I'd never heard of one back then. The calls were so persistent that I eventually sat up in bed imagining the worst, the lights still on.

"What if Cordell is somewhere nearby? What if this is a distraction while he tries to break in? What if he's trying to drive me crazy? What if he's planning to kill me *and* the kids?"

I wanted to check my front door and downstairs windows again, but was too scared. I strained my ears to listen for any unusual sounds coming from the kids' rooms. The only sound was Lamar's loud snoring. Fear gripped me, but I had to break the paralysis and peek outside. I lay down, I sat back up—going back and forth until dawn.

My strategy for the rest of the night had been to pick the phone up as soon as it rang, then quickly hang it back up. Around eight o'clock in the morning, I changed my approach. I'd listen long enough to try to hear something. I thank God I did.

"Hello?" said the male voice on the other end. I recognized it immediately because of his heavy southern accent.

"Hello," I replied, sounding surprised.

"Mrs. Walker, this is Sheriff's Deputy Monroe Demps. I was out to your house yesterday on a call regarding you and your husband. I hope you don't mind me calling you so early this morning," he said.

"Oh yes, I remember you," I replied immediately. "No, I don't mind. I've been up most of the night, anyway."

"How are you doing this morning?" he asked, sounding more polite than the previous evening.

"I'm hanging in here . . . I guess."

"Mrs. Walker, I usually don't take my job home with me at night," he said, "but I'm gonna just be flat-out honest with you. I'm worried about you."

I was flat-out stunned. It was as if he had read my mind and heart the evening before. My soul had begged for someone like him to protect me from Cordell. Someone bigger and stronger and not easily intimidated.

"Yeah, I'm worried about me, too," I replied with resignation in my voice.

"I've seen guys like your husband before. They'll hurt you."

I smiled sarcastically before replying.

"I know. That's why I've been staying locked up in this house with my kids. I really don't know what else to do."

"Well, I hope you don't mind, but I talked to some of my buddies. And they're willing to patrol the area around your place a little more often if it's okay with you. They won't be bothering you or anything. They'll just be watching out for your husband or his car."

I closed my eyes, and tears started falling. Rocking back and forth, I silently whispered over and over, "Thank-you, God. Thank-you, Jesus."

Our conversation ended after he'd given me a number. It would enable me to reach him more quickly.

"And if you don't mind, I'd like to call and check on you sometime," he said.

I wasn't sure exactly what he meant, but hoped the six foot-three-inch hunk was talking about us getting to know each other better. His thoughtfulness alone flattered me.

"Oh, I don't mind at all. I really do appreciate you doing this for me, Officer Demps. I really do."

"Just call me Monroe."

"Well, thanks again . . . Monroe," I said, still not believing what was happening.

I couldn't wait to call Lydia. She listened while I told her every detail of our telephone conversation. Puffing on a cigarette, my voice sounded more hopeful than it had in days. I could tell Lydia was smoking, too. She made the familiar sound of blowing smoke from her mouth, then gulping before she spoke.

"Now, that's the kind of stuff that lets you know that there's a God out there somewhere," she said.

COMFORT

I was still reading my Bible every day. As soon as the kids left for school each morning, I'd clean up the kitchen, then hurry upstairs to my bedroom and absorb myself in my large, four-inch-thick Bible, oftentimes reading until they returned that afternoon at three fifteen. My faith in God's word was my only hope that things would get better.

I read everything in it at one time or another, focusing on books like Proverbs and Psalms because they praised the Lord and instructed me on what to do and how to act. My Bible helped me more effectively deal with life as a single mother and gave me strength to deal with my estranged husband.

Cordell's mother had sold me the Bible when we lived with her. She had never opened it up as far as I knew. She ordered it through the mail along with a lot of other hardback books. Mrs. Walker ordered lots of books over the years and never paid for any of them. Oddly, I never saw her or anyone else in her family read them. Stacked on wooden shelves in an upstairs bedroom, the books ranged from those dealing with law and crime to cookbooks and autobiographies. Mrs. Walker had enough brand-new books to stock a small library. I always thought it was such a waste.

I fell in love with the Bible as soon as she showed it to me. Reluctant to ask her, I was pleasantly surprised when she agreed to sell it to me for forty dollars. It was the best forty dollars I'd ever spend.

A King James Version, the leather-bound Bible's thin pages were edged in gold. A color picture of cherubs inside an oval ring graced the white cover. Some inside pages also included illustrations and colored prints. I examined pictures of the Sistine Chapel by Michelangelo but didn't know anything about him at the time. My favorite was the picture of a man, his arm stretched so far that his finger almost touched a figure representing God. His arm and finger were extended, too. Every time I stared at the picture, it moved me.

The Bible had become my lifeline. In terror so much of the time, I found that it was the only thing that calmed me down. Every time I opened it up, often with no particular scripture in mind, there was always something that applied to my life.

My Bible even contained a section in the back that listed characteristics that attract and repel others. I studied them carefully and began consciously incorporating them into my life. Not only did it make a difference, I felt better. If I was afraid, I looked up "fear" in the concordance in the back. I spent a lot of time reading about faith. The scriptures comforted me like nothing else ever had. The more I leaned on the Lord and asked him to fight my battles, the stronger I became. Sometimes my nerves got so bad that I'd stop whatever I was doing and fall to my knees and pray. And without exception, the Lord gave me the strength to get through another day.

✤ A TASTE OF IT ALL

Cordell started calling me several times a day, first apologizing, then cussing me out when I refused to take him back. His calls slacked up only after I threatened to have my phone number changed to an unlisted one. Then he started sending letters through the mail. Most were written on yellow, legal-size paper and rambled on about how wrong I was for not taking him back.

"You're a selfish-ass dirty bitch," one of them said. "You know those kids need their daddy. You don't want me to call the ADC people and tell them you're an unfit mother do you? Don't make me hurt you."

I read them, then tore them up. One morning I was perched in my favorite spot on the sofa, watching my favorite daytime show, *Phil Donahue*, when Lydia called. I had been engrossed in the show because his guests were talking about their spiritual experiences and used the word "vision" to describe them. It was the perfect word for the experience I'd had several years earlier. I began to wonder if I had been called to preach.

"Jasmine, you need to come down here for a minute," Lydia said. Her voice sounded troubled.

I immediately clicked off the television, slipped my underweight body into some blue jeans and a pink top, and jaunted down to Lydia's house. She stood at the door waiting, dressed in stiff blue jeans and a navy blue pullover sweater. Lydia handed me an envelope covered with Cordell's chicken scratch-looking handwriting. A chill shot down my back.

"The mailman put this in my box by mistake," she said, as we headed to the kitchen and sat down at the table. "I didn't know you could even send some shit like this through the mail."

She lit up a cigarette. I started reading the fourteen-page letter. Cordell repeatedly swore he'd commit suicide if I didn't take him back. Once I caught the flavor of the letter, I tore it up and threw it in her trash.

"One of my biggest fears was that Cordell would go downhill if I left him. But this man has gone down much faster than I ever imagined," I said.

The idea of Cordell killing himself because of me was tough to take. But after weeks and months of dealing with his threats and bizarre behavior, I was too drained, mentally and physically, to do anything more than pray about it.

—— 2 ——

"HI BABY. Whatcha doing?" Monroe asked in a sexy voice on the telephone one evening around midnight.

"I'm sitting here curled up on the couch in the dark, playing my stereo."

"What are you listening to? 'Three Times a Lady'?" he asked softly. "I think of you every time I hear that song."

I smiled like a high school girl on a date.

"No, I'm listening to the O'Jays. I could listen to "She Used to Be My Girl" all night."

"I bet ole Cordell don't like hearing that song," Monroe said, sounding as if he was smirking. "That knucklehead sho lost out on a good thing when he lost you. I just can't imagine anybody treating you the way he did. But I've got you now. And I'm gonna do everything I can to keep you."

My new beau sure knew how to flatter me. I lay back against the pillow-backed sofa and wrapped the telephone cord around my forefinger. I didn't know I still had it in me. My fling with Jerome Taylor had been more of a sexual attraction. This had the potential to be a serious relationship.

"Monroe, I look at my marriage like this, now. Cordell didn't know the value of what he had. And if you don't know the value of something, you can't possibly appreciate it," I said, feeling more comfortable with myself than I had in years.

"Well, I'm gonna treat you like you deserve to be treated. You take good care of your kids. And I like that. If there's one thing I can't stand is a woman who lets her kids run around with dirty faces and snotty noses all day. Jasmine, you've got a sharp place, and you keep it looking real nice. That's why I like you. You're different," Monroe said.

I hadn't been courted by another man in nearly fifteen years. And I'd never lived alone and had a steady, meaningful relationship. I loved it. It was empowering.

"Can I come see you tonight?" Monroe asked softly.

"Sure you can. The kids are in the bed 'sleep. How long will it take for you to get here?"

"I'm in my patrol car now, about five minutes away."

"Give me ten minutes to comb my hair and fix myself up a little. I was getting ready for bed and look a mess," I said.

"Baby, you look good all the time. No one would ever guess that you've had four kids. But you do what you gotta do, and I'll see you in ten minutes."

The relationship between Monroe and me had become sexual within days after our first telephone conversation. The flat-footed guy from New Orleans with a dominating presence called me several times every day. I'd never received so much male attention—especially from someone as handsome as Monroe. I just knew that God had sent him to me.

I fluffed up the pillows on the back of my sofa and wiped crumbs from the cushions with my hand. I picked a dirty sock off the steps while trotting upstairs to comb my hair. I sprayed Jean Nate cologne on my neck. I brushed my teeth and gargled. Tiptoeing back downstairs, I clicked on the lights in the base of my amber-colored lamps. Their glow set a romantic mood. I flipped through my records until finding a Bobbie Womack album. I wanted it to be playing when Monroe walked through the door.

Monroe knocked. I'd barely closed the door when my honey hung his arms around my shoulders then pulled me closer and gently kissed my lips. Monroe had a sensitive touch for such a big man. We strolled over to the couch, his arm still around my shoulder. We sat down in the dark and talked.

"Has Cordell been bothering you lately?" Monroe asked, pulling me into his arms as he leaned back on the couch.

"Yeah. He's still at it."

"What's he doing?"

"He's mentally torturing me," I said quietly. "A guy from his job called me today. He was worried about Cordell and wanted to warn me."

"About what?"

"He said that Cordell constantly talks about getting even with me. I know this guy, and I trust him. We go to the same church. It's just by coincidence he and Cordell work together."

"Look baby, I keep telling you. I know Cordell's type," Monroe said, his face looking more tense, even in the dark. "He's one of those jokers who don't understand anything but a good ass-kicking."

"Let's not talk about Cordell anymore," I said, gently pressing my forefingers against his soft lips. "I don't want anything to ruin our evening."

Our conversation ended, and we started making love. Monroe's patrol car was still running in the parking lot, its yellow hazard lights flashing.

— ❧ —

ONE NIGHT after the kids and I had gone to bed, a bumping noise woke me up. I sat up in the bed without cutting on the light and listened for a few minutes. Hearing nothing, I eased out of bed and crept downstairs to check the door and windows. I rattled the doorknob. I peeked out the kitchen window into the parking lot. Nothing appeared unusual, so I tiptoed back toward the steps.

Suddenly, the crook of an arm squeezed my neck. I was slammed to the floor. Kicking and fighting in total darkness, I screamed for help and prayed someone would hear me. My assailant eventually pinned me on my back. He put his face in mine so I could see him. It was Cordell.

"I'm going to take me some, then I just might kill you, bitch," he said in a voice so cool and calm it terrified me.

But I wasn't about to go down without a fight. Twisting and turning, bucking and biting, I freed myself enough to thrust my body up, giving me enough room to breathe but not accomplishing much else. He struggled to raise my gown then ripped off my panties. Bare bottomed and fighting for my life, I kicked my legs and gouged at his eyes and begged him to leave me alone. We scuffled and rolled from one side of the room to the other. Suddenly, a light flashed through my kitchen window.

Cordell jumped up and bolted out the front door, disappearing into the frosty night and leaving the door wide open. Seconds later an officer appeared, flashing a light on me. I lay on my back, screaming hysterically and panting so hard that my chest ached.

"Are you hurt?" he asked.

"I think I'm okay," I cried. Then lost it again.

The officer radioed for backup, and within minutes another deputy rushed through the opened door. I heard them mention Monroe's name. The next thing I knew, he came charging through the door looking distraught. My six-foot-three, two-hundred-and-five-pound secret lover rushed right up to me, wide-eyed and breathing hard.

"Did he do this to you?" Monroe asked, reaching for my flannel granny gown, the sleeve ripped, revealing my flesh.

I quickly shook my head, no. My cotton gown had been raggedy for months. I liked sleeping in old nightclothes, plus I couldn't afford new ones. But I wasn't coherent enough to explain all that. Lydia and I would laugh about my old sleeping clothes several days later.

"Did he put his hands on you?" Monroe asked, his eyes looking deep into mine.

I nodded my head and looked away.

"What did he do?" he asked.

"He tried to choke me," I said just above a whisper, not wanting to share all the ugly details in front of all those men in uniforms. The whole ordeal of *almost* being raped and killed was bad enough.

Monroe's almond brown face flushed and turned red. His eyes looked wild and furious. He left me in the care of the first two responding officers, then stormed out the door.

"Monroe," I said pleadingly, but he kept going.

Calling him by his first name was bad enough. I feared saying anything else, unsure of how much the other officers knew about our relationship.

The entire time the officers were questioning me, my mind was on Monroe and what he was doing. They told me my options, which were few. I could go downtown and take out a warrant on Cordell for attempted rape and possibly attempted murder. Or I could take out some type of assault charges. Both carried prison sentences.

"Let me think about it for a few days," I said passively.

I needed to talk to Lydia first. She always seemed to know what to say and do. The idea of sending Cordell to prison scared me. Regardless of what he did, I didn't want to carry the burden of putting my kids' father in prison. I also knew the Walker family would be furious and probably retaliate.

I checked on the kids before making my call. I found Lamar standing near his bedroom door in the dark, listening. He still had trouble sleeping. I gently took my son's hand and guided him into the hallway so his brother could sleep. Whispering back and forth as we sat on the steps, he told me he had called the police.

"I woke up and heard something. It sounded like somebody was trying to hurt you, so I called them," he said defensively.

"You did just what you were supposed to do, honey. And I'm so glad that you're so smart," I said, kissing him on the forehead and hugging his frail frame.

We walked back up the steps to his bedroom. The only sound in the house was the refrigerator humming. I thanked God for my son as I watched him climb over his older brother in the dark. He scooted to his side of the bed, wiggled down into position, and pulled the covers up to his chin.

Tiptoeing back downstairs, I found my cigarettes lying on the kitchen table and lit one before dialing Lydia's number. She listened as I talked. And talked. And talked. But my sistah friend was nowhere as concerned.

"Now I know Monroe is a stupid-ass, country-ass motherfucker. But I know he ain't that crazy," she said flatly.

"I don't know, Lydia. But what if something does happen?" I said, wanting her to take the situation a little more seriously.

"Like what?"

"Like Monroe might kill Cordell. Then everybody would find out that we've been going together. Then the police would arrest me, thinking I had something to do with it. Then I'd go to prison for the rest of my life. I could lose my kids and everything."

"Well, I know you ain't had nothing to do with no murder. And I sho wouldn't lose no sleep worrying about Monroe's stupid country ass. You got enough problems to deal with. Me and you both."

I didn't want to hang up the telephone, but Lydia said she needed to iron her kids' clothes for the next day. She was good about taking care of things like that in advance. I always ironed clothes in the morning, which kept me running late.

"Oh yeah Lydia, let me tell you what Kamari said to me yesterday when she came home from school," I said in one last-ditch effort to keep my friend on the line.

"Ain't Kamari the twin who acts like RayAnna? All hyper and shit?" Lydia asked, blowing smoke from a cigarette. "You know your girls look so much alike that I ain't never been able to tell them apart. I just call them both 'twin.'"

"Don't feel bad. Most of my family can't even tell them apart," I said. "And yeah, that's her, all right. Kamari asked me, who was going to take care of them when I die of cancer from smoking cigarettes. Wasn't that deep?"

"Sho was. I know it blew your mind, didn't it?" my sistah friend asked, her tone more serious than it had been throughout our entire conversation.

— ⸎ —

NEITHER MONROE nor Cordell called that night, so my imagination ran wild. I tossed and turned all night.

"What if Monroe really did kill Cordell?" I thought. "Some of his fellow officers already know that we've been messing around. There's no way anyone would ever believe that I didn't have anything to do with it. I can see my name plastered all over every newspaper and television in the state. They'll check and find out I used to be on drugs. They might take my kids. And Lord knows I couldn't take that."

Ten o'clock the next morning, the phone rang. It was Monroe.

"I looked all over the place for Cordell last night, baby," he said, almost lightheartedly, which worried the heck out of me. "He sure better be glad I didn't find him. That joker's got a good butt kicking coming."

"Please, Monroe, just let me handle this okay? This whole thing is getting way too deep for me."

The Lord knew I appreciated everything Monroe did for me. And I told him more than once. But his anger toward my estranged husband scared me. It started out being kind of flattering, but it eventually got downright frightening.

🌸 WORKING IT

Raising four children by myself was going to require a good-paying job. And a good-paying job required a college education. I realized that immediately after the breakup. Several weeks later, I caught the bus downtown to Mott Community College to talk to a counselor about enrolling.

The counselor was a very business-like, middle-aged white man, who wore a white shirt and an ugly green tie. We talked for several minutes before he handed me half a dozen forms to complete. Unlike an incident in high school, the lengthy forms didn't intimidate me. I just took them one question at a time.

"Did you overlook the question regarding your major? I see you left it blank," the counselor said, after a cursory review of my paperwork.

I had hoped he'd miss it. It had never occurred to me to consider a career before enrolling, and I was too embarrassed to admit it. Glancing down for a second, my eyes caught sight of the words "Business Administration" in bold black print on a yellow form lying on top of papers stacked on his cluttered desk.

"Business administration," I said halfheartedly, not having a clue as to what it meant.

The counselor repeated it out loud four times as he wrote it on the forms. Every time he said the words, I cringed. It didn't feel right. I should have admitted I didn't know and asked for suggestions based on my interests, but I didn't.

"Even though I don't know what business administration is, it sounds like a career that makes lots of money," I thought, feeling woefully unprepared.

The balding counselor informed me that I qualified for financial aid and could start classes the winter of '79. The semester began in a few weeks.

That evening the kids and I discussed my returning to school in more detail as we sat at the kitchen table eating French-fried potatoes and toast, one of our favorite meals. They were so happy for me, which made me even more excited.

"All of us can do our homework together," Kendra said, flashing her million-dollar smile with the proudest look on her face.

"We can't do our homework with Mom," Lamar said impatiently, rolling his eyes at his sister. "People in college do *hard* homework."

"Our homework is hard, too," Kamari said, coming to the aid of her sister, as usual.

That night each of the kids came trotting into my bedroom, one by one, to give me a goodnight kiss and a hug. They told me how proud they were of me for going to college, and gave me an extra big squeeze. I was happy, too, but couldn't shake that nagging feeling about the major I chose.

In my prayers that night, I asked the Lord to reveal to me what to study, then drifted off to sleep. It came to me in the middle of the night. I sat straight up in the bed.

"I like to write," I said out loud. "Of course. I can get some kind of job in writing. People have always said I can write good."

It felt right. It fit right. Writing would enable me to express myself. Touch lives. Inform people. Writing would provide me with instant power and authority. I always did like the saying, "The pen is mightier than the sword."

— ❧ —

I COULDN'T WAIT to go back down to Mott Community College the next morning. I asked for the same counselor.

"I'd like to change my major to something that has to do with writing," I said with an embarrassed smile.

The counselor peered over his horn-rimmed glasses and repeated my statement back to me, his eyebrows raised, his voice bordering on indignant.

"Yes. That's right," I said politely.

He cleared his throat, ruffled through a few papers, then looked up at me again.

"Well, I guess you could pursue journalism. That involves writing," he said. " But there's a *big* difference between business administration and journalism. I suggest you go home and give this some thought before declaring a major. You've got plenty of time to do that."

I was sure and told him. About five times. He reluctantly made the necessary changes, but I didn't care about his attitude. My mind was made up. I wanted to become a writer.

— ❧ —

BEING A twenty-eight-year-old college student didn't bother me one bit. I loved college life. It felt so good doing something just for me. I also got a part-time job in the college's game room, enabling me to earn a few extra dollars, plus meet quite a few students—some of them my age. I stood behind a counter and rented Ping-Pong paddles and other game equipment to students. Being one who liked to talk, I carried on conversations with everyone, so there was always a small group of males and females standing around the counter with me.

A couple of the guys asked me for a date. I let them visit me after the kids were in bed, once or twice. But I quickly discovered that they were dealing with just as many problems as I was, so I chose to keep our relationships simply as friends.

— ℛ —

MY FAVORITE CLASS was social science. Taught by one of the most popular instructors on campus, Bill Lefler, the thirty-something-year-old man wore vests and silly hats to class every day. He gave enlightening lectures laced with humor and provided hands-on exercises that taught us concepts, such as how the rich keep getter richer and the poor keep getting poorer. I had never realized that before.

I didn't miss one of Mr. Lefler's classes. On a few occasions I had to bring Lamar with me because he was sick a lot, mainly with respiratory infections and sore throats. Another time I brought Kendra with me instead of sending her to school sick. I'd discovered that a mother's love and hugs were the best remedy for most illnesses. Each child sat quietly in the back of the classroom, often napping with his or her head resting on a desk.

I took a typing class out of necessity. Unlike my high school experience, I enjoyed the class. It was taught by Mrs. Jamison, a well-dressed, reserved woman. She was my first black female instructor ever. Appearing to be in her early thirties, she reminded me of myself—a perfectionist at heart. She was tough, but I thrived on the challenge and got my best grades in her class.

— ℛ —

MY WRITING INSTRUCTOR was a racist and didn't know it. Those were the worst kind. I never got good vibes from him but tried to ignore his condescending attitude. Short, balding, and overweight, he reminded me of Archie Bunker in appearance and attitude. The only significant distinction I saw between the two men was that my instructor didn't use incorrect grammar.

Our first assignment was to write about our neighborhoods. I wrote about Brookfield Terrace and the close relationship we single mothers had with each other. Our instructor would hand the assignments back promptly but always kept a few to read aloud. He never read any of mine. I didn't like the way he snickered at certain writings, particularly those that used "black English" and described neighborhoods with boarded-up, vacant houses and factories and abandoned railroad tracks.

"That man's got the nerve to make fun of their writing," I'd think. "I bet it was a black student who wrote that. And he knows that, too. He ain't *that* dumb."

Sometimes when he made fun of a paper, I couldn't help sneaking a peek around the room, feeling sorry for the person who'd written it. I began disliking my writing instructor the first time he did that to a student.

The Archie Bunker look-alike gave me a C on every paper. I hated Cs. Frustrated, I decided to give our next writing assignment laser-beam focus. We were to write about something we loved. I stayed up late several nights, writing and rewriting. The subject of my paper dealt with my lifelong love for drawing and writing, even though I hadn't practiced either in years. It read: *"I've always loved to draw and write. It makes me feel good inside. I can't describe it, but I have a feeling or a need to express myself in those ways. When I go inside stores, often I go to the area that has art supplies and different kinds of notebook paper. Just looking and touching them stirs up something deep within me."*

He handed my paper back with the usual C at the top of the page. And to add insult to injury, he placed a big red question mark beside my statement about art supplies and notebook paper, stirring something deep within me. I looked at the paper, then stuffed it in the pocket of my folder, almost ripping it in the process. After class, I walked down the hallway and stood facing an exit door, waiting for a female student friend who was giving me a ride home. Still stewing about my grade, I heard footsteps and glanced over my shoulder, only to see the instructor headed my way.

"I know this man ain't coming to say something to me," I thought. "He just might get cussed out today."

I kept my back turned to him, facing the parking lot. He had to walk around me in order for us to face each other. I just looked at him.

"Am I discouraging you?" he asked in a voice void of any compassion. I started to lie and say "no." A part of me wanted to be the likable student, the person who was taught to always respect her elders. Yet another part of me demanded truth. I stared him dead in the eye, then spoke my mind as clearly and as firmly as possible.

"Yes. You *are* discouraging to me. But *I* know *me*. And I don't let *anything* get me down, but for so long. I believe in taking lemons and making lemonade."

His eyes darted about as if he didn't know what to say. But he quickly recovered.

"Well, I'm sorry if I've discouraged you because that was not my intention," he said, looking dead serious. "I was only trying to help. I just don't want to see you wasting your time trying to be a writer. I'm just telling you for your own good."

I stared at him for a few seconds, trying to think of the right thing to say. I started to call him a white, stupid-ass racist. I started to tell him to shove his class up his you know what. I even considered telling him how cruel it was for him to pick out disadvantaged students' papers to read, then make fun of their work, and calling it "constructive criticism." I started to tell him that I hated his class and that he had no business being a teacher. But I didn't and forced a weak smile.

"Well, thank-you for your concern," I finally said calmly. "But with all due respect, you're the *only* person who has ever said that I couldn't write. In fact, people often compliment me on my writing—always have. But you know what? All you've done is motivate me to try harder. Cause I'm going to think about this conversation every time I feel down or discouraged. And it's going to make me even more determined to succeed."

Then I stepped to the side so that he didn't block my view and continued waiting for my ride. I glanced back once and saw him walking down the dim hallway toward his classroom.

DISCOVERY

Students in the Beecher School District attended school four and a half days a week, with classes letting out every Wednesday at noon. Calvary Reformed Church provided a Bible study for children that day from one to three. Delores Walters, a retired schoolteacher, conducted the class. She had befriended my family and me soon after we started attending the church.

"Her husband died ten years ago, and her only daughter lives in Wisconsin. She's kind of like a mother to us," I told Lydia while sitting in my living room on one of the rare occasions when she visited me.

Delores, a black woman with salt-and-pepper hair, lived across the street from Brookfield Terrace and often spent time with my kids. Her immaculate, split-level home was a three-minute walk from our front door. My kids visited her often. Before Cordell and I split up, Delores had invited us to dinner several times, but he never went. The kids and I did.

Every time Delores saw us, her face lit up with a smile. She often sat with us in church, but I never said a word to her about my ongoing ordeal with Cordell. I was too ashamed.

My kids started attending Delores' hour-long Bible study and enjoyed it a lot. I eventually volunteered to help her. She welcomed my involvement with open arms. I started out reading Bible stories but soon found my niche in drawing. I'd sketch the main characters of each story, then mimeograph copies and give them to the students to color. My drawings were a hit, and our class grew to capacity within a few months.

Of all the things I learned during that time, there was one that stood out most in my mind—my long-lost passion for drawing. Even more exciting, I sensed there were still many parts of me to know.

❧ MOMMA'S VISIT

Momma and I talked on the telephone several times a month. She updated me on what was going on in Jackson, and I filled her in on the kids and my other side of the family in Flint. Momma never did much visiting. I could count on one hand the number of times she visited me the entire eleven years I was married, even though she lived less than three miles away in Jackson. I was flabbergasted when she accepted my invitation to spend a weekend with us in Flint.

The kids and I were so excited. We had become accustomed to hosting relatives from Jackson and Lansing. My sisters and brothers had come up to visit a few times. My dad joined us, along with most of my sisters and brothers on his side of the family. We partied until the daylight hours, then bunked out all over the house. It was the first time most of my half sisters and brothers had met.

Bringing my two families together was something I had wanted to do for a long time. It felt as if my entire family had finally begun coming together.

Valerie was the first to visit after my marriage ended. It was just like old times. We hung out at a popular nightclub and stayed on the dance floor, dancing with at least half a dozen different guys. We even let a couple of them follow us home and smooched for a while.

Penny spent a weekend with us. We talked and smoked weed all weekend. Terrance visited next. Our middle brother tended to be a bit pompous and complained about everything. Keith was chatty and smiled a lot. But he missed Momma and left a day early. Yet each time a loved one visited us, the kids and I did our best to show them a good time.

Momma's visit was extra special. It was my chance to show her how grown up I'd become. It was my chance to show her that I could be a good mother and that my kids lived in a decent home. It was my chance to show off our nice town house and give our relationship a fresh start.

The kids helped me take down every curtain in the house and wash them in the new washer and dryer that Cordell bought me several months earlier. He claimed he wanted to help make things easier on us, but I knew better. The guy was trying to get back in good with me. But with no car and less money, I desperately needed the washer and dryer, so I took the gift, looking at it as the least he could do after all he'd been putting us through.

I shampooed the carpets throughout the house, then got on my knees and scrubbed our sofa so hard that blisters formed on my hands. I polished brass. I cleaned windows and glass. I washed cabinets and walls. I straightened out closets, neatly folding every towel in the linen closet, which was always in disarray.

By the time Momma arrived, our house sparkled. Uncle Darius, my dad's brother, picked her up from the bus station and drove her out to my house, about ten miles from downtown Flint. It felt good to know that Momma and Uncle Darius had remained close friends over the years, despite her difficulties with my father. Her face lit up as soon as she walked through our door.

"Everything looks so nice," she said, speaking in proper English, which she used to reserve only for white people and others she wanted to impress.

It was the first time I'd ever felt adequate in Momma's presence. It validated me as her daughter, like nothing else had. I was so happy that it was hard to sleep.

The kids barely argued the entire weekend, which was a record breaker. Ordinarily, I had to take a few lessons from Lydia's playbook and cuss them out to stop the bickering and arguing.

"The kids seemed more settled. They don't act like wild Indians anymore," Momma said.

Coming from her, that was a compliment. It also reinforced my belief that the breakup of my marriage was the best thing that could have happened for my kids and me. Lydia had made a similar remark a few weeks earlier.

We showered Momma with so much love and attention during her two-day visit that she smiled the entire time. Having planned her visit for around the first of the month, I was able to cook bacon and eggs for breakfast one morning and sausage and pancakes the next. I cooked big dinners and played Momma's favorite R & B songs on the stereo throughout her stay. It was such a comforting visit.

Lydia and three other women living in our courtyard dropped by to meet Momma. I had told her a lot about Lydia and her kids, and she seemed genuinely interested in our friendship. Another first.

Monroe even dropped by on Saturday night in his patrol car. I had been telling Momma about him and couldn't wait for them to meet.

"Oh my God!" she exclaimed with the biggest grin on her face when he walked through my door, looking like Prince Charming in a deputy's uniform.

I never felt more proud to introduce Momma to the new man in my life. She even chatted with him. Momma was so pleased with me. I could see it in her face and hear it in every word she spoke. There was not one complaint or sound of bitterness in her voice. Momma's visit was the best thing that had ever happened to our relationship.

THE BEAT GOES ON

A man ain't shit. You can go get the ugliest one you can find—thinking don't nobody else want his sorry ass. And soon as you go to having some feelings for him, he's got the nerve enough to put you through just as many changes as a good-looking one would," Lydia said, pausing to take a draw off her cigarette.

We were having one of our late-night calls. Her former boyfriend, Tiny, had called and begged her to move back down south. They had lived together for over a year, but she left after catching him "creeping" on her more than once. My friend spent forty minutes dogging the man.

"I picked Tiny's sorry ass up out of the gutter. The motherfucker had a drinking problem, no job, and was as ugly as hell. I just knew I could clean him up and *make* me a man."

We cracked up laughing.

"Girl, you got any reefer?" she asked.

"My cousin came out here and sold me a nickel bag. He's only fifteen and driving a black Cadillac. He must be making money hand over fist," I said.

"Well, I sho need me a joint. My nerves have been so fucked up the past few days, worrying about my telephone bill, that I've got to figure out something and quick. You know I can't stand nothing worrying me but for so long. Then I've got to do something about it," Lydia said.

"I heard that. Yeah, you can get one. But you'll have to run down here and get it."

"Thanks. I'll give it back to you after Mr. Dunbar comes by. I sho didn't want to call his old dried-up ass. But I need some money," my friend said.

Mr. Dunbar was Lydia's quasi–sugar daddy. Old enough to be her grandfather, the man had six adult children and three grandchildren. Mr. Dunbar visited Lydia nearly every Friday night or Saturday morning and sat at her kitchen table, talking and drinking coffee. She cooked and carried on conversations about how broke she was. Lydia swore she never slept with the quiet-spoken man, and I believed her.

"I can take sex or leave it," my friend always used to say. "It's never been something I've just got to have."

Since becoming a single parent, I was just the opposite. We laughed about that a lot, too.

— ⁊ —

LYDIA WAS A great cook and always had some southern dish on the stove or in the oven. Sometimes I'd smell her food, and my stomach growled, but I seldom asked for any. She had three other mouths to feed. Every now and then she'd offer me a plate of dinner. It was always so good and reminded me of home. Lydia taught me how to cook southern dishes like greens, fried chicken, and home-made cornbread, instead of boxed. Her kids tasted my chili and homemade pizza with biscuits and asked Lydia to get the recipe. After giving her the recipe, the next time I made them, I called my friend down to watch.

Lydia and I didn't smoke weed in front of our kids, even though Cordell and I had. Several times they walked in on their daddy and me shooting up. We'd turn our arm away, then get mad at them.

When we wanted to smoke, Lydia and I sent our kids upstairs to the bedrooms or outside to play, depending on the time of day and weather. Our kids never mentioned us smoking weed, although they could smell it. Smoking marijuana was both our families' dirty little secret.

"Do you know that cigarettes are going up to fifty cents a pack?" I asked, lighting one up, not realizing another was still burning in a small round ashtray that I always carried from room to room. "I can't afford to keep smoking cigarettes and weed."

"I know that's right," my friend replied.

We both made up our minds to quit smoking cigarettes. The Great American Smoke Out, sponsored by the American Cancer Society, was held the third Thursday in November 1978. Lydia and I both stopped smoking that day and never started again.

NO PEACE, NOHOW

Sitting in church one Sunday morning, I turned and spotted Cordell walking through the sanctuary door. The first time seeing him in a house of worship, except for a few funerals, I was scared to death.

"When church is over, leave out the side door right away," I whispered to the kids as inconspicuously as possible.

Cordell sat down on a wooden pew in the back row. I avoided looking around to see what he was doing. Church ended, and the kids did as instructed, quietly slipping through the parishioners and out the side exit. We dashed across the asphalt parking lot and through Brookfield Terrace's backyards and its cracked and pot hole–filled streets to our house.

I quickly locked the door and all the windows and prayed that he wouldn't come bothering us. He didn't, probably because Monroe had warned him, and he knew the police were still keeping an eye on my house.

"If Cordell was bold enough to come in the church, he'll try anything. And I'm sure he's watched us enough to know our schedules every day," I told Lydia, terrified that my husband was again plotting to do us harm.

The next morning I sprinted a quarter mile down the road to the kids' elementary school, looking over my shoulder all the way. I told the principal about my situation, fearing that my estranged husband might try and take my kids from school. She was more cooperative than I had expected. Prior to that day, school officials had been unresponsive to most of our inquiries and requests.

Before the week had ended, I'd also dropped out of college. My midterm grades had arrived a week earlier, and I was carrying a 3.50 grade point average. My decision to stop attending classes was made tougher by Mrs. Jamison's pleas not to quit her typing class.

"But you have so much potential, Jasmine. And you were doing so well. Isn't there any way you can continue taking classes?" she said, looking wide-eyed by all that I had revealed to her. Afraid that Cordell would be lurking around any corner at any time, I wasn't willing to chance it.

My writing instructor, "Archie Bunker," reacted completely the opposite. I spilled my guts to the man, hoping he'd feel sorry for me and give me an incomplete like Mrs. Jamison. He stared back at me blank faced, never saying a word. I never knew whether he believed me but detected a faint smile after telling him I wouldn't be back. That hurt.

❧ TO TELL THE TRUTH

Monroe claimed he shared an apartment with another officer on the force. Nearly four months into our relationship, I found out he had been lying. He lived with another woman, and they even had a young child together. I felt like an idiot.

"No wonder he was never at home whenever I called. Some guy would always answer the phone and take a message. I bet Monroe never even lived there," I spouted off to Lydia while she ran hot water in her kitchen sink.

"Didn't I tell you, Jasmine, that Flint niggahs ain't no good—especially a big, dumb, country-ass niggah like Monroe."

I couldn't help but laugh.

"Girl, you kill me talking about country people," I said. "You're from North Carolina."

"Look here," she said, laughing. "That's why I know what I'm talking about. Monroe is one of those country niggahs who come up here looking for a factory job, and somebody fucked up and gave his drunk ass a sheriff's deputy uniform and a gun."

Monroe had revealed his drinking problem to me within weeks after we started seeing each other. I'd never knowingly dealt with a straight-up alcoholic until then. He'd make promises, then break them. He'd disappear for a day or two, then turn up with a hangover and swearing he wasn't going to drink again. I tried encouraging him. I tried not speaking to him for a day or two at a time. Nothing worked.

"Monroe might be the biggest liar in town, but you gotta admit that the man sho looks good in his uniform. I love seeing brothers in uniforms," I said, trying to find some redeeming qualities in my used-to-be knight in shining armor.

"Yeah, but you take that motherfucking uniform off and Monroe looks just like any other drunk-ass, country-ass niggah," my hard-hearted friend said, steam circling her face, her hands in sudsy water, finishing up dinner dishes.

"Girl, I'm telling you the truth, these country-ass niggahs move up here to Flint, Michigan, and get jobs in the shop, making more money in one week than they made in a year down south," she said.

I'd never realized that before.

"And the first thing they do is go buy them a big shiny car so they can drive back down south to the sticks to show it off. Country motherfuckers come all out of the woodwork, too. Even the little kids be laying their rusty asses all sprawled up on the hood," she said, stretching her arms out to demonstrate, causing her long-sleeve blouses to creep up her forearm.

I cracked up laughing.

"I'm serious, girl. Then the ole stupid niggahs got the nerve to look down on women like me and you, cause we're on welfare," she said.

I knew she was right. I hated being a welfare mother. People talked about welfare queens all the time on the nightly news. Every time I looked up, some black woman living in some big city was being paraded across the television screen after being busted for welfare fraud. No one reported about people like the women in our courtyard. They were all on welfare and good mothers.

Monroe often said he admired me as a mother. We had even talked about us shacking up, a thought that intrigued me at first. But after a month of seeing the real Monroe, there was no way I'd knowingly place my kids in another dysfunctional situation.

"I know how to fix him," I told Lydia, as she sat down at the table and lit up a joint. "Every time we run into each other from here on in, I'm gonna be doing better than the last time he saw me. That goes for any man. They'll wish they still had me."

— ∾ —

WE BOTH WERE smoking joints. I loved lighting up when the kids were asleep. Lydia and I sometimes talked and smoked until daybreak. Weed relaxed me. It made me think deeper and feel more in control. On the downside, smoking marijuana messed with my memory a lot. Lydia and I often laughed about our forgetfulness after toking on a joint. Weed helped us get our housework done. We took a few tokes while cooking. It energized me when I needed to be energized and slowed me down when I wanted that.

Neither of us could afford spending five dollars on a bag of weed, so we'd go half and half on a nickel bag and make it last for several days, taking a puff or two off a joint throughout the day. We even rolled the "roaches" into joints and smoked them when we ran out. Between sharing nickel bags and frequent visits from our male and female friends—Lydia knew many more people in Flint than I did—we seldom went a day without at least hitting off a joint.

"I know that ain't Christopher up again. That boy must have drank a lot of water cause he's done trudged in and out of that bathroom twice now. Hold on, Jasmine, and let me check and see what the hell he's doing," Lydia said.

I crept in the boys' room, then the girls', to check on them. By the time I took a quick trip to the bathroom, Lydia was back.

"You see, Jasmine, you're like me. I used to talk shit to my ex-husband, knowing he was gon kick my ass. I've seen you do the same thing with Cordell. We're the type of women who'll take an ass whipping, as long as we got our two cents in."

I nodded my head. We laughed some more.

"By the way, how'd your aunt like her visit to Flint? Did she get off this morning on the bus all right?" I asked.

"Yeah. Girl, she was still talking about Flint, Mitch-again, when I put her ass on that Greyhound. My auntie is the closest thing to a momma I got. And I was glad to see her come and glad to see her ass go," Lydia said, then started imitating her aunt's voice, exaggerating her southern accent and dragging out each word.

"Lydia, chile, I sho do like those curtains hanging up here at your living-room window. What you pay for 'em? How much do people here in Flint, Mitch-again, pay for a whole fryer chicken at these here stores? Who was that on the telephone?"

"I'm used to my privacy. I've been alone too long or something," Lydia said.

My friend complained of her stomach "feeling funny." That happened a lot. According to Lydia, orange juice settled it down. She left the phone to go get a glass.

This time I waited. Smoking a pencil-thin joint, I took a few puffs, then put it out for later in the morning. I listened to see if my kids were stirring. Just Lamar's snoring. I scanned my bedroom, checking to see if anything was out of place. Nothing. I lit the joint back up. Three minutes passed before Lydia returned.

"Jasmine, I know why people always fuck over you," Lydia said, as if talking about the weather.

I laughed so hard that I swallowed some weed smoke and started choking. I squashed the joint in an ashtray beside my bed for the second time.

"Why, Lydia?" I said, laughing and coughing so hard tears ran down my cheeks.

"Cause you look like a pushover. You carry yourself all humble and shit. People look at you and figure they can do you any kind of way."

I'd never looked at it like that before. Lydia had a knack of giving me glimpses of myself, like a mirror.

I refused to believe that all men were as bad as Lydia always said they were. But the men in my life were making my argument pretty hard. Lydia was a tough debater, with quick mother wit. I knew my book knowledge and street experience. But I knew she was right about men looking down on women with kids who "lived off the state." I sensed that to varying degrees with every man involved with me.

CHECKS AND BALANCES

Raising kids as a single mother on ADC was tough. Really tough. It took planning and scheming and begging and borrowing, and lots of creative thinking. One of the most difficult challenges was making the money last throughout an entire month in order to feed my kids.

I got my check on the first of the month. Lydia's came on the tenth. Realizing that we were running out of food about ten days before our next check came, Lydia and I started loaning each other food stamps. Our borrowing averaged about twenty-five dollars a month. We also loaned each other butter, milk, and eggs, and a cup of sugar or soap powder to wash clothes. We didn't expect each other to repay the staple foods and items, only money or food stamps. Our little system worked well.

———— ❧ ————

LYDIA HAD A new man in her life. His name was William Lewis. Everybody called him Will.

She had been seeing him for three months before I agreed to meet his brother. Will was a decent-looking, well-dressed man who showed Lydia and her kids lots of attention. I admired that in him right off the bat. But I wasn't interested in meeting his brother.

"I've got my hands full with Monroe and Cordell," I told my friend every time she brought the subject up. One day I gave in and agreed to meet Tyrone that night at Lydia's place. I trotted down to her apartment after straightening up the house and the kids were settled down in front of the television for the evening. I walked inside Lydia's door, only to see this tall, good-looking man standing in her living room, wearing the biggest smile, as if awaiting my arrival. It was an instant attraction for both us.

"I had no idea this guy looked this good," I thought, kicking myself for not agreeing to meet him sooner.

Six foot three, Tyrone was a flashy dresser, showed all of his big pretty teeth when he smiled, and had a body that looked as if he worked out every day. The silky-voiced guy had worked for General Motors for seven years but had hands smoother than mine and fingernails that looked freshly manicured.

"I was born in Mississippi and buttered in Flint," he said one day, grinning from ear to ear and his chest stuck out.

Tyrone was a ladies' man and made no apologies for it. But I liked his honesty and loved his romantic nature. We started talking on the phone every day. Tyrone visited me two or three times a week, always after the kids were asleep and always bearing gifts. He gave me so much attention that it made it easier to distance myself from Monroe.

Tyrone made cassette tapes of my favorite love songs and always brought cookies or candy bars for me to give the kids the next day. Our relationship quickly grew—almost as fast as the one between Monroe and me. But there were a few problems with this one, too.

Tyrone was married and had a small son. He half worked and called in sick on more than one occasion to spend time with me. His wife pulled double shifts at General Motors in order to buy him material things, like shiny new cars with the latest sound equipment, expensive clothes, and their split-level home in Grand Blanc, a suburb of Flint.

"My wife was raised by her grandmother and was raised to think sex was bad," he told me one day. "She doesn't like having sex, so she buys me things to try to make up for it."

I envied Tyrone and his wife, even though their relationship left a lot to be desired. Both had good jobs and were able to buy nice things whenever they wanted. According to Tyrone, they didn't fuss and fight a lot, but seldom saw each other because they worked opposite shifts. The closer we became, the more he shared about his marriage. It sounded more like bribery than a relationship. Yet it became obvious that he cared deeply for his wife because he spoke of their struggle so often and with so much pain in his voice.

But Tyrone was a "good-time Charlie" in his heart and probably always would be. I knew it, so his wife had to know it as well. Women, cars, and music were his passions. Every time I talked to him he was either washing or had just washed his 1978 midnight blue Oldsmobile with lots of chrome. One day his wife promised to buy him a new car and that was all he talked about—the model, the color, the engine's horsepower, the interior. Never having much interest in cars, it meant nothing to me.

It did cross my mind a few times how big of fools she and I both were. She worked overtime in the factory to give Tyrone all the material things he wanted, and I provided him with a good time and sex. From my perspective, I had the better end of the deal. I was having fun and felt in control. I wanted *any* man, *whenever* I desired—married or not—as long as I called the shots. Lydia didn't blink when I explained my new philosophy to her.

"Most women go through a period of being wild after they've split up with their man—especially when they've treated you like a dog. I went through some changes my damn self. But I ain't gon lie girl, I wasn't as bad as you," she said, giggling.

"You go to hell, Lydia," I shot back with a smile.

"But I know how you feel," my sistah friend said. "After we break up with our man, we just need to know that *some* man, *somewhere*, still wants our tired, broke-down asses."

It was true. I wanted and needed to feel like a woman again. Realizing that marriage probably would never be an option for me because I had four kids, I felt more in control of my emotions. There was something about a relationship lacking commitment that made me feel safe.

Tyrone and I enjoyed the same kind of music and loved to talk and laugh and have fun. One time he'd come with Crown Royal. The next visit he'd bring champagne. I'd drink to be social, but preferred weed. Tyrone knew it and always came with plenty for us to smoke, too.

⁂ AS <u>THINGS</u> GO

A white family moved in directly across the courtyard from me. "Little Shirley," the young woman who had lived there with her six-year-old daughter, moved back to Texas. The new family were the only Caucasians in the complex as far as I knew.

"I see they ran that little poor-ass honkie home from school the other day, *again*," Lydia said. "Now you know they've got to be some poor-ass honkies, any time they move out here in Brookfield Terrace around a whole bunch of niggahs. Seems to me their ole nasty-ass, fat-ass momma would get tired of her kids getting their asses kicked every day and move some place else."

I felt sorry for the family, especially the kids. Nobody seemed to like them. Their faces and hands were always dirty, their noses snotty. Most times they walked around their yard barefoot and barebacked, with shorts hanging off their rear ends.

The boy looked to be about twelve years old. His younger sisters appeared to be about six and eight. The three of them half went to school and wore some of the nastiest and dirtiest clothes I'd ever seen.

One day I heard a blood-curdling scream out front while watching television and waiting for my kids to come home from school. I got to the door just in time to see three young black girls running away from the white people's front porch. One of the little white girls was standing on her steps screaming, crying, and holding her head, which could have been bleeding, but I couldn't tell.

I stepped away from the door and peeked out the living-room window, expecting an ambulance or the police. Nothing.

I called Lydia. She had heard the scream as well, but she didn't make any bones about her dislike of the white people and thought I was crazy for pitying them.

"Honkies don't ever pity us," she said. "I was born in the South, so I know all about white people. Down south, everybody knows their place. And I like it like that. Up here in the North, honkies are sneakier, but they're still some racist-ass motherfuckers."

— ❧ —

IT WAS FRIDAY night around eleven. The kids were upstairs in their bedroom watching television with all the lights off. I was downstairs lying in my favorite spot on the sofa talking to Tyrone on the telephone, the amber globe of my glass lamps dimmed. *Motown's Greatest Hits* played over and over on the stereo.

Suddenly I heard glass breaking. Then people screaming. It was coming from the white people's house.

"Somebody, please call the police! We don't have a phone. Somebody please call the police," I heard someone yell from inside the house, where only one dingy curtain sagged across the living-room window.

I darted to the window, but it was too dark to see very much. All the lights in the white people's house were off. More glass shattered and tinkled to the ground. More screaming. I ended my conversation with Tyrone and called the operator, who connected me to the police. The kids came charging down the steps, asking about the noise outside. Kendra and Kamari raced to our living-room window and pulled back the sheers to see. Lamar scolded them for being nosey and careless.

"The twins are gonna mess around and get hurt one of these day," he fussed like an old man. "They're always getting up in the window when they hear something outside. What if somebody's got a gun out there?"

After clicking off the lights in the base of my lamps and ushering the kids back upstairs, I called the police again.

"Someone's breaking out my neighbor's windows, and people inside are screaming, saying they don't have a phone to call the police. Please get somebody out here right away," I said quickly, then hung up.

"Keep your heads down. I'm gonna call Lydia," I whispered to my kids, who were sitting on the hardwood floor in my bedroom, next to my legs. Kamari leaned against them.

"That's what they get," Lydia snapped. "Didn't nobody tell them to move out here, no way."

"I'm sorry. I just can't feel that way," I replied. "I know I'd be ready to hurt somebody about my kids if they were being treated that way. There's one thing I always say—if I go to hell, it sure won't be because of prejudice."

"That's what I say about you, Jasmine. You're too damned naive about shit," Lydia said, her voice short and impatient. "Poor white honkies are the worst kind. They even got the nerve to think they're better than niggahs. They get that from their ole prejudice-ass mommas and daddies."

"But you mark my word," she continued. "These ole nappy-headed kids out here in Brookfield Terrace are gonna keep on fucking with those poor-ass white honkies until they'll want to get the hell out of here on the first thing smoking."

"Well, I called the police," I said gently. "I would have done that for anybody. That's just the way I am."

Lydia and I finished our nightly chat with an uncomfortable tension between us. Conversations about white people almost always ended that way.

—— ℯ ——

DANIEL GLASPIE was Brookfield Terrace's maintenance man and knew about most things that took place in the low-income housing complex. A short, copper-skinned man with thinning, black wavy hair that revealed parts of his scalp, Daniel probably was a good-looking man in his day, before life took its toll. Neighbors trusted Daniel. So did Lydia and I.

The Monday after the window-breaking incident, Daniel appeared at my front door unexpectedly. I was straightening up my downstairs. He looked uneasy as I closed the door behind him, but it didn't mean much to me at first.

"Hey there, Daniel. What brings you this way? It's too nice a day to be working indoors," I said lightheartedly, then returned to dusting my glass and brass plant stand, which had green, healthy plants on every shelf.

Daniel forced a smile, then put his hands in the pocket of his bibbed, denim overalls and shuffled his feet. I thought he'd come to inspect something in the bathroom or kitchen and expected him to make his way through the house as he always did. He stood there, wearing a shimmering orange shirt that was rolled up to his elbows and looked like it should have been worn at a nightclub instead of to a maintenance job.

"Jasmine, you and I get along real well. And I wouldn't tell you something unless it was true. You know that don't you?" he said, removing his right hand from his pocket and scratching the back of his neck.

I stopped dusting and looked at Daniel. His face was flushed and sweaty. My heart starting racing, and my legs got weak. I took a deep breath and braced myself for what was coming next.

"I heard some neighbors talking about you this morning. They think that *you're* the one who called the police on them the other night," he said, his eyes darting around the room to keep from looking at me.

"You mean, last Friday night when someone was breaking out those white people's window?" I asked, surprised that my identity had become known so soon.

He nodded.

"It *was* me. And like I told Lydia, I would have done that for anybody," I said, hoping that someone would understand.

"Well, I heard them say that if you don't move out of Brookfield Terrace, you're gonna be next."

Daniel's eyes looked dark and had circles. His face was strained and sad. He and I had become pretty good friends over the past two years, and it was clear that delivering the message didn't come easy.

"It's okay, Daniel. It really is. I've been thinking about moving anyway. So you can tell my neighbors—whoever they are—that they ain't said nothing but a *word*. I'm getting out of here as soon as I can. They don't even have to worry about that."

— ๛ —

MOVING ALREADY had been on my mind for several months. Daniel's news simply expedited things. The kids hated their school. There were too many fights and not enough time spent on teaching and learning. I had promised them that we'd be living in a different school district by the time school started in September.

My first idea was to move out of state, preferably to Denver or Atlanta. I had acquaintances there, but reality quickly set in. Moving out of state cost money— lots of money. We were blessed to eat from one day to the next.

Plan B involved moving elsewhere in the Flint area. I'd have my phone number changed to a private one and pray that Cordell would get tired of harassing me sooner or later. Money was still the issue.

Plan C popped up unexpectedly when Lisa and Albert called me one night, asking me to move to Lansing, where they both lived. Their call came a week prior to Daniel's visit.

"We don't like you living so far away from home by yourself," Albert said, sounding a bit impatient. It wasn't the first time he had asked me to move closer to family. He and I were very protective of each other.

Lisa had lived in Lansing since she married at fifteen. Divorced and working double shifts, my sister was raising her eight-year-old daughter alone. They lived in a huge four-bedroom home that was badly in need of repair. Lisa had taken the house out of desperation following her divorce. She'd found a smaller home around the corner and suggested I rent the one she was vacating. My sister even had gotten the okay from her landlord.

I told my sister and brother to give me time to think about it but had no intentions of moving to Lansing. I just didn't have the heart to tell them right then. But the Brookfield Terrace neighbors changed all that in one week. I called Lisa back and accepted her offer.

I wasn't thrilled with the idea of packing up my four kids so suddenly, but the Lord opened a door at the right time, and I had to walk through.

— ℀ —

THE MORNING we moved, Lydia wouldn't let her kids come outside until we had pulled off in our rented U-Haul truck. It was a sunny day in July 1979.

"It'll be too hard on them," she said over the telephone. "All three of them have been dragging around here with long faces already. I know how they feel. We all sure hate to see ya'll go."

Moving to Lansing was hard for us, too. Lydia was one of the best friends I'd ever known. It was going to be hard, not being able to call her and hold one of our marathon conversations any time of the day or night. I was going to miss our morning chats over a joint and tea in her kitchen after the kids were off to school. I was going to miss her kids.

I was going to miss Flint. Despite my troubles with Cordell, I found the people of Flint friendly—especially the men. I loved waking up to black music on the radio and listening to black DJs talk their "stuff." Music always made life more bearable for me. The kids and I had even attended a black theater production during our two-year stay in Flint. We'd never seen one before.

The flashy cars and fancy hairstyles. The dancing and partying. The black politicians. The black police. The city of Flint made me keenly aware of my racial identity but hadn't lessened my opinion of whites. I felt so good about that.

Living in Flint gave me the opportunity to know my dad's people better. I was very thankful for that because I had half sisters and brothers who had been almost strangers to me. Daddy and I had grown closer as well. We still often disagreed, but I relished and learned so much from our talks and debates. He did, too.

I would never forget the Friday morning, while living with Daddy, when I woke up earlier than usual and found him sitting at the kitchen table drinking Tanqeray gin and grapefruit juice. I was floored. That had been my favorite drink, too.

"We're more alike than I realized. It's almost scary," I thought, watching his every move while he poured me a shot.

From that morning on, we sat around the kitchen table every Friday morning, drinking and talking. He told me about his relationship with my mother, sometimes more than I cared to know. Daddy admitted to not being a good husband and had even denied being my father while Momma was pregnant, even though he was her first love and knew it. Daddy was brutally honest, and I was the same way, making for lots of interesting conversations that left me thankful to have spent time with him.

I visited one half sister Jeanette's home and discovered that we had identical lamps, only different colors, in our living rooms. Jeanette's mother was daddy's second wife. My half sister and I carried the same key chains with a big J on them. I'd never known a person with tastes so similar to mine. I'd never spent significant time around people who acted like me. Being with Daddy's family felt as if I'd found the other half of myself. And I had grown to love them like crazy.

But I was ready for a move. Flint was a party town, and I'd had my share of good times *and* bad.

"I want to be in an environment that's more education oriented," I had told Lydia several weeks before hearing the neighbors' threats. "I need to be around people trying to do more with their lives. Flint has too many distractions for me, especially when it comes to men."

Cordell had forced me to have him locked up in jail. He kept harassing me, so I finally met with a man from the Friend of the Court and told him everything. He was so scared for me that he insisted I stay in his office until Cordell was arrested for not paying child support. I never knew justice could move so fast.

Monroe and I still talked on the telephone regularly, but our relationship had become strictly a friendship. Despite his deception, I would never forget Monroe and the role he played in my life.

Tyrone begged me not to move out of town, telling me that he and his nine brothers would kick Cordell's ass if he even looked like he was going to put his hands on me again. But I wasn't about to drag more people into my problems and take a chance on someone getting hurt over me. Moving to Lansing was the best thing for everybody.

OPPOSITES ATTRACT

I t was mid-October 1979, and the leaves on the trees had turned from varying shades of green to red, yellow, gold, and orange, and appeared to burst from the treetops. They created a spectacular sight along the streets of Lansing as I rode the city bus toward downtown.

The teachers' strike had ended for the Lansing public schools, and most parents, including myself, couldn't wait to see our kids mounting the steps of school buses again. It had been a long, stressful, extended summer vacation.

I was headed to the Board of Water and Light to pay my bill before they cut my utilities off. I learned the hard way that life could be awfully difficult and boring with no lights or water. Momma always said I learned most things the hard way.

I stepped off the bus outside the green and white building, then entered the lobby and paid my bill. I was out in minutes because there had been no one standing in line. Walking toward the middle of town, dressed in blue jeans and a burgundy-and-white-striped long-sleeved blouse, I checked out the stores, wondering where to find a job. I hadn't come prepared to do any job hunting, so the idea to walk up to Knapp's, a department store, and apply for work was impulsive. They were taking applications, and a woman wanted to interview me right then.

"I'm not dressed right for an interview," I told the smiling white woman with dark hair and wearing a navy blue suit and a white blouse.

"Well, in this case, we'll just pretend we don't notice," she said, with so much confidence that I could smell a job in the air.

She read my application slowly, then looked up.

"How are you making it, raising four kids alone?" she asked, with a curious look on her face.

"It's not easy. But it's a whole lot easier than taking care of four kids *and* a full-grown man," I replied meekly.

She smiled back.

"Would you be willing to work weekends?"

"I'll work whatever hours you need me, as long as I'm home by five o'clock every day. I don't like being away from my kids in the evenings."

"Well, Jasmine, you're in luck," she said. "It just so happens that we're starting a new training class for cashiers this afternoon at one. Go home and change your clothes and be back at one o'clock for training."

———— ๏ ————

I HAD BEEN selling earrings, necklaces, and watches in Knapps' jewelry department for nearly three weeks when they called early one chilly, drizzling, Saturday morning. My supervisor asked if I could stand in for an employee in the accessories department who had stayed home sick. Needing the money, I got the kids dressed. I called up Lisa, who lived on the next street, to let her know my plans, then caught the bus to work. My sister kept an eye on my kids whenever I had to be away.

I was sorting packages of women's nylons when I noticed a short, dark-skinned guy peeking up at me as he edged his way around a display table of men's winter gloves.

"Which of these are the warmest?" he asked, marching up to me, his head high, his chest stuck out, and dangling a pair of men's wool gloves in one hand and leather ones in the other.

"I really don't know. I'm not familiar with this department. I usually work over in jewelry," I said expressionless, but politely.

"I see. Well, if I buy a pair of gloves from you today, will you get a commission?" he asked, his eyes exploring every inch of my face, then staring deep into mine.

"Nope. I get the same pay whether I sell anything or not."

"That was a very honest statement you just made," he said, sounding surprised. "You could have just as easily said 'yes' and made a sale, and no one would have ever known the difference."

"Why would I want to do that? I'd like to think that I'm a pretty honest person," I said, then started sorting packages again, wishing he would either buy something or leave me alone.

"May I ask what's your name?" he said, after glancing down at my hand to see if I was wearing a ring.

"Jasmine Walker."

"Hi, Jasmine Walker. My name is Clinton Saunders."

I softened a little. He seemed so polite and sounded so educated. He also showed no sign of letting up on our conversation.

"Are you from Lansing, Jasmine?"

"No, I'm not. I was born and raised in Jackson—Jackson, Michigan. Most people think I mean Jackson, Mississippi, when I tell them that. But I moved here from Flint," I said with an embarrassed smile.

A part of me wanted to be rude to him. He was too short. I liked tall men with light skin. He was so dark that I thought he was African, until hearing him speak. The other part of me said to give him a chance. He seemed like a nice guy.

"And how long have you been living here in Lansing, Jasmine?" he asked over his shoulder as he strolled back to the display table and neatly placed the leather gloves on a stack.

"Two months."

He walked briskly back to the cash register where I stood. By then I was busy straightening up the counter and hoping a customer would show up wanting to buy something.

"Well, what do you know," he said. "We have something in common already. I just moved to Lansing, too. Six weeks ago to be exact. I was born and raised in Oakland, California. And what brought me to Lansing, Michigan, you ask?"

I could have cared less why he ended up in Lansing. And he was beginning to get on my nerves. Yet I admired his confidence and the way he pronounced every syllable of every word with the clarity of an English teacher.

"I had two choices," he continued, without waiting for me to respond. "Stanford University told me they wanted me, but they had no money. The University of Michigan," he continued, emphasizing "the," "said, 'Come here. We've got fellowships.' So I packed up my belongings, bought me a warm coat, and here I am."

I was still wondering what "fellowships" meant, but figured it had something to do with money.

"This guy sure is pushy," I thought. "He's bordering on being arrogant and a pest."

"So, Jasmine, what do you do when you're not working?"

"You mean, like go out?"

"That, too."

"Not much. I've been out once since I've been here, and was back home before midnight," I replied.

I braced myself for the next question, knowing it had to come up sooner or later. "Do you have any kids?"

"I have four kids," I said.

By now I had learned how to minimize the impact. Say "four" near the end of the sentence, then stare the man unapologetically in the face.

He showed no reaction. He didn't blink. He didn't squirm. He didn't do anything except continue the conversation.

"I've got an idea, Jasmine. Since you and I are both new in town, how about us going out sometime? Why don't you let me give you a call some time later this evening, and we can talk more about it. How does that sound?"

I stared at him for a few seconds. My heart told me to say no. But my head said yes, so I searched his eyes behind the big glasses he wore. I wanted some *real* male companionship in my life. Tired of going with somebody else's man or husband, I wanted someone I could talk to. Be seen with. Do things that were fun, *together*.

"Sure. We can do that," I replied, after hesitating for another split second.

He smiled.

Clinton reached in his navy blue peacoat and pulled a black checkbook from an inside pocket. Taking a ballpoint pen from the same pocket, he handed them both to me with a pleased-as-plump look on his face.

"Here. Write your phone number right here," he said, pointing to a space at the top of the ledger page.

I felt a little uncomfortable giving my phone number to someone I just met. Having done it a few times since my marriage broke up and having nothing terrible happen, I was willing to take the chance again. After looking around to see if anyone was looking, I quickly jotted my name and number down and handed the pen and checkbook back.

Clinton held it up in front of him and read my number out loud.

"Five, five, five, five, zero, zero, nine," he said, then looked at me to make sure it was right.

I nodded and smiled.

After complimenting me on my handwriting, calling it "lovely," and tucking the two items back in his inside pocket, he thanked me and strutted away, swinging his arms. I said a silent prayer, hoping I had done the right thing.

— ~ —

THE WHITE ELECTRIC can opener hummed as it sliced around the top of the Campbell's tomato soup can, clicking the top off when it finished. The cans of chili beans were harder to open. They were heavier, requiring me to support them with the palm of my left hand, while pressing the silver lever down with the right. A few times, the can snapped away from the small clamp that held the rims in place, causing me to fumble them and splatter juice on the front of my yellow housecoat, which was split under both arms. I reached for the two onions and green pepper, thankful that I already had taken my work clothes off.

Pulling open the kitchen cabinet drawer, I took out a paring knife to peel and cut up the onions and dice the pepper, which felt soft and had begun to wrinkle. My eyes started burning from the onions, and I was wiping tears from my face with the arm of my housecoat when the background noise of the television in the small downstairs bedroom abruptly stopped.

"You always gotta get mad just cause your ole team lost," Kamari hollered from the area that we referred to as "the television room."

"Boston cheated," Lamar yelled back. "They always gotta cheat. They know they can't win without the umpires helping 'em cheat."

"Boy, you ain't gotta cry about it. You always gotta act like a crybaby when your team don't win. Who cares?"

Kamari and Lamar bantered back and forth for as long as I could stand it, which was about five minutes. I had hoped they would quiet down on their own, but that turned out to be wishful thinking.

Dropping the paring knife down with a clank in a metal bowel that Cordell and I had received as a wedding gift nearly twelve years earlier, I yelled so hard my throat strained. Veins bulged in my neck.

"Will you two cut it out before I come in there and beat both your behinds?"

The arguing continued.

"All right. Keep it up," I warned. "Don't let me have to stop what I'm doing and come in there. And I'm already tired, too. I'll half kill one of y'all tonight."

The voices quieted, but the arguing continued.

"That's it," I hollered from the kitchen after listening to them go at it for five more minutes. "Just wait till I put this pot of chili on the stove. I can't even cook in peace without having to stop and deal with kids who ain't got sense enough to stop before I beat their brains out. That's a doggone shame."

I put the pot, half filled with tomato soup and chili beans, on the stove and turned the black dial to "medium." Then I stomped into the living room and tried grabbing Lamar, who ducked and pulled away from me, then stood a few steps away with his mouth stuck out and tears streaming down his wide, pecan-colored baby face.

I hated it when he did that. My mild-mannered son was turning into a little maniac when it came to certain things, like baseball. At ten years old, he knew the name, weight, and batting average of every member of the Detroit Tigers baseball team. He knew Tiger trivia, their season schedules, and most other things about them, and had never been to one live game.

"And boy, you gon make me hurt you 'bout those Tigers. Stop watching them if you can't stand seeing them lose. Here we are, giving up watching our shows so that you can see *every* game they play. Then, when they lose, you get mad and jump up and click the television off so hard, I can hear it in the other room. Are you losing your mind?"

The telephone rang.

Kendra and Andre raced to answer it.

He snatched it off the receiver and dropped it. She picked it up and said a quick "Hi," before my twelve-year-old son wrestled it back. All I could hear was a man's voice on the other end saying, "Hello? Hello?"

I grabbed the phone from Andre, rolled my eyes at all four of them, then waved them away. After taking a deep breath, I cleared my voice.

"Hello," I replied calmly.

"Well, good evening, Jasmine. This is Clinton Saunders. And who is Clinton Saunders you ask?"

"Oh yes. I remember you," I said, interrupting him. "You're the guy I met at Knapp's this morning.

"Wonderful! You do remember me."

"Sure I do. You're one of the most interesting guys I've met since moving to Lansing. And you're the only black man I know who sounds white."

"Oh really now. And why do you say that?"

"Because you do," I replied. "You talk proper, just like one of them."

"Is that good or bad?"

"I don't know. Ask me a few weeks from now, and I'll let you know."

We both laughed. Surprised, and even a little flattered to hear from Clinton, I had forgotten about him until his phone call.

"This guy must be desperate," I thought. "Telling him I had four kids didn't even scare him away."

— ❧ —

CLINTON RANG our doorbell at eight thirty. He impressed me right away by being on time. We had arranged to go out for a drink at a local black nightspot in town, and I had been dressed and waiting half an hour early.

I had already talked to the kids about Clinton, explaining that we were going on a date. I also warned them not to say anything if he came inside to pick me up.

"And Kamari, I don't want you standing up in his face asking a lot of questions either. Do you hear me?" I said, giving her the eye.

"Yeah," she said, sucking her teeth and turning her head away from me, before marching back into the television room as if she were insulted by my suggesting that she would say something wrong or inappropriate. This was the same eight-year-old child who, at age three, stood in front of me, sucking her thumb and staring at a female friend who had come to visit me one afternoon when we lived in Jackson. I saw my daughter eyeing the friend, but didn't think much of it, until she spoke more clearly than she ever had.

"Is that a wig on your head?" my little darling asked.

I was so embarrassed. My friend cracked up laughing and was good-natured about the whole thing. But from then on, I held my breath whenever Kamari started hanging around company, not sure what might come out of her mouth.

"Where are the kids?" my date asked, peeking around me as he walked through the door. "I'd like to meet them."

That was not what I had in mind. Wary of exposing my kids to strangers, especially new men in my life, I preferred keeping them as far out of the picture as possible.

"They're in the back room watching Jaws on television. They've been looking forward to seeing that movie all week."

"It won't take but a few seconds," he insisted. "And I'll let them get right back to their movie."

"Okay," I said reluctantly and turned, with him following me. We walked through our sparsely furnished dining room to the darkened small room behind it.

The kids were all sitting on the wooden floor on a large, brown, crushed velvet pillow that Albert gave us. Besides the television, the pillow was the only thing in the tiny room. Nothing else would fit.

Engrossed in watching the show, they didn't even look up until I spoke.

"Kids, I want you to meet somebody. This is Clinton Saunders, the guy I told you about who's taking me out for a drink."

"Hi," they all said in unison, looking up at us for a split second, then turning their heads and attention back to the movie. I felt bad for Clinton, who had greeted them with a big smile and lots of enthusiasm.

"Well, let's get going," I said abruptly. "Can't stay out too late. We've got to go to church in the morning."

But Clinton seemed determined to make an impression on my kids.

"I'll tell you what. How about us going to pick up a snack for you all to eat while you watch your movie?" he said.

"Yeaaah," they all sang at once, never taking their eyes off the television.

So we rode to the party store around the corner on Logan Street. I suggested buying plain donuts. That was one of the few foods all four of them liked.

"What about a babysitter?" he asked as we headed back to the house to drop off the snack. "Aren't they too young to be staying home alone?"

"My sister Lisa lives right around the corner. I let her know when I'm going to be gone, and she keeps an eye on them for me. I do the same for her and her daughter. Besides, my kids are very independent and know what they can and can't do when I'm not home. We've been doing this ever since I've been on my own. It's hard to find someone you can trust with your kids these days."

—— ❧ ——

CLINTON DROVE too fast. He scared me so bad that my right foot kept pressing down on the floor board as if there was a brake on the passenger side. Three blocks from the night club, he cruised to a stop at a red light. Turning to me, he said bluntly, "Okay. Let's get this out of the way right now, Jasmine. I smoke weed. Do you?"

Trying not to show how startled I was, my mind raced for an appropriate response without sounding prudish or judgmental.

"I did up until six weeks ago," I said weakly.

"Why did you stop?"

"Because I think I've been called to preach," I said, feeling uncomfortable about revealing something so personal without knowing him better.

"A female preacher. That's interesting," he said. " I'd love to hear more about it after we get inside."

"And I love telling people about it," I said. "It all started years ago, with a vision I had when I lived in Jackson. I still find myself wondering what it all meant."

Clinton pulled out the ash tray where a joint laid inside. He pushed the cigarette lighter in then picked up the smoke. The lighter popped out seconds later and he lit up. The smell of marijuana still tempted me. I'd stopped smoking it out of guilt. Plus, memories of my vision still nagged at me. Trying to get some understanding of what it all meant, I'd even called my grandfather one morning, hoping to get some answers. There seemed to be something I was called to do but didn't know what.

"Daddy, I think I've been called to preach," I'd said, forcing the words from my mouth.

My grandfather chuckled quickly then caught himself. It shamed me for a second.

"Honey, you haven't been called to preach," he'd said, definitively.

Ordinarily that would have sealed it for me. My grandfather, the pastor of a church, would know, if anybody. But it didn't. And it wouldn't.

We sat in the parking lot until Clinton finished smoking, then climbed out of the car and into the cool, autumn night air.

—— ჶ ——

CLINTON PULLED OUT my chair for me in the nightclub. I felt a bit awkward. It made me feel special, too. No man had ever done that for me before—at least to my memory. I hadn't been on a real date since my teenage years. My idea of a date was having a man come over to my house after the kids went to bed at night. They'd have to leave about two or three in the morning, primarily because I didn't want my kids seeing a man in my bed, but also because most had another woman at home.

The club was crowded with black folks, laughing and talking and drinking at small round tables so close together that the waitresses had to squeeze through from one to the other. Lights dimmed, and as the music blared, a handful of partiers were on the small dance floor in the front of the room doing the Shing-a-Ling off "Ring My Bell" by Anita Ward.

"Do you dance?" I asked Clinton, straining to see the dance floor, yet trying not to turn my back to him.

"I try. But quite frankly, that's one of the few things I don't do well."

"You sure aren't modest, are you?"

"It's hard to be modest when you are as good as I am," he said, staring me straight in the face with the biggest smile.

"Oh my goodness," I thought. "This guy has gold teeth in the back of his mouth. Why would a man who sounds so educated put gold in his mouth?"

A waitress, appearing to be in her late twenties, nearly knocked over a chair trying to weave her way over to our table.

"I'll have Courvoisier," Clinton said. "No ice."

Not knowing what Courvoisier or most other drinks were, except beer, wine and piña coladas, I had no idea what to order. And I hadn't drank anything since Tyrone bought a bottle of champagne on one of his visits, shortly after we moved to Lansing. So I decided to play it safe and ask for white wine.

"The women on television always looked sophisticated drinking wine," I thought, as the waitress switched a smile on and off, then walked away.

"We'll have to do this more often. You're a cheap date," Clinton quipped.

Not sure whether he was being funny or what, I forced a slight smile and picked up our conversation where we had left off in the car. I talked, he listened—my favorite type of discussion. Ten minutes into my story, the waitress returned with our drinks.

"I meant to ask for a glass of water. But you don't have to bring it right now. You can bring it when you get back this way," he said, barely taking his eyes off me.

"Will you bring me one, too, please?" I asked, pausing just briefly to give the sistah some eye contact.

Clinton sat leaning forward, his arms crossed on top of the table. He seemed genuinely interested in my vision, asking pertinent questions that forced me to think more deeply.

"Well, Jasmine, you say you were called to preach, but aren't sure whose voice you heard or where it was coming from, right?"

"Right."

"Well, whose voice do you think it was?" he asked.

It seemed as if everything around me stopped.

I wanted to say "God," but didn't want to sound too crazy. It would have felt uncomfortable and even a bit arrogant to think that the Lord would talk specifically to me, particularly at that point in my life. My head tilted slightly. I thought and thought. It took several seconds for me to come up with an answer.

"I really don't know *who* it was. But whoever it was, it sounded like somebody who had a *whole* lot of authority."

We both laughed so hard, people around us turned and started looking our way. Wiping tears from crying so hard, I was still trying to regain my composure when the waitress returned with two glasses of water. I took a few sips, then immediately returned to my story. By this time, the wine must have had kicked in because I was feeling pretty good. I became so animated, waving my arms and flinging my hands, that I accidentally knocked over my glass of water. I was embarrassed but tried not to show it. Both of us calmly reached for the small white napkins under our glasses that had "The Garage" printed on them in gold. We casually dabbed up the mess, then continued our conversation as if nothing had ever happened.

Our discussion eventually turned to relationships and what each of us was looking for in one.

"I have no interest in any type of commitment," I said quickly. "I'm just looking for someone to talk to and spend a little time with. That's it. I don't have time for anything else with four kids to raise."

Clinton patted my hand and nodded his head approvingly. I talked, and he continued to listen, surveying my every move.

I talked about my faith.

"God has brought me through so many things—some things that I'm too ashamed to even admit happened. And he's still leading me. I know he is. I can feel him. And every time I get nervous or shaky about something, I pray to him, and he calms me right down. What I'm working on now is praying when things are going well."

I talked about my kids.

"Ever since we've been on our own, my kids have been my very best friends. And that's the way it's going to be from now on. We've been through so much together that sometimes I can't believe it."

I talked about myself.

"I just think that too many women get caught up in looking for a commitment from a man. I'm not like that—at least anymore. I'm learning that I need to get to know *me* before I can ever really commit to another relationship."

Clinton reached over the small wooden table and patted my hand again.

"Jasmine, I think you're *just* the person I've been looking for," he said, sounding more pleased than I understood.

After two hours of nearly nonstop conversation, I noticed that Clinton's head was getting droopy, so I suggested going home. Clinton drove me back to the house, then walked me to the door. He stood patiently beside me in the dark while I dug in my purse for my keys. Unlocking the door, I thanked him for the evening, then hurried inside.

I was relieved he didn't ask for a kiss and also a bit surprised. Watching Clinton from the window in the door, I saw him stepping high and swinging his arms as if he were as happy as could be.

The following Monday he came into Knapp's and marched up to the jewelry department, acting as if we were old friends. He kept patting my hands and calling me "sweetheart" and "dear."

I didn't like it. I never liked anybody touching me. That's why I always got a kick out of the comedian Flip Wilson's mantra, "Don't touch me. You don't know me that well." I didn't like Clinton's cockiness or his presumptuous behavior, but I bit my dry lip and endured.

Yet there was a part of me that liked Clinton. I admired his intelligence, and he was a complete gentleman. He opened doors for me. He helped me put on my coat. He loved kids and quickly started taking up time with each of mine individually. They loved the attention.

Clinton and I had been talking about three weeks when he invited me to go to Detroit for the weekend. The offer caught me by surprise.

"I guarantee that you will have a nice time," he said with so much confidence it made me sick.

I ended up going to Flint with some friends instead. We had made plans to meet Tyrone and some of his male friends at a nightclub there, long before Clinton's offer. My girlfriends and I spent the night riding around Flint, visiting different nightclubs. I rode, sitting close to Tyrone, in his newest car. His buddies and my girlfriends followed in another.

I'll never forget how proud I felt slow dancing with Tyrone in a nightclub to one of my favorite songs at the time, "Cruising," by Smokey Robinson. All eyes were on me, with a popular, tall, good-looking light-skinned man who could dance.

— ๑ —

THAT MONDAY, Clinton was one of the first people I saw. He marched up to my jewelry counter at work, trying to act unfazed by my slight.

"Good morning, dear. I hope you had a good weekend," he said in his always chipper voice.

"It was okay," I replied halfheartedly, not wanting to discuss the subject.

My weekend had turned out to be quite disappointing. Tyrone had to stay in Flint instead of driving back to Lansing with us and spending the night, as originally planned. Then I got home, only to find out that Andre had bumped his face on a door while Penny was supposed to be watching them. Both his eyes were black and swollen, plus he had a huge knot in the middle of his forehead. My son's face was so distorted that it scared me. I was furious at my sister.

"Your weekend was just okay, Jasmine?" Clinton asked. "I told you that you should have taken me up on my offer to go to Detroit. I had a great time."

That was the last thing I wanted to hear from him. But I forced a smile and carried on one of our long conversations about any and everything under the sun. I did most of the talking, and Clinton did most of the listening.

"There's a movie coming on television tonight that I've been waiting to see. Muhammad Ali is starring in it. I don't particularly care for him because of the way he treated his wife, Khalilah," I said, as if the couple had been close personal friends of mine.

Clinton was expressionless as I went on and on about Muhammad Ali's love life, but he listened. Then he invited me over to watch the movie at his apartment.

"I don't like going to guys' apartments. Too much goes on there," I said, smiling but dead serious. "The few times I've gone to a man's apartment, I've found myself in some pretty awkward situations."

"Well, Jasmine, I assure you that I would never do anything to hurt you," Clinton said quickly. "I'm the last person on earth you have to worry about."

"Yeah, well I've heard that before," I said, pulling my hands back from the counter so he'd stop touching me. "I'm not just talking about sex. I'm talking about other women calling or coming by—all that. I just don't like putting myself in that kind of situation."

"There will be no calls, I assure you. Trust me."

It was hard to say no after refusing his weekend in Detroit. So I gave myself more time to think about it.

"Call me later this evening, and I'll let you know for sure," I said, a part of me still not willing to take that next step.

Clinton called around eight, as upbeat as ever.

"So my dear, the movie starts at nine. Can I come get you?"

"Naw, I don't think so. I'm sorry, Clinton. But we ate kind of late, and I'm kind of tired. The kids are just getting ready for bed, and Andre isn't feeling well.

He tries to be tough but has always been the biggest crybaby in the family. So I need to stay home and keep an eye on him."

Clinton sounded disappointed but tried to hide it. I felt bad. I liked Clinton. We had had some interesting conversations, and I wanted to get to know him better. I just didn't want to get to know him at his place.

We talked for another half an hour, with Clinton divulging very little about himself. He didn't even tell me that he had a Ph.D. until we'd been talking for over a month. It took me another three weeks to find out what a Ph.D. was.

I told him about my plan to enroll at Lansing Community College for winter term, which started in early January. He informed me that I qualified for certain financial loans and grants.

"We can talk more about it tomorrow," he said. "I'll pick up the forms that you'll need when I'm down near the college. I walk downtown every day on my lunch hour if the weather is nice."

I wasn't used to having a man support my aspirations. Cordell had always complained that I needed a job. The few times I got one, we fought every night until I quit.

I prayed a lot about my feelings toward Clinton, particularly before climbing into bed at night. I wanted to do what was best for my kids and me.

"Lord, please show me what to do. You know that I'm terrible at picking out men. Here's a man who's never been married and doesn't have any kids. Heavenly Father, you know that Clinton shows my kids more attention than any man ever has. And I'm fighting it. What's the matter with me? Am I crazy or what?"

Lydia and I still talked on the telephone, creating havoc on our bills. We both agreed that our taste in men tended to be disastrous, and that we needed the Lord to lead us. I told Momma about the new man in my life, too.

"He's really nice, Mom. He works for the state of Michigan and has a Ph.D. in psychology," I said.

"Jasmine, is this man white?" she snapped.

"No, he isn't. He's black. In fact, he's real black."

I couldn't wait for Momma to see him. Clinton was the darkest man I'd ever dated, and the sweetest. As a teenager, Momma snapped at me one time for describing a guy with light skin and wavy hair as "fine." Momma thought I was prejudiced against dark-skinned people, and shamefully, to a certain extent I was.

❧ HELPING HAND

It was our third trip to Sparrow Hospital's emergency room in a month, and Andre was still listless and running a fever. His fair complexion looked peaked and green. I must have repeated his symptoms to the nurses and doctors a hundred times.

"My son hasn't been right since he hit his face on a door when I was out of town. He's not eating, and I can barely get him to drink anything. The antibiotic you all prescribed doesn't seem to be working, and he's been out of school for nearly two weeks."

A doctor changed the antibiotic and sent him home again. The next morning I was so broken down and weary when Clinton came by after work, he could see it in my face and body language.

"You do look a bit tired, darling. I'll tell you what. I'll stay at your house overnight and give Andre his medicine, and you can get some rest."

Clinton must have noticed the look on my face. I was all too familiar with the old "let me stay the night at your place" trick. Our relationship had been strictly platonic, and I wanted to keep it that way.

"I'll sleep downstairs on the couch. I promise. Trust me," he added quickly, looking into my big sunken eyes with dark circles around them.

I agreed. Clinton arrived at my home exactly at seven o'clock that evening, as we had agreed. I made him a pallet on our sofa with some homemade quilts that Mother had sewn, then trudged upstairs to get some sleep. Every two to four hours I could hear Clinton tiptoeing up the steps and open the door to the boys' bedroom. I listened while he gently awakened my ailing son for his dose of antibiotics and cough syrup.

I was touched.

"Here's a man, with a Ph.D. no less, who barely knows me and is willing to help me take care of my sick child," I thought while listening to Clinton quietly close the door and tiptoe back downstairs.

That was the turning point in our relationship.

—— ❧ ——

MOMMA CALLED every day to check on Andre, but he hadn't gotten any better.

"I'm beginning to think that they keep sending us home because we're on Medicaid," I told her one morning after another trip to the emergency room the night before. Medicaid was state assistance health care for people with low incomes.

"Well, Jasmine, get Andre ready. I'm gonna send Keith up there to get him. I want my doctor to take a look at him," she said, trying to hide her concern.

Momma had earned her high school diploma, then went on to become a licensed practical nurse. She worked full time at Foote Hospital. I could still remember the blue and white oblong first-aid tin she kept tucked away in her closet when we were very young. Watching Momma get it out, then meticulously care for one of her wounded children, I sensed she wanted to be a nurse.

I was giving Andre a bath when they arrived—Momma, Mother, and Keith, who drove.

"Jasmine, what have you got him in the tub for and he's sick?" Mother asked, blinking her eyes and looking puzzled.

Momma was less diplomatic. She turned to me with a disgusted look on her face before spouting, "Girl, sometimes I think you don't have a bit of sense." I just ignored her. My mind was on my son. He had steadily been losing weight, and his color was growing stranger every day.

Momma took Andre to her doctor, who immediately admitted him to Foote Hospital. He was placed in an oxygen tent to help his breathing. When I received the call at Knapp's, I dropped everything.

Keith drove back to Lansing, a forty-minute drive, to pick me up, then rushed me back to the hospital. Seeing my son was the only thing on my mind as I nearly ran into his hospital room. Sitting on the other side of his bed, in a corner, was Cordell.

I stopped dead in my tracks. As soon as he saw me, he raised up in the steel gray metal-framed chair.

"I ought to kick your ass right now for having me locked up," he snarled, giving me a dirty look.

I took a few quick steps backward, then pressed my hand against my purse as if I had a gun inside it.

"Oh yeah? Those days are over, Cordell. Cause if you even look like you're gonna put your hands on me, I'm gonna blow your brains out," I said, not batting an eye.

A second or two passed before my ex settled back into his chair. I breathed a sigh of relief. During the next half an hour, we were cordial but didn't say much to each other. Cordell did get up enough nerve to ask me something as he started to leave.

"Why don't you come on and go home with me, one more time?" he said.

I looked at him like he was crazy. Cordell left without us saying another word to each other.

— ౿ —

ANDRE STAYED in the hospital a week. The doctor had diagnosed a respiratory problem but never gave it a name. Clinton didn't hear from me the first three days I was in Jackson, so he left a message at the hospital desk for me to call him.

"How's Andre?" he asked from his office desk.

"Oh, he's better. They put him in an oxygen tent right after he got here, and I can see the difference in his color already."

"That's good news, dear. And how are you?"

It was the first time anybody had asked about me during the entire ordeal.

"I'm hanging in here," I said. "Kind of tired. But hanging in here."

— ౿ —

THE MORE I prayed about my relationship with Clinton, the more I was led to give it some time. So Clinton sounded surprised when I called on the telephone one Thursday and invited him over to my house *after* the kids went to bed. I knew the kids were usually tired near the end of a school week and would be asleep by ten o'clock. Most times, including school nights, they were required to be in bed by nine.

Working at Knapp's, I had bought myself a floor-length, cotton lounging gown, with plans to wear it when Tyrone came to visit. The gown was brown with an orange, beige, and white paisley print high neck with ruffles. Even the long sleeves had ruffles around the wrist.

After taking a long, hot bath, I rubbed lotion all over my body, greased my elbows and knees with Vaseline, then sprayed some Jean Nate cologne on my neck and wrists. I combed my hair and styled it the usual way—most of the top combed to the right side, and parted on the left. Both of us loved music, but Clinton collected jazz albums. I owned one jazz album to my name, Bob James, and put it on. Then I cut off all the lights but one in the living room and sat on my sofa and waited on Clinton.

He arrived exactly at ten. We'd never had any trouble finding something to talk about, and that night wasn't any different. Our conversation soon turned into a hilarious debate about who grew up poorest.

"Our mother used to have to cut bacon strips in half for our breakfast in order to save money," Clinton said, pronouncing each word as proper as ever.

"You're lucky. We had Oatmeal or Cream of Wheat. Bacon was a luxury in our house," I countered.

"My parents were so poor that we had to mortgage our house just to get aluminum siding put on it," Clinton said, trying to one up me.

"You had a *house*?" I asked, pretending to be indignant. "We had seven people living in a tiny, two-bedroom *apartment*. We even had to share the only bathroom with whoever lived in the other apartment. Thank God they were all relatives."

We both cracked up laughing, but I sensed that Clinton was just beginning to realize how disadvantaged my childhood had been. The beauty of it all was that it didn't seem to matter.

I dried my eyes from laughing so hard, then crept upstairs to check on the kids. They were fast asleep. After coming back downstairs and scooting closer to Clinton, I leaned over and kissed him on the lips. It was our first kiss. Within seconds, we were engaged in one of the most passionate kisses I had ever experienced. And when he put his tongue in my ear and began working it furiously, I melted like butter.

I felt weak and helpless. Chills ran up and down my back. I wanted everything he had to give. Suddenly, I pulled away from him and looked him straight in the eyes.

"Do you want to go upstairs and do it?" I asked with a devilish smile on my face.

Clinton's eyes got big, and he looked curiously at my face as if trying to read me. I stood up. He did, too.

"Sure, just show me the way," he said in a sexy, gentle kind of way.

We tiptoed up the stairs to minimize the sounds of creaking wood. My bedroom was located just to the right at the top of the stairs, so we were able to slip inside and quietly close the door.

Our passion picked up right where we had left off downstairs. Within minutes, Clinton took me to places emotionally and physically that I had never been
before—and I had considered myself to be a seasoned veteran at lovemaking.

"I thought this guy was square. Looks can really be deceiving. Here I've been
wasting my time running back and forth to Flint when I've got 'the bomb' right
here in Lansing," I remember thinking to myself afterward.

The next day I told Lisa and Valerie all about it, still grinning from ear to ear.
The female kin whom I hung out with boasted about sex, just like men.

Clinton had given me his work number soon after we started dating, but I'd
never tried to call him—until "the day after."

"This is Dr. Clinton Saunders office," his secretary said. I could tell by her
voice that she was white.

"You know what you gave me last night?" I asked in as sexy a voice as possible
when he picked up his telephone line. "Well, I want some more of that."

"Why you naughty woman, you," Clinton whispered back into the telephone.
I could tell that he was smiling, too.

"Hey, you know what Michael Jackson's latest song says, 'Don't stop till you
get enough,' and that's just what I intend to do," I said, feeling pretty darn good
about my newly found assertiveness.

I liked being bold with men. They liked it as well. I didn't want anyone—especially some *man*—telling me what to do anymore. I had paid my dues. I'd been
to hell and back. From now on, I would be calling the shots—particularly when
it came to sex. No more letting men control *when* and *where* we would "lie down."
I was going to make those decisions. And it felt good. It took me a long time to
realize it, but men were attracted to women who knew what they wanted.

—— & ——

CLINTON CAME OVER that Friday night after I had put the kids to bed around
ten. We started off laughing and talking about our escapades as teenagers. Our
chemistry was unbelievable. We grew up differently but shared many interests,
including writing and children.

One of Clinton's first jobs as a high school student was interning at the
Oakland Tribune in the sports department. He described himself as a "connoisseur
of good writing."

"My plan is to get me a college degree in something that has to do with writing. And that same energy I put into hunting down drugs, I am going to put into

pursuing my dreams," I said as we sat on the couch, with "Forever Mine," by the O'Jays, playing in the background.

I didn't learn much more about Clinton's family that night, probably because I did most of the talking. He seemed almost guarded about his personal life, which really didn't bother me. He even kept his age a secret and refused to tell me for more than three months.

"Age is just a number," he'd say every time I asked. The more he dodged the question, the more intrigued I became.

Clinton did tell me that he had three younger sisters, but they didn't grow up together. His father died when he was thirteen, and his mother died just before his high school graduation. He'd been on his own ever since, except for short stays with a few family members and friends. With no one to care for them, his sisters were placed in a foster home. Their foster parents, deeply religious and very strict, wouldn't allow them to see their brother, except in the living room of their new family's home. I think they perceived themselves as better than he was, although Clinton never said it. I could tell that experience really bothered him because he quickly changed the subject and tried to lighten the air.

It all seemed sad to me, but he wasn't seeking pity. Clinton was the most upbeat and positive-thinking person I had ever met. He walked erect, with his head held high, as if he owned the world. Clinton oozed with confidence, and I wanted some of it. I needed some of it.

A NEW YEAR, A NEW DAY

I started smoking weed again on New Year's Eve, 1980. Clinton had taken me for a late-night dinner at an upscale restaurant near downtown Lansing to celebrate the New Year. I felt as if I were dreaming.

Long-stemmed red roses sat inside crystal vases centered on each table. White table clothes with lit gold candles added a touch of elegance. A romantic from his heart, Clinton had requested a special spot when he made reservations, so our table was located in a quiet, cozy corner near the rear.

"Maybe he's beginning to fall in love with me," I thought, not believing it myself.

Clinton had too many female friends. I learned that about a month into our relationship. It seemed that everywhere we went, there was some woman who knew him. They'd hug and talk and hug some more. I stood there trying to look preoccupied with anything near me. The chatty women had big positions and degrees, like Clinton. I was still on welfare. Many of his female friends barely spoke to me, which was bad enough. But I was most humiliated by the stuck-up ones who acted as if I weren't even there, hugging and flirting and soaking up his undivided attention.

But this New Year's Eve night was mine. Clinton was the perfect gentleman—tender, adoring, and hanging on my every word. Gazing into each other's eyes, we stuffed ourselves with breads, tossed salad, and rice pilaf. Clinton ordered broiled salmon. I ate fried shrimp. At midnight, we raised our wine glasses and toasted our relationship and the new year. Life couldn't get any better as far as I was concerned.

On the way home, Clinton lit up a joint. It surprised him when I asked to take a hit.

"Are you sure you want to do this, darling?" he asked, his eyebrows raised beneath his thick glasses. "What about your calling?"

"I'm still trying to figure out what it is," I replied. "One minute I feel this strong urge to go into the ministry. The next minute I'm questioning it. If God wanted me to preach, I don't think there would be any doubt in my mind."

I reached for the marijuana cigarette and took a puff.

— ❧ —

CLASSES HAD BEEN in session a week at Lansing Community College, and I was enjoying every minute of being a college student, *again*. I carried a tote bag over-loaded with books, some just in case I found some unexpected study time. My late-morning and afternoon classes enabled me to be home with my kids when they left for school and get back home before they returned.

Every morning I walked two blocks to the bus stop on Logan Street just before daylight. Standing in the freezing morning air, waiting for the bus, I prayed that God would bless me with a car before next winter. Steady streams of headlights and cars passed me each day, some splashing rain and slush on me as they sped by.

After four babies, men still tended to give me a second look. And I had made up my mind that if someone offered me a ride on any of those mornings, I would have accepted. No one ever did. So there I stood, enduring the bitter wind and cold that snapped against my face, lifting one foot, then putting it down and rais-ing the other, constantly moving in my effort to keep warm.

"I can take it. I used to be out in the cold at all times of the day and night when I was looking for drugs. I can do the same thing to get an education," I thought.

Being a student felt natural for me. College gave me a sense of accomplish-ment and self-worth because I was doing something with my life for a change. I craved an education so badly that I kept an image of me accepting my degree in the forefront of my mind every day.

Being a student motivated me to walk straighter and not slump my shoulders or lean forward as if I were falling flat on my face. I hated the way I walked. People used to say they could recognize me a mile away. It wasn't easy trying to walk with my head held high, chin up, and shoulders back. It didn't feel natural. It was easier to do it the old way, so using correct posture was always a battle for me.

Writing 121 had me excited and nervous. The instructor was a tall white man with dark-rimmed glasses and thick, blond hair that hung on his forehead just above his eyes. He looked friendly but kept emphasizing his "high standards," and he appeared more serious than my other instructors. I liked teachers who were considered hard. I thrived on the challenge and learned more from them. But I remembered what my writing instructor at Mott Community College had said and knew that this class would make or break me.

Our first major assignment was to write a five-page paper about something we had learned to do. I couldn't wait to get started. The paper was due in two weeks. As soon as the kids crawled in bed that night, I sat on my sagging sofa, in my favorite spot, with notebook and pen, and started writing. My paper detailed how I became interested in football after seeing the Pittsburgh Steelers play.

It took me several days to complete my first draft. Being a perfectionist and a slow writer, I'd write a sentence or two, then go back and edit it several times before going on. Our instructor encouraged us to write a complete draft first, but I never could. I had to correct every misspelling and include every comma before going on to the next paragraph.

Working on the paper whenever I could—between classes, after school, and in the evenings after the kids went to bed—my most creative writing time was around four o'clock in the morning, the time I usually woke up. I'd complete my homework first and cook breakfast if time permitted, then wake the kids up around six forty-five.

The day our instructor handed the papers back, I held my breath waiting for him to call my name, nervous and praying the whole time. He finally called it, and I froze for a second or two. Slowly rising from my seat while trying to hide my nervousness, I headed toward the front of the crowded second-floor classroom. I tried to read his face when he handed me my paper, but the man who often boasted of his German heritage was expressionless. Scared, I waited until sitting back down to look at my grade. The instructor had written a big A in the upper right hand corner of my paper in red ink.

I sat at my desk bewildered. I had expected a decent grade, but I never dreamed to do that well. My heart leaped. I kept thinking, "I knew I could write. I knew I could write. That instructor in Flint was wrong."

My confidence was boosted even more by the comments written below my grade. "Excellent! Good wording. Good style. Good job." I felt like jumping up and giving everyone in the room high fives. I must have read his comments half a dozen times before our class ended, unable to concentrate on our instructions for the next paper.

I read my essay to my kids as soon as they settled in from school. Proud of their mother, they starting clapping and patting me on the back when I finished. I called Lydia in Flint and told her. School never fazed her, but my good grades always made her proud of me.

—— ๏ ——

ONE EVENING we had just finished a dinner of black-eyed peas and cornbread with fried chicken—thanks to my food stamps. Clinton had been in Washington, D.C., for a week, so I had cooked a special dinner to welcome him back. The kids were cleaning up the kitchen when I called Clinton into our living room.

"Clinton, will you take a look at this paper I wrote for class? It's due tomorrow, and I think it still needs some work. Be honest and don't worry about hurting my feelings. I learn from constructive criticism."

Clinton's chest stuck out, and he flashed a smile when I handed him my eight-page paper. But his face became serious after he started reading. A few pages later he looked up at me with a startled look on his face.

"You wrote this?" he asked, his small eyes nearly twice their normal size.

"Yes," I replied, wondering what was coming next.

"I didn't know you could write."

"But I told you that I'm taking classes in order to get some job that has to do with writing," I said, feeling a bit offended.

It seemed that every time I told somebody, especially a male, about my plans to become a writer, they'd nod or smile politely, then go on to another subject. Clinton had been different. He asked probing questions like, "What type of writer do you want to become?" and "What kind of company would you like to work for?" I had even boasted about the A and the comments my instructor had made on my first paper, so Clinton's surprise at my writing ability disappointed me a bit.

"But darling, I've done lots of traveling and seen lots of writing. And this is good writing. I had no idea you could write like this," Clinton said, my paper still in his hand.

My heart danced. His comments flattered me. Clinton made me feel prouder than ever and helped me know for sure that I could write.

—— ๏ ——

THE SMALL greeting-card store in downtown Lansing was crowded with last-minute shoppers like me. We were all looking for just the right Valentine's Day card—taking one off the shelf, reading it, and putting it back to pick up another. When I finally found the card that expressed how I *really* felt, I realized that I had fallen in love with Clinton.

The card had splashes of color, predominately red, with black script lettering. It indicated how wonderful life had been since he and I had met. The card ended with "I love you." Considering we had agreed to no commitment, I wondered whether to buy the card and read a few more. None of them said what I felt in my heart, except the one I continued to hold in my hand.

Taking the card up to the register, I paid the cashier and walked out and boarded the bus at the corner of Capital and Kalamazoo streets. All the way home, I wondered how Clinton would react to my card.

— ‰ —

CLINTON PICKED me up on Valentine's Day dressed in his typical work attire, a sharp, three hundred–dollar suit, starched white shirt, and silk tie. Sporting a fresh haircut and shave, he waited patiently, chatting with each of the kids, while I finished cooking one of their favorite meals, hamburger gravy over mashed potatoes, string beans, and warm rolls.

It was a school night, so I stuck around long enough to supervise the boys washing and drying dishes, and the girls sweeping the floor and wiping off the kitchen table and counters. There was no such thing as "boys'" chores or "girls'" chores in our house. I wanted all my kids to be able to take care of themselves with no help from anyone, if it came to that.

By the time it was dark, Clinton and I had arrived at his apartment. I laid in his arms on the living-room floor, listening to jazz. We talked about our day. During the conversation, Clinton reached over me and picked up a medium-size, thin bag that had been lying on the table near us and handed it to me.

Inside was a red heart-shaped box of chocolate candy with a card taped to it.

I couldn't wait to read the card. Sliding my long, slender fingers under the flap, I opened it, ripping the envelope nearly in half. My heart fell when I read the words "Thank-you for being my *friend*," and could barely finish reading it. Clinton's card made me even more nervous about giving him mine. But I had mentioned my card to him already. He had seemed pleased, saying, "How wonderful, my darling!"

I rose from the carpeted floor and slowly picked up my black, imitation-·leather purse that had been sitting on the end of his sofa. Clinton got up and strolled into his bedroom, then returned carrying a letter opener. I reluctantly slid the red envelope out of the side pocket of my purse and handed him the card. He lay on the sofa. I scooted in front of him on the floor, praying he would be happy to know my true feelings and hoping I was doing the right thing.

He took the letter opener and ran it along the crease at the top of the envelope. Unlike mine, his envelope was cut so perfectly I could barely tell it had been opened.

I watched and held my breath as he read it to himself and would never forget his face when he looked up. It was as if he felt sorry for me.

"I'm sorry, dear, but I don't want you to fall in love with me," he said, staring me straight in the face. "There's no way we can do that."

"Why?" I asked, barely above a whisper, my heart pounding so loud I thought he could hear it.

"Because we can't. We had an agreement that we wouldn't expect any commitment from each other. And I've told you before that I have lots of female friends," he said, his voice sounding more firm, the pity evaporating from his face.

I had prepared myself for that possible reaction. So it didn't devastate me like it could have. But it was the pity in his eyes that bothered me most. I didn't know what it meant.

"Then I'd like to know where you see our relationship heading," I said, each word choking my throat to come out. "I don't understand how you can expect us to spend as much time as we do together, and do the things we do, without eventually falling in love."

I don't think he answered my question directly, which was unusual for him. He mumbled something about "being hurt before," and gave me no reason to think that our relationship could grow to the point of him ever falling in love with me.

༉ <u>MORE</u> GRACE

S pringtime on the Lansing Community College's campus was beautiful. Tulips and daffodils in full bloom protruded from cement planters, huge cylinder-like structures that sat outside each brick building. It was May 1980, and we had been having picture-perfect days for a couple of weeks. I loved walking across campus, especially carrying my large, brown art portfolio, made of imitation leather. It was about four inches thick and zipped along three sides. I felt like an artist in the rough.

My art class frustrated me. Every student in there could draw better than I could and appeared much more relaxed in the art studio. I was being particularly hard on myself one afternoon and mentioned to the instructor my thoughts of withdrawing from the class.

"Oh no. Please don't do that, Jasmine," said the redheaded female, reaching for my shoulder, her half-dozen bangle bracelets jangling on her wrist. "Just give it until the end of the term. And if you don't see any growth in your portfolio, then I can see you doing that. But please don't give up so easily. You have lots of potential."

I decided to stick it out and was glad. Art became my outlet. I could lose my-self drawing a still life or human figure for the entire four-hour class. Although twelve years older than most students in my class, I made several friends, male and female. One student, Nancy Helou, was an excellent artist. We started talking during our fifteen-minute break every class.

"You're raising four kids by yourself?" the blonde, slightly overweight woman asked me one day, appearing stunned by my revelation—like most people. "But you don't look old enough."

"I just got started young. Then didn't know how to stop," I said lightheartedly. We both laughed.

— ℘ —

CLINTON COACHED ME through the process of applying for a federal student loan. Although my tuition and books had been paid through grants, I had no idea that I qualified for additional monies.

"Now remember, dear, this is a *loan*. There's a big difference between loans and grants. Grants are given to you. Loans you have to pay back, starting six months after you graduate."

I didn't care. Graduation seemed a long way off. I was dealing with the here and now. If it weren't for Clinton lending me money, we would have gone hungry the last few days of the month, for sure. He'd pick up bread or milk at the store. He bought hats and gloves for the kids. He often lent me money for art supplies, which were expensive. I always tried paying him back. Sometimes he refused the money.

"I pray that by the time I graduate, I'll be able to find a good-paying job within six months. Then I'd be able to pay off my student loans," I told Clinton.

The loan was approved, but it took another six to eight weeks to get the check. I'd never had fourteen hundred dollars, to spend as I pleased, in my entire life. Excited, I started telling Clinton all the things I planned to buy with the money. My "list" became an inside joke between us.

"But darling, your money will only go so far. You'll be broke before you get halfway through all the things you're talking about buying," he cautioned each time I added to my list.

That didn't matter. I enjoyed just pretending to be able to buy certain things. The check came in late May, and reality set in. I needed a car more than anything and couldn't take my mind off those cold winter mornings I stood at the bus stop before daylight.

One day I mentioned to Nancy that I was having no luck in finding a decent car that I could afford. Her face lit up.

"My uncle has a car he's planning to sell," she said. "I can call him and arrange to take you out to his house to look at it."

— ℘ —

NANCY'S UNCLE, a retired college professor, was a distinguished-looking man who lived in the suburbs. He was looking under the hood at the engine when we pulled up in his driveway. His head popped out, and he smiled as we walked toward him.

"Hi, Uncle Frank. This is the friend I told you about," Nancy said, trotting up to the tall, rosy-cheeked man, whose only hair was a white layer around his ears and the back of his head. She stood on her toes to give him a quick hug, then turned and introduced me.

Nancy's uncle was a warm and friendly man who liked to talk, especially about his hobby—tinkering with cars. He pointed out every part he'd ever put on the 1972 Oldsmobile Delta Eighty-eight, then explained why he did it. He chatted about changing the oil himself, every three thousand miles, and spark plugs and cylinders. I liked the color, yellow with a green vinyl top and dark green uphol-stery. The backseats were spotless, looking as if no one had ever sat on them.

"There's not a dent or rust spot on this car," I said, walking around it with Nancy and noticing that their garage was also spotless.

I waited until we were ready to go before bringing up the subject of money. The uncle looked deep into my eyes and spoke.

"Nancy told me that you are raising four kids and trying to go to school. And that you're doing it all by yourself," he said in a soft, serious voice.

I nodded my head.

"I had planned to advertise it in the newspaper for eight hundred dollars. But I'll sell it to you for four hundred," he said.

I jumped at the offer. Clinton took me back to his house around seven o'clock that evening. I brought Nancy's uncle the money, and he gave me the title to the car.

WHO <u>KNOWS</u> WHOM

The admission and financial aid forms for Michigan State University (MSU) were long and required lots of time and thought, but I was determined to read and complete each one. It was the end of June 1980, and I had successfully completed two six-week terms at Lansing Community College, and was ready to take the next step.

"I don't have the luxury of taking my time to get a bachelor's degree. I've got to graduate as soon as possible so that I can get a decent-paying job," I thought over and over again.

Clinton encouraged me to get my application in as soon as possible, saying many college students already had probably applied, some as early as February.

Forms and applications made me nervous, often overwhelming me. As a senior in high school, in the fall of 1966, I wrote Flint Junior College, requesting an application for admission. My plan was to move in with my dad after graduating from high school and to attend junior college in Flint. School officials promptly mailed me a brown, legal-size envelope, thick with application forms. Excited at first, I took it to school the next day and started trying to complete the information during my free time.

Questions about my parents' income, taxes, and other things troubled me. I had never asked Momma anything about her income. My dad's either. Many questions on the application forms didn't apply to our household. Others, I didn't understand. Halfway down the first page I got so frustrated that I crumpled the forms into a ball and threw them in a wastebasket near the door as I walked out of a classroom. Although that was fifteen years earlier, it had been the one of the biggest mistakes I'd ever made in my life. I wasn't about to repeat it.

It took me more than a week to complete all the forms MSU sent. When I finished and finally dropped a large white envelope in the mailbox, I felt so good and very hopeful. Clinton called me up and invited me to dinner to celebrate. All I talked about at the restaurant that night was becoming a Michigan State University Spartan.

"Darling, you're the most focused person I've ever met in my life. And you're just a wonderful mother. I've always said that all you need is an opportunity," he said, patting my hands as we sat at the restaurant table. I had gotten used to Clinton's touchy-feely behavior. Now, it felt good to me.

A month passed before the mailman delivered a letter to my house with the MSU logo on the envelope. I tore it open immediately, and the words stunned me.

"Unfortunately, your request for admission has been denied at this time."

My mind went blank for a few seconds, then I burst into tears. I called the number at the bottom of the page and talked to a man who looked up my records. He said the admissions committee based its decision on two things: I had been out of high school for over ten years, and I had dropped out of Mott Community College in the winter of 1979.

It had never crossed my mind that MSU might turn me down. My grade point average at Lansing Community College was 3.25, and my midterm grade point average in Flint had been 3.50. Devastated, I cried so hard that at one point, it became hard to breathe. Still whimpering and feeling sorry for myself, I dialed Clinton's number at work.

"I'm so sorry to hear that, dear," he said, sounding disappointed, too. "But don't ever give up. Remember that. Don't ever, ever give up. Besides, I've got some friends who work out there on campus, and I'll give them a call right now. I promise to do everything possible to get you enrolled in Michigan State University this fall. Trust me."

—— ℅ ——

I WANTED TO believe that there was still a chance for me to become an MSU student, but things hadn't been going well for me the past several weeks. Two months behind in my rent, I received a summons to appear in court. A sympathetic judge dropped one month's rent after I told him all the cleaning and painting we'd done in the house prior to moving in—without any compensation from the landlord.

The judge ordered me to pay two months of payments—one month back rent and the rent for June, totaling $430, which included $40 court costs. There was no way I could pay that much and still feed my kids. My ADC checks on the first and sixteenth combined only came to $396. That, plus $330 in food stamps, still wasn't enough to feed four growing kids.

Midway through reading the rejection letter from MSU for the fifth time, I fell to my knees and started praying and crying until the pain of disappointment eased up and I was exhausted. I had four kids to think about. I had to fix dinner. I had to get clothes ready for the next day. I had to keep moving or it seemed as if I'd die.

Just before five o'clock that evening, I received a call from Ann Merriweather, a friend of Clinton's who worked at MSU. He'd never mentioned her name before. A college administrator, Ann worked in admissions.

"Jasmine, would you be able to meet with me tomorrow?" she asked, after informing me of her conversation with Clinton.

"Sure."

"In the meantime, I'm going to start making some contacts," she continued. "It's nearly July, and they'll need to reconsider your application right away if you want to enroll for fall term."

Ann and I met the following day at two thirty in her office. It was located on the second floor of one of the oldest buildings on campus, halfway down a dim, narrow hallway. A petite female, Ann didn't look a day over twenty-three. Clinton had told me the night before that she was twenty-nine. They had met while working at Dartmouth College in New Hampshire. She was very friendly and spoke optimistically about my chances of being admitted.

I told Ann about my lifelong dream to graduate from college. I told her about my kids and my turbulent marriage.

"I would be the first person in my huge family to earn a four-year degree," I said, my eyes wide and expressive.

Ann listened silently, occasionally nodding her head or raising her eyebrows. I felt comfortable talking to her. It never took me long to decide whether I liked a person or not. I liked Ann.

Our meeting ended with her suggesting that I write a letter to the admissions department, explaining my reasons for dropping out of Mott Community College.

"You don't have to go into a lot of detail, but just give them the basic facts," she said.

I drafted the letter that same night and drove down to Clinton's office the next morning to type it. He read the letter and made a few suggestions while smiling at me.

"Beautiful, you're so sweet. If people only knew how good you are. I keep saying, all you need is a chance," he said, embracing me in his arms.

Two anxious weeks later the mailman delivered another letter bearing MSU's logo. The letter informed me that the admissions committee had reversed its decision and that I could register for fall term, 1980.

"Please be aware that you will be placed on academic probation for one year," the letter read.

That didn't bother me one bit. I had convinced myself several months earlier that if anyone else could earn a college degree, I could, too.

Clinton kissed me when we saw each other right after he got off work. I dressed up in my nicest black slacks with a matching black-and-white-checked jacket, tossed a red scarf around my neck, and we went out for dinner and a drink that night to celebrate.

OKEMOS

The want ad section of the Sunday *Lansing State Journal* offered two pages of apartments, houses, and town houses for rent. Most of the decent-sounding places were too expensive, required a one-month security deposit, or didn't rent to people with children or pets. I needed to get moved and settled before school opened and my MSU classes started.

My eyes caught a large ad for apartments in Okemos. I'd heard of Okemos, but had no idea where it was. In tall script letters the ad read, "Conveniently located near MSU and city bus stop," but anywhere past Aurelius Road was out in the boondocks to me.

Centered in the three-column page ad was a sketch of a lovely brick apartment building with a balcony and surrounded by flowers and trees. After reading the words "No security deposit required" underneath the picture, I picked up the telephone so quickly that it fell off my glass coffee table. It was still dangling by its cord while I was trying to dial the number at the bottom of the ad.

— ❧ —

ALBERT AND PENNY rode with me twenty miles out to the complex after Sunday worship service. My Delta Eighty-eight hummed down the long stretch of highway. The rental office manager, a dishwater blonde woman who appeared to be in her late thirties, took the three of us on a tour of a three-bedroom "garden level" apartment that had been recently painted. It was the only one available.

"Do you accept people on ADC?" I asked, holding my breath.

She answered yes so casually that it took me by surprise. I was used to getting a pause, at least. I wasn't thrilled about living on the garden level, which was the basement as far as I was concerned. But I fell in love with the place and its L-shaped floor plan immediately. It was bright. Cheery. Lots of space.

"I could cook in the kitchen and watch television in the living room," I thought as we strolled from room to room. Two bedrooms were on one side of a hall and faced the bathroom. The master bedroom was at the end of the hall and had its own half bath. It would be our first time living in a home with more than one bathroom. I welcomed anything that would help alleviate the morning congestion when all five of us were trying to get dressed at the same time.

Many of the apartment dwellers were college students, the kind of learning environment I wanted for my kids and me. With central air conditioning and free utilities, Valley View Apartments seemed to be the perfect place to restart my life and college career. I prayed that my credit would be approved. Several days later it was. Another miracle.

My check came eight days later, on the first of August. The kids and I were beaming as our trusty car cruised down the highway. Twenty minutes later I was paying the office manager my first month's rent. She handed me the keys. I walked, and the kids skipped beside me, to see our new home.

— ॐ —

THE BEAT-UP truck that Albert borrowed from a friend was loaded and ready to go by eight o'clock one Saturday morning in August. He had to return it by five. The kids and I climbed into our Oldsmobile and drove the long stretch of Mt. Hope Road to Okemos. They had been chattering and arguing about who was going to get which bedroom before we pulled out of our driveway.

"Okay you guys. You've got to settle down now. We're almost there," I said, after passing the "Welcome to Okemos" sign.

Silence.

The scenery was beautiful: long fields of green, freshly cut grass, its smell drifting through our open windows. Big brick homes. Subdivisions. Parks. Even a small wooden bridge. The upper-middle-class community looked enchanting.

Albert, Penny, and I unloaded the sofa and carried it out of the parking lot and down a few steps. We were walking down the long sidewalk leading to our apartment when the sound of Roberta Flack singing "The First Time Ever I Saw Your Face" came floating from an upstairs window. I closed my eyes and thanked God for such a beautiful welcoming. The skies were blue, and the sun was shining. I felt in my heart it was going to be a good move for all of us.

Albert, Penny, and Terrance helped us put up beds before going back to Lansing. The kids and I worked feverishly until well past midnight because I wanted all my furniture to be neatly in place before retiring for the night. It was. Most of our clothes were hung up or put away in drawers by the time the kids started bickering and arguing with each other. I knew they were tired, and it was time to quit for the night. The clock said two eighteen.

—— ℅ ——

"I WANT YOU to stay inside and settle down for another day before going outside to check out the neighborhood," I explained the morning after we moved in. "You're still a little too excited. These people out here don't know anything about us, and I don't want them thinking that we're a bunch of rowdy folks."

Their faces dropped in disappointment, but they understood. I cooked chicken and dumplings for dinner, and we spent the day relaxing and watching television together in our new home.

The next morning, the kids got up before me. Staggering into the living room, I was surprised to find my four darlings dressed and ready. Their cereal bowls were in the sink. The twins had combed each other's hair, something they had done since age seven. Their ponytails stuck out and hung just above their shoulders and even had barrettes, turned backward, on the ends.

The boys had brushed their hair as well. Andre loved his wavy hair and had put so much grease in one spot that it was slicked to his head. I had taught them to keep their naturally dry skin oiled. Their faces, tanned by the summer sun, were shining from putting on too much petroleum jelly.

It was a Kodak moment. I felt proud of my kids for being so independent and became more determined than ever to continue raising them that way. Still feeling a bit uneasy, I looked each of them over carefully, hoping to find any excuse to keep them in a little longer. None. Their ears were clean. Their teeth were brushed. They had even slung their washrags over the towel bars in the bathroom, rather than leaving them in a heap in the tub or on the floor. I had to keep my word.

Looking each of them straight in the eyes, I told them that we needed to have a quick talk. I started with, "I need y'all to listen to me because this is very, very important." Those words usually got their undivided attention.

"I don't want y'all talking loud and arguing with each other out there. These people out here probably aren't used to a lot of noise and confusion. And keep in mind that somebody's always gonna be watching you cause you're the new kids on the block. So don't leave away from the sight of our building, and you all know better than to go up in somebody's house."

The temperature in Okemos had been dropping, according to the local weatherman on TV. The sky looked gray, so I went outside to check before giving the kids the green light. Though it was the first of September, I insisted that the kids wear their jackets. They hustled back to their bedrooms, quickly returned, each struggling to get into a jacket. Andre was first. Kendra was second. Lamar and Kamari tore out of the door together. I held my breath.

Less than an hour later, they knocked on the wooden door. Opening it, I knew something was wrong by the looks on their faces. The most vocal, Kamari spoke up before I could close the door behind them.

"Mom, don't none of these white people around here like black kids," she said dejectedly, attempting to pull her arm from her jacket sleeve.

My heart started pounding. Afraid to ask the next question, I had to.

"Why do you say that?"

"Cause everybody we tried to play with said that their parents don't allow them to play with black kids," she said, slinging her jacket on the closet floor.

My mind flashed back to Lydia's comments about white people. I fought my sense of panic and turned to God instead. My knees were so weak they trembled. We gathered around the kitchen table first, held hands, and prayed. Then we had one of our long, serious, talks.

"If the kids around here don't want to play with y'all, that's their loss. There's enough of you to play by yourselves. None of you have to beg *anybody* to play with you. Being prejudiced is stupid and based on ignorance," I said, getting madder the more I talked.

"But why are they like that?" Kendra said, contorting her face, then thrusting herself against the back of the kitchen chair. "We ain't never did anything to them. It's not fair."

My heart wrenched. Tears welled up in my eyes. Lips trembling and scrambling for words, I tried my best to explain.

"I know it's not fair, honey, but that's just the way life is sometimes. It's not always fair. And it's okay to be hurt and disappointed," I said, struggling to maintain some sense of composure. "But you can't let this get you down too much. You just *know* and keep *believing* that you're all wonderful kids. I know it. And God knows it. And quiet as it's kept, that's all that really matters."

"Besides," I continued, "I don't want you playing with people who are prejudiced anyway. I want you to stay as far away from people like that as possible."

By then all five of us were crying. I thought my ordeal with Cordell was hard on us. This was just as hard. We were living half an hour from Lansing in a lily-white community that seemed to despise us simply because I was a black woman on welfare raising four children alone.

I couldn't tell whether my kids were listening or not. Andre hung his head and kicked his feet back and forth under the table. Lamar sat slumped in his seat, picking his fingernails, a nervous habit he picked up from me. Kendra sat staring down at the table, her arms folded tightly across her chest. Kamari was the only one who looked at me from time to time, while drawing imaginary circles on the table with her finger.

ON MY MIND

Clinton was trying to put some distance between us, and I could tell it. He still called nearly every day, but he visited mainly during the week. He had started spending his weekends out of town again, driving to Detroit, Ann Arbor, and Ypsilanti, his old stomping grounds.

One afternoon he called and invited me to meet him for lunch in a downtown Lansing café. We were laughing and talking in the small sandwich shop when a woman he knew, dressed to the hilt, strutted up to our table, her open-toed high heels clicking on the tile floor. They laughed and talked for ten minutes, never even acknowledging my presence until Clinton remembered and introduced us. That happened a lot. Each time it made me madder and madder.

"It's disrespectful to me," I explained to him during the drive back to my house. "Those women know exactly what they're doing by ignoring me. Women can be very sneaky and conniving toward other women. Trust me on this one. I'm a woman. I know."

"This is just the way I am," Clinton replied. "I'm just a charming guy who tries to be a kind, caring, and loving person to everyone."

"You call it *charming*. I call it being extremely flirty," I snapped.

Silence. Tension. Regret. I hated arguing with Clinton. When our relationship was good—which was most of the time—it was *really* good. Sometimes I couldn't believe that the Lord had sent someone so wonderful and loving to both me and my kids.

Our arguments were so rare that when they did occur, the emotional pain tore me apart. My stomach ached. My heart felt like lead. I'd wake up in the morning, and as soon as reality hit, a dark cloud hovered over my heart. I felt as if I'd lost my best friend. It never seemed to bother Clinton, though. He had other things on his mind—women, women, and more women.

—— ❧ ——

LOSING CLINTON'S affection was hard, but I had to keep moving forward. Pressuring a man for attention just wasn't my style anymore, regardless of how much I loved him. No more begging men to spend time with me. No more putting a man before my kids. No more yelling and cussing about other women. No more sitting around waiting and wondering what my man was doing. Cordell's craziness put an end to all of that.

But never in my wildest dreams did I expect to run across someone like Clinton. He was everything I wanted in a man and a father. With no kids of his own, Clinton spent more time with my kids than any man ever had. He took the twins to work with him one day, simply because they were so curious about what he did for a living. Kendra came home saying, "When I grow up, I'm gonna get a Ph.D., too."

Clinton took Andre to a youth leadership workshop in Pontiac one afternoon. He presented leadership workshops to students around the state. Andre came home impressed and would talk about Clinton's exciting presentation for years afterward. Clinton took us all to our first live Detroit Tigers baseball game and even arranged for Lamar to meet Rudy May, a New York Yankees pitcher. Clinton and Rudy had attended Castlemont High School in Oakland, California, at the same time. Rudy graciously spoke with us for several minutes at the wire fence before the game and even signed a baseball for Lamar.

Clinton definitely had a good heart. He was an outstanding role model for my kids and an absolute inspiration to me. But the man stayed up in women's faces all the time, grinning and hugging them during their entire conversation, while I stood around looking stupid.

"It's one thing to give a person a hug. It's another to just wrap yourselves up in them—especially in my presence. I don't know what kind of women you've been dating in the past, Clinton, but I don't believe they took this kind of behavior off of you. And even if they did, I'm not," I said after every party or social event we attended.

Unlike Cordell and I had, we didn't we cuss or call each other names. Arguing always made Clinton uncomfortable, and it showed. And when a cuss word did pop up during a heated discussion, it usually came from me. It was still hard for me to argue without swearing. Using profanity was a habit that was difficult to break, but I was determined to do it. The only real issue in our relationship was Clinton's behavior with his female friends. And he made it clear over and over again that there was no room for compromise.

"This is the way I've always been, and I'm not going to stop now, just because you have a problem with it," he'd say, his whole demeanor tensing up.

I didn't like it. So I gave him his space and focused my attention on moving and getting prepared for classes. We still saw and talked to each other regularly, and our sex life was still like fireworks in July. But I sensed Clinton's attention turning elsewhere and wasn't about to run after *any* man anymore. I had set some new standards.

—— ≈ ——

CLINTON STUNNED me one Sunday morning by joining Grace Baptist Church. I had joined a year earlier. He'd been going consistently for several months. I was so happy for him. Clinton had first joined church at an early age, but like me, he had stopped going. He thought that most ministers took advantage of their congregations. He never called them pimps, but that was the impression I got from him.

"How is some man going to tell me how to live my life when he's doing things just as bad, if not worse, than me," Clinton would say.

"See, that's the big misunderstanding about church. People think we go because we think we *deserve* to be there. We go because we know we *need* to be there. We know that we're sinners and need God in our lives," I'd counter.

But there was a more personal reason why I loved and trusted the Lord, and it had nothing to do with preachers or church.

"I'm not going just by what someone told me or what I read. I'm going based on my own personal experiences. I know what the Lord has done for me in my life. He has brought me through so much pain and turmoil that sometimes I can't do anything but drop to my knees in awe. I'm just so grateful for his power and mercy, and thankful to know him," I had said during one of our late-night discussions in Clinton's bed. "There's no doubt in my mind that there is a God who's been looking over me—even when I didn't have sense enough to look out for myself."

Sure enough, Clinton eventually started going to church. We seldom sat together. I figured he didn't want to be seen with me and all my kids. But that was okay. At least he was going. That was the most important thing.

One Sunday he approached me after church and told me that we needed to talk. Clinton seemed unusually withdrawn and uncomfortable. All afternoon I thought about what he might say. After driving the kids home and getting them fed and settled in to watching television, I waited for Clinton to pick me up. It was well past three o'clock when he drove me to our favorite eating place.

"Maybe he finally realizes that he is in love with me, and plans to propose," I thought on the way. "Or maybe he's going to say that he'll stop seeing other women. That would be almost as good."

I was wrong.

"Jasmine, I don't want to see you anymore," he said, staring straight into my eyes as I nibbled on a warm croissant.

Startled, I looked around to see if anyone else had overheard his statement. A middle-aged white woman, sitting alone at the table next to us, glanced at me with pity in her eyes, as if she couldn't believe her ears either.

"Is there someone else?" I asked, feeling as if my world had shattered.

"No."

"Then why are you doing this?"

"I just don't want to see you anymore. That's all," he said, looking a bit nervous.

Despite his denial, I suspected he was seeing another woman. A part of me wanted to beg him not to do that. I loved every minute we spent together. We were so different, yet so compatible. But the bigger part of me wasn't about to beg.

"Well, if that's all you needed to talk to me about, I guess there's nothing left to do but take me home," I replied.

There was very little said between us during our fifteen-minute drive back to Okemos. Clinton came inside and talked to each of the kids for a few minutes, then left.

"I'm not going to call him or anything," I thought. "I don't need anybody who just pops up out of the clear blue sky and says we're through. I know he's got somebody else. But he's going to be like all the rest and find out one day that I'm a hard act to follow. And by then, it'll be too late."

On Sundays, I barely spoke to Clinton at church. But he went out of his way to be nice to me, probably out of guilt. I missed Clinton—a whole lot. But something deep inside of me wouldn't allow me to want someone who didn't want me. Been there, done that.

"Lord, if it's meant for us to be together, I know that you will see that it happens. And if it's not meant to be, please help me to accept your will," I prayed throughout the day and every night before going to bed.

Three weeks after Clinton dumped me, I rode down to Jackson with Lisa, Penny, and the kids after church. I parked my dependable but twice-dented car on the street alongside Penny's house on Pennsylvania Avenue. My life still felt empty without Clinton, but I kept putting one foot in front of the other. I had to. We returned from Jackson after dark, and I noticed a letter stuck under my windshield wipers when pulling off in my car.

Folded and written on yellow, legal-size paper, Clinton's letter finally said some of the things I desperately wanted to hear.

"I want you to see you again, Jasmine. I know that now. My life isn't the same without you," I read, my heart beating a mile a minute. "I don't know where this all will lead. But the only thing I know for sure is that I want you in my life."

That was good enough for me. One month later, we were seeing each other regularly again.

egistering for classes at MSU took every bit of eight hours. I was there when
the doors opened at eight o'clock in the morning. When I came back out,
the sun was setting in the west, casting an orange glow over the landscape.
Trudging a mile back to my car, I smiled at my picture identification card most of
the way. It looked just like I felt—tired and sweaty and relieved.

Clinton was waiting for me when I got to my car. It was a nice surprise after
such a grueling experience.

"Well, beautiful, you've done it. You're an official MSU student now. Con-
gratulations!" Clinton said, with a look on his face as proud as mine.

"Thanks. I feel like I just worked an eight-hour job in a factory somewhere.
But it was well worth it," I replied.

By this time we were face to face—almost nose to nose. He reached out to
me, and I rushed into his arms, feeling an incredible sense of accomplishment.
We stood there a minute or two, hugging and gently swaying to our spiritual
rhythm and saying nothing.

There was a time—not long before—when I would have felt uncomfortable
embracing in front of people, particularly for any length of time. My relationship
with Clinton was changing all of that.

"Let's go to dinner to celebrate," he whispered in my ear. I nodded.

Clinton arranged to pick me up after I had cooked dinner for the kids. They
ate homemade spaghetti and cornbread. We took turns washing dishes, so it was
the boys' week. By the time Clinton had arrived at seven, the kitchen was clean,
and the kids had started on their homework. I didn't feel as comfortable leaving
my kids alone in Okemos. The problems with our neighbors had grown much
worse.

One afternoon my kids came running home from the school saying some adults met them at the bus stop carrying baseball bats. They scared my kids to death. The following morning I walked them to the bus stop and watched them board the bus. A half a dozen women had congregated and blocked the sidewalk when I turned to leave. I walked right through them and cut my eyes at one woman who had come to our house and welcomed us to the neighborhood a week earlier. She looked embarrassed and dropped her head.

"I can't believe that people are still so prejudiced. Here it is 1980, and these people out here act like the racists you see on television," I told Clinton as we headed out the door to celebrate.

Turning to the kids, I gave them some last-minute instructions.

"Remember. Don't tell anyone that I'm not home, except Lisa, Penny, and Albert, if they call—nobody else. And don't let anybody in this house, and *do not* go outside," I said firmly. "The last thing I need is for something to happen and I'm not even home."

Clinton chose a nearby restaurant and ordered his usual broiled salmon. I ordered my usual fried shrimp, although both of us read our menus carefully. That was one of the many things we had in common.

After dinner, Clinton made a toast, raising his glass of white wine and clinking it against mine.

"To your success as an MSU student, to your continued success as a mother, and to your future success as a professional writer," he said, beaming with pride.

—— ℘ ——

FRESHMEN CLASSES started at eight o'clock every morning, which was fine with me, being an early riser. The first one up, I'd iron the kids' clothes and fix breakfast before taking a bath and dressing. By seven fifteen I was ready to leave for campus. The kids' school bus came a little over an hour later, so most times they'd sit and watch cartoons until it arrived.

Monday through Friday I drove a mile down Okemos Road to the parking lot of a large supermarket. Leaving my car, I then caught the city bus to MSU because of difficulty finding parking on campus. I had the routine down pat and even managed to study during the half-hour bus ride to campus. I had learned to study whenever and wherever possible.

I loved walking to classes across MSU's campus. The smell of foliage, the energy of students rushing by, the cars, the bikes, it felt invigorating. I felt as if I belonged there. Making my way through throngs of students, some walking, others dodging me on bikes, and a few gliding around the campus on roller skates, I soaked it all in. Everything.

My most difficult class was Natural Science. It was hard for me to visualize how cells functioned within the body. Understanding how plants turn sunlight into food was just as challenging. My brain just didn't work that way. One day I sought help from my science professor, who was floored when I mentioned being a single mother raising four kids.

"Oh my God!" she exclaimed, laying her hand against the side of her face. "And I thought you were one of these twenty-year-old students running around here."

Most people thought the same thing until I told them differently. Looking nearly ten years younger turned out to be a good thing after all. Once I revealed my age to my fellow classmates, they treated me with more respect. That was a pleasant surprise.

Most enjoyable was my art class, because I could lose myself for four hours, forgetting about everything around me. It was incredibly therapeutic. I thanked God many times for the art instructor at Lansing Community College who had convinced me to stick out her class for at least one term. Through art, I learned that my strength was working with color, design, and large spaces.

It seemed that every student I befriended—black or white—knew more about black history than I did. It was embarrassing. Wanting to learn more about my heritage, I decided to do my research papers on some aspect of black history whenever possible. It was very enlightening and helped me realize how strong we really were. The more I learned, the prouder I became.

❀ OKEMOS'S SECRET

Okemos was a small, quiet community where elderly couples walked down the roads hand in hand after dark. Parks and playgrounds were filled with children and parents playing ball at dusk. Joggers pounded the pavements at five o'clock in the morning, sweatbands around their heads, earphones to their ears. If there was such a place as utopia, Okemos appeared to be it. On the outside.

There was an undercurrent in the small, upper-middle-class community, invisible to the naked eye and probably most of its white residents. I felt it everywhere but most often while shopping, especially with food stamps. Cashiers stared down at my primary food source with disgust written all over their faces. A few had the nerve to snatch my stamps from me without looking up. They saw food stamps and a black woman using them. That's all they needed to know.

One female cashier, who looked around my age, had the audacity to sling a loaf of bread at me.

"I'd like it in a bag," I said, just above a whisper.

She rolled her eyes and started grinning and talking to the customer behind me. Both were white. I'd been tiptoeing around Okemos, trying not to cause any trouble, even though most of our neighbors seemed hell-bent on running us out. But I couldn't let her get away with treating me that way. I'd seen white people treat dogs better than they were treating my family and me.

I sought out the manager and told him what had happened. The chubby white man looked down his nose at me. No apology. No bag. I doubt that he even bothered to say anything to the rude cashier. She watched me storm out of the store with a smug look on her face.

It didn't take my kids long to figure out whom to play with and whom to keep a safe arm's distance away. They made lots of friends—kids and adults alike. But they learned that some adults could be cruel, especially when they drank.

One day a twenty-something-year-old guy who they thought a lot of was standing on a nearby balcony with a group of friends. All of them had cans of beer in their hands. He beckoned Andre to come closer, then called him a "baby slave." My oldest son came in the house and told me, looking so hurt.

I started to say something to the guy, but my better judgment said no. I called the rental office for the fifth or sixth time, and the lack of response told me that they were growing tired of us, too. This was October, a month and a half into the school year.

Even the schools gave us the blues. Other children taunted and called my kids names nearly every day. I'll never forget the day Andre came home with a surprise announcement that underscored our entire experience.

"This is the first time that I went the whole day at school and no one called me a nigger," he said.

— ፰ —

I WENT TO CAMPUS to get a library book one Saturday morning and returned to find all of my kids locked up in the house, looking scared to death.

"Trevor Brooks and some of his friends threw Kamari in the dumpster," Andre said, wiping tears from his light brown eyes. "I told them to stop, but they wouldn't listen. And we weren't even messing with them. We just were playing kickball at the playground."

By the time they told me the whole story, I wanted to kill somebody. First, the white teenage boys took their kickball. When Kendra insisted they give it back, they started bouncing it off her head—and laughing about it. That's when Kamari stepped in and told them to stop. That angered the teens. They called some little girls playing on the playground and ordered them to beat my daughters up.

"And if you try to fight back, we're going to beat your little black asses," the bullies had said.

Tears filled my eyes when Lamar told me how my poor children stood by helplessly while some girls, with whom they had been previously playing, started hitting and kicking my daughters. It reminded me of lynch mobs I was reading about in the South.

"And when this girl started choking Kendra and pinching her neck," Kamari said, her eyes big as balloons, "I told her to stop hurting my sister. That's when Trevor picked me up and carried me over to the dumpster and threw me in."

Her face scratched and bruised, she looked terrified. I tended to her wounds and examined her broken eyeglasses. My next instinct was to hunt down the culprits and try to kick all of their asses. But I had sense enough to know that acting crazy out in Okemos wouldn't get me anything but some jail time. I had to say a quick prayer to calm down before speaking.

"That's what they expect black people to do—act a fool. But we're not going to do that. We're going to call the police and let them handle it. That's how you deal with racist people," I said while thumbing through the phone book for the Meridian Township police's number.

One of my biggest mistakes was explaining my complaint over the phone. We waited half an hour, and no one came. Knowing the small police station was only two miles away, I called again. And again. And again. I made four calls before a policeman showed up at our door, two hours after my initial contact. By then I was so mad, I wanted to cuss him out, but didn't. I kept my cool, keeping in mind that my kids were watching and we still had to live there.

The responding police officer looked like the all-American guy—tall, dark hair, and clean cut. His chest stuck out. I was disappointed when he refused my offer to come join us around the kitchen table. He stood near the door, as if he thought he'd catch something or was uncomfortable being there. That hurt—all of us. I could see it in my kids' eyes.

I began telling the officer what had happened and became so emotional that I started crying, barely able to finish. The kids panicked and rushed over to me and started patting and rubbing my back, trying to console me. Then they started crying, too.

Still standing at the door, the officer was expressionless, almost looking bored. I wanted him to say something comforting or at least give my family hope of living in Okemos in peace. But he didn't. He just stood there looking at us as if we were from another planet, taking no notes and asking few questions. I had to offer the boy's name.

"Well, I'm sorry, ma'am, but maybe you need to start keeping your kids closer to home. That's what most parents are *supposed* to do."

It couldn't have hurt worse if he had slapped me. Our whole little corner of the world seemed to be going crazy, and there was nowhere to run or hide.

"You mean to tell me that a sixteen-year-old boy can throw my nine-year-old child in the trash, and there's nothing you can do?" I asked with indignation and disbelief. "What about her glasses? I'm on ADC and can't possibly afford to replace them."

He might as well have said the whole thing was my problem.

"We don't have enough manpower to go knocking on doors, looking for kids who got in a little spat. Besides, it's her word against his."

I wanted to spit on him. He was so cold and detached that it scared me. I broke down crying again. I started begging.

"But we have witnesses. My kids saw it. Their friends saw it. So it's not just one person's word against another," I sobbed uncontrollably.

The man waited until I finished, then repeated his characterization of the incident as "kids' spatting." By that time I was ready for him to leave. I thanked him for his time and opened the door. He left without saying anything else. It was the most frustrating and disappointing encounter I'd ever had with a police officer in my life. And during my drug-using days, I'd had many.

"He acts like he don't like black people either," Kamari said as soon as I closed the door.

I agreed. But I wasn't about to let the whole thing go. I called up some of the kids who had witnessed the incident and found out where Trevor lived.

"Tomorrow, we're going to pay Trevor and his parents a visit after church," I informed my family after hanging up.

The next day we all put on our Sunday best and went to church. I prayed and prayed and prayed about our situation, feeling pretty good about my Christ-like approach. After worship service, I drove the kids back to Okemos and decided to drop the boys off at home. I didn't want Trevor's parents to see five black people standing at their door and panic.

"Now, I want ya'll to let me do the talking," I reminded my unusually subdued daughters as we slowly trekked the winding sidewalk to Trevor's apartment. "Just listen and pay attention."

I knocked on the door several times before we heard a woman's voice ask, "Who is it?"

When I said my name, the door flung open.

"May we come in? I'd like to talk to you about your son, Trevor," I said as politely as possible.

"No, you cannot! I don't allow people like you in my house," snapped the brown-haired white woman who wore a green printed housecoat.

"But I really need to talk to you about your son. He threw my daughter in a dumpster yesterday . . ."

"No, my son did not!" she yelled, cutting me off. "And don't you dare try to say that he did, or you'll be sorry you did."

Boom! She slammed the door in our faces.

I was stunned and humiliated. So were my daughters. I didn't know what to do. But we quickly left the apartment building out of fear that someone would call the police on us.

I felt even worse for my daughters. They had to stand there and watch their mother get humiliated trying to "teach them the right thing to do." We walked back to our apartment building without saying a word. My heart felt so heavy I thought it would drop to my feet. I had no idea that racism still ran so deep in this country, let alone this state. It was like being hit with a brick between the eyes.

We walked through our front door, and the boys knew by our silence and the looks on our faces that things hadn't gone well. I briefly told them what happened without stopping, then dragged myself to my bedroom and closed the door to cry.

I don't know how long I was on my knees, crying and begging the Lord to help us out of our latest ordeal, before I realized the house was completely silent. I got up, threw some cold water on my face so that my eyes didn't look so puffy, then eased to the girls' bedroom and cracked open their door.

My daughters were sitting side by side on one of their twin beds, tears pouring down their faces. I felt physically sick, hurting so badly that I could barely speak. But I had to comfort my daughters in some way. Hurrying to the bed, I sat down between them and put my arms around their shoulders.

"Don't worry. It'll be all right. I promise you, it'll be all right," I kept saying over and over, not knowing what else to say.

I don't know how long we sat on the bed, crying and rocking in each other's arms, but it would never erase what we'd just experienced. It just didn't make any sense. It was crazy. Insane.

"What kind of message will they get from this?" I wondered as we sat there silently, rocking from side to side. "Will they end up hating white people? Will they grow up believing that there is no such thing as justice for black people in this country? Will they resent me for having moved them out here?"

The boys had gone to their bedroom, too. They weren't crying, but they weren't watching television or wrestling or sprawled out on the floor playing with their race-car set or other toys like they usually did. They were sitting there on their full-size bed, looking just as stunned and worried. And they hadn't heard half the story.

"Some people won't like you no matter how hard you try or how nice you treat them. And it's sad to say, but it's true—only because of our skin color," I said, trying to get the words out without breaking down again. "But you don't want to be like them. So you've got to work real hard at not letting it bother you *too* much. Cause if you start hating all white people, you will have become just like the racist people that we're dealing with out here. Then they've won the battle for sure."

Andre wanted to move again. The thought had crossed my mind after the first problem arose, but I often sat in my classes wondering how I was going to feed my kids when I got home. How could I afford to *move* anywhere?

"We're just going to have to watch our p's and q's and pray a lot," I told my kids after informing them that we wouldn't be going anywhere for a while. We were trapped in a place where people despised us, and all of us knew it.

— ๏ —

I WAS LYING across my bed with the door closed, studying for my Natural Science exam. Books were sprawled everywhere. Science had always been my toughest subject.

The kids were at a Christian youth group called AWANA (Approved Workmen Are Not Ashamed), held at a local church. It was nearly six o'clock, and the bus had just picked them up, so I had two whole hours to spend studying. I had been cracking the books for half an hour or so when someone knocked at the door.

Not expecting any company, I crept to the door and peeked out through its peephole. It was Trevor's mom and another woman. I wasn't sure what to do. So I did the Christian thing and opened it.

"Yes? Come in," I said cautiously, hoping they'd come to make peace.

Wrong.

"No thank-you," Trevor's mom snapped. "We just came by here to let you know that I've talked to a lot of the mothers in this apartment complex. And if you call the police on my son again, they're all gonna say your kids were beating up on ours."

I slammed the door in their faces. They yelled and shouted obscenities in the ordinarily quiet hallway. Their anger and bitterness astounded me, especially when it was *my* kids who were being victimized. I thought I had seen it all.

"I've got a whole new respect for those blacks who were bold enough to integrate lunch counters and schools back in the 1950s and 1960s. Cause there's some crazy white people out here in this world," I thought nearly every time I stepped foot outside my door.

I didn't tell the kids about the encounter. They were scared enough. I prayed one of those "I need you right now, Lord" prayers, then tried to focus on my exams. I tossed and turned all night.

The next afternoon I dragged myself out the door to catch the bus to campus. I felt like the weight of the world was on my shoulders. Head hung and feeling as if I were fighting a losing battle, my heart begged God for some sign of hope. I couldn't afford to move. I didn't want to bring my family and friends into the situation any further, fearing things would only escalate. I was tired of complaining to the rental office. Nothing was ever done as far as I knew.

I neared the laundry room when the door closest to our apartment opened. A woman in her mid-twenties called my name.

"Jasmine, can I talk to you for a minute?" she asked, her dark brown glasses nearly the color of her short-cropped hair.

I stopped and braced myself.

"I overheard what those women said to you out here in the hallway last night," she said. "I heard the whole thing. And if it comes down to it, I'll tell anyone that I did. Don't let them run you out of here. That's giving them what they want. You and your kids have a right to live here, just like the rest of us."

I could have kissed her. I needed that like a river needed water.

"Thank-you," I said. "Thank-you very much. You have no idea how much that means to me right now."

I caught the bus, rode to campus, and took my exam.

✿ ROSES AND WEEDS

he air was damp and cool, and the trees were bare in late December 1980. The MSU campus was quiet, like a baseball field after a game had ended and everybody had gone home. A few students, professors, and employees still trickled in and out of the ivy-covered brick buildings. Most had gone home, happy to have a two-week Christmas break.

I was happy, too. But most of all, I was thankful. My dream of going to college had become a reality, and I had successfully completed my first term. I knew I could do it. That's the way I looked at most things those days. I was so thankful for that.

Our battle with racism in Okemos still brewed beneath a surface of serenity. My soul ached every time I thought about all the taunting and abuse my kids were enduring in the community that I once thought was heaven on earth. But in the midst of it all, we were growing closer and stronger—mentally, emotionally, and spiritually. God had brought us through tough times before. And I knew he'd get us through our latest struggle, too. Somehow, someway.

And Kamari, my darling angel, Kamari. She may have been a talkative nine-year-old who could pluck a person's last nerve because she stayed so busy. But her heart was kind and loving, and she was always thoughtful of everyone at the expense of herself. She bore the brunt of the whole sorry mess in Okemos. A white bus driver had ordered her off the bus because "her cello took up too much space." Some white neighbors labeled her a troublemaker, even though she had earned the respect of most people, including adults, who took the time to know her.

I was learning to lean on God more and more each day. My faith told me that if we kept him at the center of our lives, we'd make it through and come out even better people. That was his promise. And I was eternally thankful for that assurance.

My final exams were over. I had just finished taking my last one, a Western Civilization exam, and felt pretty darn good about it. Another reason to be thankful.

Clinton and I still had a passionate thing going on. Where it would lead to, nobody knew but God. I was thankful for our relationship. I was thankful for Clinton. He was by far the best thing that had ever happened to me in the skin of a man. We still talked nearly every day and saw each other at least twice a week. But he had his life—especially with all his female friends—and I had mine. Our lives were vastly different. But so far we had made it work and had managed to grow from each other at the same time. I was extremely thankful for that.

Being a single parent kept me on my knees. Between Andre's football games, where he was a star linebacker for the middle school team, Kendra and Kamari's violin and cello recitals, and Lamar's challenging intellect, I felt like an octopus with arms being pulled in all directions. But I was determined to stand firm on God's word.

I prayed before any big decision, and many little ones as well. My kids and I still attended church most Sundays, driving to and from Lansing—sometimes not sure whether we had enough gas to make it back home. Things were tough. Really tough.

I still smoked a little weed to take the edge off, but I knew that sooner or later I'd kick that habit, too. All human beings had their struggles. I used to think there were big sins and little sins. But sin was sin. And everyone did something they wouldn't want others to know about. Whew! That was a liberating thing to finally realize. I was extremely thankful for that as well.

I was just "Jasmine Walker." The girl who grew up hating herself and loving every minute of it. The teenager who was determined to ruin her life, and smile at her mother while doing it. The young mother who started out with big, brown, starry eyes and grew into an adult with red, teary ones.

I had bounced back from it all, with God's help and by believing in myself.

I had sought out people and things to make me happy, not realizing that happiness came from within. I reached for men, and they made me a puppet. I reached for drugs, and they made me a slave. I reached for God, and he comforted me and gave me peace. Most amazing is that he was there all the time, and I didn't even know it.

But I was thirty years old now, walking across one of the most beautiful campuses in the world, my head high, my life humbled—realizing it was all a gift from God. I was so thankful.

My future looked brighter on that dreary late afternoon as I walked across campus to the bus stop to wait for my bus ride back to Okemos. Staring out the window, I smiled, thinking about the poster that hung on my kitchen wall. Using chalk, I had sketched a picture of a white, shaggy dog on a large piece of black poster board. He was holding a red rose in his paw, and his head was tilted modestly. Underneath it were words I copied from a card in a Hallmark store in Lansing one day, which read: "I may not be perfectly witty, or perfectly wise, or perfectly wonderful. But I'm always perfectly me."

And for that I was extremely thankful.

—— ℯ ——

II CHRONICLES 20:15 (KJV): "Be not afraid nor dismayed by reason of this multitude; for the battle is not yours, but God's."